The DARK THAT HIDES US

The DARK THAT HIDES US

ANDY DARCY THEO

GALLERY YA

SIMON & SCHUSTER

London New York Amsterdam/Antwerp Sydney/Melbourne Toronto New Delhi

First published in Great Britain in 2025 by Simon & Schuster UK Ltd

1 3 5 7 9 10 8 6 4 2

Simon & Schuster UK Ltd
1st Floor, 222 Gray's Inn Road
London WC1X 8HB

www.simonandschuster.co.uk
www.simonandschuster.com.au
www.simonandschuster.co.in

Simon & Schuster Australia, Sydney
Simon & Schuster India, New Delhi

The authorised representative in the EEA is Simon & Schuster Netherlands BV, Herculesplein 96, 3584 AA Utrecht, Netherlands. info@simonandschuster.nl

A CIP catalogue record for this book
is available from the British Library.

PB ISBN 978-1-3985-3187-1
eBook ISBN 978-1-3985-3185-7
eAudio ISBN 978-1-3985-3186-4

Printed and bound in India by
Replika Press Pvt. Ltd.

For anyone who has ever felt like giving up,
but was too stubborn to quit.

AUTHOR'S NOTE

This story is one of battle. A battle to persevere, to seek light, even when all we see and feel is darkness. It is a battle that many of us will face, or have faced already, at some point in our lives. Some of these wars are fought on the surface for all to see, but for the majority, they are waged far beneath the surface. If there is one thing you take from reading this book, it is to ensure that, no matter how fierce the opponent, you do not yield, and should you fall, you get back up and continue the fight.

PROLOGUE

Eleven years ago

Blaise Ademola's parents were certain their son was the happiest and bravest boy there was, completely and utterly fearless.

They were wrong.

Blaise was petrified of *everything.*

So when he heard a person in his house whose voice he didn't recognise, well after midnight, Blaise flew out of his bed and dashed into the wardrobe. He pulled the door almost shut, plunging himself in darkness, save for the small nightlight in the corner of his bedroom, which illuminated the walls with an orange-red glow.

Blaise had always been scared of the dark; the only fear his parents didn't attempt to condition out of him. Even in their bedrooms, where they slept separately due to his father's snoring, they themselves left a small light on. It made Blaise feel like he wasn't the only one who felt uneasy in the shadows.

Everything else, however, all of Blaise's other fears, those were things they did not stand for.

Most recently, his mother had caught him squirming at the sight of a dead pigeon on the side of the road. The next day, when he came home from primary school, there it was, its bloody entrails sprawled out on the patio garden. Blaise had been forced to sit there and stare at it for hours on end until he said it didn't bother him any more.

'Face your fears.'

That's what they drilled into him. It seemed like that was the only thing they were concerned with. So long as he ate what they told him to, slept when they instructed and kept up a rigorous level of daily physical activity, even on the days he was unwell, Blaise's parents took very little interest in their only son.

If Blaise ever complained or asked any questions, they would tell him that the strongest little boys were beautiful and fearless. Nothing more and nothing less. After a while, Blaise learned to stop asking questions; being strong and beautiful and fearless seemed to be the only things worth caring about. The only things of any value.

But Blaise didn't feel fearless most of the time. Certainly not now, as his body trembled inside the narrow wooden wardrobe. He allowed the clothes on their hangers to drape over his head, another layer of concealment. If he listened closely, he could make out a conversation between two people.

He could hear his mother. Blaise's small shoulders relaxed slightly with relief. *Who is she talking to?* It wasn't Blaise's father; the accent was similar, but the voice sounded deeper. Blaise hadn't ever heard anyone else who spoke like his parents, not even people who said they were born in Nigeria where his parents said they were raised. Even in the Nollywood films they sometimes watched, no one sounded quite like them.

Why is a man in our house so late? Blaise's parents wouldn't even let him invite friends over, not that he had many.

'May I see the boy?' asked the man from downstairs. There was a creak from the bottom step beneath his weight.

‘He will be sleeping now,’ came his mother’s reply. ‘But you may look.’

She sounds different, Blaise thought, although he couldn’t describe how or why. All he knew was that he would be in big trouble if she caught him awake.

As Blaise heard footsteps approaching, he tore out from the wardrobe and clambered into his bed. He had barely thrown the duvet over him and shut his eyes by the time the bedroom door opened gently, flooding his room with light from the hallway.

Blaise’s heart thumped in his chest, but he urged himself to stay still. He was already sweating under the covers, his body temperature hot at the best of times, but he couldn’t risk his mother catching him out.

The man let out a soft gasp. Blaise could feel him drawing nearer, blocking out the hallway light. *He smells of firewood*, Blaise thought.

‘Beautiful,’ said the man under his breath in awe.

‘He really shines in the summer season,’ Blaise’s mother reported. ‘His seventh birthday is approaching soon. We work every day to build his strength and remove his fears for when the time comes.’

‘He looks strong,’ the man agreed, his voice so low that Blaise could barely hear it. Blaise felt a hand touch his pyjama top and he prayed his face didn’t portray his startle. The neckline of his top was pulled down slightly to reveal the deep-red triangular amulet that rested on his chest: the necklace he wore every day; the necklace his parents forbade him from ever taking off. ‘Beautiful,’ the man said again.

Finally, after what seemed like an eternity, he let go of

Blaise's top. 'You have done an incredible job, My Queen. I consider it an honour to have laid eyes upon him.'

'An honour you must keep to yourself,' hissed Blaise's mother in response. 'Should anyone know you have been here and met the boy, should the king find out, my hand would be forced.'

There was a rush of air. Had the man bowed to her? 'Of course, My Queen. I promise to speak no word of this encounter to the tribe.'

Blaise needed air. He could feel himself wet all over with sweat. He needed them to leave so that he could breathe properly. There was so much he didn't understand: who was this man and what did he look like? Why was he calling Blaise's mother a queen? What was a tribe? And why was he here? But most importantly, when would he leave?

As if he'd willed it, he felt his mother and the man withdraw from his bedside and heard the door open and close again. Their voices grew muffled, barely audible over his own anxious breathing. His mother sounded like she was giving the man orders and he was murmuring in agreement. Blaise heard his mother's faint laugh, or at least he assumed that was what it was because it wasn't a noise she'd ever made with him or his father.

Blaise wondered if his father knew this man. A friend from work? Blaise's parents often went on extended trips that took them away from him for weeks at a time. Most of the time, one went and the other stayed, but there was one time when both of his parents had gone and Blaise had been so overwrought with the fear that he had been abandoned that he hadn't left his room for a whole day, not even to go to the toilet. '*Work*,' they had said when he asked, and then they shut the conversation down and swiftly moved on as if it had never happened.

Blaise could no longer hear them. He knew he wouldn't be able to sleep until the man was gone, so he crept out of bed and padded to the door. It hadn't been shut properly. All he needed to do was press his fingertips against it and push it lightly to see out.

He could see two figures at the top of the stairs. At first Blaise thought they were hugging, arms wrapped tightly around each other and bodies pressed close. But then the angle of their heads shifted slightly.

And kept shifting. Over and over again, their faces squished together, mouths slightly ajar every time they met. Blaise stared in horror, unable to move. Each kiss was hungry. Passionate. Like they would stop breathing if the other pulled away.

Emotions that Blaise didn't recognise flooded through him, making his eyes burn. Many of them he had never felt before and didn't have names for. He would later learn what they were: shame, anger, confusion, embarrassment, fear. Always fear.

Blaise blinked away tears and when his vision cleared, he saw that his mother's eyes were open and were staring straight at him. He stumbled back, retreating into his room. His mother mumbled something to the man and a moment later, the door to her bedroom clicked as it shut.

'Blaise, what are you still doing up?'

Blaise backed into his bed, his heel kicking the sturdy bedframe as his mother entered the room. She wore a long, colourful dress he hadn't seen before. An explosion of reds and oranges and yellows hanging loosely from her tall, muscular frame. He noted the bright lines on her face and thought it looked a bit like face paint, although he didn't know what all the swirls and points were meant to make her look like. Great golden chains dangled from her neck, decorated with numerous jewels that glinted in the glow of his nightlight.

She looks like a firework, Blaise thought. No wonder the man had called her a queen. She looked like one.

'I asked you a question,' she said, stepping closer.

'I couldn't sleep,' Blaise replied, his voice coming out high-pitched. He placed his hand on the mattress behind him to steady himself. 'I heard a man. I thought he was Father. Who was he?'

'A friend,' she said noncommittally. 'Let's get you into bed; you're up far later than you are allowed. We've got a big day tomorrow, lots of walking and climbing.'

Blaise got beneath the covers, but he stayed upright. 'Why were you kissing him?'

A look passed across his mother's face, one he couldn't decipher. 'What did I tell you about asking questions?'

Any other time, Blaise would have dropped it and done as he was told, but he couldn't shake the unease he felt in his gut at what he had seen. He felt deeply as though it was something he shouldn't have. He didn't know why it made him want to cry.

Questions clamoured inside his head; questions he was too afraid to ask out loud.

Why are you dressed like that? When's Father home? Do you love him?

Blaise's mother knelt down beside his bed. She rested her hands against his shoulders and pressed gently until he was lying down flat. He thought she would be cross, but she wasn't frowning. In fact, her face looked sad almost.

'Love isn't as simple as you think, Blaise. Not for adults. You won't ever understand – love is not important to you. You are meant for greater things. You are to forget tonight and all that you saw and never speak a word of it again. Is that understood?'

The tone of her voice was one Blaise knew better than to argue with. He nodded, the fear swirling in his chest, tears pricking at his eyes.

'Good,' she said. Her hand reached towards him and Blaise thought, *hoped*, it was to caress his face. Instead it went to the fiery amulet at his chest. She twirled it between her long fingers, inspecting the stone with fascination and wonder. She had never looked at *him* that way.

'Good,' she repeated, letting the amulet fall between her fingers. She rose to her feet and looked at her son. 'You are so pretty and so strong, Blaise. You are lucky: that is all the world will ever want or need from you.'

Eleven years later

Blaise was a pretty boy. This he knew was undeniable, confirmed in the eyes of anyone who saw him, anyone he graced with his charm or subjected to a flirtatious smirk. He had grown into a young man who was *actually* tall, dark and handsome. A muscular build from years of training, maroon eyes, chiselled jaw, flawless skin.

It was all he had ever been told. His defining characteristic. Not wise like Caeli or honourable like Demi or thoughtful like Alexis.

No. Beautiful. Handsome. Pretty.

So why bother trying to be anything else? Why waste time on anything other than his looks? Why be anything more than what was expected of him: a pretty thing to be stared at?

Blaise wished that was all he was. Life would be easier if he did not feel so deeply. He constantly compared himself to the people around him, petrified they would outshine him or, worse, grow bored of him. That was why he had so few friends. That, and their jealousy.

Minus Alexis, of course. Alexis had an irresistible quality that made Blaise gravitate to him. Blaise wanted to impress him . . . or maybe he wanted to be him. Not that he'd ever share that. To the outside, Blaise was as his element implied: bright, bold, brilliant.

That was why it grated on him so much that the girl whose door he had been knocking on for the last ten minutes still hadn't opened it. She was in there; he could hear her walking around. He didn't want to be alone that night, not after everything that had happened on the quest. It was normal to need a little comfort, no? Mortem had plans to imprint any person with a drop of Elemental blood come the summer solstice, which just so happened to be in less than two days. Blaise needed to not be alone.

The door to the room of the girl he wished to distract himself with remained firmly shut in his face. He couldn't understand why though. She had called him beautiful. Wasn't that enough?

She must be playing a long game. The thought came as a cool, calming tonic. *Two could play that game.* Besides, Blaise had always enjoyed a little competition.

He turned and stared down the length of the corridor. Perhaps, he thought, he could start walking. Perhaps he shouldn't stop walking. Leave the Haven and get away from Stonehenge before Mortem and the Shadowless came to poison it in a little under two days' time. He had to stay alive and stay alight. Let others do the fighting; he wouldn't risk extinguishing his flame for anyone. If that was selfish, so be it.

Blaise Ademola was a pretty boy and he wanted to stay that way so he didn't end up a pretty corpse.

After all these years, it appeared that he was still very much afraid, and the larger his world got, the more he had to fear.

PART I

1
INDURATIZE

Induratize (v.) *Latin origin*
To make one's own heart hardened or resistant to someone's pleas or advances, or to the idea of love

'Valentina?'

If he called her name one more time, she would consider slitting his throat. Maybe then he would get the message.

Blaise Ademola had been knocking on the door for a while now. In that time, Valentina had changed out of the rags tossed her way in Mortem's castle, taken her first shower in a week, changed into the clean clothes Ziya Parashakti had given her and braided her long black hair into a simple plait that fell down to her waist. If there was one thing about Valentina everyone could agree upon, it was that she was efficient.

'Valentina,' Blaise said again, drawing out the end of her name playfully. 'I don't know if you're still awake, but did you want to talk?'

And if there was one thing Valentina knew, it was that this beautiful boy, born from the fires, did not want to talk. Valentina knew by the way he had looked at her: lust, provoked by a girl who could resist his good looks and charm. This must be a rare occasion.

Valentina had half a mind to let Blaise in. Let him drive out her anxieties and quieten her rage. She did like him, and it would be entertaining to watch the fallout if his girlfriend found out. Getting under her skin had been one of the few things that had brought Valentina joy recently.

Would it be greedy to ask Alexis Michaels to join? He looked like a man who would worship the woman he was with. Would he kiss her all over and tell her he loved her?

No, because she was not Demi.

Blaise's footsteps retreated in reluctant defeat, and so too did the image of the grey-eyed Caeli Doran – a girl who knew nothing of her own heritage or of the waves her ancestors had made that had torn apart their community centuries ago.

For what felt like the first time ever, Valentina was left with her thoughts; her *own* thoughts.

They say when you are born into a burning house, you think the whole world is on fire. But the scars from the flames stung that much more when you trusted the people who poured the gasoline.

Valentina had been in the shadow of abuse so long, it almost felt comfortable . . . *safe*.

No. More.

There had been no place for her at her home.

That was why she burned it to ashes.

Dignity and hope had once sustained her through every act of disrespect and desecration. Not any more. The only thing that kept her going now was revenge; a thirst that could only be quenched with the bloodshed of those who had harmed her.

Mortem Arcangelo needed to pay for what he did to her.

For what and who he took from her. But he wasn't the only Arcangelo who threatened her safety.

Incantus had seen the scarification on her wrist before they came to the Haven, as had Alexis. The burned tattoo of a dragon coiled into a circle, forever chasing a flaming pearl. Incantus would know what it meant, what it symbolised. As for Alexis, she didn't know him well, but she could tell the type of person he was.

He wasn't like others, satisfied with the illusion of the show, blissfully happy to remain naive to what went on backstage. He sought what was behind the curtains. She recognised it because she was just the same, yet that filled her only with unease.

She liked Alexis as she did Incantus. She respected them more than most, but she couldn't trust them to keep her secret. She couldn't trust anyone, not even Ziya, who had done her very best to make her feel welcome.

Despite everything, Valentina had found Ziya oddly endearing, showing her around the Haven, to her room. She was authentic to her core in a way Valentina had always been discouraged of. If Valentina had planned on sticking around, maybe they would have grown to be friends.

But trust was hope personified: a virtuous but innately vulnerable gift to entrust another with. Gone were the days of allowing someone to hold that kind of power over her.

Valentina would be gone by morning. She couldn't guarantee Incantus would conceal her identity from her enemies, who would not rest until they punished her. She couldn't risk Alexis asking questions, discovering the truth of who she was and what she had done.

It was a secret she would kill to keep buried.

For one night only, she would sleep in a warm bed, comforted by the certainty of safety her locked door brought her. Then she would leave to enact her revenge on the man who had enslaved her, before the summer solstice stole her opportunity from under her.

But by then, Valentina had to make one more choice.

Was it just one Arcangelo she was going to kill ... or them all?

2

ANABIOSIS

Anabiosis (n.) *Greek origin*

Return to life after apparent death; suspended animation

Alexis Michaels buried his blade into his opponent once again and watched as its body disintegrated into pixilated cubes onto the grass in the centre of Stonehenge.

Sweat plastered his dark wavy hair to his forehead. He pushed it from his eyes, soreness and exhaustion doing their best to cripple his body after hours of fighting. He clenched his teeth. Rather the physical pain than the mental. Rather pain from the present than pain from the past.

The private Training Academy of the Haven was quiet save for the sound of his heaving breaths. No one was around at this hour. He alone stood within the projection of Stonehenge, which was as convincing as the real thing, accurate to the very last detail, even to the touch. The perfect replica, printed by the Academy devices. Alexis had come as soon as the nightmare ripped him out of his slumber at sunrise, little after half four in the morning.

The vision of a young Mortem and Incantus awakened him as it had every night since his memories began, although this time, as the body of Nero was clawed apart from within, the pain Alexis felt was infinitely more vivid. He was almost relieved when the boy who would grow up to be Mortem finally fell off the cliff and crashed into the black sea, an end to both of their torment.

'Send me another,' Alexis demanded, swinging his bi-sword, equal halves bronze and steel, in an arc. The Haven's projector immediately printed another corporeal combat bot that raced towards him, sword in hand, but Alexis shattered it without so much as a glance over his shoulder.

The bots weren't enough of a match. He needed something better.

Alexis pressed his palms together and thought of the only person that would provide a challenge.

Himself.

His proxy appeared in front of him wearing nothing but a pair of grey tracksuit bottoms that hung loose at its narrow waist. With its toothbrush still in its mouth, it blinked wildly and took in its surroundings before its blue-and-black-ringed eyes settled upon Alexis. It frowned slightly. 'You're still alive.'

Alexis gave an exaggerated thumbs-up. 'Fantastic observational skills. You would've known otherwise as proxies cease to exist if the Elemental dies.'

Alexis sized up his double. It was risky to have summoned it without warning. What if it had been with his parents or Jason? How would they react to seeing who they'd thought was Alexis suddenly vanish into thin air?

'How are Mum and Dad?' he asked, readjusting his grip on the hilt of his sword.

His proxy eyed the bronze-and-steel blade, holding its toothbrush similarly at its side. 'You should ask them yourself now that the quest is over.' It wiped the frothing toothpaste from its mouth. Unlike Alexis, the proxy showed little emotion in its expression and held no real conviction in its voice. It was simply a superficial reflection after all.

Alexis almost envied it. What he would do to feel nothing.

'I should've checked in with them before I left,' Alexis admitted guiltily. 'But I was worried they might sense something was wrong. Besides, it's your job to keep up my mundane appearance.'

The proxy hummed in agreement, but it was otherwise transfixed on the circular monoliths of the holographic Stonehenge. 'It's so real, I can't even see the walls of the Haven beyond it,' it said, placing its hand against the stone. 'Why am I here?'

Finally.

'To be my distraction,' said Alexis, splitting his bi-sword down the middle and throwing his proxy the bronze half.

'Bit of an unfair duel,' said the proxy, pocketing its toothbrush and gesturing to its half-naked body. 'We last synchronised over a week ago, so your most recent memories haven't transferred over. I'm already at a disadvantage without your powers.'

Both powers, Alexis thought, dropping his gaze. The proxy noticed the minute change in his expression; annoyingly, it was as observant as he was. To prevent the impending question, Alexis tucked his sword beneath his arm and extended both hands outwards. The proxy matched him until their palms were touching.

There was a soundless exchange as Alexis harmonised with his reflection, encoding its memories and experiences from the previous week. It had argued with his dad for getting into a fight with Jason and had spent most of its days hanging out with Demi or reading. Nothing unusual or exciting, but that was a good thing.

Alexis's own memories were crawling up his spine, stretching out like taloned claws around his throat, hoping to suffocate him. He had to silence them.

The proxy stared back at him, its head slightly tilted, full lips pressed into a sympathetic line. If it had been human, its eyes might have looked sad. 'You don't really want to fight,' it said with a sigh. 'And you're not sure if you really want to live, either.'

Alexis swallowed the lump in his throat and steeled himself. He then swung his sword at his proxy.

His proxy reeled back, barely missing the blade. Alexis swiped at it again, but his blade cut into one of the giant monoliths. He was surprised when it did not disperse into holographic pixels as the training bots had.

His proxy lunged at him, but when it swung its blade, it was with the flat edge. Alexis parried it away and threw a punch with his free hand, but the proxy ducked beneath it gracefully. It darted to the vacant centre of Stonehenge to free itself up some space, but Alexis advanced on it again. He swung his blade down lightning fast, relishing in the surge of blood and adrenaline that pumped through his muscles and preoccupied his mind. He had to keep moving, keep fighting, keep acting, or risk remembering the icy powers of darkness at his fingertips.

The proxy shuddered under the weight of the incessant strikes, its mortal body struggling to compete with one of the famed Children of the Elements. It staggered backwards, blocking each blow just in time but unable to return any of its own.

'Hurting me isn't going to make you feel any better,' it said, gasping after Alexis kicked at its stomach, forcing it to keel over. It looked up at him. 'We need to talk about what happened at the waterfall.'

Alexis's breathing hitched in his chest as memories flooded his mind, the dams of his resistance crushing beneath the overwhelming weight of what he had endured during the quest for the Elemental Gems.

The vacant expression on Demi's face as the arrow struck her through the chest. Holding her limp, soaking body in his arms after catching her in the waterfall, praying to the god she believed in to take him instead. The collective powers of the four primal elements destroying the darkness poison and reviving her. The prophecy the Woman of the Water had disclosed to him.

'*By the blade of darkness, you will fall, wielded by the one you expect the least.*'

The proxy tackled Alexis to the ground. His head smacked against a fallen monolith of Stonehenge's inner circle and his vision exploded into undulating flashes of light and dark. Fighting to stay conscious, he jabbed the hilt of his sword into its side. Its weight shifted for only a second, but that was all Alexis needed to thrust his hips and heave it off, pinning it down by its arms with his knees.

The proxy shared every feature of Alexis's face. The tan of his skin, the curve of his bow-shaped lips and harsh contours of his cheekbones. Yet in that moment, Alexis saw the flash of another's face: sunken eyes, bulging cranium, a line of phlegm dripping from its nose. As Alexis drove his sword down, he saw Mortem's assassin, Sinner, in front of him, and a sword made of shadow in his hands.

The blade stabbed into the floor millimetres from his proxy's neck.

'Enough,' Alexis whispered, releasing his sword, his hand coming away trembling violently. He tapped his thumb to his index finger, then the middle finger, then the next. Over and over again, synchronising it with slow and steady breaths.

The proxy stayed pinned beneath him, breathing heavily from equal parts exertion and fear. It sat up slightly, the hard muscles of its abdomen tensing as it attempted to gauge the panicking Elemental.

'What if people find out what I did?' Alexis said through ragged breaths, staring at his hands as if darkness would suddenly start seeping from them. 'What if Incantus knows I used my shadow powers? What if my old psychiatrist caught me on camera? To Dr Dash, it must've looked like I killed a defenceless man for no reason. What if I'm no different to Mortem?'

What if I'm worse? he thought, unable to say it aloud, not even to himself.

'You did what needed to be done,' reasoned his proxy. 'That doesn't make you an evil person.'

'All sinners look innocent standing next to the devil,' Alexis cut back.

'You did it for Demi. You would do anything for her.'

Although Alexis knew its words to be his own, he still dismissed them. No sane person could justify the act of cold-blooded murder. No sane person could enjoy using a power sworn to corrupt its user, a power intrinsically unnatural, the power of death and shadows. The depth of the guilt he now felt was matched only by the rush of pleasure he had experienced in that moment.

The proxy took Alexis's shaking hands in its own. Despite there being a replica of a beating heart within its chest, nothing could simulate the trueness of the living, and so its hands were cold and lifeless around his.

'Try it,' said the proxy. It pulled free the amulet that lay under Alexis's compression vest, the carved fragment of the Water Gem, cut into the shape of an inverted triangle. When Alexis's sleep had been restless, which was more often than not, he had examined his amulet, turning over the pendant, inspecting it for any traces of discolouration. It was now as it had always been: a swirling mix of cobalt, azure, cerulean and all shades of blue in between.

'Try it,' the proxy repeated, remaining on the ground even as Alexis drew to his feet. It nodded in encouragement as it stared up at the amulet it would never possess, that would never glow under its touch.

So he did. Alexis lifted the chain from around his neck and lay the stone flat in his palm. He closed his eyes, attempting to channel the power that had been written into the very fibre of his being, the power of the ancestors he had never heard of or met, the power only *he* had the ability to create. Darkness had been the last power he had used. He prayed it hadn't eclipsed the former.

A gasp escaped him when a small ball of clear water bled into the palm of his hand. Not a manipulation of the water vapour in the air or the sweat from his skin, but a liquid conjured from nothingness, birthed into existence at his will. He poured more and more into it, spurred on by its crystalline colour, a smile flourishing upon his face. It fountained in the air, flowing in between the illusory stone monoliths, washing over their surface until they glistened.

Alexis could feel the tide of his element cleansing his mind and body. With its current, he came to appreciate the fundamental nature of his element: water would only keep clean if it flowed. If it fell still for too long, it would become stagnant, infected. As would Alexis. To be still was to suffer.

'*Sink or swim*,' as Incantus had said on his first day of training.

Alexis pulled the water back with the closing of his palm. It swept into his amulet, where it was absorbed with a flash. 'Thank you,' he said, finally helping the proxy to its feet.

The proxy's eyes lifted from the amulet to meet Alexis's. There was something in them, Alexis noticed. A glint. It lasted only a second, but Alexis saw it nonetheless; it was the first time that the proxy looked like it had felt. Like it had *wanted*.

'Thank yourself,' it replied. It gestured to the sword Alexis had almost speared it with, still embedded into the ground. 'For a second, I thought you were really going to stab me. You know I don't feel pain to the degree that you do, but that would've still hurt and you would've remembered it when we next synchronised.'

Alexis knew that.

After all, it had been his intention to strike true. If only his hands hadn't been shaking so much, he would have hit his target.

He clasped the hilt of his sword and pulled it free from the grass that sprouted between the rings of the three-dimensional projection of Stonehenge. As he drew the blade away, he flicked his wrist and brushed the tip of the blade against the bare neck of his proxy. It was only a superficial cut, but it was enough to make the proxy grunt in pain.

Alexis was almost surprised when he saw blood trickle freely down its neck.

The proxy took a few paces back, its hand clamped to its neck. Its expression was somewhere between shock and anger. 'What was that for?'

Alexis didn't blink at his reflection when he looked it in the eye. 'To remind me that I can't trust anyone . . . not even myself.'

3

YA'ABURNEE

Ya'aburnee (phr.) *Arabic origin*
'You bury me'; a declaration of one's hope that they will die before their lover because of how unbearable life would be without them

'Lexi . . . can I join you?'

Alexis knew it was her without having to look up; only she and his family called him by that name. His heart swelled at her voice. Demi Nikolas stood tentatively in the doorway to his bedroom. Incantus's loyal dire wolf, Gibbous, stood at her side and nuzzled into her palm, his snowy-white hind nearly as tall as she was.

Alexis was torn a hundred ways to reply. Conjuring the right combination of words to express how much he wanted her there with him felt impossible. Instead, he just offered her his hand. They both knew Gibbous wouldn't follow her inside, partially because he wasn't Alexis's biggest fan, but mostly because he preferred his spot in front of the ever-burning white hearth of Incantus's library office.

Demi lightly kissed the wolf's forehead before parting from him. She took the short steps that bridged the single-lane pool that split the two halves of Alexis's bedroom and joined him at the foot of his bed, holding his hand long after the customary welcome Caeli or Blaise would've given.

'I thought you'd be back on Valerian Lane by now,' he admitted once he realised Demi hadn't planned anything to say. He gestured after Gibbous as he trotted away. 'Gibbous kept you company last night?'

Her damp curls brushed her bare bronzed arms as she nodded. Sat so close, Alexis could smell the floral scent of her lavender conditioner. 'I don't know if I asked or he offered or Incantus told him to, but Gibbous hasn't left my side all night. I think it has something to do with my Gem. Since connecting with it, I can better understand the nature of the Earth's creatures.' She wrapped her arms around herself as if acutely aware of Gibbous's absence. 'I know a seventeen-year-old with the power to create earthquakes shouldn't need a fluffy animal in her bed to help her sleep. I guess, even after everything we've survived, I'm afraid to sleep alone. Silly, isn't it?'

She said it lightly, but her words fell flat when unaccompanied by her typical radiant smile. Her pain was cellular. Alexis could see it somehow; it permeated her aura that had once glowed yellow as spring but now hung dark.

'A month ago, we had a conversation beneath the oak tree in my room,' she said abruptly, crossing her legs beneath her. Alexis remembered the secrets they had traded, of fathers and faith. 'I swore to never take the life of another human. I was so certain in my conviction that there wouldn't ever be a situation that justified such an innately immoral act.' She shook her head, cursing herself. 'All of you were right. I was naive to think I would be able to fight for my life without ending another's. The embarrassment, the fall from grace, hurts as much as that arrow in my chest.' Her breathing hitched. 'And the weight of this guilt is suffocating.'

Her voice broke. Alexis could see tears that hadn't yet fallen lining her thick eyelashes. Somewhere beneath her loose green pyjama top, he knew there was the scar that sat between her crucifix and her amulet. A scar that divided her faith from her duty, inflicted by a man *she* thought she'd killed.

'Do you want me to get Incantus? Or I could call your parents?' He felt far too inadequate to help her through this grief.

Demi's intense green eyes found his. 'No,' she said firmly. 'It's you that I want . . . to talk to.' She looked away just in time to miss the flush of red that rose to Alexis's cheeks. His skin had tanned during the quest, but he knew the blush would be unmistakable.

He cleared his throat and shuffled to sit directly opposite her. 'Demi, I know you feel bad, but don't you think Sinner deserved it?'

'Does anyone really deserve to die?' she replied, her dark eyebrows furrowing in consideration. 'Doesn't that make us just as bad as them? I'm not stupid; I know he was a monster. I can't even imagine the things he's done. At the time, I thought I was doing it to protect Caeli and Valentina, but now . . . I don't know if it was just for revenge.'

Dead eyes and a punctuated blood-soaked canvas for a chest was all that Alexis could see in his mind's eye. *That's the difference between you and me*, he realised. Demi's attempt on Sinner's life had been desperate and necessary. It was grounded in instinct, fight or flight. And even so, she was ashamed of it.

When Alexis had seen Sinner on the riverside, he'd

made sure his murder had been intentionally slow to ensure Mortem's assassin felt a fraction of the pain he had inflicted on others. Alexis didn't feel guilty for doing it; he felt guilty for enjoying it.

Demi tilted her head up in stubborn refusal to let her tears fall. 'In light of everything that we've discovered – Elementals, creatures of legend, powers and all of that – I have held on to my faith. I still believe in God, *my* god, and have found a way to reconcile Him with this world just as I do with science. But that is what is tearing me apart.' Her throat bobbed and her next words came out as gasps as she fought to breathe. 'Now I know I can't go to Heaven. I've done something unforgivable. He brought me back from death only for me to take another's life. And now I'm going to spend an eternity in darkness.'

The shame of it all came crashing down. A loud sob escaped her, a savage, unrestrained cry that came from her core and shook her shoulders.

Alexis wrapped his arms around her, hoping that if he held her tightly enough, she wouldn't fall apart. She breathed hard, ragged breaths against his chest as he stroked her hair, his lips on the top of her head, uttering reassurances she likely couldn't hear and probably didn't believe.

He should tell her. He should tell her that he was the one who had really killed Sinner and absolve her of her guilt.

I can't, shouted the fearful part of him.

That would destroy the image she had of him. It would confirm the suspicions the Women of the Elements had about him – that he was a tainted product of the corrupted waters. That he was just like the person they had set out to stop. That all those years his adoptive parents had spent raising him to be a kind, honourable man meant nothing against the influence of his blackened blood.

To admit his guilt was to admit to his shadow; a shadow he didn't cast. Was it selfish to keep it from her, to let her think she was a murderer? Alexis rationalised that telling the truth would bring her no relief. It was the intention to murder that was hurting her just as much as the act itself. Sinner would've died from his wounds even if Alexis hadn't finished him off. Demi's guilt would only turn to horror at what Alexis had done or shame that he had done it for her.

He wasn't convinced that what he was doing was the right thing, but if he was certain of anything, it was that to lie was to conceal, and to conceal was to protect. He had protected his parents by concealing the existence of his nightmares, which remained even after the *Shadow Man* had disappeared. Now he was protecting himself and protecting Demi by concealing the existence of the blade of darkness he had swung.

'Demi,' said Alexis, cupping her face in his hands, wiping away the wetness on her cheeks with his thumbs. When he spoke soft words to comfort her, he desperately hoped they would comfort him too. 'You are a good person. A pure person with a virtuous soul and incredible morals. You light up any room you walk into and light up the people around you. If you weren't a good person, then you wouldn't be feeling as bad as you are right now. You did what was necessary to save us and save the world. So thank you. In my eyes, you are a hero.'

Alexis gently pulled on the thin gold chain around Demi's neck until her crucifix emerged. He could feel her eyes on him, staring intently, but he couldn't bring himself to meet her gaze, not when they were sat so close. He didn't trust himself. So he stroked his thumb across the length of the crucifix and finally leaned back.

When fresh tears rolled down Demi's cheeks, they were not from sadness. They bled into her full lips that now curved upwards into a faint smile. 'That was why I came to you,' she said, slowly sitting upright. Her eyes remained trained on his. 'Incantus healed my body, and my parents and Kallisto will heal by heart, but you always have a way of healing my soul.'

With her words, all thoughts of shadow and death recoiled from Alexis's mind. If he hadn't known otherwise, he would have been certain that it was Demi who possessed the angelic power of light.

'Forget whatever the Woman of the Water said to you,' she told him, gripping his hand with a force as unyielding as the ground beneath them. The sadness of her voice had withered away, replaced by the stubborn tone of conviction Alexis had always associated with her. 'Forget about the darkness that may exist far beneath the surface. Forget about all of that. Don't let anyone tell you any different. You are perfect, Lexi.'

At what point in the quest or during their training had Alexis realised his true feelings for her? Feelings that had been shoved aside for years; feelings he thought were too ludicrous to even consider. Feelings he now wondered, *hoped*, might be reciprocated.

He thought back to the waterfall, to the moment she'd sat up after being healed. To the feel of her wet lips on his. She hadn't kissed him back, and at the time, he thought it was because she didn't care for him the way he had and would always care for her.

But what if she does? If she could someday?

It wasn't fair to Demi to ask her about it though, not when she was already processing so much else. She seemed more herself now than Alexis could have hoped for and he didn't want to risk overwhelming her.

Even so, Alexis couldn't help but smile and foolishly believe that for a brief moment, there may come a time when they could go back to chasing sunsets, only this time, as something more than friends. He squeezed her hand back, knowing that it wouldn't break no matter how tightly he held it. Knowing that the *Shadow Man* could never reach him as long as he had her.

'Believe me,' he replied, 'the perfect part of me is you.' And then, for reasons he knew not, he added, 'If you decide to spend another night at the Haven, don't ask Gibbous to stay with you. Ask me.'

He felt his pulse thrumming in his throat, but he forced himself to keep her gaze. Demi didn't look away either, not even as her expression darkened from one of softness, of bashfulness, to an intense, brazen seriousness to match his.

They remained like that, locked in limbo for many moments, until eventually Demi replied. 'Didn't think I'd need to ask.'

4
EXHȲDRIA

Exhȳdria (n.) *Greek origin*
The winds which are accompanied by rain

Even though her room was only across the hallway from his, Alexis walked Demi to her door. He lingered by it long after she left.

Incantus wants to see you all in the lab before you leave, read a message from Ziya on his phone. Demi said she would join once she'd done her make-up and finished packing her bags for home. Alexis didn't plan on doing either one of those things, although the former might help in hiding the dark circles beneath his eyes.

He was just about to knock on Blaise's bedroom door to ask to walk with him when he heard the slow creak of Caeli's door opening from further down the corridor. The figure that emerged from her room was not who Alexis had expected.

The tall man with floppy blonde hair froze when he saw Alexis, his pale cheeks deeply flushed.

'Alexis! Hi!' said Joe Coin, in an unusually high-pitched voice. With the hand that wasn't holding his shoes, he reached hastily for the open buttons on his shirt. Behind him, Alexis caught a glimpse of Caeli's long platinum hair as she shoved

Joe out then slammed the door shut, leaving him to explain himself.

'Morning,' said Alexis, stifling a smile. 'You're here?'

Despite Joe being several years his senior, and an Elemental with the ability to change the properties of his skin to be impenetrable to any blade, he tripped over himself to answer Alexis's question. 'Yes! The Haven graduates that assist the Security Council of the High Order were sent back here late last night. Mr Arcangelo must have convinced them we need to be here . . . for tomorrow.'

A solar eclipse on the summer solstice: the day the Prophecy of Light and Darkness referred to. Or so Alexis had been told. He hadn't heard the direct translation of the Prophecy himself. The day that Mortem would make his way to Stonehenge and unleash his powers of darkness, imprinting all Elementals to be nothing but mindless puppets, instruments for his influence. The only thing that stood a chance in stopping him was Incantus, supported by the Gems collected by the Children of the Elements.

'I'll be seeing you on the battlefield then,' said Alexis, declaring his decision to stay for the first time.

Joe's eyebrows lifted. 'You're going to fight with us?' The corner of his mouth curved into a smile. 'Brilliant. We could use your help. Mr Arcangelo told me he's got me stationed near the front lines with Althea. It means we've got a better chance of wringing the neck of that incel, Ezra, for betraying us.'

'You'll have to fight me for him.'

Alexis truly meant it. He wanted to punish Ezra Alastor for allowing Mortem to invade the Haven and imprint the

Leaders and murder Teller Sagen just as much as he wanted to confront Mortem.

Joe didn't say anything; he only grinned.

'So . . . that explains why you're here,' Alexis went on, his voice teasing as he gestured to the corridor that led to the Haven's hive. He then pointed to Caeli's room. 'But why were you *there*?'

Joe stammered, casting a wayward glance at the closed door behind him. Almost as if answering his silent distress call, the door was thrown open.

'You don't have to answer to him,' said Caeli, spearing Alexis with a cutting side-eye.

Then, much to Alexis's surprise, Caeli tiptoed to plant a soft kiss to Joe's cheek. A frown flickered across Alexis's brow at the genuine display of affection.

'He's toying with you in the name of his own warped sense of humour,' Caeli added. She lightly pushed Joe on. 'Go. I'll find you later.'

Alexis stepped aside to allow Joe to pass. The fair-haired Elemental placed a hand on Alexis's shoulder as he slipped past.

'Good to see you again. Congratulations on the quest, by the way.'

Alexis nodded in thanks, but he was already making his way up the stairs towards Caeli's room where she had disappeared.

'Not your usual morning cardio, Cae.'

'Mind your business,' she warned, slamming the door with a gust of wind conjured from her hand. Alexis caught it before it shut, slipping inside. Caeli took a seat in front of her vanity and started brushing her hair. She sighed when she saw him, but she didn't look surprised.

'Now when have I ever done that?' Alexis folded his arms as he leaned against the side of the wall. He would've taken a seat on the bed, but the unruffled sheets and the sight of a discarded sports bra made him change his mind.

Each of their bedrooms was unique in its own way, suited to their powers. Alexis's housed a wide, arcing pool; Demi's grew a twisting oak tree in its centre; and lines of coal and a long hearth patterned Blaise's. Caeli's room was a stormy grey colour and mostly bare save for the dresser, wardrobes and a king-size bed. Instead of a ceiling, the walls vanished at the marking of the white chalk characteristic of the teleportation lines. In its place was a cloudy early morning sky, breathing in gentle gales of fresh air to the training facility far underground.

'So . . . Joe again.'

Caeli ran a finger along her sharp jawline before pressing it against her chin. Noticing that all of her nail varnish had been scratched away, she quickly shut her fist. Through the mirror, her hooded grey eyes found Alexis's. 'Yes. And what? It's none of your business who I'm with. And it's none of Blaise's.'

'I never said anything about Mr Ademola,' Alexis said coyly. He really was doing his best not to smile.

'Yeah, but I know you're thinking about him,' she snapped, getting to her feet. She stalked past him and walked straight out of her room, forgetting to pick up her suitcases. Alexis had to jog to catch up to her as they walked in tandem down the pristine corridors of the Haven towards the hive.

'I'm just surprised, that's all,' Alexis admitted, trying to engage her. 'Less than a week ago, you broke up with Joe because you said there was "no fire". After everything that happened between you and Blaise on the quest, I thought it would be the last push you both needed to finally get together.'

Caeli turned on him. 'So did I, Alexis! So did I. After years of trying to pretend it would never happen, I thought we could finally just admit it. I thought he realised that too.' The words tumbled out of her, taking them both by surprise. 'But last night after we all went to bed, I heard his door open, and I knew he was going to see if he could find *Valentina*.' She almost spat her name. 'Turns out that it was nothing more than a holiday romance when there was no one else around.'

Caeli started walking again, raking her fingers through her hair, leaving long strands of silvery blonde floating in the air.

Alexis would've let her be any other time – it was foolish to approach a storm – but she had chosen to walk when she easily could have flown from him. Maybe it wasn't that she wanted to be alone; maybe it was that she wanted him to prove he would stay, even if she pushed him away.

'Blaise only went after her because he knows she's not an option,' he said softly. 'Not really. It's easy for him to be rejected by someone he doesn't care about than to risk being rejected by you . . . by the only person he really wants.'

'I'm tired of watching him chase everyone else,' Caeli retorted. 'Joe isn't afraid to show me he cares about me. And I'm starting to care for him too – he's sweet and attentive and disgustingly attractive. If Blaise wants to pursue things with a random stranger he met once instead of make any effort with me, then I won't be the one to get in his way.'

'Would you waste your time chasing after something you thought you could never get?'

Caeli went to react, her face beginning to contort into

disagreement as she inhaled. But as Alexis tilted his chin up at her, she slowly let go of her breath. She shook her head. 'The fire boy that's scared of getting burned and the sky girl who changes her mind like the wind. What's the likelihood of that working out?'

'I think if he knew there was even a sliver of a chance, you could count on Blaise to play those odds.' That pried a smile from her lips. Alexis squeezed her arm and decided he should stop meddling in his friends' love lives. It wasn't like he was well positioned to give anyone relationship advice. 'I just want you to remember that tomorrow could be our last day. Who would you want to spend it with?'

Caeli arched an impossibly high eyebrow as she smirked. 'Hypocrite.' She turned on her heel, raising her hand to silence whatever excuse he began to conjure. 'Let's go before the bloody eclipse starts.'

'And she's back.'

The bright core of the Haven radiated with a hum of energy, fuelled by the powers of all who resided within. It was a place of contradictions for Alexis: it felt both grand and homely, ancient and modern, a place for everyone, but also as if it had been built for him and him alone.

Alexis and Caeli ascended one of the many marble staircases that weaved across its hollow centre, connecting its multiple levels in a lattice of Grecian white and gold.

'I forgot to ask you about your dad,' said Alexis, suddenly remembering a conversation they'd had during the quest. 'Did you want to talk about it? I know you still don't know anything about him, but drawing on my own experience, sometimes it's better to have no dad than to have a murderous, psychopathic one.'

Caeli shook her head firmly as they approached a short, round woman who stood at the highest level of the Haven, talking with a muscular dark-skinned boy with a red-stone amulet. Ziya Parashakti gave Alexis a slight wave as they drew closer.

Caeli's eyes were trained on Blaise. 'I'm not wasting my last couple of days thinking about the men who didn't care enough about me to stick around.'

'Hello,' said Ziya at their arrival. Her arms were folded awkwardly in front of her chest, her dark hair tied into a taut bun on top of her head. Something about her was off, Alexis noted immediately. Usually, she was giddy to spend time with the Children of the Elements. Why was her mouth settled into a frayed line?

'Hey, bro.' Blaise smiled. Alexis clasped his calloused hand that was forever warm to the touch. 'What's up with you, Cae? Not happy to be going home?'

Caeli crossed her arms as she glared at him. 'You are not worth the air it takes to converse with.'

Blaise looked at Alexis quizzically, as did Ziya. Ziya could read several languages and half a dozen books in one day, but she had never been good at reading the room, which meant the scathing look of disdain Caeli was giving Blaise was universal in all languages.

Demi waved at them from the far end of the walkway as she approached. She took a deliberately large step away from the edge to avoid seeing how high up she was as she adjusted the strap of her bag on her shoulder. 'Sorry I'm late. Where's everyone's stuff?'

Blaise turned his back to Caeli before answering, 'I'll probably head later. Got no reason to go home; my parents will be out anyway.'

Alexis avoided the question by asking another. 'Is everything all right, Ziya?' She was playing with her sleeves, pulling them over her hands methodically as if the motion of doing something would occupy whatever was on her mind. 'You don't seem yourself?'

The young Indian woman raised her head, meeting Alexis's eyes. She never looked at him in the eyes, not for longer than a transitory glance. He was almost taken aback by it.

'It's Valentina. She's gone.'

5

SCHWELLENANGST

Schwellenangst (n.) *German origin*
Fear of embarking on something new; fear of crossing a threshold

'What do you mean, "She's gone"?' Blaise asked.

Caeli scoffed and muttered something inaudible under her breath. Blaise shot Alexis another confused look.

After a long pause, Ziya replied in her usual rapid fashion, running out of breath at the end of her sentences until she was physically forced to inhale. 'She left. We had a really nice conversation last night. Really nice. I told her about the Haven and she gave me some advice and . . . we kind of bonded. Or at least I thought we did.' At that, she shook her head. 'But this morning when I went to her room to check on her, she was gone – no note or anything. And the night before, she said there was no one she needed me to call, so I've got no clue where she could have gone. I'm sure she can handle herself just fine, but it's not safe out there for powerful Elementals this close to the solstice.'

'Oh, bless you, Ziya,' said Demi, placing a hand on her slumped shoulder. 'I'm sure she'll be okay. She looks like she can handle herself better than anyone.'

Alexis knew that Ziya hadn't left the Haven in years; she had told him that during one of their first conversations. Despite the Haven's immeasurable size, the outside world must be an overwhelming place to imagine after so long.

'I went to check on her last night to see if she had settled in,' said Blaise, looking at anyone except Caeli as they started making their way down the long corridor that led to Incantus's office. Caeli cut Alexis a look as if to say, *I told you so*. 'She didn't answer, but I could hear the sound of her shower. She must have gone early morning.'

Alexis spoke his thoughts aloud. 'I wonder if she's in trouble.' The last time he had seen her, he had noticed the dragon-shaped branding on her inner wrist. He remembered the look on her face when Incantus seemed to recognise it. Perhaps it was something she could be identified by, like a family tattoo. Maybe she didn't want to be found.

'She must be,' Ziya agreed. 'She's an Elemental that can portal anywhere, including places she's never been before. Ezra's powerful, but not even he can manage that. How could Mortem capture and imprint someone like that?' She clenched her jaw at the mention of the man who had killed her mother, and left her and her sister orphaned. 'I'm just worried that she left because she thought she had to and not because she wanted to.'

Caeli threw her hands up. 'Who cares anyway.' She observed the looks on her friends' faces. 'What? It was obvious she didn't want to stay. Don't pretend like you're all best friends with her; we barely knew her. She portalled us right into the hands of Dr Sinner and the Shadowless, *and* she nearly broke my nose. Why are you all so forgiving, considering what she did?'

Blaise made a noise of disgust. 'You can be so cold sometimes.'

Caeli tutted, but otherwise didn't retaliate. She attempted to catch Ziya's eye, but Incantus's protégée had them fixed on her own footsteps.

'Would you be able to find her?' Alexis asked, steering the conversation back. 'Track her using aura maps or something?'

It was a redundant question. He knew she could. He had asked Incantus to do the very same thing but with his birth parents nearly a month ago. He didn't know how difficult it could be or how long it would take, but he couldn't shake the feeling that Incantus hadn't tried very hard. Maybe it was because he knew Mortem was Alexis's father and he didn't want to confirm it.

Whatever the reason, Alexis had agreed to let Ziya take over the task before he left for the quest. Still, she hadn't mentioned anything to him since then. By all accounts, his birth parents had been ghosts. It was as though he was a product of the tsunami itself, birthed from the seas and abandoned in the wreckage from the tidal wave he likely caused.

'I could try,' Ziya decided eventually. She had been staring at him and he averted her eyes when he zoned back in. 'All portallers are legally required to inform the Transport and Portalling Council of the High Order of their whereabouts, you know, so that they don't go around breaking the law. I presume she hasn't, which would make breaking into their database relatively useless.'

'You can break into the High Order's database?' Caeli asked, with much more enthusiasm than was customary of her. She let out an impressed hum. 'The skill *and* the readiness to do so . . . You never fail to surprise me, Ziya.'

For what was probably the first time since they'd met, Ziya smiled with pride. 'You've got your powers; this is mine.' She tapped the side of her temple and grinned when both Demi and Blaise shook her shoulders in cheers. 'Not that I ever would,' she added hastily.

Behind them, Alexis smiled to himself. Despite their flaws, his friends had a way of bringing out the best in people, celebrating their achievements as much as they would their own. They had done it for him and now they were doing it for Ziya. *Not a bad batch of people to spend my last few days with*, he considered.

Incantus Arcangelo was waiting for them at the end of the corridor. He was every bit as beautiful and impressive as he had been the first day Alexis met him, as if he had been carved by the angels themselves. Incantus's pale shirt was rolled three-quarters of the way up his forearms, displaying the taut muscles and veins that snaked down to his wrists, his hands clasped together. Gibbous stretched by his side and yawned as they approached, his tail wagging idly.

'Brilliant; you're here,' he said, an easy smile spreading across his ageless face. He brushed a strand of frosty white hair from his eyes, tucking it behind his ear where it had grown over the course of the summer, giving him a 'classic old-money look' as Caeli had called it.

The door to Incantus's office folded away at his presence, revealing his grand, warm headquarters that looked more like a lived-in library than someone's workspace. More cluttered than ever, papers upon books upon battle plans were scattered across whatever surface there was. From the zigzagging floor-to-ceiling bookshelves to the aged brown leather sofas, Alexis dreamed of spending hours there consuming everything he could get his hands on.

'Mind the mess,' said Incantus, snapping his fingers. A white mist trickled from his hand and coated the surfaces. Encompassed in its glow, the files and books started to stack themselves, tidying away or flinging themselves into the fireplace that blazed white beside his desk.

Caeli's mouth hung open, her eyes wide in marvel. 'You need to teach me how to do that; it would honestly solve at least half of my problems.'

'Only you get that excited about cleaning,' noted Demi, patting the taller girl's back.

'Are we getting another proxy?' asked Blaise, but Incantus led them straight past the door to the Proxying Chamber.

'Elemental law states you're only allowed one proxy,' Ziya reminded him. She trailed after them, walking alongside the white dire wolf, scratching him behind the ears.

The tall walls of bookshelves towered over the Elementals like an assortment of ceiling-high mazes, forcing them to walk in single file as they followed Incantus deeper into his office. Alexis caught glimpses of the book spines as he walked, lagging behind the group as he tried to read them through the thick layer of dust. Most were intact, some had withered with years, and about half were partially burned, scorched black as though they had come from a library that had gone up in flames.

'Have you read all of these?' Alexis asked, not bothering to hide his wonder. He jammed his hands into his pockets after the thin, papery spine of an old book written in hieroglyphics tore away at his touch.

'Most,' Incantus called from the front of the line. He had

come to a stop at the plain back wall. 'Some are historical; some encyclopaedias; others are sacred texts preserved for thousands of years dating back even to the beginnings of literature. I take a great comfort in books, as does Ziya. Maybe after all of this, I will write one about our story.' He winked at the young Elementals before pointing at Alexis. 'Feel free to borrow them, although for every book not returned, I will sever a finger.'

Alexis's hand clamped into a fist. 'Most bookstores just give out a fine,' he mumbled.

The far wall before Incantus glowed white at recognition of his power. A tall section of it opened inwards with a soft click, revealing a sterile, rather bare room that was no bigger than a store cupboard. The only thing it contained was four metre-tall marble Corinthian pillars, one at each corner of the room.

'All this space for dusty books and you crowd us into this cramped space?' Blaise moaned as they filed in behind Incantus. At Incantus's presence, the walls of the room illuminated with a steady white glow. Caeli thrust Alexis in front of her so she wouldn't have to press up against Blaise.

The grooved marble pillars bulged as if they contained something, like a clam holding on to a pearl. They looked like pods, Alexis observed, shuffling closer. Behind him, the door shut slowly, sealing off Ziya and Gibbous as she waved goodbye.

'Are our Gems in there?' Demi asked, placing her hands against the column that her amulet pulled towards. Her amulet had lightened to a rich green glow at the proximity to the Earth Gem, as did the other amulets to their corresponding Gems.

'Yes, being examined to ensure they are stable to be used

without your guidance,' Incantus replied, shifting from in between Caeli and Blaise.

Noticing there was now no one between them, Caeli took a step back as Blaise simultaneously put his hands up to protest and turned away from her. Alexis caught Caeli's eye, but she just shrugged at him. If she thought she had hidden her look of disappointment in time, she hadn't.

'This is the White Room,' said Incantus, snapping his fingers to garner their attention. 'A housing place for the Gems, and the oldest and most secure part of the whole Haven. Sitting directly beneath the centre of Stonehenge, it is protected by the sacrifice the First Borns made aeons ago when they first vanquished the shadows with your powers. It is the only place in the world where you will be safe from Mortem's imprinting powers should we fail during the solar eclipse tomorrow.'

'There's barely enough space for us,' Demi stated, her eyebrows drawing together. 'I'd want my parents and sister here – *all* of our parents, and Ziya, and . . . Wait. Who else knows about this?'

Incantus shook his head. 'Only us. Everyone else, if they are of age, will be fighting tomorrow, alongside the operatives of the Security Council of the High Order. In a few hours, my dear friend Serena Aevum and the Elementals of the Sanctuario will join us for final battle strategies.'

Alexis recalled Aevum's name from Teller Sagen's stories of the Quinate. He imagined the female counterpart of Incantus: strong, famed, brilliant. And powerful. If she was anything like the other members of the Quinate, Alexis couldn't wait to meet her.

'As I have said, staying to fight tomorrow is not something I have ever or would ever ask of you,' Incantus continued, offering them a small, sincere smile. 'You have made enough sacrifices for our world with your quest and I should be able to fulfil the Prophecy with the power of the Gems in your absence.'

The decorative heads of the four Corinthian columns slid away to reveal the Elemental Gems. Glowing steadily and humming with limitless power, they beamed green, grey, red and blue from each corner of the White Room, painting the monochrome walls with splashes of colour.

Between the Woman of the Water's revelation, his fight against the Serpent, the unhinged murder of Sinner and his old psychiatrist spotting him in the jungles of South America, Alexis hadn't had a moment to appreciate how entrancing his Gem was. How its colour swirled beneath the surface of the stone. All he had to do to feel its immeasurable power again was touch it to his amulet.

A flicker of jealousy crossed Alexis's mind. Incantus and Mortem didn't have stones to inhibit their abilities; they had their eternal powers within their grasp at all times.

'You haven't been raised powerful,' said Incantus, studying his face as though he had Akili Pierce's mind-reading abilities. 'You have obtained your power recently. Despite all you have learned from your past month of training, one thing you cannot rush is time itself. Once you have learned to completely control your elements, then you will be free to access all that you are entitled to and become "Omni": it's a name I'm trying for when you wield your Gem's inexhaustive power over your element. But I can't sanction that unless I am certain it won't cause corresponding and potentially catastrophic effects across the natural world.'

'Why show us the prize we fought and nearly died for, and then tell us we can't cash it in yet?' asked Blaise, crossing his muscular arms.

'Tomorrow, Elementals and our allies will be fighting to prevent Mortem from entering Stonehenge. If he unleashes his power during the few minutes of totality, all of us will be enslaved by his powers.'

'We all remember what Akili said last night,' said Caeli grimly.

'In your absence, I hope to weaponise the power of the Gems to safeguard Stonehenge.' He clasped his hands. 'That is why I have brought you here before you go. The last thing I ask of you is to help me harness your elements to protect Stonehenge.'

'Of course,' said Demi without a second thought. 'We'll do everything we can to help you.'

'I want to fight.'

It wasn't until Alexis saw his friends turn to face him that he realised it was he who had spoken. Paranoia and insomnia had weakened his inhibitions. He had planned on telling his friends at some point before they left, but he would rather have waited so they wouldn't have the opportunity to argue with him, which was exactly what they proceeded to do.

'Alexis,' said Incantus, a kind but sad smile adorning his face. 'You don't have to, son.'

Blaise backhanded him, his fear masked with protective anger. 'Are you crazy? I know it's fun being the "Chosen Ones" and all, but we've done our bit.'

'Why would you risk being anywhere but here during the eclipse?' added Caeli, elbowing Blaise out of the way so she could get closer. 'No offence, Incantus, but I am not chancing losing my mind if you fail out there. Let's stay here in the White Room where we know we'll be safe if Mortem succeeds.'

Demi spoke last, and although she was quietest, her words were the ones that had the greatest impact. 'You are admirable for wanting to stay, Lexi, but this won't be like the quest. Thousands of people and *things* will be out to hurt you to settle the Prophecy in their favour. The bloodshed will paint the fields red.' She swallowed hard. 'Wouldn't you rather spend the day with your family as fate decides which side the coin lands? Aren't you sick of the sight of shadow and death?'

Alexis thought of his mother in her scrubs and his father stroking her hair as he showered her face with gentle kisses, declaring his love for her between each one, refusing to accept that she was the one who 'loved him more'. The smell of home-cooked food and the sound of explosions from a superhero movie Jason had picked out for them to watch. Falling asleep on the sofa yet waking up in his own bed. Strong arms around him and assurances that he was safe. A childhood of care and a lifetime of love.

Stephanie and Jackson Michaels had done everything for him, for a child they didn't birth. They had made so many sacrifices for him.

It was only fair that Alexis made this sacrifice for them. To grant them a world and a future where they could bathe in the glow of sunlight until they were old. They may not have powers, but the world as they knew it would be forever changed by Mortem's success. Alexis could not sanction that.

'I will fight for every Elemental who will lose their shadow if Mortem wins and every mortal who will grieve the loss of a person cursed with a gift they did not mean to inherit,' he said, hearing the waver in his voice. But that was another thing his parents had taught him.

Shout, even when your voice shakes.

'I won't judge you for your decision, so don't judge me for mine,' he continued, looking between his friends. 'I have a chance to make a difference out there tomorrow and I'm going to take it. Incantus, you can attempt to stop me, but we all know how hard it is to try and hold water in your hands.'

His words rang out against the hard walls of the White Room. The five Elementals had fallen still, but their beating hearts had synchronised into a crescendo conducted with the wave of absolution and purpose. Alexis could feel it; he could sense the pulses within their bodies quickening to match his own. But did their hearts race from fear or from conviction? Perhaps it was both.

Even though he had never explicitly asked his friends the question, he received their answer.

'Well, when you put it like that, I guess we have to now as well,' decided Caeli with a roll of her eyes. She picked up the grey glowing Gem of the Air. 'So long as I get to go Omni again. I want the world to know how powerful I can become.'

'We'll make a big difference on the field,' Blaise confirmed, turning to look back at Incantus, who'd put a hand on his shoulder. 'It should be a wash if we've got the backing from the High Order too. We won't have to do anything with them there. I don't know about you guys, but I don't feel scared. You didn't see us on the quest, Incantus – we were on fire. Or at least, I was.'

‘I’m sure you were.’ Incantus beamed, gesturing for him to pick up the Fire Gem. He looked towards the only person who hadn’t yet spoken. ‘Demetria, you can still go home and be with your family – it is completely your choice.’

Demi shook her head. She clenched her strong jaw and took the Gem of the Earth into her hands where she held it just millimetres away from her amulet and her crucifix. ‘If I go home, I know I won’t come back. I’m not leaving my friends. If we fight, we fight together.’

Incantus’s pale blue eyes glistened with pride. ‘If you are to stay, you must adhere to my conditions. No questions, no compromise. Understood?’

They nodded. The outline of Incantus’s body began to whiten as he spread his arms out for them to take, ready to light-jump them to Stonehenge to begin their defences.

Alexis was the last to join the circuit of Elementals. The current of his thoughts had pulled him into a whirlpool that he couldn’t escape. When they vanished from the Haven and reappeared in the centre of Stonehenge, he uttered a silent prayer that his friends and mentor would never discover the other reason he had agreed to fight. They wouldn’t find him so honourable if they did.

It had not been for peace, but rather for chaos. For death and not life. For revenge on the man who had plagued them, the father who had abandoned him, the enemy who sought to harm them.

And perhaps for the chance to kill Mortem with the shadows he had spent years tormenting Alexis with.

6

TUKO PAMOJA

Tuko pamoja (phr.) *Swahili origin*
'We are together'; a shared sense of purpose and motivation in a group – it transcends mere agreement and implies empathetic understanding amongst the members of the group

There was an explosion.

A soundless, silent explosion. It was as if a grenade had been thrown into the centre of the five Elementals as they light-jumped from the White Room. A white blast flung them outwards like ragdolls in a hurricane beyond the ancient circle of standing stones above ground.

Alexis slammed to the ground, hitting it so hard that the air fled his lungs in a sweeping exodus. He gasped as he blinked bright spots from his vision. Somehow he had managed to keep a hold of his Gem, which thrummed with power. He glanced down at it and was surprised not to see the deep blue it usually pulsated with. Instead, a shimmering white glowed back at him.

He drew to his feet, shaking off the after-effects of the light-jump that still made his stomach feel like it had been pulled inside out. It didn't help that Caeli was retching not too far from him, whining that Incantus had forgotten to bring her internal organs with them.

Demi coughed from somewhere in the distance, saying something in Greek before switching to English. *Dare it be a swear?* And then she said, 'What in the world . . . ?'

Stonehenge was shining with the light of an exploding star. It poured out from the stone structure in heaving ebbs, flooding the scene and overwhelming every one of Alexis's senses. He had to shield his eyes with his arms as he took cautious steps closer.

When he reached the outermost ring of stones, he realised that it was not the ruins that were glowing; it was Incantus. He was kneeling in the very centre, huge white wings pouring from his hunched back, looking like an angel cast down from the heavens.

'Incantus?' Demi called softly, rolling her shoulder with a grimace. She looked unsure of whether to run to his aid or flee from him.

'Can you turn it down, please?' Blaise shouted, rounding Stonehenge to join the others.

Incantus grunted from exertion as the light that made up his wings slowly dimmed, snaking lines fading beneath his skin as his power was painfully reabsorbed. Alexis couldn't do anything but watch his mentor struggle to prevail, and when he finally did, Alexis also let out a deep sigh of relief. He went to him the moment he thought it safe.

'What the hell just happened?' Caeli asked, rubbing her eyes.

Incantus didn't seem to hear her. He hadn't looked at the Elementals. His hands were on his knees, supporting his weight as he stared at the ground, head tilted in thought. He glanced at the Elemental Gems in the hands of his students, then again at the circle of standing stones around him.

'I know what it means,' he declared, sucking in a sharp breath. 'I understand it now.' His eyes found Alexis. 'I know how we can destroy the shadows.'

'What do you mean?'

'It's the Prophecy.' His hands were at his head, then down again at his sides. 'The Prophecy of Light and Darkness.' He shot to his feet. 'We knew what Mortem needed to happen to succeed – to be in the centre of Stonehenge during the eclipse to cover the world in darkness and imprint us all. But that was it; we could only thwart his plans, not outright destroy him. What just happened is how we can defeat him!'

Blaise shook his head in confusion and let out a huff. 'Boss, you still haven't explained what's going on.'

'You have to stop,' Alexis demanded. Incantus fell still, turning to him. 'Ever since we discovered who we were and where we came from, you've refused to tell us the Prophecy in full.'

'Alexis, if I could tell you, I would—' Incantus began, but Alexis cut him off.

'I know you said people shouldn't know their fates, but if that's the case, why did the Women of the Elements tell us ours?'

Incantus's head dipped. 'Told you what?'

'They offered it as a gift,' said Demi. The muscles in her jaw tensed. 'I think they hoped it'd bring us peace ... offering a glimpse into our future. A personal prophecy of something that will one day be important to us. Mine already happened – back at that waterfall.'

Alexis watched Incantus's eyes narrow. 'And the rest of you?'

'The Woman of the Fire said I'd be "*the first to go dark*", whatever that means,' Blaise answered. He was holding the Fire Gem with both hands, looking into it intently as if it still held the answers.

'All of ours are so vague,' Caeli added. 'The same will probably be true about the Prophecy of Light and Darkness. We might as well know. In fact, I'm not agreeing to anything more until I do.'

Alexis remembered his prophecy from the Woman of the Water. He wouldn't ever forget it.

'*By the blade of darkness, you will fall, wielded by the one you expect the least.*'

There were only two people that wielded that power. Mortem and himself.

'I did not know,' Incantus said slowly, crouching to meet their eyeline. He shook his head. 'I am sorry, my children. There is still so much we need to share with each other.' His pale blue eyes found them, each look filled with nothing but genuine, paternal care. 'Only a select few have heard the Prophecy in full over the years and they have guarded it with their life. I wouldn't even allow Secretary-General Kleine of the High Order hear it, which he was none too happy with. As for sharing it with you, there have been people in the past who have gone crazy trying to fulfil or avoid their fortunes – I couldn't risk that.' He sighed and placed his hand on Caeli's folded arms until they relaxed. 'But if the Women of the Elements disclosed your own prophecies to you, maybe I should too. After all, it is the reason why you are here.'

Incantus shut his eyes and brought forth the ancient words

of the Prophecy of Light and Darkness. When he spoke, his voice was distant, reciting from memory as if the lines had been etched into his very being.

In a way, they had been.

Raised apart from their powers,
The Children of the Elements will meet,
The birthplace of Light and Darkness they seek.

When the sun meets the moon,
The Gems of creation will unite,
Falling on a day equal or longest from night.

Once the four corners rally,
A world of light or dark will be lain,
By oneself is how the other will be slain.

When Incantus reopened his eyes, Alexis had his face to the sun. It was the first time in what felt like forever feeling the mild warmth of the English sunshine. He never thought he would long for it. Despite how he treasured seeing the world in all its grandeur, far beyond the confines of Protegere, it was the familiar outdoors of the country he had been raised in where he felt most comfortable.

'You're right,' said Blaise, breaking the silence as he gawked at Incantus. 'We don't understand it.'

'At least the Women's prophecies were just one line,' Demi muttered.

'How do you know it's legitimate?' Caeli added.

'It was a Prophecy passed on by my mentor, Sapientis Aevum

himself,' Incantus replied. He gestured for the Elementals to take a seat on the lush grass while he perched on the edge of the huge fallen altar stone in the very centre.

'Before we get started, where is everyone?' Alexis asked. The others looked around, only now recognising that the sea of fields surrounding Stonehenge were vacant of the hundreds of tourists that usually marked it.

'The High Order's enforced the road closure ahead of the battle and had the Erasers put up a shield that will make anyone coming this way forget why and turn back.'

Alexis shrugged and took a seat beside his friends. He started picking at the grass until he noticed Demi giving him a withering glare. After that, both he and Blaise decided to sit on their hands as Incantus spoke.

'Sapientis Aevum is the eldest and most knowledgeable Elemental to ever live,' he began, his fingers scratching the growing salt-and-pepper stubble along his jaw. 'Grandson to the First Borns, his lineage has inherited the power of energy and time. Manipulate it, slow it, even see through it. His prophecies over the centuries have become famous in the Elemental and mortal world alike, but his most important was always the Prophecy of Light and Darkness, for that foretold the fate of our people and reunited the powers that birthed our kind and all of creation.'

'Let's break it down to decipher it,' said Alexis, looking at Caeli and nodding.

Demi forced herself into his eyeline with an eyebrow raised. 'Blaise and I will just go home then, shall we? You two might be book smart, but don't count us out.'

Blaise was otherwise too busy trying to conjure a ball of

flames without his hands to contribute besides humming in agreement. Demi sighed audibly.

Incantus flashed a spark of bright light before Blaise, stealing his focus. 'All prophecies are open to interpretation. We don't know if this is the way it should be read, but this is what the few who have heard it make of it. The Prophecy speaks of the Children of the Elements, born to the four original elements, coming to Stonehenge, the birthplace of light on this world. On a day when a solar eclipse falls on either equinox or the summer solstice.'

'That's why we went on the quest,' Caeli added, thinking aloud. 'To retrieve the Elemental Gems for this eclipse . . . from the world's "four corners". On a day where the sun meets the moon.'

'What about the rest of it though?' Demi asked. She pinched Blaise's arm when he incinerated a patch of daisies before him. With a delicate sweep of her bronzed hand, she bore new ones from the earth that were even brighter in colour.

'We haven't figured it all out yet,' Incantus admitted. 'We may not uncover the truth of it all until after the eclipse. But just now, we made a huge step towards unveiling how to destroy the darkness for good.'

'That explosion thing?' Blaise asked, sitting up straight

'Yes!' said Incantus. He sprang to his feet. 'Your powers combine to make light, yes? That was how the First Borns defeated the darkness aeons ago.'

'*Delayed*,' Caeli corrected.

Incantus powered on. 'Well look what just happened when *we* were in the centre of Stonehenge on an insignificant day. And that was without you being Omni – when you weren't connected to the Gems' full powers. The solstice is a powerful time for Elementals, but for a solar eclipse to fall on the same day? We knew it would supercharge Mortem's powers of darkness in a way that the world had never seen before, and should he be here in the centre of Stonehenge at totality, he could rewrite the very laws of nature. But maybe it's not only Mortem's powers that will be amplified by Stonehenge tomorrow. Ours should be too!'

'So there's a way to put him down for good?' Blaise asked. 'Not delay, but actually destroy?'

'I think so. And I think the only way is for *us* to be here during totality, together, to reignite my eclipsed light until it is so strong that it will erase the shadows from the world for ever.'

'It's a good thing we all agreed to stick around then, isn't it?' remarked Caeli with a pout.

'But how do you know that our combined power, while in our Omni state, won't destroy you and everything else in the process?' Alexis asked.

He recalled how invincible he had felt when he had synchronised with the Water Gem's unlimited energy. Like he could cast tsunamis so great, they could shake the very Earth itself. How was Incantus expecting to contain four times that amount of power while at his weakest? Visions of him exploding into nothingness at their touch swarmed Alexis's mind, unable to be shaken away.

'I'll do my best to contain it or die trying,' Incantus replied simply, interlocking his fingers in front of him. A brief look passed across his face. It wasn't surprise or fear. It was resignation, like that of a senior teacher at the end of their working days.

'No,' Demi refuted. She shook her head as she stood, loose, brunette curls swaying from the movement. Her glowing green Gem rolled off of her knees, briefly illuminating the individual blades of grass in concentric rings when it thudded to the earth. 'No, we're not doing that. We're not going to risk killing you. We're not going to risk killing anyone else.'

'Babe,' Caeli said softly. She reached to take a hold of her hand, but Demi snatched it away.

'No! No one should have to die. You said it yourself; you don't know if that's the accurate interpretation of it. There must be another way to try and do this. Like . . . like if we held Mortem off until after the eclipse and then locked him up for ever.' She looked frantically between Incantus and her friends. She saw only sympathy cast across their faces. Tears of frustration rose to her eyes. 'I know you think I'm foolish, but just because I cry, it does not make me weak.'

'Of course it doesn't, my dear,' said Incantus, offering her his hand.

After wiping at her face, she took it and held it tight. 'I'm not giving up on you. You deserve a better fate than this. You deserve to grow old and see the world you sacrificed yourself for. There has to be something else we can do.'

'I already am old, dear, even if I don't look it.' Incantus's smile failed to reach his eyes. 'I'm afraid this might be the only way. It is a sacrifice I am willing to make, one the Prophecy may require. But I can only do it with your support. All of you. The alternative is complete and utter darkness for us all.'

The anger slipped away from Demi's expression, and as it did, it pulled down the corners of her mouth, transforming her face into one of grief in limbo, as if she had just been told a loved one had received a death sentence. She allowed Alexis to come up beside her and wrap his arm around her waist as she rested her head against him.

What Demi didn't know was that she was supporting Alexis just as much as he was supporting her; he couldn't fathom a world without Incantus Arcangelo. Not Incantus the head of the Haven, or the Elemental of light, or even his uncle. But Incantus his mentor. Incantus his guide, his companion, his inspiration. His friend. He knew they would each suffer his loss, but he was certain he would take it worst of all. Incantus was all he had ever hoped to be, the binary opposite of the father and fate he thought he had inherited.

'Who knows, maybe we pull it off and it all works,' Demi offered. Even now, she remained hopeful. Alexis envied it as much as he adored it. 'It says only one power will remain in this world. We'll just have to make sure it's yours. If either you or Mortem need to destroy the other to survive, it has to be you that triumphs.'

That was one part of the Prophecy they hadn't discussed. Alexis realised it and he was sure Incantus had too.

'*By oneself is how the other will be slain.*'

Alexis hadn't yet told Incantus what he had learned about himself on the quest. That he possessed the shadow power, just like Mortem. Now here they were. The implications.

Perhaps Incantus wasn't the one prophesied to kill Mortem after all.

Alexis was.

7

MAMIHLAPINATAPAI

Mamihlapinatapai (n.) *Yahgan origin*
A look shared by two people, each wishing that
the other would initiate something they both desire,
but which neither wants to begin

'So tell us how we're going to defend Stonehenge then,' said Caeli, standing beside Alexis and Demi. She, too, appeared to be in denial about the possibility of anything bad happening to Incantus. 'We don't want Mortem getting anywhere close to us or to you, old man. And hey, if we can hold him off through the eclipse, we've won, right?'

Incantus seemed grateful for the initiation of a new task, one that would preoccupy them. 'In theory, yes. Although I have no doubt that if Mortem is allowed to go free after tomorrow, it won't be the last we hear of him. Either way, our plan of defence is as follows. One by one, you will infuse Stonehenge with your primal elements.' With beams shooting from his hands like torchlight, he split the circular structure into four distinct quarters. 'Mortem will find a way to teleport his army using Ezra or any other portaller he has convinced or imprinted. This site will be guarded from all sides by our army; everyone we have recruited, Elemental and magical alike, and Mortem won't be able to teleport into Stonehenge directly. So if you are certain you wish to join us, it will be on the condition that you remain the last line of defence where I know you will be safe, deep in the centre. Here, and not a foot beyond.'

'Wouldn't exactly call anywhere on a battlefield "safe",' Caeli murmured.

'Where will you be?' Demi asked.

'The front line.'

No way, thought Alexis. 'I don't want to wait here on standby while others give their lives to protect us,' he said. It wasn't right. The prospect of battle shook him to his very core, it made him want to run and hide, but how could Incantus expect them to do nothing? If Incantus was on the front line, Alexis wanted to be right there with him.

Blaise joined the others in standing. 'Nah, I agree with Incantus. We should stay here, but so should you.' Blaise looked at his mentor as he crossed his arms across his chest. 'I know you're the most powerful, but if you've got to get back here in time when you'll already be powerless from the eclipse, do you really think it's a smart move being so outfield?' He raised his eyebrows self-importantly when his friends stared at him in surprise. 'Yeah, I listen sometimes.'

'It's for that very reason, Mr Ademola, that I need to be at the front – because I am the most powerful,' Incantus replied with a growing smirk. 'Trust me, I'll be able to handle my brother and the Shadowless up until the start of the eclipse.' It wasn't often that Incantus said something with complete self-assuredness. Most of his accomplishments had been relayed by others, namely Teller or the Leaders or Ziya. Hearing him speak now made Alexis grin despite everything.

He had nothing to worry about. His angel wouldn't be going anywhere anytime soon.

'Mortem will likely bide his time and send his forces forward to clear his route to the centre ahead of the eclipse,' Incantus went on. 'But if there's a chance for me to rescue the Leaders and take him down before the eclipse even begins, before I am robbed of my powers, I have to take it. And if I don't manage to do this, then I need you as close to Stonehenge as possible, ready for me. Totality lasts for no longer than seven minutes – we cannot waste a second of it.'

Incantus yawned and stretched his arms wide so that the bottom of his shirt pulled up, revealing his toned, muscled lower abdomen. Blaise made a high-pitched wolf-whistle, and he tugged it down before pointing them each to one of the four segments of the monolithic ruins while he remained in the centre.

Alexis called to his friends, 'It's like we're back in training.'

'He better not throw us in the ocean again,' Caeli warned, tying her silvery hair into a ponytail.

'To ensure Stonehenge remains as protected as it can be, I want you to use the power of the Gems to guard it,' Incantus instructed, slowly turning in a circle as he spoke. 'Mortem will have to get through our entire army to reach the centre before the eclipse, but we can't underestimate what tricks he may have up his sleeve or the powers he has at his disposal. You and your defences have to stand, even if everyone else falls. Create your defences how you see fit, ensuring that no one except yourselves can enter through your respective quarter. Be imaginative; utilise your gifts in ways that would complement you best. It has to be strong enough to stop the entire Dark Army.'

The Children of the Elements got to work at the birthplace of light, the gravesite of their ancestors, constructing their defences to ensure it wouldn't be theirs come tomorrow.

Alexis manipulated the energy of the Water Gem to flood the land just in front of his quarter of Stonehenge. It poured freely as if it came from an inexhaustive faucet, glistening in the midday sunlight. The force of the water excavated the soil, and in its place, there soon lay a deep, arcing pond that bordered his section of monoliths. Alexis could've stopped there, but he knew it wouldn't be enough to hold back Mortem or the Shadowless.

He brought forth a second cool wave from the Gem to bathe the great standing stones with a shimmering curtain of water. For his first defence, he had pulled on thoughts of home, of his room in the Haven and the pool he so often bathed in. For the second defence, he thought of the final stage of the quest where he had almost lost his life.

Alexis's fingers shivered from the frost as he plummeted the temperature of the waterfall over Stonehenge. Tendrils of ice stretched out between the rocks like desperate, drowning hands reaching for each other in the chaos.

Alexis panted from exertion, his hands on his knees for support as cold sweat trickled down his spine. Each breath turned to mist as he stared at the hardened wall of ice before him, so thick that it stood as solid and unbreakable as the stones that pillared it.

Try and get through that, Father, he thought, stepping out of the shadow of Stonehenge and into the sunlight.

Once the Children of the Elements had finished their defences, Incantus made them follow him around the circumference of the stones and asked them to explain how they had transformed it into a structure almost unrecognisable from what it had been for millennia.

The north-east quarter, which faced nothing but miles of mowed fields, had been guarded by the Earth Gem. A magnificent oak tree stood before the outermost circle of rocks. Its trunk was more than a metre in width, shielded in thick layers of dark bark, and a gnarling tangle of roots split the ground beneath it. Great twisting arms broke off, riddled in thorns as sharp as needles, and draped with long-stemmed lianas that hung over the branches like vines.

Alexis marvelled at its beauty, the shelter it provided and the confidence with which it grew. It was a product of nature as breathtaking as its mother; wild and imposing. He noted its inspiration – the Tree of Life that had grown beneath the ground when the Woman of the Earth had appeared to them, although this was a far more threatening apparition. It seemed as though Demi had also drawn on her experiences and the greatest feats of her element to protect her during the battle.

Moving clockwise to Caeli's quarter, a hazy double image shimmered before the outermost circle of the monoliths, refracting the light like a mirage along the horizon on a hot day. The greyish borders of the force field clearly marked the edges of her section, with the highpoint reaching far overhead beyond Alexis's Elemental eyesight. Beside it, Blaise's stones that faced south-west had been ignited, burning with bright red and yellow flames, wisps of fire flicking dangerously tall into the sky. Although the rocks of Stonehenge didn't burn or scorch, the fire crackled on, spitting embers as soon as Blaise moved close to show it off.

Lastly, Alexis presented the pool of water and ice wall that guarded his side, to drown or to freeze. In the back of his mind, Alexis already anticipated that Mortem would approach Stonehenge through his quarter. *Call it irony or nostalgia*. He also knew no matter how strong his defences were, they wouldn't be enough to hold him off indefinitely. He was sure Incantus was thinking the same thing too. Nevertheless, the mentor praised him for his efforts just as he had done his friends.

'Well done. All of you,' Incantus continued, the late afternoon sunlight making his ruffled white hair glow. 'Very well done. You have certainly deserved the rest of the day to yourselves. Spend your afternoon as you please. I will call you when the Elementals of the Sanctuario arrive so that I can introduce you to them and to Serena. She is most eager to finally meet you.'

Tendrils of white light spread from Incantus's palms and coiled around the Alpha team. Once the five Elementals were connected, in less than a heartbeat, they were returned to the White Room.

They each returned their Gems to the sealed capsules without complaint, wanting nothing more than to get out from the confined room. Alexis watched as the casing of his container closed, shutting off the Water Gem's luminous blue hue, storing it until the time came tomorrow where he would need it again.

'So what should we do now?' Blaise asked, looking to Alexis as the four friends reached the peak of the hive.

Despite his tiredness and his anxiety, Alexis couldn't help but smile. In that moment, he wanted to hug Blaise tighter than ever, but there was no way that he could without being probed for questions as to why a simple question elicited such a strong response.

Alexis didn't want to explain how he had spent so many years dreaming of having friends that, even after spending the whole day with him, still wanted to be in his company. It was something he always longed for but was told by the *Shadow Man* he'd never have. With half a mind, he wished it could see him now: powerful, loved, safe – all the things it said he'd never deserve.

'It's one of the only times we've had more than a few hours to ourselves since we got here,' said Caeli. She picked at her cuticles and made eye contact with Blaise for the first time all day. She then looked away. 'I should probably put a few extra hours of training in. Can never be too ready, can you?'

Demi took her hand. 'You've trained enough,' she said. 'We should rest. Actually, we should celebrate!' She reached out with her other hand for Blaise. 'Any suggestions?'

'We should drink,' Blaise announced, making Caeli smile despite herself.

Alexis noted how jittery Blaise had been since they'd returned to the Haven, how he couldn't stop shuffling his feet or darting glances between them. He looked like he was worried they would suggest to go their separate ways, leaving him alone to comprehend and contemplate the dangers they had agreed to face together. Although Alexis would've preferred to spend some time by himself, possibly reading, which always seemed to calm his anxious mind, he was more than willing to make this silent sacrifice for Blaise, even if that meant joining his friend on a venture that seemed extremely unwise.

'Okay, maybe underage drinking isn't the best thing to do

the day before a battle,' Demi began, glancing at Alexis for support.

'No, I think that's exactly what we should do,' decided Alexis, making Blaise cheer. Demi rolled her deep green eyes, but her mouth had curled into a wide-toothed grin. 'Last week, Teller gifted me a bottle of wine and said we should open it when we return successful from our quest. I can't think of a better way to honour him.'

For hours, the Children of the Elements joked and teased and laughed as normal teenagers would, without the weight of the world and its future on their shoulders. They sprawled themselves across the sofas of Demi's warm, flower-filled room in a haphazard arrangement, arms and legs layered over one another.

Demi's room seemed to reflect her mood, and more than it had ever before: the flowers lining the edges of it blossomed beautifully, and the vines that adorned the walls stretched and curled into spiralling patterns that looked almost like a thousand wide smiles. Card game after taunt after story filled their time, not a dull or quiet moment falling amongst them.

Demi protested her turn at first when the bottle was passed her way, but before long, she was helping herself to large swigs.

'Eugh!' she shouted, shaking her head as she hiccuped so deeply, she startled herself. 'I can't be hungover for tomorrow.'

'Too late,' Blaise pointed out, throwing down the last card in his hand and sitting back against the couch. Alexis put his arm over him, feigning an embrace in order to snatch the bottle from his hand.

'I'm not even sure what a hangover is, to be honest,' Demi admitted.

Alexis wiped his wet lips with the back of his hands. 'It's when you drink too much alcohol and need water.'

Demi reached for the bottle again. Her hand closed over Alexis's where he held it, and – call it Dutch courage – but he didn't immediately let go.

'I always need water,' she said quietly, her eyes trained on the bottle as a blush rose to her cheeks. No matter how intently Alexis looked at her in the seconds that followed, she appeared too bashful to meet his eyes until he had relinquished his hold on the bottle and she had sat back again. Only then, after taking another swig, did she return his look and grin.

'If we survive the eclipse, we should go away!' Caeli suggested, although it sounded more like a command than a suggestion.

Over the course of their drinking, Alexis had noticed how Caeli and Blaise had drawn closer together – as had he and Demi. Caeli lay slumped atop Blaise's lap as he stroked his fingers carelessly through her hair, a smile etched onto her face that she didn't bother to conceal.

'We've travelled across the world in a weekend,' said Blaise, looking down at Caeli, his gaze unwavering. 'I'd like to stay here for a little while and remember what it's like to be normal.'

Caeli used her powers to float the nearly empty wine bottle from Demi's hand and guzzled it from the air. A small amount dripped from the corner of her mouth. Blaise met the drop before it fell, brushing it away with the delicate stroke of his thumb, his eyes not leaving hers once. Alexis felt like he was intruding just by watching, but he couldn't look away. Not when the air drew still, not when the temperature of the room skyrocketed.

Go on, Blaise, he wanted to shout. *Show her how you feel.* Demi nudged his leg with hers, then elbowed his side, any and all subtlety flung out of the window. She was doing everything in her power not to scream in vicarious excitement as their friends slowly leaned towards one another, eyes closed, lips puckered—

'What do you think you're doing?' boomed Incantus's voice from the doorway.

The four friends scrambled to their feet, none too gracefully. Caeli thrust the empty bottle into Demi's hands. She fretted with it for a moment before tucking it behind her back, her timing so far off that Alexis had to look away so that he wouldn't giggle. He could only imagine what they looked like. There couldn't have been a worse time for him to catch them.

'Move your big arms out of the way, Ian, I wanna see 'em,' snapped a woman in a thick Scottish accent, shoving him aside.

Incantus spoke through gritted teeth as he glared at them. 'Children of the Elements, meet Serena Aevum.'

8

GEBORGENHEIT

Geborgenheit (n.) *German origin*
To feel completely safe, like nothing could ever harm you; security, comfort, trust, satisfaction, acceptance and love from others

The glass bottle slid from Demi's grasp and smashed on the floor as noisily as it possibly could. Demi showed no reaction other than a slow, regretful blink, as if that would mean Incantus didn't notice.

Much to Alexis's surprise, what followed was the loudest, most unrestrained laugh he had ever heard. It cackled around the room, thumping against the walls as if produced from a heavy-bass speaker.

'Brilliant!' bellowed Serena Aevum.

The eldest daughter of Sapientis Aevum was like a small ball of fire, barely half Incantus's height. Pale-skinned and covered in freckles, her bushy ginger hair was streaked with grey and stood out untidily. Cloaked in a brightly coloured pashmina, the old, rounded woman radiated a vitality almost as strongly as Incantus.

'Don't encourage them,' Incantus chastised, putting his hand over hers to stop the booming sound of her applause. 'This is not what I expected from the four of you when I said enjoy the afternoon. Underage drinking? You have the most important day of your lives tomorrow. A day that will dictate the future of our whole world.'

'Oh stop being such a bore, Ian,' Serena said, waving him away, uninterested. Alexis had only ever heard Teller speak to him like that, yet apparently Incantus didn't seem to mind at all. In fact, he looked like he expected her to do so. 'Don't you remember what shenanigans we five would get ourselves into in our spare time? You've been caught in far worse positions, if my old memory serves me correctly.'

At that, Incantus slowly closed his mouth, receiving a self-satisfied 'hm' from Serena in return. The closer she came towards them, the more awake Alexis felt, as if her presence supercharged him. With wide, owlish eyes, she looked upon each of the young Elementals, taking them all in. Her grip was hard and warm around Alexis's hand as she shook it with a strength that didn't match her age.

'Pleasure to meet you all. An honour. I would've introduced myself prior to your quest, but I've been so busy with the Sanctuario on the other side of the world and I know you have been equally as busy. I want to hear all about you! But first, my Elementals need some good food and I need several bottles of wine. And, most importantly, I need to see my granddaughters.'

Alexis and his friends followed the two elder Elementals from Demi's room, stifling their smiles as they apologised to Incantus. His disappointment was short-lived. With Serena's arm around his, the odd pairing of the handsome middle-aged man and the woman old enough to be his mother painted an unusual but amusing picture.

'I didn't know she had granddaughters here,' Alexis said to his friends. 'Wonder who they are?'

'I'm pretty sure that if they were anything like her, then we definitely would've noticed them,' Caeli added under her breath. She and Blaise walked at a slightly slower pace behind them, his arm loosely wrapped around her waist. They had been thieved of the opportunity for their first kiss, but with this much tension between them now, Alexis was certain it wouldn't be long.

When they reached the hive, Alexis was met by more Elementals than he had ever conceived of existing. There must've been thousands of them, so many that the ground level of the hub had disappeared, no longer visible beneath the swarming crowds that dotted the benches that made up the huge reformed dining area. The buzz of the two training institutes resonated throughout every crevice of the Haven, radiating like a star in the sky or a whistle in a cave.

'I had no idea there were so many of us,' Demi said with a gasp. 'They must be from the Sanctuario!' She pointed to the gathered mass of Elementals wearing similar monochrome uniforms to those at the Haven, only in a deep navy instead of black.

'Where is it?' Blaise asked. 'Never really paid attention in Taranis's Scholar sessions.'

'Shock,' Alexis commented, receiving an amused side-eye from him.

'It's the partnered Haven beneath the great stone heads of Easter Island,' Serena answered from ahead, beaming proudly back at them. 'It's not significant to our people and our history in the way Stonehenge is, but it's still the only other Elemental training facility that isn't overseen directly by the High Order – Teller made sure of that when he was the secretary-general.'

One by one, the crowd began to notice the Children of the Elements, flooding them with customary stares and exclamations. Alexis wasn't one for big groups or attention, but he couldn't deny the contentment he felt when he observed the proud, excited looks on their faces. Whether or not he was deserving of it, it still felt nice to be regarded as a hero.

'Speech time,' Serena said to the young Elementals. 'Join your comrades while this one does what he's best at.'

'Inspiring others?' Demi suggested.

Serena scoffed. 'Stealing my limelight.'

Alexis and his friends made their way down the golden marble staircase until they reached one of the bridges that crossed the hive the level above the crowd. Blaise instantly set to work, revelling in the attention, expertly conducting the masses' gasps and cheers with his red-glowing hands. Elementals of the Haven and Sanctuario alike called to them, shouting greetings and asking questions in more languages than Alexis could count. Caeli took flight over the crowds, swooping like an eagle in the sky, while Demi waved and shook hands with as many people as she could reach.

Alexis could admit that he probably wasn't the best conversationalist of the group, especially with people he didn't know. Having spent much of his early childhood conversing with only three people (one being his brother who, for many years, couldn't speak back), Alexis didn't feel well-rehearsed in making small talk. So instead, he searched the hundreds of faces below him for anyone familiar.

'Alexis Michaels,' called a nearby woman with a deep Southern drawl, 'Tide Caller, Lord of the Seas, Serpent Slayer, and tormenter of Joe Coin.'

Directly beneath them, standing taller than most of the crowd, was Althea Orenda. Blaise noticed her too and gave an awkward wave.

'Never officially called things off with her,' he mumbled to Alexis.

'I'm fairly certain you weren't official with her to begin with, and even more confident that she'll survive somehow,' Alexis said with a grin. Blaise rolled his eyes and went back to addressing the crowds.

Althea swept thick dreadlocks from her face and beamed at Alexis as he knelt down to clasp her hand in greeting. She also must have been called back to the Haven, relinquishing her assigned post as personal guard of the British prime minister. Alexis did his best attempt to sound innocuous in his reply. 'Only you and Joe were brave enough to get involved with either one of them.' He gestured to where Blaise was exploding fireworks in the sky as Caeli dipped and soared. 'Or was it stupidity?'

Althea scrunched her nose and shrugged. 'What can I say? I'm a witch and a bitch.'

As Alexis laughed, he spared a moment to skim the rest of the crowd. Not even the Haven was able to contain them all if many more arrived.

Why haven't they opened the Garden? he wondered.

In the far corner, past the clustered banqueting tables and chairs, stood the great archaic stone archway that had once led to the wondrous enchanted forest. It remained unlit, dull without the typical glow of the teleportation line that had once powered it. 'The Garden's still sealed?'

Althea followed his gaze. 'It's warded off. People were saying they weren't comfortable with it, said its pureness was tainted after Mortem's invasion and Teller's death. Incantus closed it down to make the younger ones feel safe again.'

'But Mortem could only enter because Ezra granted him access from inside the Haven,' Alexis protested, watching as Althea shrugged. He knew how much Incantus loved the Garden, how he had once said it was his favourite place in the whole world. It would be a shame to never see the beauty of it again.

'I know a lot's happened with you guys, but you've also missed a lot here too. People are petrified. It is far easier to fear the nightmare than it is to treasure the dream.'

'Elementals!' came Incantus's thunderous voice from the peak of the hive, stealing the undivided attention of all those gathered. 'Thank you for joining me today. As you may have noticed, here with us now are all those from the Haven and Sanctuario who have agreed to fight tomorrow. Let's show Serena Aevum and her Elementals the welcome they deserve!'

The crowd erupted into a cheer. High-pitched whistles and war cries flooded the area with excited noise. The spirited reactions were infectious, filling Alexis with purpose and courage. To see the army of warriors he would be fighting beside, soldiers as young as fifteen and others well over a hundred years old, blossomed a pride within him that affirmed his decision to stay.

Blaise whistled to catch the attention of Althea below them. 'What's Aevum's power again?'

'Not even a "hello, how are you?"' Althea tutted, but there was no malice in her words. 'Energy, pure energy. Convert its form, even create and destroy it. Teller would never admit it publicly, but he used to say she could rival Incantus if you got her angry enough. Or drunk enough.'

Serena cleared her throat and took a step forward. She radiated authority, aristocracy, and she barely needed to make an effort to raise her voice to be heard. 'This is a reminder for you all. Every single person here, whether you are fighting at Stonehenge or guarding the Haven beneath it, is doing their bit to save the world. You have the evening to rest and reconnect with friends, to share in the contagiousness of hope. For tomorrow, when the solar eclipse meets the summer solstice, the fight of our lives takes place and we cannot lose! We have the Elementals from the Haven and the Sanctuario, the support of the High Order, and the help of the magical communities across the globe!'

Incantus swooped in and gestured to Alexis and his friends. Their amulets winked with power back at him. 'And of course, as you can see, the Children of the Elements have returned victorious from their quest and have declared their place beside us tomorrow. The Prophecy of Light and Darkness is unravelling and there is only one outcome we will accept!'

The ear-splitting roar of the Elementals thundered throughout the Haven and shook the marble arches that bridged the hive. Alexis wasn't sure how long they had all been cheering, but his throat was sore by the time the noise began to fade.

'The moon will begin to block the sun just past four o'clock,' Incantus said, reengaging their focus. 'From then on, my power will wane as I get weaker and Mortem stronger. Once totality begins, there will be *seven* minutes where the light from the sun is entirely blocked by the moon, where the world will be cast into complete shadow. Until then, Mortem and his army will be battling across the fields towards Stonehenge. If he reaches its centre, he will use his powers to cover the world in permanent shadow and imprint all those with Elemental blood. Seven minutes, that's all he has. Arrangements have already been passed on to you. Familiarise yourself with them; they are different from how they once were when the Leaders were with us. Any questions should be directed to Miss Parashakti in my absence. But as for now, dinner has been served!'

While he and Serena had been conducting the crowds, the Elementals hadn't noticed the rows of tables at the back of the hub slowly fill with bulging platters of meats and fish, salads and pastas and vegetables. The head chef, Libero, his equally huge proxy, and dozens of the Training Academy sparring bots – printed by the numerous projectors around the hive – were adding the final trays to the serving tables, beckoning the Elementals over.

The crowd moved as one, swarming across the hub and filling their plates before dispersing to find their seats.

'The best perk of being a celebrity is not having to wait in line,' said Caeli. '*Very Important Elementals* coming through!' With a flick of her wrist, the air shifted beneath Alexis and he felt himself lift off his feet to join her, Blaise and Demi. In a fraction of the time it would have taken otherwise, they collected their dinners and settled on the high-table most central in the room.

The young Elementals squeezed onto the bench, shuffling against each other's shoulders and nudging each other apart when Incantus and Serena later joined them. Serena barked an order at an Elemental nearby to bring her two plates of food before she stretched out on the row opposite the Alpha team and downed a glass of wine without taking a breath.

The unmistakable reaction to Gibbous from the Elementals in navy suits signalled his arrival. Dozens fled from the intimidatingly large wolf, while others stood immobile as he strode brazenly past them. He nearly knocked Serena over as he tried to lick her face in excitement. Only when he got in the way of her taking a sip from her drink did Serena finally order him down, keeping him at arm's length so his wagging tail didn't sweep the tabletops.

'The old boy's going to outlive us all,' she said, throwing Gibbous a whole rotisserie chicken. 'That should fill you up for the next half hour.'

Incantus raised his eyebrows. 'Indeed.' His mouth grew into a sly smile.

'What?' Serena asked, adjusting the tower of cushions she sat on that helped her see over the table.

'You've got fatter.'

Serena dabbed at her mouth with a serviette before chucking it at Incantus's face. 'When you're this powerful and experienced, you don't need to do all that running and jumping.'

Alexis had assumed that one of the dozen daughters of the esteemed Sapientis Aevum would hold herself with poise and grace. The fact that she didn't made him warm to her even more. It helped distract him from the wandering hands and heated whispers passing between Caeli and Blaise beside him.

At the other end of the row, Demi leaned back to catch his eye and feigned a gagging action. The Haven had hundreds of rooms to choose from – couldn't Caeli and Blaise excuse themselves to find one?

There was a series of grunts and shuffling footsteps as the crowd of Elementals nearest to their table was shoved aside. Althea emerged, trailing an apologetic-looking Joe Coin behind her.

'Here they are,' Althea said, gesturing to the table eagerly.

The colour drained from Caeli's face.

'Hey, Joe, good to see you're back,' said Blaise, removing his hand from Caeli's thigh to greet him.

Alexis swore he could hear Althea cackling shamelessly as she wedged herself back into the crowd.

'Thank you, Blaise,' Joe replied. He cleared his throat. 'Caeli, is it all right if I have a word with you?'

Caeli had started running her fingers through her hair over and over again. 'Joe . . .' Joe rested his hand against her shoulder, but removed it immediately when her storm-grey eyes met his.

'Caeli, please can we just talk?'

'*What's going on?*' Demi mouthed to Alexis from the other end of the bench, her eyes darting between Caeli, Joe and Blaise. Alexis stretched the neckline of his T-shirt and pressed his lips together. Alexis knew Demi had figured it out because her mouth dropped open.

Blaise looked Joe up and down, his jaw clenching. 'Take a hint, bud. She's over you.'

Joe's eyes darted to Caeli. 'That's not what she said last night.'

Serena gasped, not even pretending to give them any privacy. Incantus, on the other hand, gave them the courtesy of acting like he was deeply interested in rearranging the remaining food on his plate.

It was as if Blaise had been slapped across the face. His focus snapped to Caeli as she cringed beside him. His shoulders slanted slightly. 'Are you kidding me, Cae?'

Alexis saw the top of Althea's head poking out from the crowd. When he flashed a sarcastic thumbs-up for instigating it all, he heard her cackle again. By then, Alexis had already got to his feet and was guiding Joe away from the group. 'It's time to go.'

'But I didn't do anything wrong,' Joe protested, looking over Alexis's shoulder to try and catch a glance from Caeli. 'She's the one who invited *me* over.'

Demi appeared at his other side, guiding him onward. 'Now's not the time, Joe, I'm so sorry.' They returned to the others just as Caeli began shouting.

'*What?* I did nothing wrong!' Caeli's voice rang out. Her demeanour had been quickly replaced with a brazen ignorance, the kind that she only used when arguing with Blaise.

'You literally just told me you wanted to talk privately. That you've got something "important" to tell me as your hands stroked *very* high up my thighs,' Blaise retorted scathingly. His eyes had reddened to a deep maroon as the muscles of his eyebrows came down in a frown. 'Was it to tell me you got back with your private-school boyfriend?'

'No!' Her voice carried over the bustle of the hub, turning the heads of those close by. 'You know what, it doesn't matter what I was going to say. You're probably too busy obsessing over whoever next walks through the door.'

'Damn right I will,' Blaise replied, crossing his arms across his chest. 'Why shouldn't I? All everyone does is treat me like a piece of meat. That's all I'm good for, isn't it?'

Caeli pressed her lips together into a thin line and shook her head. 'Classic Blaise, unable to wager on a fight he's not guaranteed to win.' Her hair whipped around violently, but she didn't break her stare. 'You've just made it *so* much easier to give up on boys whose egos are as fragile as their dicks are small.'

Red wine shot from Serena's nostrils and soaked the table cloth. Incantus glared at her, but he couldn't stop her shoulders from jostling from laughter.

'The second-hand embarrassment is killing me,' Demi muttered.

Alexis put his arm around Blaise when he got to his feet. 'I don't get her, I really don't,' Blaise seethed through gritted teeth, throwing his napkin down. 'If you're going to insult me, at least make it accurate.' Alexis could only shake his head in the hopes to pacify him.

Behind them, Caeli was spitting insults to Demi, also not bothering to keep her voice low. 'I'm being so serious, Dem. I am giving up on men.'

'Let's go for a walk and meet some new people,' Alexis suggested. He looked for an opening in the crowd before Blaise ended up incinerating the table.

'There they are!' Serena exclaimed just as the crowd parted before her. She rose to her feet, smiling so widely that creases formed at the edges of her eyes. 'There are my beautiful granddaughters!'

Alexis turned to follow Serena's gaze and was shocked to see who was standing there. The direct descendent of one of the most powerful Elemental bloodlines ever to exist, the eldest daughter of the newest generation of Aevum. The person who, despite that, did not possess any powers of her own.

'Hi, Grandma,' said Ziya.

9

SHAKTI

Shakti (n.) *Hindi origin*
Power; energy; Hindu goddess of creation
and all dynamic forces in the universe

'Why has it been a whole month since you last came to see me!' Serena beamed, enveloping Ziya and Parvati, Ziya's younger sister, into a tight embrace.

Ziya's head was turned at an awkward angle to avoid the gawks from her friends. Side by side, she bore no resemblance to Serena other than her rounded, short stature and large, owlish eyes. Her brown skin and dark hair must have come from her father, but Alexis knew that Ziya had kept secret who her famous grandmother was not because she didn't inherit her looks, but because she didn't inherit her power.

'I've missed you, Grandma!' said Parvati, giving her a second hug. Where Serena squeezed her back so tightly, the action disturbed the placement of Parvati's left hearing aid, and together they helped to readjust it.

'Remember what I said, dear,' said Serena, using her hands to sign fluently as she spoke, likely having an awareness that the loud background noise might be making it harder for Parvati to hear her clearly. 'Don't call me Grandma. Makes me sound old.'

Parvati giggled. 'How old are you again?'

Serena waved her hand dismissively. 'I stopped counting once it got to three digits. Have you both been well?' She held on to each of their arms to help her sit down on the bench, piling pillows beneath her before freeing her hands again to sign. 'Are you both happy? I hope Incantus has been treating you right. Especially you, Ziya, with all the new responsibilities I hear you've undertaken.'

Ziya nodded enthusiastically. 'He is. I'm almost finished with my training to be a Leader here. And Parvati's been doing *so* well. She's come so far recently, you would be so proud of her. Tell her, Ti.'

'I can restructure objects now!' Parvati boasted as Alexis forced a reluctant Blaise back on the bench. 'I can't change their material . . . not yet. Can I show you later?'

Serena clapped so loudly that it made the table reverberate. 'You'd better do, little lady. I'm also going to remind you that you can move to the Sanctuario anytime. It's not as lavish or big as this, but it'll be much warmer on the surface.'

'Hey!' Incantus shouted, pausing his conversation with a group of Elementals a couple of tables away. 'Stop trying to steal my students! Ziya is my protégée; she's not going anywhere. Not if she's one day going to take over the mantle of this place. And Parvati is showing the greatest promise of any Elemental I've ever seen at her age. They're staying here with me.'

'Not if I can help it,' Serena said, her eyes glinting with the prospect of a challenge.

'Do you want to meet my friends?' Parvati asked, tugging at Serena just as she pressed her lips to what was possibly her third glass of wine.

Sighing, Serena got to her feet. She turned to Ziya and said, 'I guess I've got to show my face, do the rounds. Don't want your mentor showing me up. That's the annoying thing about tall people – they cast awfully large shadows.'

Ziya grinned and only then did Alexis notice the similarity between them. In their smiles, how it encompassed their whole face. Serena kissed Ziya's cheek and said, 'I'll come find you later,' before nodding towards the Alpha team and being whisked away by Parvati.

With both Incantus and Serena filtering through the maze of tables, Caeli practically leaped from her seat to sit as far as she could from Blaise on the opposite side of the table. It was impossible to ignore the shooting daggers they sent at each other, occasionally catching Alexis and Demi in the crossfire.

Ziya cleared her throat as she stood to leave. Demi caught her hand and said, 'Join us.' Without waiting for an answer, Demi launched into conversation as Ziya lowered herself back into her seat. 'Your grandmother seems so lovely! So, how have you been? Busy day, I'm sure.'

'Yeah. Super busy,' Ziya replied, glancing between them. 'I've been making sure everyone is prepared for tomorrow. Getting the Centauroi and Amazons together again has been rough with their long history of conflict. And then there's negotiating with the Fae. And I'm still trying to contact the Elemental Tribes, but—'

'So how come you don't have powers?' Blaise asked, interrupting her. Alexis shoved him in reprimand as Caeli tutted. 'What? We were all thinking it.'

'You don't need to answer that,' said Alexis.

'No, it's fine.' Ziya shrugged, her eyes fixed on the table.

'Everyone who knows asks me that. *I* ask myself that. It's one of the first things Ezra ever said to me. Truthfully, I don't know why. I know I should, considering the Aevum and Parashakti blood in me. Sometimes Elementals' powers can be suppressed if they've experienced trauma, but I didn't show any signs of power even before Mortem took my mother. I'm just unlucky, I guess.'

Alexis remembered meeting Ziya on his first night in the Haven. Her embarrassment then paled in comparison to the shame she now showed. She hadn't met her friends' eyes once since sitting. *As if we would think any less of her because of this?* Alexis had to show her how untrue that was.

He spoke with conviction when he said, 'Incantus may be the head of the Haven, but you are its heart, Ziya. Its centre of gravity. You are what makes this place home.'

At that, Ziya met his gaze and saw that he wasn't looking at her with judgement or pity. He truly meant what he said and he hoped she believed him. She nodded her head, smiling as the rest of the table heartily raised their drinks in agreement.

Blaise soon struck up another conversation about the magical creatures that had pledged to fight alongside the Elementals. As he did, Alexis found Demi staring at him, a glint in her eyes. The way she looked at him made him feel as though the spring season had taken permanent residence in his chest, bringing with it the prospect of something novel and beautiful. He would sooner go blind than risk losing that look.

Not long after, Serena came swaying through the dining area, almost snapping the wooden beams of the bench when she slumped to her seat between Ziya and Caeli. 'She's got your mother's defiant boldness,' she said to Ziya, generously pouring herself another drink before 'spilling' some of it into the rest of the Elementals' glasses. 'Your mother got that from me.' She sat back proudly. 'And you have her compassion – I don't know where she got that from.'

Ziya shared a silent, intimate smile with her grandmother. It only lasted a few seconds, but it was long enough for Alexis to see how deeply they both must miss her and how much Serena sought to ensure that Ziya kept her memory alive, despite how long it had been since her disappearance.

'Now,' Serena started, changing subject before any tears dared ruin her night. She slammed her hands on the table and looked between the Children of the Elements. 'Tell me all about you! Your battles, the victories, the little affairs in between. Tell me about your quest!'

'And me!' Ziya added. She curled close to Serena's side and beamed when her grandmother draped her pashmina shawl over her shoulders. 'I can't believe I still haven't heard it properly. I want to know everything!'

And so they went on, divulging the details of their expedition. The mantle of speaking passed fluently between the four of them, taking over when it came to describing the Woman of their Element and the corresponding Creature they took on. As the story evolved, carrying them through what happened over each portal from Greece to China to Tanzania to Argentina, the surrounding Elementals gathered around them like moths to a flame.

Soon enough, they had to project their voices to speak to the entire crowd, with Blaise once again taking pleasure in his exaggerated descriptions. He had always said to never let the truth get in the way of a good story.

Alexis indulged in enjoying himself, seeing his friends' eyes light up with the affirmation of others and the animated squeals and gasps coming from Serena and Ziya. Incantus perched on the edge of the neighbouring table to listen with wide-eyed fascination, beaming with pride from the very first moment they had started their story.

When the time came to explain what had happened at the top of the waterfall, just after Demi had been shot and the Serpent had been let free, the whole crowd fell silent.

'Sinner?' Serena gawked, waiting for confirmation. 'You took out Sinner? With his own arrow?' Demi didn't respond, falling in on herself slightly, still racked with a guilt that looked as if it made her feel cold all over.

'You lucky girl!' Serena exclaimed after a long pause. 'I always wanted to be the one to do it!'

The crowd erupted into a cheer as she shook Demi's hand with such a force that Demi had to hold on to Blaise's shoulder so that she wouldn't fall over. There was a flicker of a smile on Demi's lips that couldn't be suppressed.

When their story came to a close and they broke off into smaller conversations with the remaining Elementals around them, Alexis saw Serena turn to Incantus and take his hands in hers. 'Incredible job, Ian, you really did it! They make some of our missions pale in comparison, aye?'

Incantus chuckled. 'Some of them, yes.'

'Here comes the most important question. Who is more powerful: the Quinate or the Children of the Elements?'

Incantus shook his head. 'Always a competition with you,' he said fondly. 'We trained for our whole lives. They trained for a fraction of the time and look at what they've achieved.

They froze a waterfall, shook the surface of the Earth, caused a volcanic eruption, and created a tornado in the sky. They are more than we were at their age – and maybe even us now.'

Serena reached out to cradle the side of Incantus's face. 'You really love them like they're your own, don't you, my dear?'

Incantus's smile softened. He spoke quietly, unaware that Alexis had been listening in. 'I may not be their father, but they are certainly my children.'

Surrounded by a sea of motion and noise, Alexis noted that the two old friends were faintly glowing, their powers amplified by the presence of all the Elementals around them. Alexis hadn't seen his mentor look this happy in what felt like a long time. It reminded him of the kind of synchronicity he had with Jason. After a lifetime spent squabbling, he wished for nothing more than the opportunity to argue with his brother once again.

Alexis pushed the thought from his mind and turned to Serena. 'Teller would always go on about the missions you went on together. I spent hours by his side hearing about them. Akili would deny them and Incantus would just say that he was exaggerating. So you've got to tell me a couple.'

'I've *got* to tell you a couple?' Serena repeated, reaching across to steal Incantus's glass.

'Yeah, you have to,' Alexis replied, matching the challenge in her eyes as he too took a sip of a drink that tasted far too sweet to be good for him. 'Purely to confirm Teller's stories.'

She laughed heartily. 'Ah, I loved that man.' She raised her glass, catching Incantus's eye. 'To Teller. And to Akili, for we shall soon have him back by our side.'

Incantus nodded, his smile a beautiful juxtaposition of grief and hopefulness.

'And to Darcy,' Serena added, her voice softer, sadder this time, and desperately watchful of Incantus's reaction.

Incantus dropped his gaze at the mention of her name. The lightness of his expression vanished in a heartbeat as Alexis watched the breath slip from his lungs. Suddenly, he looked very small, very old. Very powerless.

'For the Quinate,' Serena said for him, taking his hand and gripping it tight. They shared a look like no other, like two people who had relied on each other throughout decades, surviving everything from childbirth to heartbreak to the death of a loved one.

In that moment, Alexis saw their true age, and all that they still stood for despite what they had lost. With goosebumps running down his arms, he joined in the cheers.

'And for Aadya,' Serena added, her other hand taking Ziya's. 'And everyone else we will avenge tomorrow.'

To that, the Elementals celebrated, raising their drinks in salute and finishing what was left of them. Incantus didn't stay for much longer. He and Gibbous slowly filtered through the crowd of Elementals. When Alexis asked if he should follow him, Serena simply said to let him be, that he wouldn't want others to see him when he was like this. With the masses soon dispersing, the kitchen staff, led by Libero, began cleaning up. Alexis and his friends lingered to the last, but once Blaise told them he was getting a phone call from his proxy and swiftly exited, the rest decided it was time to go.

Caeli and Demi bade Alexis goodnight when he said he'd stay to wait for Blaise to return. In all but ten minutes, the majority of the dining hall had been emptied. Only Alexis and Ziya were left, unable to interrupt a drunken Serena from reliving the old days.

Once Serena had finished her glass, though, she was gone to wander through the vacant tables in search of any remaining bottles. Alexis had been waiting for the right moment all evening to catch up with Ziya, and this was it. 'I've been meaning to ask if you managed to find out where Valentina was going? Or where she was from?'

Ziya shook her head, ensuring that her grandmother was out of earshot. 'I'm not exactly sure. I haven't had much time with everything going on today. I did manage to search through the Haven's copy of all recorded teleporters and portallers though. Her name didn't appear and there's less than a dozen portalling families out there. I'm going to continue dating back, but it looks like she must have changed her name or deleted her file somehow. For what reason, I'm not sure, but it seems like she was trying to hide herself from someone, even before Mortem captured her.'

Alexis said nothing in response, taking in her words and going over anything about the way Valentina had acted or what she had said that could have been a clue as to her past.

'And another thing.' Ziya spoke cautiously as though unsure of how to word her next sentence. 'I haven't forgotten about what you asked Incantus to do. What he passed on to me. You know . . . about your family history. It's not much, but I think I've found something on that front too.'

Before Alexis could ask what it was, to find out why Ziya had shifted so awkwardly in her seat and was unable to meet his gaze, worried that whatever she had to say would send him into a spiral of questions, Blaise returned.

He approached the table, his phone held idly in his hand. His dark skin was washed and his aura was lacking its typical flair. He looked like a candle whose flame had blown out: naked and oddly vulnerable.

Alexis frowned. 'Blaise, what is it?' It was rare to catch him looking anything other than confident or cheerful. Now, Blaise's expression was vacant, as still as the ash on coal long after a bonfire had burned out.

'That was my proxy,' he said dully. 'It just spoke to my parents. About everything. About Elementals. About the battle tomorrow . . .' He met Alexis's worrisome eyes. 'Guess what they told it? They knew this whole time.'

10
SAUDADE

Saudade (n.) *Portuguese origin*
'The love that remains'; a nostalgic longing to be near again to something or someone that is distant, or that has been loved and then lost and will never return

Blaise Ademola was furious. He felt as if someone had lit a fire beneath him and the smoke was slowly choking him, following him everywhere he went.

He met Alexis's open-mouthed expression of shock and went on. 'They only stayed together, they only had *me*, because they knew I was going to be one of the Children of the Elements. They're a part of this world, Al. They're from the bloody Fire Tribe. And now that my proxy has spoken to them, they're returning to their tribe . . . and they're not coming back.'

Alexis rose to his feet and went to put his arm around him, but Blaise shoved it off. 'I want to see Incantus,' he demanded. He didn't need comforting; he wasn't a child. He'd just found out that his parents were abandoning him and he would never see or hear from them again. He needed to vent. He needed to blow off steam. He needed to explode at someone, and Incantus seemed like the only person who could take it.

Blaise's day had gone from bad to worse. He never should

have agreed to fight in the battle. What was he thinking? He wasn't thinking; that was what it was. He had conformed to save face so that his friends wouldn't think he was a coward.

Somehow, after setting up the defences at Stonehenge and after seeing the thousands of Elementals that would stand in to defend him, he had convinced himself that he wouldn't even get close to the battlefront, that everything was starting to look good again.

And then Joe had come and taken Caeli from him just when she was almost his. No, he couldn't blame Joe. It was Caeli. She was the prize and she was the opponent. Blaise was as angry at her as he was at his parents.

Blaise never knew why he had grown up to be so sceptical of love, why he was convinced it didn't exist the way he wanted it to. Lust: that was all there was. This only consolidated that core belief.

Serena stalked over to them, stumbling slightly as she waded her way through, using the chair tops and tables for support. 'What do you need Incantus for? I know you wouldn't dare think of being rude to that man – not in my presence.'

Despite having to crane her head to look up at Blaise, there was a fierce protectiveness in her eyes that he didn't dare challenge.

Blaise took a deep breath before replying, this time without the armour of anger to disguise his sadness. 'Why did no one tell me that my parents knew all along? They said they recognised it was my proxy the minute it went home in my place and they waited until *today* before they said anything. They could have told me years ago and given me a lifetime of training instead of a single month!'

His amulet sparked scarlet as his fists erupted into flames. They climbed his muscular arms and would've charred his T-shirt had someone not taken his burning hand in theirs. Alexis. He clenched his jaw as the fire bit into him, steam billowing from their contact.

Blaise gasped from a sudden cold as Alexis's hand froze over, but also from the realisation that Alexis would go as far as to scald himself in order to show Blaise that he was there for him. Somehow it extinguished Blaise's fury. He wished it hadn't. He knew how to deal with anger. This . . . he wasn't so sure.

Alexis guided him to the table where Ziya was. Blaise had grown fond of Ziya, even though she was strange – the polar opposite to anyone Blaise would typically associate with – and although he convinced himself he didn't care about anyone's opinion, he wanted as few people as possible to see him like this.

Alexis picked up on Blaise's discomfort. 'Ziya, is it okay if we catch up later?'

'I'm sorry, I'll go,' she replied, shooting to her feet.

'Sorry, Zee,' Blaise mumbled, but otherwise didn't look at her.

'Don't be; it's a private thing. I hope you're okay.' She awkwardly waved goodbye to them and gave her grandmother a kiss on the cheek before leaving the dining area. Alexis looked after her as she left, as if she had something he wanted, but Blaise didn't know or care enough to think about what that was.

'So what happened?' Alexis asked, turning back to Blaise, locking in on him. He rotated his wrist and the temperature of the air around them cooled, going some way to combat Blaise's temper. 'Did your proxy confront them?'

Blaise was quiet for a long time. His nostrils flared as he breathed, his dark maroon eyes on his hands. 'Yeah,' he said, with a shrug. 'It just couldn't hold it in any longer; I know I wouldn't be able to either. It turns out that they were both born and raised in the Fire Tribe. They'd always told me we were Nigerian, but maybe the tribe is hidden nearby somewhere. I don't know – I don't care about the geography of it all. They said they were arranged to be together from a young age just so they would continue the line of full-blooded Elementals. It's like they didn't even have me because they wanted me, but because they had to. I feel like I'm some sort of . . .' He searched for the word as if it was somewhere in the air.

'A pawn?' Serena suggested knowingly.

Blaise snapped his fingers. 'Exactly. Like I'm a pawn. A trophy. A box they can just check off.' Blaise moved from the bench, unable to sit still. 'Who does that? Who gets together just to have a kid they barely pay attention to and then leave when the world needs them most? When I need them most?' He kicked a nearby wooden bench, splintering it into burning embers that soared across the vacant dining area. 'And now they're going back to their tribe, wherever the hell that is. They're not going to fight in the battle with us because apparently "*the elements are meant to create and not destroy*", or some crap like that. Is it really like that, Serena? That this whole time, they just stayed with each other for me and nothing else?'

Disbelief and pain gripped Blaise's voice, making it break towards the end of his sentence. It was easy to reinterpret his pain as anger in the daylight when surrounded by others he sought to impress. But as the night grew dark, the lights of the

Haven dimming at the hour, it became all that much harder to obscure his hurt.

He had asked his proxy these same questions, and apparently his proxy had asked his parents this too, but it was met with the same response Blaise had always received. *Don't ask questions.*

Somewhere deep in his mind was a vague memory of a colourful dress and a man he didn't recognise with his hands on his mother's body and her lips on his. Blaise had kept his mother's secret, even from his father, but something about what he had seen that night had changed him, in ways he was only now beginning to realise.

Despite all she had drunk, Serena seemed surprisingly steady as she pulled Blaise into the seat next to her. 'Not everyone gets together for love, dear boy. Not in this world. The partnership with my husband was arranged by my father too. To join two noble, prestigious bloodlines of Aevum and Parashakti. I didn't love him, but I did love what we created together. My beautiful daughter.'

She squeezed her eyes shut, and each hollow breath seemed to cause her effort that was laborious to muster. Ten minutes earlier, she had been a fiery ex-warrior, revelling in her conquests. Now, as they sat in silence, she looked tired, still haunted with the grief of outliving her only child. 'I am sure that it is the same with you,' she continued, her wrinkled eyes fluttering open as if remembering the point she was trying to make. 'Your parents, while they might have been instructed to have you, must love you very much. Don't let emotion cloud your knowledge of that.'

Blaise pressed his lips together and nodded. 'They did make my proxy promise to tell me that.'

Whether or not he truly believed that was another thing. He was sure the thing they loved most about him was his strength and his beauty and his power, for that was all they'd ever praised him for. Blaise didn't particularly feel like he exhibited any of those traits now.

Serena pressed two fingers to Blaise's chin and forced him to look up at her. 'Just so you know, you do not *need* anyone, young man. The Elemental Tribes are selfish zealots who believe that through their practice and pacifist ways, Mortem's powers won't reach the four corners of the world where they reside. To hell with them, I say. You are strong enough for them all.' Serena gripped his hand tightly, almost popping his knuckles.

Grimacing under her grasp, Blaise looked at Alexis for confirmation.

'I know I'm not much, but you've got me,' Alexis offered softly. 'I'll be your family.' Alexis's cheeks visibly reddened, but still he went on, like it was important Blaise knew this. 'I'll scold you for staying out late and comfort you when you're sad. I'll cheer you on and have your back, just like you've had mine. In times of darkness and times of light. You've got me, Blaise. You've always got me.'

Blaise's eyes stung with something foreign. He felt a deep pang in his chest that was unfamiliar to him. It was an emotion, that much he recognised, but he couldn't name it. All he knew was that despite having tears in his eyes, Blaise felt a vivid sense of belonging and comfort that he hadn't felt with anyone before, not even with his parents. He didn't trust his voice enough to reply; he only nodded and bumped shoulders with Alexis to let him know he had heard him.

'Consider yourself lucky to have a friend and a brother in one,' came Incantus's voice from behind them.

He looks worse than me, Blaise thought as he turned. Incantus seemed utterly sapped from energy. He no longer radiated his usual aura of light and power. Gibbous stood particularly close, the top of his hind brushing against his arm reassuringly.

Incantus and Akili Pierce had been the first role models that Blaise truly looked up to. Incantus for his power, and Akili for his strength. Blaise didn't like how so many things were changing around him. Usually he felt like the world moved at a much slower pace than he did, but this night, he couldn't help but feel like he was falling behind.

'Treasure what you have,' Incantus added as he placed a hand on Blaise's broad shoulder. He was wearing a withered brown knitted blanket around his neck that Blaise thought was possibly the ugliest thing he'd ever seen, but Incantus seemed fond of it. 'Ziya told me you might need me. How are you, son?'

'I'll be fine,' Blaise replied. He cleared his throat and shrugged. 'My parents came clean to my proxy that they're from the Fire Tribe. But I guess you know that. It's probably the same for Demi's parents and Caeli's mum as well, isn't it?'

'I'm sorry you had to find out that way,' said Incantus, his hand to his chest. 'That is something they should have told you in person.'

'Yeah, well they didn't do anything in person all my life anyway,' Blaise muttered. He wondered if it counted as abandonment if they hadn't been around much in the first place. 'They said the house and enough riches to last me a few lifetimes will be left in my name when I turn eighteen in a couple of months, if I choose to stay here.' He picked at the wood of the tabletop, carving his initials into the side of it with a scorching finger. 'It's just annoying. They could have dumped me here when I was younger to have a proper upbringing. At least I could've got more practice in that way.'

'They were acting in accordance with the Prophecy once I informed them that you would be the Child of the Fire and gifted you your amulet,' Incantus replied, as if there was nothing more to it. 'The Children of the Elements were to be "*raised apart from their powers*". Your parents had to leave their family and all they ever knew to raise you in the mortal world so that you would meet your friends and come to Stonehenge when the universe deemed it was time.'

'But we really haven't had enough time,' Blaise protested, looking to Alexis for support.

'There is never enough time,' Incantus said quietly, hugging the brown blanket tighter. 'You should get some sleep, boys,' he advised, squeezing Blaise's slumped shoulder. This time, his hand glowed lightly and a white energy bled across Blaise's back. The healing effect was fleeting, lasting only as long as Incantus had a hand on him, but the relief was great enough to make Blaise smile and find the strength to get to his feet.

'Come on then, Al.' Not knowing quite how to thank them, Blaise just dipped his head at the two elder Elementals before parting. He stopped a few tables away when he noticed Alexis hadn't yet moved. 'You not coming?'

Incantus had already steered away from the group, leaving with Gibbous at his side. Alexis was staring after him longingly, but Blaise couldn't figure out why. There was so much that hid beneath the surface of his face and it was hidden so well. Blaise couldn't help but show everything he felt, clear as day. His happiness, his anger, his fear. He couldn't deny that it unnerved him slightly, that a war could be raging inside Alexis and no one would ever know.

'You know I do all my best thinking at night,' replied Alexis with a faint smile. 'I'll join you later.'

Blaise hesitated, but then decided to go on ahead. Alexis looked like he needed to be alone, which was yet another thing that confused Blaise. *How could anyone bear the silence of being alone?*

Blaise soon reached the hallway to the bedrooms of the Children of the Elements and noted Caeli's door was shut stubbornly before him. Despite everything, he wanted to speak to her. To argue with her and shout at her and be shouted at by her and hold her and be with her. He wished that he could bring himself to say it to her. If only he could knock on her door and just *tell her.*

No. She didn't want him, and up until today, until they were so close to being together, Blaise hadn't been sure who he wanted. Something new or something for ever. Someone who told him he was beautiful as soon as she had laid eyes on him or someone who infuriated him and tormented him and ridiculed him. Only Caeli could get under his skin like that. Only Caeli could make him feel ways no one else did.

Only Caeli . . .

Before he knew it, Blaise had walked up the stairs to her room, his fist poised to knock on her door.

Until he heard a laugh. Her laugh, and then Joe's.

Blaise withdrew as a crushing pressure weighed down on his chest, squeezing the air from his lungs and extinguishing the delicate flame that had been flickering there.

Caeli had chosen her happiness, one that came simply and easily and without complications. Blaise wanted to hate her, but he couldn't.

That was the thing about fire – Blaise realised as he opened the door to his own, empty room – one could admire it, but only at a distance. Come too close, and it'll burn you, and when it does, you will no longer seek the warmth of its flame or miss the light of its glow. Instead, the spite of its kiss will be all you remember.

Such a shame, for it was not the kiss that Blaise had ever intended to share with her.

11
NEPENTHE

Nepenthe (n.) *Greek origin*
Medicine for sorrow; a place, person or thing that can aid in forgetting your pain and suffering

Alexis Michaels gazed at Incantus as his mentor walked towards the engraved stone archway of the Haven. Blaise had not long left, but Alexis was in no hurry to call it a night.

Serena didn't need to look to know that Incantus was reactivating the chalk line far behind her, nor did she need to ask whether she should stay. Instead, she kneaded her pashmina shawl and asked Alexis, 'Ready for tomorrow?'

Alexis shook his head. 'You?'

Serena smiled, but she also shook her head.

'Ever since I got here, I've been so busy learning and training for the quest that I've barely had time to think about my parents. I guess with Blaise talking about his, it's reminded me how much I miss mine.'

Serena wiped the crumbs from her cloak and loosened it where it clung to her rounded belly. 'You are adopted, aren't you?' She paused before she said the word 'adopted', as so many people often did.

'It's not a taboo word,' he said politely. 'I am adopted. My parents didn't birth me, but they are the ones who raised me. Blood has no bearing on that.'

Serena smiled into her drink as she finished off the remains of someone else's wine. 'Still waters run deep,' was all she said, and although Alexis didn't know what she meant, he took it as a compliment.

'Serena, why are so many of us orphaned or without a parent?'

'With our duty to protect the world from all things that would seek to harm it, sacrifice is required,' Serena answered simply. 'Some have children out of love; some, obligation to continue their bloodlines, like Blaise's parents. That doesn't always make for good parenting. Ian can testify to that better than anyone.'

A wave of bright white light flashed from the archway as Incantus disappeared through it. Incantus had only mentioned his father once or twice to Alexis, but it had been enough to know that he had been torturous, abusive. Being raised in a home like that, it was easy to see why Mortem turned out the way he did. It didn't justify it, but Alexis could understand it.

Serena went on, slurring her words as she spoke, making it even harder to understand her Scottish accent. 'Some say that the true transfer of our powers is not through blood or DNA, but through childbirth. It's not uncommon that a mother may not survive birthing a powerful Elemental. It happened to my mother with me; it nearly happened to me with Aadya. It happened to my baby sister, the only one I cared for out of the bunch, with her daughter. When her mortal husband took my niece from this world before I could even meet her, not wanting her to ever be a part of it, I was not surprised. The life of an Elemental is not one all people desire, with its pressures and its dangers. Sadly, though, not all of us have a choice in what our fate dictates.'

Serena drew to unsteady feet, forcing Alexis, who had been looking over to where Incantus had been, to meet her gaze. Alexis understood she wanted him to fully feel the weight of what she was about to say. 'Do you know how easy it would have been for him to turn out exactly like his brother? It wasn't his power of light that kept him good. It was his character. This world will never know how much that man has sacrificed. And if it comes down to it tomorrow,' she said, taking a step closer, lowering her voice despite there being nobody about. 'If it comes down to allowing him to sacrifice one more thing for us, then I will do everything in my power to ensure that thing is not his life.'

Alexis rose to his feet and bent over to kiss her cheek, catching a whiff of her: rosemary and wine. She held him for a moment, her small hands warm against his back, containing within them a limitless supply of energy that hadn't dissipated with age.

'Now, if you don't mind me, I'm going to find my granddaughter. It looks like she needs reminding who she is: an Aevum woman. Powerful, even if she is powerless.'

Alexis smiled at the thought as he made his own way towards the dully glowing archway at the back of the dining hall, grateful that Ziya had someone who loved her as fiercely and unconditionally as her grandmother. Just before he passed through the white haze, he caught himself against the stone frame and turned around.

'Serena?'

She stopped, her hand on the banister of the hive.

'Who was Darcy Raphe to Incantus?'

A long silence passed between them. Alexis could see her eyes fill as she searched through an infinite number of ways to describe her, him, them. With the resounding tone of grief filling her voice, she finally replied.

'She was his light.'

12

ODNOLIUB

Odnoliub (n.) *Russian origin*
Someone who only has one love in their life

The Garden was devoid of everything that once made it beautiful. The glow of the fairy lights that the Elementals had hung between flourishing trees had blinked out, the excited twittering of the tree nymphs had fallen quiet – the very things that had made it magical had long been extinguished.

Although it had been less than a week since Alexis had been there last, the feast on the eve of the quest felt like it had been an eternity ago. The night that Ezra broke Mortem in; the night Teller had died and the Leaders had been taken.

'Now, how did I know you would follow me?'

Incantus sat on one of the circular wooden tables. Beside him, Gibbous's tail wagged at Alexis's arrival. The young Elemental had been so deep in thought, looking out towards where the moon lay over the river beyond the canyon, that he hadn't noticed Incantus had been waiting for him.

'Maybe after all those years you picked up on Akili's telepathy,' Alexis replied, making him smile.

'Or maybe I have just come to know you better than you thought,' Incantus countered, his eyebrows raised. 'Come on then,' he said as he rose to his feet. Gibbous neared Alexis's side, nuzzling to be stroked as the three of them walked side by side.

Grass turned to dirt as they left the forest and the clearing behind. They took a seat on the cliff edge which overlooked the river that snaked between the swooping mountains far below. Incantus stretched the blanket over them both, tucking the corners beneath them despite the sticky evening heat. Gibbous deeply sniffed at it, closing his eyes at its lingering scent before licking Incantus's hand once more.

'Which existential question shall it be tonight?' Incantus asked, failing to convincingly fill his voice with humour.

Alexis shook his head. 'I wanted to check up on you,' he said. He watched Incantus's face soften. 'For the past however many years, you've been preparing for this. We've had it rough recently, but you've had it much harder. And earlier ... when Serena mentioned Darcy ...' Incantus's eyes dipped. 'You deserve to be considered too, Incantus.'

A long, deep sigh escaped the handsome, white-haired Elemental. After, he seemed smaller somehow. 'This was our place, you know? She loved it here – said it was the place she wanted to raise our family and be put to rest.' He toyed with the weaving of the blanket as if searching for any trace she may have left behind. He shook his head ever so slightly. 'She was my angel, my curse, my most holy sin. I might be an Arcangelo, but she was truly a gift from the heavens.' Incantus looked to the stars, his voice falling hoarse. 'And now I have grieved my wife for longer than I knew her.'

Wife. In all the stories, Teller had never once mentioned that Incantus had been married. The revelation took Alexis by surprise. How had he not known this? How much more did he not know about his mentor?

She was his light. She *was* his light. She was *his* light. She was his *light*.

Alexis wanted to ask what happened to her, what made Incantus become a widower, how long he had been without her – but he knew now was not the time. An old grief had reared its head, its talons sharp and unavoidable, sinking Incantus beneath the surface once again, no matter how much time had passed.

Alexis could understand it. Not because he had experienced anything like that in his life, but rather because he knew that if his mother or father lost one another, they too would never truly get over their sorrow.

That was what he knew of true love. He wondered if anyone would ever feel that way about him? Was it selfish to want someone to grieve him so deeply? Hearing the pain in Incantus's voice and seeing the emptiness in his eyes, he decided he'd much rather be forgotten about than grieved, for he wouldn't want the person he loved most to experience an ounce of the suffering Incantus did.

'You don't see it, do you?' Incantus said, the conviction in his voice returning. 'I watch you, Alexis, and when I can't, I hear it from your friends. How you help them. You let them feel heard and give them the advice they need to hear, not because you need them to fight in quests and battles, but because you care. Because you love them. And it's an incredible thing to love so boldly. So altruistically. Please tell me you know that.' He paused to stroke the top of Gibbous's head, smiling faintly when the old wolf hummed in contentment.

'Despite the darkness you now know lives within you, every day you choose to be a good man, and that is what makes your light shine even brighter.'

Alexis wasn't sure at what moment his eyes had begun to fill, but by the end of Incantus's speech, he found himself doing all that he could to not let the tears fall. Clenching his jaw as he blinked them away, he gave himself a moment to consider what he had been told. To truly process what someone else was saying to him rather than cast the compliment away as he usually did.

Ever since the Woman of the Water revealed the duality of light and darkness existing within him, and even before then, Alexis had doubted the state of his soul. It wasn't something most children considered growing up, but for some reason, it had been a question he had asked himself for as long as he could remember. To hear Incantus confirm it, to hear him say that he was a good person despite the parts of him that were corrupt, felt like a pressure he never knew was weighing him down finally be eased.

He cleared his throat to make sure his voice didn't break. 'The others told you?'

'I sensed the darkness within you the first day we met,' said Incantus softly. 'And noticed the absence of your shadow as soon as Stonehenge unlocked your powers.'

Alexis frowned. Why had Incantus kept it from him this whole time? Did he not trust him to keep the darkness locked away?

Alexis then remembered what he had done soon after discovering it himself, how he had smiled as Sinner's eyes widened when the blade of darkness punctured his heart.

Incantus had, of course, been right to be sceptical of another Elemental with the power of water.

'The Prophecy states, "*By oneself is how the other will be slain*",' Alexis recalled, moving on before Incantus somehow sensed the blood beneath his fingernails or the shadow of death lingering on his hands. 'I can imagine that might have factored into your decision to keep it from us. From me.' Incantus's silence was enough of an answer. 'Does that mean I have to be the one to kill Mortem with the shadows?'

'I wondered that for a time,' Incantus said with a nod, running a hand across the light stubble that had grown on his jaw. 'But it can't be true. He and I are afflicted with the Curse of Raphe. Only I can kill him, and only he can kill me. That is our gift and our curse, written into existence long before you were born. The Prophecy also states the need for the Children of the Elements, however, including and especially you. Perhaps that is the meaning of your role in this.'

Alexis hoped it to be right. He wasn't totally convinced, and he had never heard of the Curse of Raphe before, but it was the truth he decided to accept. Between himself and Incantus, only one of them had a fighting chance of succeeding in defeating Mortem.

'Would you do it?' Incantus asked. The question was posed absent-mindedly, idly, but Alexis sensed the true depth of it. 'If it had to be you, would you be able to take up the sword against Mortem.'

'Why wouldn't I be able to?' Alexis challenged. He wanted him to say it, to admit to the secret he had kept from him. He wouldn't blink or look away until he did.

'You know why, Alexis,' Incantus replied. His eyes softened, but he did not drop his gaze either. 'I suspect you've known ever since you saw him wearing a face similar to yours, or perhaps even before that, when you came across a photograph of two boys from a hundred years ago, a photograph I left for you to find. The Haven, in order to operate independently from direct High Order interference, is required to declare any and all Elementals housed here, including details of their heritage and the powers they display. I have done neither in the case for you, for we both know what would be revealed and the implications that may have.'

Incantus reached for the blue stone that hung from Alexis's neck. He turned the triangular amulet in his hand, watching as it pulsed with the power of the seas at his touch. All the while, Alexis remained still – so still that he didn't realise he had been holding his breath until Incantus withdrew and he was able to inhale deeply enough that he felt his lungs physically swell.

'It's true then,' Alexis said, more to himself than to anyone else. He buried his hands beneath Gibbous's furry neck so that Incantus couldn't see him tapping his fingers to his thumbs. 'The reason I have his powers. The reason I have dreamed of him every night for as long as I can remember. Mortem really is my father.'

Incantus let his amulet slip between his fingers. His dark eyebrows knitted together, his blue eyes squinting in question. 'You dream of him? Even before you knew you were an Elemental?'

Alexis was confused by the intensity of Incantus's stare. Of all the things they had revealed, how was his nightmare the most shocking?

'Of you both.' He shuffled to sit across from Incantus to

see his reaction more clearly. For once, he felt as though he knew something his mentor didn't, something important. He proceeded to say his dream aloud, hoping that hearing it back would allow them to make sense of it. 'Ever since I can remember, I've had this nightmare of me as a boy falling off a cliff while trying to tear my body apart. It's as if there is an evil within me fighting to be let out – the darkness. I wake just as I crash into the sea far below.'

Incantus hadn't taken his eyes off him, his body impossibly still, so much so that Gibbous had stirred and placed his large paw into his lap to garner his attention.

'All my life, I thought it was me in the dream. I feel his pain and see through his eyes. Knowing I was found after that tsunami, it made sense that that's where I could've ended up. But now I know it can't be me because, in the dream, you are there as a boy, watching it happen, running towards me to try and catch me before I fall.'

Alexis wasn't sure if he was shivering from fatigue or from speaking about the nightmare that haunted him, but either way, he was grateful to have the blanket to provide him some comfort. He wrapped it around his hands, stilling them from shaking just as Gibbous moved closer to him, his breath warm against his skin.

Incantus scratched at his knuckles so hard that Alexis was worried they would bleed. After a long while, head still shaking slightly, he finally replied. 'What you have just said has stirred a memory I have long forgotten. You're right, Alexis. The nightmare you have isn't one of your memories. It's one of Nero's.'

'You mean Mortem?'

'Yes, technically. In my head, I still think of them as two different people: one, my brother; and the other, my enemy.' Incantus chewed the inside of his cheek and looked out towards the valley of sloping mountains. 'When we finally found Nero that day, he was different. Changed in a way I didn't see at first and refused to admit long after. First Borns, I barely even remember it. How could you have known of this?'

'I have no idea. I don't know why I suffer from a memory that isn't my own.'

'Possibly it's a result of your shared powers ... water and darkness ... There could have been some sort of memory transfer. A displacement. Why this memory, I do not know. Maybe because it almost took Nero's life? His first encounter with the darkness.' Incantus scratched the square of his jaw before running his fingers through his pale hair. 'I'm afraid I don't know much more than that, son.'

That Alexis could get his head around. What he didn't get, however, was how he had been allowed to connect the nightmare to Mortem in the first place. 'Why did you leave the photograph for me to find when you could've just told me? The night we sat here when I asked you to find out who my birth parents were, after my very first day of training, you could have said it then rather than setting Ziya on an aimless task to discover it. I think she was going to tell me that earlier before Blaise came back.'

'I guess leaving it in your room was my way of letting you figure it out for yourself while allowing you the chance to deny it should the truth be too much. Had I known of your nightmare, I would've been more transparent with you. I never wanted you to be burdened with the truth, and yet I know that it can be healing in its own, vulnerable way. I am deeply sorry for keeping this from you, Alexis.' He spoke sincerely and Alexis knew him to be telling the truth. 'I didn't even know Mortem had a son until you washed up on that beach. I couldn't risk you refusing once learning this. Please forgive me, but also understand that if I had to, I would make the same decision again.'

It was easy for Alexis to get angry at being lied to, to call Incantus names or to walk away rather than to stay calm, for the tide of the ocean was by nature more destructive than any other element. Maybe it was due to forced maturity or possibly a greater perspective, but Alexis realised he no longer wanted to be angry. Not every misstep deserved a reaction. Sometimes, forgiveness and acceptance served the dual role in absolving the guilt of another as much as it healed the grudge held by oneself.

Alexis wasn't angry with Incantus for doing as he did, for not coming forth and telling him the truth. What if he *had* objected? It would be condemning the entire world to eternal shadow.

'I would've done the same thing, Incantus, if I had been in your position. You don't have to worry; this doesn't change anything. Not after everything he's done. From now on, though, know that you can trust me with anything, even if it's bad. There's nothing I hate worse than being left in the dark.'

A wave of relief washed over Incantus's face, relaxing the tautness of his expression and allowing his shoulders to sag and eyelids to close. Leaning over and shaking Gibbous's paw, Alexis played with his matted fur as he asked Incantus his final questions of the night. 'Do you know who my birth mother is? Or was? Do you know if she was the reason why I escaped from him and was found alone after that tsunami?'

Alexis felt his throat threaten to close. He didn't want any hope to blossom, nor to allow himself to start painting a picture of what his mother could look like. What she would be like. If she was anything like Mortem at all or if she had been imprinted. Was she even still alive?

'Ever since I first saw you, brimming with a power I never thought I would see again, I have wondered who your mother could be,' Incantus answered, his eyes fixated on the blue amulet resting against the centre of his chest. 'I don't know who she is or where she could be. On the First Borns' sacrifice, I swear this.'

Alexis shrugged it off, forcing himself to swallow despite how dry his mouth was. 'It's fine,' he said. 'I've already got a mum anyway.'

When Alexis asked to be alone sometime later, Incantus agreed without question. 'Stay as long as you like,' was all Incantus said as he tousled Alexis's hair. 'Nephew,' he added, making them both smile.

Without Incantus or Gibbous to distract him, Alexis was left alone with his thoughts, with only the distant glowing moon to keep him company. He knew Blaise would try and stay up, hoping Alexis might join him in his room, but there was much he wanted to savour on what might very well be his last night. The sound of the water rushing far below, the unrestricted freeness of his breathing, the smell of the forest at night, and the lightness in his chest from being unburdened by secrets.

For the first time since stepping – or falling – into the Elemental world, Alexis felt safe. He felt like he was home. It was a feeling he recognised all too well and missed oh so much.

It wasn't until he heard his mother's voice that he realised his phone was in his hand and he had called the people who had taught him what home was. Not a place or a people, but a feeling.

'Lexi, darling, are you okay?' said Stephanie Michaels. She sounded startled as though she had just woken up in a hurry.

Alexis nodded despite her not being able to see him, glad that he was seated for he was sure he would have sunk to his knees if he hadn't been. He didn't expect to feel such a pain in his heart, but upon hearing her voice, a rush of emotion rose to his face, prickling at his skin. With his breathing unsteady, he did his best to sound normal, sleepy even. 'I'm okay, Mum. Just wanted to say goodnight.'

Her audible concern wilted. 'You're such a sweet boy. I hope you're having a good night round your friend's house. Blaise sounded upset when he came round to pick you up, not quite his usual, cheeky self.'

Blaise's proxy must have gone to see Alexis's about what he had learned, just as Blaise had come to see him. 'He's better now. Don't worry, we're going to sleep soon. How's Dad? And Jace. I miss them.'

He could hear her laugh on the other end of the line. 'You miss your brother? Now that's a first. And Dad's good, not long come in from work. Love, it's Lexi.'

He wasn't prepared to hear his dad's voice too. Would this be the last time he would ever hear from them? A single, soundless sob rocked Alexis's body, and he had to press the face of his phone against his leg so that they couldn't hear him weep for them.

Alexis's father's reply came through muffled. 'Lexi, what you still doing up? Not about causing havoc, are you? I'll get you both arrested for underage drinking if you are.'

Alexis wiped the tears from his face and rubbed his eyes until he saw yellow dots. He collected himself as quick as he could, pushing the phone close to his ear so that he could be comforted by the sound of his dad's breathing on the other end of the line. 'Of course not, never me,' he countered. How could he imagine ever replacing either one of his parents with anyone else? 'I just wanted to check in.'

'We're all good, my boy,' Jackson said through a yawn. 'It's so nice for us to hear you speak kindly about Jason,' he added, forever doing his best to force his two sons to spend time together. 'I want you home tomorrow though. Bring Blaise if his parents aren't back, but you're coming home. I feel like we've hardly seen you recently.'

'I feel like I've hardly seen you too.'

'We're off to bed, darling,' called Stephanie. 'Sweet dreams. Love you and see you tomorrow.'

'Good night, my boy,' Jackson added. 'Love you.'

Alexis's reply was barely a whisper as he repeated what his parents had always said to each other and to their sons. 'Love you more.'

He held the phone tightly in his grasp long after they'd hung up, the corner of it pressed against his chin. Only then, only after speaking to his parents himself and not through the dulled surface of his proxy, did he finally feel the imminence of what the following day would bring.

The summer solstice. The Battle of Stonehenge.

A whooshing noise stirred Alexis from his introspection. It was so faint that he almost hadn't heard it, but the night was silent, and his Elemental senses were attuned to pick up even the faintest changes in his environment.

Have Incantus and Gibbous returned?

It couldn't be. Incantus's footsteps were soundless and Gibbous's pawprints beat with a heavy rhythm. This was a noise of air being sucked out of a vacuum, of a transport of something, of someone, who hadn't been there moments before. Alexis didn't need to turn around to know who was behind him.

'*Alexis.*'

In one moment, Ezra Alastor had said his name; in the next, Alexis had thrown him off the side of the cliff.

13
KAIHO

Kaiho (n). *Finnish origin*
A hopeless longing – an involuntary solitude in which one feels incompleteness and yearns for something unattainable or extremely difficult and tedious to attain

Alexis's shoulder struck the lanky young man in the stomach with a force that made him gasp. Had he cracked Ezra's rib? He hoped so.

Alexis had underestimated his own strength, and the momentum of his lunge carried both him and Ezra over the side of the cliff with not so much as another word.

As they plummeted towards the river in the canyon far below, serrated nails raked down Alexis's face as Ezra clawed at him, but he refused to let him go. He wrapped his legs around him and grappled with his arms so that if Ezra cast a portal or teleported, Alexis would go with him.

'Get off me!' Ezra shrieked, spitting in his face.

Alexis retaliated by slamming his forehead against Ezra's nose, which exploded with the wicked sound of cracking bones. The pain in Alexis's head was worth the sight of blood pulsing from the centre of Ezra's face.

The walls of the canyon drew closer the further they fell,

jagged cuts of rock whistling past them, threatening to shred their bodies apart. Seconds before the surface of the river would've smashed them into pieces, Alexis extended his hand. The water shot into the air in one great stream, catching them in its tide. Ezra grunted as it redirected their weight and thrust them across its surface.

Alexis solidified the surface of the river so he could stand, but granted Ezra no such mercy.

The moonlight barely reached them, providing only weak patches of illumination that reflected atop the water's broken surface. Ezra's overgrown black hair clung to his face as he battled to stay afloat, fighting against the whirling torrents Alexis had started to spin. Without a spare moment to concentrate, Ezra wasn't able to teleport away.

'Have you not hurt us enough?' Alexis shouted, his hoarse voice booming across the canyon, its sound fractured by the thousand juts and angles of the mountainous rocks that loomed above. 'You betray us, get the Leaders imprinted and Teller slaughtered, and now what? Back to gloat? To finish me off before the solstice?'

He hurled a torrent of dark water at Ezra, forcing him under. He resurfaced a few seconds later, spluttering and coughing. Alexis beat him down with another tide. All around him, the river pulsed in synchrony with his wrath.

'Stop!' Ezra screamed between mouthfuls of water. His resistance wouldn't last much longer. He was skinnier than he had been while at the Haven, the angles of his cheekbones and jaw that much sharper. Aided with the ability to see, even in the dark, Alexis saw the deep-set rings that hung beneath his eyes; eyes that had never been black.

'You're a coward,' Alexis spat with disgust, spinning the whirlpool faster and faster. He didn't know if Ezra could hear him, but still he went on, his anger surpassing the sadness that had stilled his body just minutes before. 'You're a traitor. And now you'll die before you get the chance to see the world you traded all of us in for.'

'I wish I could take it back!' Ezra shouted. He had given up trying to teleport away, his body no longer shimmering bronze with power. He used whatever remained of his energy to stay afloat. 'He told me I was special! He told me I would have power. I-I thought what I was doing was right.' He tried to say more, but he didn't have the breath in his lungs.

I should kill him, Alexis thought, curling his hand into a fist and plummeting the temperature of the water so low that it would feel like Ezra was being charred by a vice of frozen blades.

This was the punishment he deserved, Alexis was sure of it. What if Alexis hadn't bested him? What if it had been someone else out here for him to sneak up on: Blaise, Caeli, Incantus . . . Demi?

Ezra's head dipped underneath the surface, his arms flailing above in helpless surrender.

He must have been sent to murder whoever he could to thwart their plans of resistance. There was no other reason why he would be here. This would be the only chance Alexis would have to defeat an enemy too dangerous to let free or attempt to imprison.

He should kill him.

He must.

So why couldn't he?

He had killed in cold blood before, so why, despite his rage, did something inside Alexis's chest hold him back?

'*Every day you choose to be a good man*,' Incantus had said to him.

Alexis had so desperately wanted to believe him. Maybe this was how he could. Ezra had sold them out, but there was something about the conviction in his voice when he said he thought what he was doing was right that made Alexis still the river's surface and dissipate the whirlpool.

Ezra had been alone and in need of a purpose. He had been promised greatness by one of the most powerful and revered Elementals in the world – sold an ideology that was far from unpopular. An ideology that made him feel *needed*.

Ezra had been indoctrinated, Alexis realised; radicalised while no one at the Haven paid him enough attention to teach him otherwise. If Alexis had been raised the same, without parents to guide him or friends to care for him, would he also have fallen prey to a person too brutal to refute or defy?

Ezra's hands were no longer waving above the water and the bubbles had ceased. Alexis wasn't sure if he was making the right decision, but that would be for future-him to deal with.

He dived into the river and didn't come out until he had Ezra's limp body slung over his shoulder. He set him down none too gently on a stretch of land adjacent to the riverbank. In the faint moonlight, Alexis saw just how pale he was, and when he started doing chest compressions, after leaching the water from his lungs, he was worried of pressing too hard to risk fracturing his chest.

'Don't make me go through the moral dilemma of saving you for nothing, Eczema,' Alexis grunted, counting almost thirty compressions to no sign of movement. He gritted his teeth as he pinched Ezra's bloody, broken nose, hoping it hurt him. 'I can't believe you're going to make me kiss you.'

Alexis pressed his wet lips against Ezra's and exhaled two deep breaths.

Ezra's chest rose and his eyes shot open. He sucked in gulps of air as Alexis backed away, putting as much distance between them as he could. They watched each other as if they were both wild animals, venomous and unpredictable.

Neither of them said a word for the longest time until Ezra eventually stopped coughing. Finally, he croaked one word. 'Why?'

Why what? Why did Alexis try to kill him? Or why did he save him? The answer was the same.

'I don't know. Why did you come here?'

Ezra's eyes darted to the floor. 'I don't know.' He pressed two quivering fingers against his lips and let out a sigh that left his head hanging and shoulders slumped.

Alexis felt the pressure in the air around the other Elemental change. The frame of Ezra's body began to shimmer with bronze specks. Alexis made no move to stop him.

'The High Order,' Ezra blurted out, as if he couldn't stop himself in this moment of exhaustion. He looked at Alexis again and spoke through gritted teeth. '*Don't trust them.*'

Ezra teleported before Alexis's question ever left his lips.

14
AGAPI

Agapi (n.) *Greek origin*
The highest form of love; selfless, sacrificial and unconditional love

Alexis didn't go to his room that night. He didn't go to Blaise's either.

He closed the teleportation line to the Garden after the long journey back to the clearing. As he walked through the sleeping Haven, he took his time to admire everything about it: the golden bridges that arched across the hive; the infinite expanse of it that somehow never compromised its homeliness; the magic and power intertwined with its design, as if the residue of its residents had rubbed off on it.

Alexis couldn't imagine anyone not feeling at home here, and yet Ezra had.

Ezra had given him a warning about the High Order, the international governing rulers of the Elemental community. Alexis knew little of how they operated, having struggled to pay attention in Taranis's Scholar training sessions where he discussed their role in dictating the laws and regulations of Elemental-kind. Alexis simply thought of them as the Elemental equivalent of the United Nations, a centralised international body that aimed to maintain the peace and security of their people and that could be subdivided into smaller councils: Erasers, Justice, Transport and Portalling, Knowledge, Security, and so forth.

So why would Ezra urge Alexis to not count on their support? They would absolutely have to in light of Mortem's true plans to imprint every Elemental. Had Ezra said that to plant a seed of doubt, to make them turn on their allies? Or had it been a fleeting moment of morality to return the favour of Alexis sparing him? And why had he come in the first place?

Alexis was tired of thinking. He was tired of everything. He would discuss it with Incantus in the morning, but now, at this hour, he wanted nothing more than to rest before the dawn broke and brought with it a day of death and darkness. Incantus deserved that much too.

He didn't knock when he reached the door to Demi Nikolas's bedroom. He knew she would already be fast asleep. It was foolish, inappropriate maybe, to be here. This he knew. Yet with just as much certainty, he also knew that he would not get a wink of sleep unless he saw her.

Faint fairy lights were strung around the giant oak tree, illuminating the room with a soft yellow glow. Alexis drew closer to the bedside to see her at a closeness he didn't have the chance to when she was awake. His breath caught in his throat.

Nothing in the world can compare to her beauty, he thought. *Not the seas nor the sky, not the forests or the fires.*

There was much Alexis didn't know, but this he was certain of.

The moment felt sacred, stolen. If there was a way he could preserve it, he would do everything in his power to freeze it in time.

Her hair was sprawled across the pillow, lines of caramel streaking through dark brown, sun-dyed from their quest. She was curled on her side, her bare arms and legs wrapped around a pillow, her skin tanned to a beautiful bronze. Her chest rose and fell as she breathed, and the light snore that escaped her made Alexis's heart swell with a kind of happiness no combination of words could adequately express.

But it was Demi's lips that Alexis spent the most time looking at. It was what he loved most about her face. The shade of them: a pale rose so she never needed to wear lipstick. The shape they always took: a hanging crescent; a smile that rarely wavered, even in her sleep. The words that came from them and the laughter that sang.

Alexis wished he could dance to her laugh and sleep to her voice. A sound that stirred and settled his heart all at once.

I should go.

Demi stirred as if awoken by Alexis's presence or even his thoughts. Her eyes adjusted to the darkness before they fell upon him. He watched her, and she watched him back, neither one of them moving, locked in that moment for an eternity, until finally, Demi made the slightest gesture of invitation. She pulled back the duvet cover for him.

Alexis lifted his T-shirt over his head and dropped it to the floor. He took slow steps towards her before lowering himself in the bed beside her, where he then pressed his bare, broad chest against her back and draped his arm over her, feeling the warmth radiating from her body. He could see the pulse thrumming in her neck. He could almost hear her heartbeat rising and rising.

Was she waiting for him to say something? To do something?

All Alexis could think about was the look in Incantus's eyes as he spoke of Darcy Raphe. If Darcy had been Incantus Arcangelo's angel, then Demi was surely his.

He wondered if others saw that same look on his face when he was with her. His mask was capable of shielding many things: his past, his hallucinations, his fears and insecurities. But a feeling this strong, could anything truly hide that?

'You called me "*my love*".' Demi's voice came out as barely a whisper, so quiet that Alexis wondered if he had imagined it. Her eyes were still closed, but Alexis felt the ache of his heart abate the moment she pressed herself against him, deeper into the curve of his body. It could've been as natural as her readjusting herself to get comfortable, but he hoped it was so they could be even closer, to feel like one entity of yin and yang. Good and bad. Whole and broken. When she said it again, he knew he couldn't be dreaming. 'When I was dying, you said "*my love*".'

Alexis wanted to declare it. To tell her he was hopelessly, utterly, completely in love with her. That in a world so dark and cruel and lonely, she had given him comfort and shown him kindness and blessed him with the light of her smile and warmth of her embrace.

His voice came out deep, drowned by all the things he wanted to say to her but couldn't. 'I did.'

From where he was lying, Alexis saw her throat bob as she swallowed. He could feel the flow of her blood pulsing over her body where he held her. He wondered if she could feel his heartbeat thundering against her back, threatening to burst free from the ribs that constricted it.

A lifetime later, Demi spoke again. 'I need time to process everything that's happened to me. Everything that is yet to happen. I don't know who I am any more. I-I need to focus on me.'

Alexis withdrew his arm from around her, but she caught it, guiding it back to where it had just been, tucked around her waist, grazing the skin of her bare stomach. Alexis sucked in an intake of air, and prayed she hadn't heard him gasp.

'It's not a no,' she whispered, and then kissed his fingers with a painful gentleness. 'I can't ask you to wait for me—'

'You don't have to.' He buried his face in her hair, his skin alight with electricity and bristling with goosebumps. He returned the kiss to the base of her neck. 'I will wait. I always have and I always will.'

With that promise, they didn't say another word. After a long time, they simply fell asleep, their breathing falling into synchrony, Demi in Alexis's arms, his heart in her hands.

The earth and the seas.

PART II

15

EUNEIROPHRENIA

Euneirophrenia (n.) *Greek origin*
The peaceful state of mind after having pleasant dreams

In the early hours of the summer solstice on the twenty-first of June, when the dawn ignited the sky, Alexis's unconscious anticipated the return of the nightmare. The cold darkness of the picture, the vividness of the pain. Even as he went to sleep, comforted by the feel of Demi in his arms, he knew that sooner or later, the nightmare would rip him from his slumber.

But the dull, monochromatic scene of Nero on the cliffside never came.

Colour burst from all around, every shade of blue Alexis had ever seen before and could ever imagine. The light glowed with a fierce power, reflecting off the glistening walls of the cave he recognised all too well as the place he had met the Woman of the Water. If he listened closely enough, he could hear the rush of Iguazu Falls in the distance.

His hands were his own, calloused and mature with age. Alexis was himself, he was sure of it. He looked out through his own eyes and saw his reflection against the blue-shining walls. On his chest, his amulet pulsed with a heartbeat of its own.

The Woman of the Water stood beside him within the circular trickling waterfall in the middle of the hollowed cave, exactly where Alexis had seen her last, her body swirling with the same transcendent colour as his amulet.

When she spoke, the sound came from all around as if the water itself had spoken. 'Hello, my child.'

Alexis knew he must be dreaming, and yet . . .

The intensity of the colour, the intricate details of the cracks and fissures on the walls, even the chaotic movement of the water made it seem too perfectly illustrated to be a figment of his imagination. Never had the hallucinations of the *Shadow Man* come so close to reflecting reality in such a way that it was tangible to his every sense, even his newfound Elemental aura. It was as if the Woman of the Water had come to him to save him from the nightmare herself.

There had to be a reason why.

'Are you real?' he asked.

Her crystalline blue eyes blinked slowly. 'As real as I was the first time we met,' she said.

'What's wrong?' He couldn't waste time with greetings and formality. Incantus could wake them up at any minute to make sure they were prepared.

'You are in danger.'

'Yeah, I figured,' Alexis replied before he could stop himself, his voice dripping with sarcasm. In his dream, his conscious inhibitions were also snoozing. He hoped he hadn't offended one of the primordial beings that gave birth to a quarter of all creation. What would his punishment be? Frozen in time for ever? Drowned in a puddle? Having his powers sealed off from him?

The Woman only shook her head, causing rivulets of water to wash over her bare shoulders. 'This day shall be doomed unless you heed what I have told you.' Her voice was devoid of mortal passion or sentiment, but there was a pleading in her eyes. A desperateness in her expression that implored him to recall every word she'd said to him.

'Help me,' he asked. His memories of their last interaction were clouded with the exhaustion from the quest, residual panic from thinking he had lost Demi, and the shock of the Woman's revelation of his powers over the shadows. 'What did you tell me?'

'Remember,' she urged him, her speech reverberating throughout the walls, shifting its colours. 'Things do not need to be real for someone to think they are. Illusions of the mind can be just as convincing as reality, especially if what is shown is that which a person believes they deserve.'

Alexis's mind's eye was flooded with the image of the *Shadow Man* as if she had called upon it herself. Since seeing it again in the Garden after meeting Mortem for the first time, Alexis still wasn't sure if it had been nothing more than a hallucination, a projection of his mind, or if it had been cast by the person whose body it reflected. Mortem. Regardless of whether it was real for anyone else, it had been real to him.

Illusions of the mind were powerful, and projections could be just as convincing as reality. The Woman of the Water had tricked Mortem with a clone of the Water Gem. There had to be a way Alexis could mislead him too.

Individual streams of thought slowly channelled into one encompassing river. Alexis looked up to see if the Woman could read his mind. She must have seen the spark in his eyes as an idea came to him, hard and fast, a plan that could work, one which could help them to win the battle during the eclipse, or at least help them stall Mortem for time.

The Woman of the Water smiled and Alexis smiled back at her.

'Thank you, thank you for coming to me,' he said, pressing his hand over his heart, wishing there was a more sincere way to express his gratitude without hugging the Woman. He was fairly certain that if he did, it would be considered a wet dream, which was not what he was after.

The image before him was already starting to fade. The blueness of the colour was washing away, darkening at his periphery as though his eyes were slowly closing despite him feeling more alert than ever. There was still one thing he had to ask her before he woke up.

'*By the blade of darkness, you will fall, wielded by the one you expect the least.*'

He tried to speak as quickly as he could, but it was like trying to swim against current. 'The prophecy you told me . . . about my falling by darkness.' Even his words came out slurred. 'Does this happen tomorrow? By someone I don't expect? Will I still be able to stop him?'

The Woman of the Water's eyes were already shut. Her aura and the water amulet on his chest were the last two things to be glowing.

She didn't answer his question. Or rather, she didn't answer it in a way that he would understand. 'Even when you feel most powerless, know with certainty that the waters will always be there to cleanse you. Your element will never abandon you; it will always be enough. Do not be a fool and turn your back on it. The consequences of this betrayal will only bring about suffering for you and for everyone you hold most dear.'

She pressed a light kiss against Alexis's forehead like his mother used to before parting for bed. The Woman's cryptic words had stunned him into a silence, but he felt peaceful in the knowledge that their meaning would never truly be clear to him. At least not yet.

The striking blueness of her power, *their* power, swept across the cave and poured over Alexis. It washed away the shadowy tendrils of his nightmare that fought to steal him away in its cold clutches.

The Woman's last gift to Alexis was the blessing of his first dream in colour, his first sleep without pain, and first morning without panic.

If this was to be the last time Alexis ever slept, he was grateful to experience the novel awakening to the gentle warmth of the light.

16

PERTINACIOUS

Pertinacious (adj.) *Latin origin*
Stubbornly unyielding; to hold firm to a view, decision or course of action

The beauty of the divine was replaced by another equally as breathtaking, although Alexis knew this image before him was very much real.

At some point, Demi must have turned around in the night, for when Alexis opened his eyes, her face was inches from his. She lay slightly atop him so he could feel the weight of her on his chest, her hand cupping the nape of his neck, the top of her head pressed beneath his chin. Long lashes curled over her closed eyes that moved back and forth beneath the lids as she dreamed.

The walls of her huge vine-covered, flower-streaked bedroom were glowing with a soft green lightness that reflected the hour of day. Alexis had never slept through sunrise, but somehow the Woman's power must have prevailed over the nightmare long enough to stop it from forcing him awake.

This must be what it feels like to wake up for everybody else, Alexis realised, taking a moment to listen to the slow beat of his heart and calm rhythm of his breathing. The peaceful awakening was the most unusual yet serene experience, one that he wanted to prolong, especially with Demi beside him. If there was ever a moment Alexis could bottle and keep for ever, it was this. But despite his body screaming at him to stay in her embrace, he knew he had to leave.

Dreams were for the night. The day had begun, and Alexis only had a short window of time to take action before the Haven roused.

Cupping Demi's face in his hands, Alexis pressed a feather-light kiss against her forehead. She let out a faint hum as her lips curved into a smile, eyes still closed and mind still asleep. Alexis left before the temptation to kiss her a hundred times overtook him.

Heart full of yearning and thoughts somewhere in the clouds, Alexis didn't notice Ziya Parashakti standing in the corridor between the bedrooms of the Children of the Elements. She walked into his path just as he was about to ascend the steps to his own room. She let out a little yelp as she bumped into him, then let out a louder one after he steadied her and she saw that he was shirtless.

Alexis backed up as she averted her eyes, her cheeks flushed. Behind her at the foot of each of the four staircases was a small parcel, wrapped neatly and tied with a bow that matched the colour of their amulets.

'I'm sorry, I thought you'd all still be asleep!' She glanced at him, then at the symbol on Demi's door, and then back at her feet. She didn't say anything further. Alexis knew what it must look like.

'Why are you here so early?' he asked, hoping to steer the conversation away. He had a newfound empathy for Caeli and

Joe when he had caught and tormented them the day before. 'What are those?'

Ziya turned to pick up the parcel outside Alexis's room with the blue ribbon. 'They're your new Haven suits. Raeve designed you some especially for the battle, in case we ended up needing to fight. I was just dropping them off. I know how it seems . . . but I promise I don't wait around for you to be . . .' She gestured to his shirtless body and appeared to forget the words needed to finish her sentence.

'It's my bad,' Alexis replied, taking the parcel from her and using it to cover himself. 'I was actually hoping to run into you.'

Ziya cleared her throat. 'Me? Why?' She finally met his eyes and saw the intensity of his gaze.

'I need your help, Ziya.'

Ziya agreed to wait for Alexis while he washed and changed into his new Haven uniform. It was similar to his last – the same soft, durable fabric dyed charcoal black – only what distinguished his from those of all other Elementals of the Haven was its additional colouring. Towards the cuffs at the wrists and trouser legs, it appeared as though it had been dipped in a sea-blue ink, which doused the sleeves to the elbow in a gradual gradient. Inspecting it more closely, Alexis noticed a tiny inverted triangle on the inner wrists that matched his amulet.

Alexis pictured Raeve making these with a determined look on her face, ensuring they made the Children of the Elements stand out, divergent from everyone else on the battlefield. He didn't think she would ever imagine fighting on the opposing side as them, stripped of her shadow and enslaved by the man she trained them to stop.

Alexis forced her and the other Leaders from his mind. No amount of mental fortifying would prepare him for seeing them, so better to not think of them at all. He only hoped he wouldn't have to face them directly. Not just for his own safety, but also for theirs.

'Thanks for waiting,' he said to Ziya, shutting the door to his room. He joined her, but didn't stop to wait around. 'If you're ready, let's go.'

'Where are we going? And what are we doing?' Ziya hurried after him, doing her best to keep up with his pace. It was little after 5 a.m. and he didn't want to risk anyone seeing what he was doing and report it to Incantus or his friends.

'It's for the defences at Stonehenge,' he replied, not wanting to say too much. When they got to the hive, he took two steps at a time as he descended the great spiral stairway. 'I need to add to it. It's for a back-up plan.'

'A contingency plan?'

'A contingency plan!' He came to an abrupt stop just before the level for the Training Academies. 'But before I tell you, you have to promise me you won't say anything to the others about it. They can't find out about it. Not yet.'

Ziya frowned, clearly unaccustomed with the seriousness of his expression. Alexis didn't have the energy or desire to mask his face with his typical unassuming façade.

'Why me?' she asked, her voice quiet. 'Why are you asking *me* to help you with whatever you've got planned? If you don't want your friends to know, it must be risky. I'm . . . I'm not even going to be on the battlefield. You should tell Incantus. Does he know?'

'You're the only one who can help me, Ziya,' Alexis replied in all sincerity, reaching to take her arm. He looked into her huge owlish brown eyes and added, 'I need you. This plan might save us all from Mortem and I'm powerless without you.'

Ziya's jaw clenched at Mortem's name, just as Alexis knew it would. He felt bad for using it to manipulate her, but it was the only way to get her to agree to help before she knew what it was she was agreeing to. This would be her way to fight without setting foot on the battlefield, to thwart the plans of the man who had kidnapped and murdered her mother.

'Okay.' She undid her black hair from its bun and retied it much tighter. 'I swear to not say anything. But you have to tell me what it is you're planning and why you don't want Incantus and the others to find out.'

Alexis swallowed hard. 'I will,' he said, his heart rate picking up again. 'I'll tell you it all, but you aren't going to like it.'

A light layer of dew covered the grass on the sea of surrounding fields. It was cold to the touch, as was the brisk morning air by the time that Ziya and Alexis finished adding the final touches to Stonehenge.

She had instructed him to stand back, that she would be able to get it done quicker if he wasn't there beside her. Alexis did as ordered, instead admiring the clear sky above him as its colour changed from golden yellow to a brilliant blue. He took in the distant warmth of the sun against his face, listening to the rhythm of his breathing. The comforting inhale that expanded his chest and the exhale that deflated it.

Despite all that he had gone through, all the hardships and the sorrows and the darkness, Alexis was grateful to be alive. Now that he knew that this sunrise could be his last, that his time in the light was finite before the eclipse cast them into shadow, the impermanence of it all made it that much more beautiful.

'I've done it,' Ziya announced, pulling him out of his trance. She had spent the better half of their time muttering to herself and shushing Alexis anytime he breathed too loudly or asked a question. Alexis found it oddly refreshing, even amusing. 'It should work just like you wanted it to.'

'I trust that it will.' He came closer to see the finished product – from a distance, it was camouflaged so well that he wouldn't have seen it at all had he not been the one to place it there beside his wall of ice. 'Thank you again, Ziya.'

'I'll transport us back down,' was all she said. She waited until Alexis stood beside her before she pressed the screen of the Haven command disk. Two round circles illuminated underneath their feet, and in less than a second, they were transported underground, finding themselves back in the laboratory on the top floor of the Haven.

'As much as I hate this plan, I can't deny that it is ingenious,' Ziya admitted. 'I don't like the position it puts you in, though. I-I don't see you surviving.'

Alexis offered her a lie that came all too easy. 'I'll be okay, Ziya. By tomorrow, we'll all be sitting in the Garden toasting our success. Don't you worry about me.'

Whether she believed him or not, Ziya nodded and left Alexis at his request, saying she had to wake Serena, who was sleeping off her hangover.

As soon as Alexis was alone in the white-walled laboratory, he called his proxy. After a couple of rings, he heard his own voice speak to him.

'You okay?' said his proxy. It sounded like it had just woken up. Alexis remembered his mother saying that it spent the night round Blaise's house – it was likely they had been up late talking about Blaise's parents leaving.

'I'm fine—'

'Of course you are,' the proxy interjected, somehow able to convey Alexis's sarcasm to a realistic degree. 'If there's any day to not be okay, it would be today.'

'Thank you, but that's not why I called you, unfortunately,' Alexis replied. He started walking, following Ziya's footsteps at a distance. He reached the point where the hallways forked, one end heading to the centre of the Haven, and the other to Incantus's office. 'How's Mum and Dad?'

'Normal,' said his proxy. 'Kind of. Mum and D—*your* mum and dad,' it said, correcting itself, 'have been a bit weird the last couple of days. Your dad's got the day off and they want me back as soon as I can be. I don't think they know anything about what's going on in your world, but maybe they're scared because the news has been reporting a lot of natural disruptions across the globe this last week.'

Its tone was accusatory. Incantus hadn't mentioned any impact of their usage of the Elemental Gems while on their quest, and Alexis was grateful, for it was one less thing to fill his mind.

'Look, I have a favour to ask you,' said Alexis. 'You're not going to like it, but I'm only going to say it once, so buckle up and don't hate me too much. If all goes to plan, then we win. If it doesn't, well then I'd sooner stab myself in the chest than be imprinted.'

Alexis heard his proxy sigh. 'I knew it was going to be a bad day when I woke up to Blaise's ashy feet in my face.'

Alexis switched off his phone and pocketed it when he got to his bedroom. He crashed onto his own bed, revelling in the coolness and minimalism of his room in contrast to Demi's. He had nothing to do but wait until he was called by Incantus or Ziya.

He tried to stomach breakfast, knowing he needed the energy. He ate purely for sustenance and then made sure he used the toilet. There probably wouldn't be much opportunity to relieve himself once the fighting commenced, and the sight of Mortem and his army of Shadowless would certainly make him need to.

Finally, with nothing else to do except ignore the static feeling of anxiety that crawled beneath his skin and unsettled his stomach, he reached for the photograph that lay hidden in his bedside drawer. The picture meant more to him now that he knew for certain who it was. The fondness of the smiles between the two boys, the way the young Incantus had his arms wrapped around his brother. Mortem. Nero, rather.

Alexis stared at the Arcangelo brothers who would grow up to be men on opposite sides of a battle, and tried to prepare himself for what was to come. For what he would have to witness. What he would have to do. And who he would have to kill.

17
PHILOTIMO

Philotimo (n.) *Greek origin*
'Friend of honour'; complex array of virtues that encompass honour, dignity and pride in one's responsibilities and duties

'At least we'll die looking good,' said Blaise as he flexed in front of the mirror in his red-tiled bathroom. The cuffs of his new Elemental suit were painted a fiery vermilion, which coincidentally matched the beads of blood that dotted his neck from where he had nicked himself with the razor.

'If you insist on shaving the two pubes you have on your face that you call a beard, let me do it so you don't slit your throat,' said Alexis, snatching the razor out of his hand before Blaise went in again at a toe-curling angle.

'Fine,' Blaise conceded. He followed Alexis into the bedroom and sunk into the plush maroon-coloured, long sofa.

Alexis washed the razor with a splash of water from his palm. He tilted Blaise's chin up and wiped away the spots of blood, before gently shaving the dark coiled hairs at his neck.

'You ready for today?' Blaise mumbled, his eyes fixed on Alexis's. 'How do you think it'll be? Bet it lasts all day. We'll be fine though at the back, won't we? Everyone will keep us safe from Mortem. Do you think he'll target any of us when he sees us to prevent the Proph—'

Alexis clamped his hand over Blaise's mouth. 'If you keep talking and I slip up, then *I'll* be the one who prevents the Prophecy.'

Blaise's throat bobbed.

Alexis knew Blaise well enough by now to identify with ease the signs of his fear and his attempts to conceal it. Where Caeli blamed others and Demi went quiet, Blaise's reaction was to talk. *Incessantly.* Alexis was usually happy to entertain it, but not if the topic of conversation was Mortem.

Instead, now that he had one of the few opportunities where Blaise would be forced to listen and not speak, Alexis seized the chance to do some last-minute meddling in his friends' love lives.

'You're going to hate yourself if you die today having not tried things with Cae.'

'What . . . ?' Blaise began, shifting in his seat.

Alexis steadied him with his other hand, locking him into place. He lightly brushed the blade across the square of his jaw and continued. 'She wants to be with you, but only if you show her that you want her too – and not only in the absence of other options.'

'Then why did she get back together with Joe?' Blaise snapped, his bushy eyebrows pulled together. He resisted Alexis's hand to sit up properly. Despite his tone of annoyance, Alexis noted the vulnerability in Blaise's disclosure. 'I heard her with him again last night. Doesn't sound like she wants me at all.'

Alexis rolled off a number of possible reasons as to why:

'To feel desired, for revenge, to serve as a distraction. Either way, she told me that it'll never work with him or with anyone else because there wasn't any *fire*. It's you that she wants, but she's not going to sit around and put her life on pause while you figure out what you want.' Blaise had fallen silent as he listened. In between Alexis's sentences, only the crackling of the wall-length fireplace that encircled his room made any noise, loud and nervous. 'You're brave enough, and irritatingly handsome enough, to go after any girl you meet, even if there's no chance with them. Even if it's right in front of her. So it's not fair to hold it against Caeli when she does the same.'

Blaise went to retort, but he caught himself before the words came out. He sat back, resting his head against the back of the chair, staring at the ceiling. His mouth then curved into the faintest of smiles as he asked quietly, 'She told you there wasn't any fire with anyone else?'

Alexis shaved the last section of his face and nodded. He returned his smile. 'She did.'

When Ziya notified them that it was time to gather at the hive, Alexis found it as packed as it had been the evening before, teeming with thousands of Elementals suited in Haven black or Sanctuario navy. Only today, things felt different.

A low cloud of anxiety hung over the crowd, ridding the Elementals of their typical buzz. The glory and passion of the previous night had been washed out, replaced by clipped messages and lingering embraces. As the Elementals of the Haven said their goodbyes to their younger siblings or grandparents who were too old to fight, a silent web of fear stretched between them. Or at least it did until the crowds looked up to see the four Children of the Elements.

Alexis and Blaise joined Caeli and Demi on one of the golden-lined marble pathways that bridged the hive. They had exchanged greetings, but otherwise didn't say much, opting to stand stoic and powerful, their amulets displayed clearly on their chests. It worked well enough for Caeli and Blaise, who were continuing to ignore each other.

Alexis and Demi, on the other hand, were looking at each other as if they were the last two people in the world. Alexis wasn't sure if his face betrayed the series of questions he hoped to conceal; questions that arose from his deepest insecurities as if spouted by hot water springs.

Should I not have come last night?

Should I not have left?

Slipping into her bed the night before felt like a fever dream. If Demi wanted to pretend like it hadn't happened, Alexis would respect that, even if that made him feel as though his heart hadn't the strength nor the will to beat again.

'Everyone okay?' Demi asked after a long period of silence. She looked between them as they secured their weapons to their Haven suits: Caeli's quiver of arrows strapped to her back and her two-metre-length double-edged spear; Blaise's mighty flame-resistant axe; and Alexis's bi-sword of equal halves bronze and steel. She fiddled with her own liana whip and tried to secure it to her hip. 'We've all had something to eat and had plenty of water?'

'Yes, Mother,' Caeli replied.

‘Let me help you with that,’ offered Alexis. If they were going to act like they hadn’t slept in each other’s arms all night, then they might as well go back to being best friends.

He took the thick vine from Demi and moved to stand behind her. Her dark hair was tied into a curly ponytail, with a simple plait on either side of her head that met together at the back. As he coiled the whip tightly around his hand, it was impossible to not breathe in the floral scent of her hair he’d smelt upon waking. He fought to stop his hands from shaking as he clipped the wrought liana to the curve of her hip. He stood back, his head lowered.

Demi let out a long sigh that made Alexis wonder if she had been holding her breath. ‘Thank you, Lexi,’ she said, looking up at him. She hadn’t taken a step back and neither had he. ‘How did you . . . ? Did you sleep well?’

Alexis met her doe eyes, the same colour green as her emerald amulet and the sleeves of her suit. She focused intently on him as if she was sending him a message in a language he had no experience in reading.

‘I did.’ He swallowed and watched her do the same. ‘It was the best night’s sleep I’ve ever had.’

‘Mine too,’ she said.

‘Lucky you,’ said Blaise loudly, interrupting the moment. ‘I had the worst gas all night.’

Caeli tutted and shook her head as the others laughed.

Heavy footsteps strode across the suspended walkway towards them. ‘Good morning, my dears,’ said Serena Aevum groggily.

Caeli gasped as she looked the famed Elemental up and down. ‘Serena! You look like a queen!’

Serena did indeed look magnificent. A vintage grey cloak was stitched to her shoulders and elbows and swept the floor, the inside threaded with a deep regal purple. Beneath it, she wore a white patterned undercoat, adorned with a myriad of golden jewels.

Lastly, sitting just over her left breastplate was a magnificent, intricate brooch. Dotted with fine crystals, the metal curved in the shape of the letter 'A', surrounded by two angel wings that spread out proudly in the shape of a circle with twelve indentations marking the border.

'I've never been a big fan of all this clothing,' she grunted, flapping her arms once. From one of the many inner pockets, she pulled out a leather-wrapped flask and took several large sips. She cradled it between her hands as though it were the only thing that could give her energy, despite that being the inexhaustive power she had at her fingertips. 'But it beats wearing one of those gimp suits you've got on. Although, I'm sure if I squeezed into one, it would be enough to send half the Shadowless running for the hills.'

'That's such a stunning brooch,' said Demi, stepping closer to admire its design.

'An Aevum family heirloom,' Serena answered. She turned when Ziya approached them on the walkway, her hands held awkwardly in front of her as though she was unsure whether she had any place amongst them. 'Passed down to the eldest daughter. Trust me, when there are only women in your family, it becomes difficult to hide. One day when I pass, it shall become yours.' She stroked the side of Ziya's face before lifting her chin so she was no longer looking at her feet.

Alexis noticed the Haven command disk in Ziya's pocket.

He knew she had spent the better half of the early hours accounting for the magical creatures of their world that had agreed to fight on the Elementals' behalf. 'How's it looking up there?'

'Nearly two thousand Centauroi, Amazons, Seelie Court of Fae, and all other beings combined,' Ziya replied, reciting the numbers off the top of her head.

'Fae?' Blaise interrupted, looking between Alexis and Demi as if that was a joke. 'As in fairies? As in tiny little pixies? What are they going to do? Take their teeth out?'

Serena laughed as though the questions were utterly preposterous before she gestured for Ziya to explain.

'We should consider ourselves fortunate the Seelie Court have come to our aid,' said Ziya matter-of-factly, back in her element in teaching. As she spoke, Alexis thought of how great a Leader she would be, if there was still a Haven to lead. 'Over the years, Incantus has struck up an alliance of sorts with them, whereas the Unseelie Court and the High Coven of Witches, with whom they are associated, have opted to remain neutral until it is clear who the victors will be. They argue that they have wasted enough blood on Elemental wars.'

Alexis was listening intently, making mental notes to understand the world he was a part of but had experienced so little of. He had to kick Blaise's heel to recruit his attention as Ziya continued. 'Seelie Fae look like us, only a hundred times more beautiful and a thousand times more devious – although I'm sure those statistics aren't totally fact-checked. Regardless, a world without Mortem plaguing it will be far more enjoyable for them, so they have chosen to join us, which is especially useful as they are far stronger in the spring and summer seasons.'

'Is it true they can't lie?' Alexis asked, remembering all that he could from the stories he used to read that he once considered 'fantasy' and now would count as 'non-fiction'.

Serena snapped her fingers in front of Blaise's face, making him startle. 'Yes, although they choose their words carefully, so don't allow yourselves to be tricked if you engage with one. And don't slight or offend them. The Fae have a long memory and their support is vital for us.'

'Don't they love all pretty things?' Blaise asked with a smirk as he puffed out his chest.

If only he had turned slightly, he might have seen Caeli smothering a reluctant smile. She cleared her throat to mask it and then asked, 'What of the number of Elementals?'

Ziya glanced skywards and recalled, 'With the Haven having around three thousand eligible recruits – fighters, healers and scholars alike – and the Sanctuario having just over two thousand, the Light Army stands strong even without the High Order against the anticipated size of Mortem's.'

'*Don't trust them.*'

Ezra's warning of the High Order beside the river last night rang out through Alexis's mind, puncturing his memory.

'When are the High Order expected to join us?' he queried. 'Surely they should be here from the start in case Mortem tries to seize Stonehenge well before the eclipse.'

Ziya frowned slightly at him. 'Secretary-General Kleine has assured us that the operatives of the Security Council will arrive as soon as they have secured all of their facilities and locked their records away to prevent any potential breach should Mortem's imprinting succeed.'

'Reassuring,' Caeli mumbled.

Alexis wanted to probe further, to find out how much Incantus was relying on the High Order, but Ziya was already getting ready to go. She hugged each of them as she said, 'I wish you all good luck. It has been an honour getting to know you. The best time of my life. I am forever grateful for your friendship and for the kindness you have shown me.'

She hugged Alexis last, crouching in on herself, becoming even smaller. When they parted, she looked Alexis dead in the eye and added, 'When you see Mortem, hit him for me and my sister.'

'I will,' he promised.

Ziya stepped away from the Children of the Elements to converse with her grandmother as Incantus arrived, Gibbous at his heel. Dressed in his bespoke crystal-white Haven suit, he looked angelic, brimming with power. His salt-and-pepper beard had been tidied, angled sharp along his cheekbones and jaw. His bright blue eyes surveyed the crowd below as he smiled at them encouragingly.

Incantus exchanged final words with Ziya. After she finished speaking, her face soon crumpled as her hands rushed to cover it. He bent down, whispering something in her ear, something that made her nod and stifle her tears. He pulled her into a tight embrace and as he held her, Serena pulled out the pins that kept Ziya's long black hair taut in its bun and stroked through it.

Ziya stayed for a moment longer to hug her grandmother

and then wrap her arms around Gibbous's neck and kiss the side of his face as he tried to lick her. She then hurried away from the hive and made her way towards the laboratory where she would be able to watch as the day unravelled.

'It is time, my children,' Incantus said gravely as he and Serena came to stand beside them.

Incantus stretched his arms wide. Slowly, a dense white fog escaped from the cuffs of his suit, falling towards the ground. It kept low to the base level, lapping over itself like a thick body of water, spreading out to all corners of the hive. The smoke encapsulated the thousands of Elementals as another tendril meandered towards Serena and the Alpha team, immersing them in the connected web of mist.

'Brothers and sisters in arms,' Incantus began, his voice reaching every corner and crevice of the Haven, reverberating through the empty halls, echoing along the sanctuaries where the Elders and young children remained. 'You know your mission. You know what we need to do. Fight for each other. Protect one another. This is not a battle that will be without sacrifice and blood.'

The white fog pulsed as he spoke, his voice rippling through the smoke. Alexis tried to see through it, but his sight went no further than to make out Demi's figure beside him. She turned to look at him, her amulet glowing softly like a faint lighthouse in the night. He placed his hand over the cool metal of his sword and gripped it tightly.

'Fight for your friends, for your families. Fight for your home, your Haven. Fight for yourselves and your futures. For even when the day goes dark, the light of our lives will shine on and we will burn brighter than the dark that hides us!'

The fog flashed with a brilliant white light. In a fraction of a second, the army light-jumped from the Haven.

With the midday sun beating down upon his face, the coolness of fresh air ruffling his hair, Alexis opened his eyes to see that lying out before him was their battlefield. Their arena. And for many of them, their deathbed.

18
TACENDA

Tacenda (n.) *Latin origin*
Things better left unsaid; matters to be
passed over in silence

Alexis half expected to be transported into the middle of a battle sequence. He was almost disappointed by the absence of Mortem and the Shadowless on the fields surrounding Stonehenge. Now he simply had to wait.

Alexis loosened his grip on his sword and accounted for the sun's position in the sky. The total eclipse would commence in just over five hours, but the moon would begin to block the light before that, waning Incantus's power and amplifying Mortem's. Alexis assumed Mortem was conserving his efforts for such a time.

Coward.

'File out in formation,' Serena ordered, her voice booming across the ranks of Elemental soldiers. They dispersed like a colony of ants, tracing around Stonehenge where Alexis and his friends stood, forming hundreds of ringed rows between the monoliths and the sea of magical creatures that spread out across the flat grassy fields. No longer was Alexis surprised at the existence of such creatures, but seeing them in such a great number truly took his breath away.

Centaurs whinnied at the arrival of the Elementals, who formed the front rows. They were most noticeable, standing far taller than their human half-relatives, hides shining black and brown and golden in the sunlight. With human hands, they greeted their comrades and bowed at their declarations of gratitude.

It was as though every creature from the myths and legends Alexis had spent his childhood reading about had found their way on to the fields to support the Elementals: fauns with the legs of a goat, and dryads made of tree bark and leaves. Alexis could easily identify the Seelie Court of Fae dressed in their finery, wings thinner than a sheet of paper folded behind their backs, each pair a unique colour shared by no other. Their critical eyes surveyed the might of the youthful Elementals and Alexis shivered beneath their hungry stare. He was glad they kept their distance, even if many of them appeared to be mesmerised by his and his friends' arrival.

'Why did so many non-Elementals agree to fight with us? *For* us?' Alexis asked the moment Incantus and Serena appeared to be free.

The most experienced Elementals filled in the ranks at the rear of the Centauroi, while the youngest, aged no less than fifteen, were ushered by the Haven and Sanctuario Leaders to the very back of the army, closest to Stonehenge. Both Joe Coin and Althea Orenda gave Alexis and his friends a parting wave as they advanced far beyond the lines.

'Many are repaying their debts owed to our people over millennia,' Incantus answered, guiding a particularly nervous-looking Elemental boy to the final row just before Stonehenge.

'Others have stepped up because they know Mortem doesn't

distinguish between those who stand by and those who stand against him,' Serena added. 'And they all understand the destruction his reign will bring, even if his imprinting powers don't affect them.'

A towering brown-skinned woman with arms as muscular as Akili Pierce's came forth and shook Incantus's hand. She was followed by an even taller golden-haired centaur who was covered head to hoof in silver armour, which had more scratches on it than he had wrinkles on his furred face.

'We've even got Amazons and Centauroi fighting side by side,' said Incantus, greeting them both. He inclined his head. 'Queen Otrera. Chief Sophos.'

'There are few things more important than centuries' worth of fight: this is one of them,' responded the giant warrior woman.

The elderly centaur hummed in agreement. 'Indeed.' He then turned to the Children of the Elements. At the sight of Demi's amulet, he bent his great stallion legs and knelt to a low bow. The Queen of the Amazons also bowed, her crown tilting forward slightly.

'Lady Earth,' said Chief Sophos. 'Your powers brought life to us creatures of the land. My people are at your command long after our death.'

Demi gawked at Alexis awkwardly. She shrugged before clearing her throat. 'You are very welcome . . . Thank you for your service. I hope it will not come to that.'

Alexis winked and gave her a thumbs-up. While she may not have noticed it, Demi's presence on the battlefield and the aura of her amulet must have attracted the animals from the wild, as from across the meadows, swathes of mundane creatures had gathered around her, everything from stray foxes to a herd of stags.

'Shame we aren't fighting underwater with my people,' Alexis mumbled as the Amazon Queen and Chief Centauroi parted from their group.

'At least you've got people,' Blaise complained, pulling a disgruntled face. 'What creatures do you know hang about in fire? Cockroaches are all I'll have fighting on my side.'

'What about me?' Caeli added, adjusting her quiver of arrows. 'We're not anywhere exotic. This is England. I'll be lucky to have a flock of pigeons swoop in and shit on Mortem's army.'

Demi barked a laugh when Blaise shivered. 'Anything but pigeons,' he grumbled, making Caeli laugh too. This time, she didn't try and hide it.

Alexis noticed Serena standing from a distance observing them, having that same look on her face Incantus so often did when seeing them laugh together. She caught his eye and took a step towards them.

'I can see now why Teller, Akili and Incantus sent so many messages about you. My boys were right. You truly are the ones worthy to take on the mantle we once held.'

Alexis didn't know what to say, so he just let Demi take her hand and squeeze it as he smiled.

'Incantus, where are our Gems?' Caeli asked once he returned from his lap around Stonehenge. It seemed as though the Elementals had been trained well enough to know the exact formations to fall into. There wasn't much left he needed to do.

'Oh yes, one moment.' He closed his eyes in concentration

and clenched his jaw as four tall golden staffs flashed into existence before them. Secured to each top was one of the glowing Elemental Gems.

Alexis eagerly reached for his and at its contact, an electrifying current swept through him with a force so powerful it tensed every muscle of his body. His amulet sparked, awaiting the transferral of the Water Gem's infinite powers.

'You can take from it your omnipotent powers as you so wish,' Incantus sanctioned with a cautious smile. 'Use it to guard your stations. You can also use it as a weapon to maim rather than to kill if you are able to make the choice. It may come of particular use against those who have been imprinted and are acting in the agentic state at Mortem's command.'

'Already bloody hot in this,' Serena interrupted. She beat her grey-and-purple robe before finishing the last of what remained in her flask.

'I'd be too nervous to drink coffee . . . makes me need the toilet,' muttered Demi distractedly.

Serena leaned in close so that Alexis could smell the wine on her breath. 'Good thing it's not coffee.' She gestured the four young Elementals to her and pulled them into a tight embrace, one Alexis imagined only a grandmother could give. 'It's been a privilege meeting you all. I shall see you at the end.'

'I guess it is time,' Incantus said somewhat reluctantly as Serena pulled away. He squatted to his knees before the Children of the Elements and spread his arms wide so that they formed a circle. 'I am so proud of the four of you,' he said, passion in his voice and emotion in his eyes. 'I have learned from you as much as I have taught you. Please remember my instructions and obey my orders today: keep yourselves safe and protected at all costs until the time comes. No matter what happens, make sure we are all inside Stonehenge during the ecl—'

His sentence was cut short, interrupted by a great disturbance in the crowd.

A tide of gasps erupted across the Light Army, followed by a chorus of screams and the crumpling of bodies. The fear was tangible, like the smell of decay in the air or the taste of bile. It was contagious, flooding though the ranks of soldiers in seconds.

As Incantus slowly rose from his crouched position, Alexis sensed the presence of darkness even before he could see it. Incantus gave him one last look, his face a blend of conviction and courage, before he and Serena began to make their way to the front of their army, Gibbous striding in between them. It was only when the crowd parted to let them through that Alexis could see what was happening beyond.

He immediately wished he had closed his eyes, for in this instance, the fear of the unknown was far less terrifying than what lay before him.

A monstrous cloud was sweeping across the fields like a sandstorm in hurricane winds, bathing the ground in coiling blackness as it traced around the outermost ring of the Light Army. Once the shadow band connected, there was a flash of black, followed by an ear-shattering eruption that violated the oppressive silence and forced the ground to quiver.

The wave of shadow tore the grass from the earth as it rippled closer and closer, a destructive force of nature too fast and too powerful to be stopped.

There was a flash of light, and then a boom from above.

Alexis's eyes were too slow to follow, but he felt the heat of Incantus's power as he shot into the sky. With a bellow, Incantus swept his arms wide and an explosion of white light burst from his back like great, sweeping angel wings. Layer upon layer of glowing beams of white struck the ground surrounding the Light Army, encasing them in a protective dome seconds before the darkness hit.

The two primal powers collided with a thunderous crash, climbing higher to dominate the other until only the wisps of light remained. When the black smoke finally dispersed, the true nature of the Dark Army was revealed.

Ziya's prediction of their numbers had been wrong. So wrong.

The Dark Army stretched out further than Alexis's eyes could make out, an endless sea of enemies, an infinite number of foes. And yet amongst them all, it took Alexis only a moment to find Mortem Arcangelo.

The beautiful fallen angel of darkness stood at the forefront, facing him, not a couple of hundred metres away from the outermost point of the Light Army. His black dire wolf, Crescent, stood to his left side, a great, fearsome beast matched only in size by Gibbous.

Dressed in royal robes that cloaked his shining black-plated armour, Mortem somehow looked fearful, even in the light of day. The rigid scar that curved from his square jaw down past his neck gleamed in the sunlight, the only crack in his otherwise perfectly sculpted appearance.

Alexis had forgotten how striking his eyes were, identical to his own. A combination he had never seen in another person, with blueness in the centre fused with an outer ring of blackness, mirroring the arrangement on the battlefield. Alexis knew them as well as he knew his own.

Father, we meet again.

Demi gasped at Alexis's side, her hand clamped over her mouth. 'My God, my God, what has he done?'

Only then did Alexis take notice of the first wave of the Dark Army behind Mortem.

An army of the undead; the Nekro. The things that had killed Ezra's parents. Human bodies devoid of humanity and light, of life and sentience.

They appeared as mangled reanimated beings, barely held together by strings of muscle tissue, rotten skin and broken bones. Where limbs had been torn or destroyed, sharp metal fragments jutted out from the sockets, misshapen and reddened with dried, coagulated blood. Alexis had to swallow to keep down the vomit that threatened to spill.

He couldn't see much beyond the Nekro, but he knew there stood hundreds of Mortem's devout followers, the Shadowless. Whether they had been imprinted already or they had chosen to follow Mortem, they posed a greater threat than the Nekro. They possessed their Elemental powers. Alexis wondered how many of them were innocent, enslaved by Mortem to be his pawns. Alexis made a small, silent vow to himself to save as many of them as he could, to take caution where he could and not gravely injure a single person with eyes infected black and shadow stolen away.

'Dr Sinner left his boss with a few parting gifts,' Blaise scathed through gritted teeth.

Sinner's brutal experiments – the mutilated Hybrids. There were more than Alexis could count, each a vile amalgamation of the most adaptive and destructive components of different species. They were as sickening as the Nekro, if not worse.

Incantus spoke first. If he was afraid or intimidated by what lay before him, he did not show it. 'Where are my Leaders?' he demanded, his voice thundering across the battlefield.

Mortem tilted his head to the side. The Nekro parted to make way for Akili Pierce, Raeve and Taranis. Their eyes gleamed black in the daylight and they displayed no more humanity than the Nekro that stood amongst them.

'This is the only chance I am going to give you,' Mortem announced, addressing them all. 'Join me now and avoid this fate. I do not wish to kill you all. I promise that if you come freely, you will not be imprinted upon the eclipse. Betrayal is the cost of survival. You would be fools to turn this offer down.'

Serena called out indignantly, 'Your name means "death", you pompous psychopath! No one with half a brain would follow you.'

Alexis heard Mortem chuckle with genuine amusement. 'Long time, no see, Aevum. Are you here to join Akili or do you wish me to send you to Teller? You would've been so disappointed to see the look on his face when I struck my scythe through his chest.'

A lesser woman would've dropped to her knees, but Serena spat on the ground. 'I will dance on the day of your downfall, scum, don't doubt that for a second. They will tell stories of how you begged for mercy at my hand. Akili, have no fear, I'll get you back to us.'

The muscular black Leader's face grimaced in confliction, but so close to Mortem's side, any resistance of Akili's true self was quickly subdued, replaced once again by the vacant look shared by all of the imprinted.

There would be no fleeing, no going back from this point on. There was only a moment of standstill, this moment, after which chaos would ensue.

'This fight is between me and you,' Incantus called. 'Let us send our armies away. If you truly wished the best for our people, you would not send yours to the slaughter.'

Mortem spread his arms wide. 'Have you seen my army? It is your people who will be slaughtered. I will start with you and end with the precious Children of the Elements.'

Over my dead body, Alexis thought, which was likely exactly what Mortem was hoping for. At the touch of the Water Gem to his amulet, his body trembled with power. Everything around him intensified, as did his awareness of his element. He suddenly locked in on the sweat across his brow, his heartbeat drumming thunderously in his ears, the dryness of his mouth. This was *power.* He only hoped it would be enough.

Blaise, Caeli and Demi followed suit, absorbing the extent of their eternal powers and becoming Omni. Together, the four Children of the Elements glowed brilliantly from the centre of Stonehenge, illuminating their sides of the battlefield. Slowly, they turned to one another.

Demi shook her head as though trying to find words that evaded her. 'I . . . um . . .'

'You don't need to say it,' said Caeli, taking her hand. 'We know.'

The four friends exchanged a lasting look before reluctantly parting to make their way to their quarter of Stonehenge, where the elements they had used to defend their section sprang alive. Alexis stayed where he was, glancing at the people nearby. He nodded at them in consideration. For all he knew, they might be the last people to see him alive before the day was up.

No one had noticed what lay hidden between his defences at his section of Stonehenge. To everyone else, it was just the wide burrow of water and the great wall of ice interconnecting his stone pillars. He hoped it would remain that way.

'I already broke into your Haven,' taunted Mortem, his voice deepening as shadows rose from his robes in the form of wings, twisted and clawed.

On the other side of the battlefield, Incantus took Serena's arm.

With her free hand, Serena slammed her palm against the ground. Ripples of golden energy erupted from her body, sending great shockwaves undulating across the entirety of the Light Army behind her. As it rolled through Alexis, the energy infused him with a surge that made him feel as though he would never tire, as though his chest could barely contain the beating of his heart. Serena's power amplified him with a strength equal to that of Incantus's light, close to the inexhaustive powers of his Elemental Gem. It made him as prepared as he would ever be.

The moon was visible in the sky, a small white sphere against the blue canvas, already on its path towards the sun. Alexis accounted for its location again, counting down the hours until it would begin to eclipse the light and cast the world into a shadow that may never leave.

At the front lines, Incantus had shaken his head. 'No,' he

said, eyes fixed on the man who had once been his brother. 'We are the Haven.'

Gibbous and Crescent howled into the air and the Battle of Stonehenge finally began.

19
NEART

Neart (n.) *Irish origin*
Strength, power, might, energy

Five hours until totality

Through the lines of battle as the armies of Haven and Shadowless collided, Alexis watched Incantus Arcangelo. With Gibbous at his side, they tore ahead at a speed unmatched by any other, knocking aside Nekro like they were nothing more than flies to be swatted.

Crescent bounded from Mortem's side and collided viciously with Gibbous. Gibbous sank his huge jaws into Crescent's chest, forcing him to howl in anguish. By the time Incantus reached Mortem, Alexis's sight was obscured, and he could only pray that the fist Incantus had pulled back to punch struck true and hard.

Seconds later, the sound of metal striking metal erupted across the battlefield as the Dark Army crashed into the Light, sparing only Stonehenge, the eye of the storm, the still centre of the chaos. Fae and harpies ravaged each other in the skies while the Nekro, Hybrids and Shadowless savaged the front lines of the Light Army. Flailing winged bodies and carcasses fell like bloodied hail to the ground. And all Alexis could do was wait and watch.

As Chief Sophos of the Centauroi galloped forward, he linked arms with Queen Otrera of the Amazons and swung her up onto his hind. The giant woman roared a battle cry, forcing her warriors to follow her as she somehow got to steady feet on top of the centaur's back, crouched to keep her balance, thick, dark hair swept back in the wind.

Serena Aevum miraculously kept up with the military front's charge. She clapped her hands just as Akili Pierce's astral projection leaped at her. A reverberating band of gold boomed from her fingertips, overpowering Akili's telepathic power and throwing him against the ground with a force that would have broken any human's body.

Even from the centre of Stonehenge, Alexis heard Serena scream, 'Fight against it, love!' as she dropped to her knees and clamped her hands either side of Akili's face, forcing him to look at her through tortured eyes. Meanwhile, the Amazon Queen leaped from Sophos's back to intercept Raeve just as wild bolts of wicked blue-and-yellow lightning erupted from Taranis.

Alexis couldn't keep up with it all, no matter how hard he tried. He scaled his wall of ice, but that provided only little improvement in his vantage point. He felt as if he was dishonouring each and every person on the battlefield if he didn't consider them, if he didn't acknowledge their individual fights, knowing that it may be their last, knowing that it was to safeguard him and his friends. But trying to observe it all was like trying to count each small wave in the ocean's tide. Naturally, his eyes fell to whichever wave, whichever battle, was largest as it crested and crashed, soon to be replaced by another.

There was a parting in the warzone, long enough for Alexis to see Incantus and Mortem again, this time with weapons in hand, their wolves engaged in a brutal brawl beside them. Incantus had manifested his broadsword of light while Mortem drew his scythe of shadows, the very same that had taken Teller Sagen's life.

When they met in battle, it was like nothing Alexis had ever seen before. There was no restraint; there was no reprieve. There was only pure fury. Brothers turned into something far worse than enemies. They moved like lightning, battling so quickly, their blades blurred into indistinct shapes, each blow hoping to be the final one as it swung for the other's head. They had exchanged ten before anyone else around them had taken their first. It was horrifying. It was mesmerising.

Alexis had thought he'd seen true power before. He thought he himself was on his way to becoming a respected Elemental. Yet to watch the Arcangelo brothers, even at a distance, was almost too much. No one dared to approach as they duelled with a ferocity that shook the very ground, their blades casting out shards of light and shadow around them every time they met. Alexis was glad when they disappeared from view again and his breathing could resume.

A huge explosion from the south-west stole his attention. A fiery wave erupted into the sky as Blaise's hands ignited into billowing flames of black and red.

Blaise turned to his friends on the other sides of Stonehenge. The burning rocks of his quarter shimmered from the heat of the blaze. 'We have to do something to help!'

Blaise pointed his staff to the sky. The Gem of the Fire gleamed as he catapulted an array of smoking firebolts from it.

They hurtled towards the canopy of naked harpies, dispersing those who managed to evade its burning path.

'You're Elementals, aren't you?' Blaise shouted to the soldiers lined before him. Alexis saw them nod, moving their bodies for the first time since the wolves howled to commence the battle. Blaise swept his arms wide, the boldness of his element masking the fear Alexis knew he was feeling. 'Then use your goddamned powers!'

The Elementals stationed to defend him followed his command. Rays of coloured lights erupted from those who could conjure their abilities at long range, firing deep towards the masses of the Dark Army.

Caeli acted as soon as she saw Blaise had. She shot into the air, joining the airborne warriors in her region. Her long hair shimmered in the sunlight, accented a deeper silver by the glow of the Air Gem atop her staff.

Alexis saw her twist it in her careful grip, and as she did, the air around her sharpened into a number of distinctive points. It was like crumpling a sheet of paper, only her canvas was imperceptible to the naked eye, made only visible when it pinched into pointed edges. Caeli swept her arms wide, sending the needles of wind flying. They thudded into the mangled bodies of the Nekro, tearing apart their decomposing flesh and crushing much of the first row to the ground.

'I guess we're next,' called Demi.

The grass at Demi's feet swayed as if blown by the wind, but Alexis knew that Caeli had nothing to do with its manipulation as the blades were plucked from the earth one by one. When they began to encircle Demi as though she was the sun conducting a ring of asteroids, Alexis raised his staff into the sky to bring together whatever moisture there was in the air. Rain clouds drew within seconds.

Demi hurled the blades of grass so they shot like bullets, and Alexis unleashed a tide of frozen icicles from above. Even from a distance, Alexis heard the trampling of bodies as they collapsed to the ground. He felt a surprising burst of adrenaline intermixed with the dopaminergic rush of satisfaction. It was like the video games he used to play with Jason. He could shoot as many times as he wanted, never fearing that he would come to any real harm or run out of ammunition. It was thrilling without it ever being dangerous.

The battlefield was a huge painting of colour, cut into four segments surrounding Stonehenge. Shimmering razors of wind, blazing firebolts, flurries of grass blades and pikes of frozen water flooded the scene, commanded by the Elemental Gems wielded by the descendants of the First Borns. Alexis's amulet hummed against his chest, vibrating with the thunderous power of a flowing river.

And yet, it was not enough.

New waves of Nekro and Shadowless came quicker than the former fell. Shadowless tore through the Light Army with their powers while Nekro savaged any in their way. Soon enough, Alexis saw the first rows of Elementals meeting the unrelenting tide of Mortem's army, barely holding their ground. As powerful and trained as they were, it wouldn't be long until they were swamped with more opponents than they could hope to keep at bay.

A petrified howl echoed across the battlefield. *Gibbous.* Alexis watched as Incantus turned to his wolf just as an elephant-rhino Hybrid attempted to trample both him and

Crescent. That split second of Incantus's divided attention was all Mortem needed. Alexis tried to call out, but his voice lodged in his throat as darkened daggers lashed out from Mortem's robe and tore into Incantus, throwing him deep into the masses of the Dark Army.

Alexis needed to go to him, to save him. But the only way to do that was to kill Mortem, and he knew he had no hopes of that in open battle. No matter what Incantus had said, Alexis felt a certainty in the core of his being that in the end, he would have to be the one to destroy Mortem with the power they shared. Incantus had mentioned something last night that tied him and Mortem together – the Curse of Raphe. Alexis wished he had asked about it then, but even so, it didn't shake the sureness in his belief that his role was greater than that of the other Children of the Elements.

There might be only one chance for Alexis to face Mortem and stand even the slightest chance of victory, and that was to stick to the plan he and Ziya had implemented that morning. A plan that hopefully wouldn't come into action until the very last few minutes of the eclipse. He would have to pray that Incantus would be able to stay alive until then.

Faith and prayers, however, were not something Alexis could rely on, not as his eyes caught on the carnage that surrounded the former Leaders of the Haven. Chief Sophos lay smoking on the ground, his body charred and torn apart where his human and stallion halves had once met, his legs twitching as the last of Taranis's lightning rippled through him. Not far off, Queen Otrera screamed as she fought to escape the purple iron chains that bound her at Raeve's command.

But then came an explosion of gold that shook the

battlefield, its force so great that it toppled Taranis, Raeve and the collapsed Akili. Even deep in the centre of Stonehenge, Alexis felt its aura thawing the iciness in his chest. Perhaps faith wasn't something he could rely on.

Serena Aevum, on the other hand, was.

The small woman bellowed something indiscernible at Mortem as she heaved bolt after bolt of energy at him, forcing him to stagger backwards. Where he deflected the golden beams, the fragments of her power raced past his sides, tearing apart the Shadowless and Nekro behind him.

Mortem looked . . . *scared.* It was a sight most magnificent to witness.

There was a high-pitched shriek from above, loud and dangerously close to Alexis, forcing him to look to it. Two harpies dived beneath the faeries, sweeping low to rip at the faces of the Elementals. They were small, hunched-over beings with human legs gnarled into eagle talons and vulturous wings that were covered in ruffled black feathers. They soared towards Demi, fangs bared.

But Demi needed not raise a hand to react. When they drew close, the great oak tree that bordered her quarter of Stonehenge whirled to life. The lianas drooped over its branches sprang forward, snatching the harpies from the sky and crushing them into each other with a bone-crunching thud.

'Where can I get one of those?' Alexis asked, looking at his immobile wall of ice with mild disinterest. He noted the nearby Elementals of the Haven shuffling further from the tree, glancing over their shoulders every few seconds to ensure it didn't strike them next.

'Sorry, it's pre-order only,' Demi replied, patting its

bark-covered trunk. 'Helps me to focus on subduing any humans when they reach us.'

Alexis didn't know if it was foolish or admirable of Demi to try to distinguish between human and otherwise in the middle of a battle, but he did not challenge her. Hopefully, neither would come close enough to force her to figure it out.

Caeli's voice boomed in overlapping soundwaves that made it difficult to understand her at first. She remained in the air, but was hovering closer to Alexis and Demi. 'It's not looking good from up here! The Elementals from my side will be breached in the next half hour, probably less.'

Alexis turned back to where Mortem and Serena had been battling. Serena's onslaught didn't falter for a second as she continued to press him back, shouting obscenities that Alexis couldn't make out no matter how hard he tried.

There was a flash of bronze. One moment, Mortem had been there, shouting a word, a *name*, and the next, he was gone. Seconds later, just as Incantus emerged blood-soaked through the fields of battle and reached the fallen bodies of the Leaders, they too disappeared in the blink of an eye with a glint and a whoosh.

It seemed as though for Ezra Alastor, fear was a harsher dictator than redemption, and all the more easy to obey.

Alexis's attention was pulled just as he saw Incantus and Serena embrace one another fiercely, unaware of the wars that raged around them.

At least they are together; at least they are okay, Alexis thought, his chest finally allowing him to take a deep breath.

'Where the hell is the High Order?' Blaise demanded. He jogged over to Alexis's ice wall just as Alexis dismounted it.

'Incantus said we're counting on them to hold back the Shadowless,' said Demi, crossing Stonehenge to meet them. She ran her fingers through her hair and Alexis noticed how pale she looked. It was more than just fear. It was the copious amounts of blood that was poisoning the earth.

'Without divine intervention, I don't think we'll make it to the eclipse!' Caeli shouted, dropping to the land to join her friends.

Alexis clenched his jaw so hard, the muscles began to ache. 'We can't count on them.' He had to get to Incantus to inform him of what Ezra had said. Let it be up to him to see if there was any truth in it.

'Al, what's up?' Blaise asked as Alexis grabbed the hilt of his staff and thrust it into the air. He waved it side to side, hoping that the glow of his royal-blue Water Gem would catch Incantus's attention.

'You're right,' he said. 'We can't stay here and wait as the Shadowless eat away at our armies until they reach us. We have to do something.'

'You saying we should go outfield?' Caeli asked, eyebrows lowering over her hooded eyes.

Alexis swallowed. 'I'm saying we have to.'

20
VERSCHLIMMBESSERN

Verschlimmbessern (v.) *German origin*
To make something worse in an attempt to improve it

Four and a half hours until totality

The tightly packed rows of Elementals that guarded Stonehenge parted, and through them came a bloodied Incantus, Serena and Gibbous. Relief washed over Incantus's face at the confirmation that the Children of the Elements were seemingly untouched and together.

They rushed to meet each other and Incantus spread his arms wide to embrace them all. 'As far as birthdays go,' he said, his voice tight as they squeezed him, 'this is by far my least favourite.'

After several belated 'happy birthdays' and 'why didn't you tell us?' complaints, the Alpha team released Incantus.

Demi winced when she saw the dried blood at Incantus's sides, then again at the sight of Gibbous limping. She dropped to her knees to see if the red that stained his white coat was his own.

Caeli wasn't tactile at the best of times, but even she made an attempt to touch Incantus's shoulder lightly as she asked, 'What happened?'

‘I had them,’ Incantus said, his voice low. ‘Serena was more than handling Mortem, and I was *this* close to extracting the darkness from the Leaders, but they managed to get away. Mortem’s many things, but he’s never been one to flee from a fight. He’s planning something.’

Serena didn’t add anything, her eyes transfixed on a distant point on the ground as though she was in a haze, her flair from earlier ruthlessly extinguished. *What could be so frightful and shocking to have silenced her?* Alexis wondered, suddenly aware of how dry his throat was. He pooled several floating bubbles of water for them to drink from and splash against their faces.

‘Are you hurt?’ Demi asked as she rustled for something in her pockets. A moment later, she pulled out a small yellow healing crystal and a long string of cloth that was slightly damp with a balm likely concocted in the Healing Sanctuary. She looked to Incantus, but he gestured to Gibbous instead.

‘I’ll be fine,’ he said with a fleeting, appreciative smile. Already, his wounds were starting to heal on their own, erased by thin white-glowing lines of his own immortal power. He ran a hand through Gibbous’s matted fur as Demi bound his front paw as delicately as she could. ‘You fought well, old boy.’

‘Mortem’s wolf?’ Blaise enquired. He had never been a huge fan of Gibbous, but even he patted his tall hind supportively. ‘Crescent?’

‘Gibbous wished for me to spare his brother,’ Incantus replied. He added no further detail, leaving Alexis to wonder whether Incantus had granted the wish or not.

‘What’s the High Order’s ETA?’ Alexis asked, hearing the concern in his own voice.

‘I spoke to Secretary-General Kleine just before we left the

Haven,' Incantus replied. 'The Security Council operatives should arrive around the same time as our Elemental front lines are breached, hopefully sooner.'

'And what if they don't?'

Caeli tilted her head at him. 'Why are you so sceptical?'

Despite being the Elemental with the power of water, Alexis found it hard to swallow. There wasn't a way to say it without sounding complicit in Ezra's betrayal. How could he tell them what he knew without revealing he had also let Ezra go? Not only let him go, but also saved his life.

It didn't matter. The truth was more important than how he looked. He would just keep the details to a minimum.

'Ezra came to the Garden last night,' he said. He powered through while Demi gasped, ignoring Caeli's questions and Blaise's swears. He did his best to maintain eye contact with Incantus, but he struggled not to falter beneath his stare. 'We fought, and I almost killed him, but he got away. I don't know what he wanted, but just before he left, he said not to trust the High Order.'

Demi grabbed Alexis's arm and forced him to look at her. There was an intensity to her eyes that revealed her realisation – this had been before he had gone to her room and he hadn't said anything. To Alexis's relief, she didn't mention it. Instead she asked, 'Do you think he was trying to warn you?'

'Traitor was probably trying to screw us over just like he did before the quest,' said Blaise, his hands in fists that smoked at his sides. 'I wish I had been there. I would've fried him.'

'I'm with Blaise,' Caeli agreed, surprising Blaise so much that he didn't know whether to frown or smile. 'People like that don't do anything unless it feeds their own self-interest.

He was just trying to get in your head so you wouldn't bother to fight.'

Incantus raised his blood-specked hand to silence them. 'There is a chance of redemption in everyone, especially the young,' he said. 'I believe it may have been a fleeting moment of morality. I saw him just before, and this is clearly not what he could have anticipated.' He looked to Serena. 'With Teller gone, we have few people in the High Order we can trust with confidence to tell us if there is any truth in what Ezra said. Alexis, you should've told me this earlier.'

Incantus needed not say anything further to express his disappointment, for it was written clearly across his face.

The heat of shame prickled at Alexis's cheeks. 'I'm so sorry.'

He didn't bother to offer excuses, nor did he take offence that no one had asked him if he had been hurt in their fight. He had put his own selfish desires for a night with Demi in his arms above his duty to find Incantus as soon as it had happened, and for that, he didn't deserve to be forgiven, not if it cost them the battle.

'So what do we do now?' asked Blaise, shifting the focus away from Alexis's regret. 'I don't fancy sitting here until Mortem rocks up again.'

'Let us go out, Incantus,' Caeli pleaded. 'That's why we signalled you back here. We can help. You know we can.'

Incantus went to respond, but Serena placed her hand on his chest. 'They're right, Ian,' she said softly. 'Let them do what they have been trained to do. We are surrounded on all sides and we can only guarantee the support of the people we have here right now.' She turned to the Children of the

Elements and spoke with a regal voice of authority. 'You go no further than the front line of the Haven and Sanctuario. Understood?'

Despite her words and the way in which she spoke them, she still inclined her head to Incantus. Incantus sighed and begrudgingly acquiesced. 'You are the only way we win today. Do not put yourselves in jeopardy, not for anyone. And do not feel obliged to go either just because the others are,' he added, looking at Demi. She gave the slightest of nods. 'In the meantime, Serena and I will continue the search for the Leaders. If I can destroy Mortem's influence over them, their support will be immeasurable.'

Caeli pointed to the sky over Alexis's shoulder, her mouth agape. Her voice came out hoarse when she said, 'You won't need to search hard.'

Alexis turned. About half a mile away on the horizon came a huge billowing cloud of cosmic purple fog. Raeve's outline glimmered just beneath it, her arms raised as she swept the bulk of the giant levitating blanket over the battlefield.

As the wave loomed closer, the fog suddenly disassembled into thousands of smaller moving shapes. It was then that Alexis realised it was not a cloud at all, but a roaring sea of ravens; ravens that squawked before hurtling to the ground and pecking at the faces of the Elementals with their sharpened beaks.

Serena made a noise of disgust. 'I hate witches.'

Taranis soared into the sky to join Raeve, his messy blond hair static with electricity. He threw his hands forward and shooting from him erupted a great crack of lightning. The bolt struck the ravens, interconnecting them in a lattice of screeching birds that dived at the ground and exploded when they made contact.

The Light Army east of Stonehenge could barely raise their defences in time to shield themselves from the tide of exploding kamikaze birds. Even the faeries had to pull back before the currents ripped through their featherlight wings.

'I've got this.'

Caeli shot into the air before anyone could stop her, a sonic boom bursting after her. She held her staff at its end with both hands and Alexis could see her slender body shuddering under the force of power she was mustering. With a scream, Caeli swung the golden staff in a huge arc towards the oncoming wave of birds.

Bursting from the Wind Gem poured a hurricane that swept through the skies. The storm threw the electrocuted ravens against each other, detonating them mid-air, far away from the Elementals below. Even Raeve and Taranis struggled against the gales, halting in their assault to fight to stay in the air.

On the ground, Blaise's body ignited into red-and-yellow flame, burning so hot that Alexis felt his cheeks sear from the heat. He too took to the skies, shooting into the air like a firework, using his staff as a flamethrower to spit streams of fire against the new tide of ravens.

'You going to be okay here?' Incantus asked, tearing his eyes away from Caeli and Blaise.

'We'll be fine. You go,' Demi affirmed. She went in for a quick embrace with Incantus, then with Serena.

'Incantus, I'm sorry again—' Alexis began, but he was swiftly interrupted by his white-haired mentor.

'Just stay alive.'

At that, Incantus and Serena disappeared through the ranks of Elementals with Gibbous leading the way in pursuit of Raeve and Taranis, who had begun to retreat at the appearance of them.

Alexis turned to Demi, who was already staring at him. Her eyes were wet with emotion, and Alexis knew her well enough to know why that was.

'You can do this, Demi,' he said, taking a step towards her, forcing her to look up at him. 'You're the strongest person I know. If there is a way for you to help by not taking another human life, you will find it. The Nekro are already dead, so you can't kill them again, and the Hybrids are so unnatural, so . . . poisoned and tormented. Consider this putting them out of their misery. As for the Shadowless, imprinted or otherwise, I know you'll be able to subdue or trap them. You're an incredible fighter, you can do this, but you are just as good a healer.'

The corners of her lips were downcast, a shape so different to that which Alexis knew her for. 'I feel so small,' she said so quietly that Alexis had to strain to hear her over the chaos of the battle. 'I feel like a child – like the earth is going to swallow me whole and I don't know if I'll stop it.'

Alexis took her hands in his. He squeezed them tightly and looked into those bright green eyes that he had come to associate with the safety of home and budding life of spring. 'The earth beneath your feet has never once failed you, so why do you doubt it now?'

She glanced at the shining amulet on his chest, and then to her own, cut in its identical upturned shape. Her jaw set, and when she looked up, there was the stubborn determination back in her eyes.

‘You keep safe, Lexi,’ she said, squeezing his hands once before stepping back.

‘And you, Demi,’ he replied, voice laden with the weight of the three words he couldn’t bring himself to say.

He started towards his quarter of Stonehenge, turning back to see if she was still there. She was. Her eyes were closed and she was muttering something with her hand to her chest. It took Alexis a moment to realise she was holding her golden cross and was praying. Once she’d finished, she strode past the tree that defended her without hesitation in her step and disappeared through the ranks of Elementals on the way to the battlefield.

Alexis didn’t believe in her god, but nonetheless, he prayed for Demi Nikolas.

For her life, for her soul. For her to come back to him.

21
MORRIÑA

Morriña (n.) *Galician origin*
A deep nostalgic and melancholic homesickness
experienced as one intensely longs to return home

Four hours and twenty minutes until totality

When Alexis reached the battlefront, the breath fled from his chest.

The rich coppery scent of blood filled the air and the mutilated carcasses of the fallen littered the ground – Nekro, Hybrids, Elementals on both sides. It was hard to distinguish between them and harder still for Alexis to find space to stand without fear of tripping over.

Althea Orenda was at the front line, hastily tying her long dreads away from her face. 'Alexis, what are you doing here?' she yelled. She shouted something in a language Alexis didn't recognise before the tip of her wand rocketed an explosion of light. It blasted into the underside of a mangled Hybrid, spraying acidic green blood across the Nekro that surrounded it.

'You're not supposed to be here!' added Joe Coin, appearing at his side just in time to stab through a Nekro that had been crawling towards him. Joe's skin was pale and matte in texture, and Alexis knew that as long as he kept up his power, no weapon would be able to harm him.

Alexis had deposited his golden staff back at Stonehenge, and he now gripped his bi-sword with both hands. 'I've come to help,' he said.

He then charged before they could stop him.

He collided with a Nekro and swung. His sword cut through its flesh with ease, severing it in half. The stench of its rotting body was so potent, it brought tears to his eyes, but he quickly swept it away. Another reared up behind him. His mind was tapped into a primal drive and he reacted instinctively, a javelin of ice growing in his hand as he turned. He buried it into its cranium and stepped back as it dropped to the ground.

Alexis raised an eyebrow at Althea and Joe. Althea rolled her eyes, but she could not conceal her grin.

'Yeah, I think you can handle yourself,' Joe decided with a shrug. He nodded once to Althea, and the two of them leaped into action beside Alexis.

Alexis split his sword in half as he advanced to defend a young centaur. He raked his blade against the armoured back of a Shadowless soldier. The man turned, locked eyes with his glowing amulet, and then spat at his face. Alexis barely ducked in time as acid shot overhead, corroding the patch of ground he'd just vacated.

Alexis clashed his blades against the Elemental's broad sword, getting a measure of his fighting technique instantly, just as Raeve had taught him. He caught the back of the man's leg, cutting through muscle and making him drop. Alexis cracked the hilt of the blade against the back of the man's head, knocking him out flat, but not before he gobbed another mouthful of acid. Alexis caught the liquid and hurled it at the Nekro that had forced Althea to the ground. It disintegrated its shoulder, giving her the space to stab her wand into its eye.

Heaving from the smell, Althea scrambled to her feet and gave him a thumbs-up. She scanned the battlefield, and tore to Joe's aid when she saw him in a three-way battle against a tall Shadowless woman and a Nekro that didn't discriminate between who it feasted upon.

Alexis didn't doubt they could handle themselves. He turned back to face the Dark Army just in time to see that looming before him the size of a small bus was a disfigured amalgamation of a rhino and a hippopotamus. And it was charging towards him.

Alexis threw himself aside and thrust upwards with one of his swords, but it barely scratched the surface of its leathered skin. The Hybrid charged again, but this time, Alexis changed tactic. Water burst from his palms, pouring in limitless supply with a force so great, it toppled the beast.

Alexis struck while the iron was hot, or rather, while the water was cold. He swept up the creature, imprisoning it in a giant ball of water. With both hands wavering as he held the great weight, more of the Dark Army advanced on him, but the Elementals of the Haven stood in their way to defend him.

With a bellow, Alexis slammed the suspended Hybrid against a horde of Nekro and froze it just as it crushed those beneath it. He staggered back to admire the makeshift ice sculpture he had created, noticing it had made enough space for the Haven to move forth several metres and take a moment of reprieve.

'You're a hero for this,' said Joe, running his hand through his blond curtains, the surface of his skin returning to normal for a few moments as he caught his breath. 'Thank you. But we can't risk any of you dying. Go where you're needed – we'll be okay here.'

Alexis returned his wide smile. 'Between you and Althea, I trust you will.'

'How are the others? How's Caeli? Is she —?'

Alexis frowned as Joe coughed, choking on his words, unable to get them out.

'Joe?'

Then all at once, Alexis noticed the blade protruding through Joe's chest, the blood on his lips, and his eyes rolling to the back of his head.

Alexis found himself paralysed as Joe slumped to the ground without a word. The battle continued to rage on around them with no thought, no consideration, no beat of silence for Joe.

Why hasn't it all stopped?

Alexis's shock wouldn't allow him to look away from Joe's unmoving body at his feet. He'd always thought of him as being quite tall, but curled on the ground, he seemed so small, so young. Joe was a good man, a kind, honest, brave fighter, and yet he had fallen and not a single person seemed to notice or care as he had gone from someone who *is* to someone who *was*.

In his place, holding the dagger that had ripped through his back, rose a Shadowless solder. Alexis was still immobilised, his brain trying to catch up to reality, replaying Joe's smile as it faded from his face and how his last thoughts had been of Caeli.

Alexis didn't have time to react when the Shadowless lurched towards him with the dagger pointed at his throat. His amulet pulsed with a blue glow that created an impenetrable shield around him. The tip of the dagger slid uselessly against his aura. It gave Alexis the moment he needed to register what had happened and work out what he was going to do. With the noise of the battle rushing back, his focus returning, he stepped towards the man.

In one swift motion, Alexis froze his own arm to ice and drove it through the gut of the Shadowless.

Alexis stared into his eyes as he gasped. Only then did he realise the grave mistake he had made. The blackness of his irises faded away to reveal the true colour underneath, to reveal that he had been imprinted, acting against his will.

He had been innocent, and Alexis had just killed him with his bare hands.

Wisps of parasitic darkness oozed from the man's chest, fleeing now that its host could no longer sustain it with life. 'M-my family,' he stuttered, dropping to his knees. Alexis dropped with him. He moved his mouth to speak, but no words came. His eyes, brown now that the black had cleared, looked frantically at Alexis, urging him to understand what he didn't have the energy to say. 'Katie ...'

Alexis could feel the man's blood slowing around his hand, still embedded in the man's stomach. He forgot that he was in the middle of a war – that there were people all around him engaged in battle, fighting with everything they had to survive. He could only focus on the man and nod.

The man's grip slackened and his face fell flat as Joe's had. Just like that, he was gone.

Alexis staggered backwards, staring at his arm, slick with the man's blood.

Had blood always been this red? It seemed odd to Alexis that the body, something so complex and intuitive, relied on the flow of this crimson liquid, and that it could cease to function so easily. It was almost funny.

It must have been funny, because Alexis found himself laughing. His chest rattled as he laughed so hard, he found it difficult to breathe. He buckled over from it, holding himself up by pressing his hands against his knees. He sucked in air, but no matter how hard he tried, he still couldn't breathe.

He.

Couldn't.

Breathe.

Suddenly, it was no longer funny.

This wasn't like Dr Sinner. This hadn't been the darkness that had taken a life. This wasn't something Alexis could distance himself from.

Spouts of panic rocked his chest until he was gasping for air, like he was drowning on the inside from the weight of his regret. With each gasp, his mind froze and fractured and froze again. How could he survive this day?

Do I even want to? I don't deserve to.

Why had he been such a fool to agree to this and twist the arms of his friends to do so too?

This wasn't a game he could restart or a film he could fast-forward. This was his life. This might be the end of his life.

Alexis wanted to be brave. He wanted to be strong, but there was carnage everywhere he looked. Bodies dropped like rain, and blood soaked the ground faster than the earth could absorb it. He couldn't deal with it all. Noise everywhere. Blood everywhere. Death everywhere. He regretted ever setting foot outside of his home in Protegere. He had been safer when tormented by the *Shadow Man* than here in the Elemental world.

In the chaos of the battle, all he wanted to do was curl into a ball and weep for his parents.

But something would not let him.

His amulet beat with power, and he was forced to look at it, to see himself in the reflection of its crystalline surface and to remember. To remember who he was and what was at stake if he stayed down. To remember to hope. To remember what Incantus had told him a lifetime ago.

'*Light will always find a way through the darkness, and if you can't find it, become it.*'

He was Alexis Michaels. He had survived the tsunami that stole his memories, a demon that defiled his childhood.

Perhaps hope isn't a delicate thing, he realised for the first time, feeling for the tether of light that dangled before him, just within reach if only he looked up. It wasn't a child's dream or a shaky voice in the night or a distant friend that never returned your calls. Hope was hard. It was gritted teeth and ripped clothing, dirt on the face and aching legs that refused to buckle. It was stubborn and determined and unwavering, the polar opposite of delicacy.

Hope was strong. Hope was all he had.

'Get up, Lexi,' Alexis whispered to himself as he tapped his fingers to his thumbs, swallowing his panic and his fear with every tap. '*Get up.*'

So he did. Alexis got up. And he kept fighting.

22
KUEBIKO

Kuebiko (n.) *Japanese origin*
A state of exhaustion inspired by acts of senseless violence

Three hours until totality

Alexis didn't know how much time had passed since the Dark Army descended. All he knew was that his side were losing.

No matter the hundreds of Nekro and Hybrids he killed or the dozens of Shadowless he incapacitated and subdued, many more soon took their place. The Dark Army pressed on and the front lines of the Haven and Sanctuario were succumbing to the tide.

'We're getting annihilated out here,' Alexis said over his shoulder to Althea.

A ripple of magic tore from her wand, stunning her opponent and sending them careering to the ground.

'You have to find Incantus,' she grunted. 'At this rate, Mortem and the Shadowless will reach Stonehenge long before the eclipse starts.'

Alexis couldn't let that happen. Despite every fibre of his being wanting to stay there on the front lines to protect his people, he knew he had to find a way to tell Incantus they needed a change of plan. He also wanted to make sure his friends were okay, that they had kept themselves safe and hadn't endured what he had.

'Will you be okay?'

'I'll be fine,' Althea said. 'Besides, I haven't seen Joe in almost an hour. I need to make sure he hasn't bailed on me to go after Ezra. He promised me we'd take him down together.'

The truth swelled in Alexis's throat and he forced himself to choke it down. He couldn't tell her that her best friend was already dead. He could only give her a brief hug, wish her safe, and promise himself that it hadn't been for nothing.

Alexis slipped through the barracks of petrified Elementals lying in wait, ready to fight, until he eventually found his way back to Stonehenge. The wall of ice before the stones of his section remained magnificent, barely a scratch on its surface. He hurried around the rim of it and his heart skipped a beat when he found Blaise, golden staff in hand, shooting down harpies and ravens with beautiful accuracy.

'Where the hell have you been?' Blaise called without turning to him, swathes of flames encircling his arms.

Alexis took a deep breath, grateful for a pause from fighting. 'You don't want to know.'

Blaise looked at him and his eyebrows shot up. 'Al, you okay? Is that your blood?' He reabsorbed his flames and used his sleeve to wipe away the red that splattered Alexis's face – blood that may well have been Joe's, the imprinted Shadowless he had killed with his hands, or any of the countless bodies he had defeated.

Alexis stepped away. 'I'm fine. Where're the others?'

Blaise rubbed his sweaty face with his hand. 'Cae keeps

flying off even though we're getting swarmed up there. I'm not taking the same reckless risks for the attention or approval from others.' He exhaled anxiously. 'She's being stupid, trying to prove herself or something.'

The sky above Caeli's quarter was besieged with Fae against harpies, creating a cloud so dense that they covered much of the ground in moving shadow. Flashes of grey light and great torrents of wind tore through the flurries of ravens, but the swarm from the Dark Army was incessant. Alexis didn't know how much longer Caeli could keep them at bay.

'Boys!'

Demi rushed to them, her staff gleaming brilliantly in her grasp. Alexis instantly searched her for any sign of harm, but she appeared unscathed. 'No one got near me. With the Gem's powers, it's like my body acts without me even thinking. But no matter how many of them I knock out, it's impossible to keep them back. They're surrounding us from all sides. We need back-up now.'

A rumbling from the sky interrupted her. At first, Alexis thought it was thunder, but as he listened more closely, he realised it was more like the distant sound of stone scraping against stone.

And then he saw it. On the horizon, soaring towards them came a dense haze of grey and black, carrying with it a roaring louder than that of the battlefield.

'Taranis?' Blaise asked, scanning the sky above Stonehenge for Caeli. 'Mortem?'

'I don't think so,' Demi mumbled. She squinted at the cloud as it drew closer, trying to make out its composition. 'What the . . . ? Are they gargoyles?'

The cloud split apart and charged into the airborne Dark Army with an ear-splitting crash. Alexis only caught glimpses, but it was enough to see the animated stone-carved grotesques colliding with the harpies and ravens, crushing them beneath their solid weight.

Caeli dropped to the ground beside them, her knees almost buckling from the impact. She clutched on to her staff for support, her hair darkened by sweat and blood, and cheeks dotted with red blotches.

'I don't know how you've called them from neighbouring cities, but it's genius, Dem,' she said breathlessly.

Alexis shouldered Caeli's weight as he produced a stream of water for her to drink from.

'I'm not doing that,' said Demi, equally as stunned. There wasn't an Elemental in the Haven with the power of rock or stone as far as Alexis knew – maybe it was someone from the Sanctuario? 'But whoever is has got to be exceptionally powerful to animate so many of them.'

They watched as a gargoyle with the wings of a horned beast crashed into a cluster of shrieking harpies. Its stone body knocked two out of the sky, casting them down somewhere on the battlefield, but it was immediately leaped upon by the remaining harpies. They thrashed their daggers against its side until it cracked apart and fell to rubble.

'What the hell do you think you're playing at?' Blaise demanded, whirling to Caeli. 'Incantus said to stay back and you're up there putting yourself in danger. Is it your fatal flaw to feel important? Or are you doing it for attention?'

Caeli's eyes were so wide, Alexis feared they would pop out of their sockets. 'There aren't nearly enough of us that can fly as there are on land. And who are you to tell me anything? Call me an attention-seeker all you like, but at least I'm not a coward.'

Blaise bristled, Caeli's jibe having struck a nerve. 'I'm not a coward. I'm doing as we were told. Something you seem to be incapable of.'

Alexis sighed. 'You really need to start scheduling your domestics for when we aren't in danger.'

'We're always in danger,' Caeli cut back.

'Back to more pressing matters: what do we do now?' asked Demi. 'We have to find a way to hold back the Shadowless at least until the eclipse begins. I don't know if our defences at Stonehenge will stand indefinitely if they're breached.'

If only we could create a barrier in front of our army similar to the shields we've built around Stonehenge, Alexis thought. He chewed his lip as he turned the thought over in his head. 'Caeli, fly us up.'

The air surged beneath them and the four Elementals instantly shot into the air. The wind swept them higher and higher at Caeli's command until Alexis told her to stop once he could see the entire battlefield below.

Stonehenge lay untouched in the centre, protected by the enchantments they had created and dozens of rows of Elementals from the Haven and Sanctuario. They were all that remained between Stonehenge and the invading ring that was the Dark Army.

'We create a blockade before our army,' said Alexis, his jaw ticking as he brainstormed. 'We go to the battlefront and use our Gems' powers to create a barricade to hold back the Dark Army. It gives our people time to rest and recover while delaying the Shadowless from ever reaching Stonehenge.'

‘Easier said than done,’ said Caeli, lowering them back down to the ground within Stonehenge. ‘We’d have to ask Incantus.’

‘Ask me what?’ said Incantus from behind them, making Caeli yelp. ‘I saw you all gathered in the sky. Is all well?’

‘Splendid, just enjoying the weather on this peaceful day,’ Caeli said helpfully.

‘Lexi had an idea about holding back the Dark Army,’ said Demi.

Incantus’s eyes fell upon Alexis, and his mind went blank. Or at least he wished it had.

The image of the imprinted man he had killed burst to the forefront of Alexis’s mind, unable to be blinked away. *Could Incantus tell somehow?* He had strictly told them to not take the lives of anyone who had been imprinted, for they were under no more control of their actions than the Leaders were of theirs. Could Alexis really justify it as self-defence if his aura had protected him and he had wanted revenge on the person who had just killed his friend?

Can Caeli sense that Joe is dead? Should I tell her?

So many questions, so many secrets, so many missteps. Alexis couldn’t deal with them, so he didn’t. One thing at a time, that was all he could manage.

Alexis finally found his voice, but he could not meet Incantus’s eyes. ‘It’s basic, probably too simple, but I was thinking we could force them backwards with the Gems – we extend the defences we constructed around Stonehenge to act as barriers to defend the front of our army.’

‘An honourable yet extremely risky battle tactic,’ said Incantus, cracking his knuckles and scratching off flakes of dried blood. ‘If you go ahead with this, you have to ensure our people are behind our barricade – we can't allow for any collateral damage or for anyone to be left to die.' His intense gaze levelled against Alexis, and with that, Alexis knew that he could sense the blood that stained his soul or smell the death that swathed him. Incantus placed both hands on his shoulders, but what he said was not what Alexis had expected to hear. 'Well done, my boy.'

'How's Serena?' asked Demi after retrieving Alexis's staff for him.

Before Incantus could answer, a distant bright gold explosion boomed. They heard the distorted screams of a couple of Nekro and the animalistic screech of a Hybrid in answer.

'Does that answer your question? Scottish women; built with steel,' said Incantus, a smile forming despite himself. 'She's been out of the game for a while. I think she's enjoying herself.'

'Who's controlling the gargoyles?' Demi asked just before he left, still engrossed in their animation. 'Is it you?'

Incantus pursed his lips knowingly, but even before he said anything, Alexis knew from the glint of his eyes that it wasn't going to be something he'd share with them. 'No, it is not me controlling them.' He didn't elaborate. 'I'll inform Serena of the plan. We'll go clockwise covering the north-west and south-west sides of Stonehenge, marking clear borders for our Elementals to remain behind. You four stay together and do the north-east- and south-east-facing sides. Once your lines are clear, use your Gems, and show Mortem who he's dealing with.'

'Guys . . .'

It was Caeli who had spoken. Alexis turned at her tone, one

of equal parts confusion and concern. Her grey eyes scanned the group and then fell on the space beside her, the space that Blaise should have occupied, but no longer did.

Alexis's heart dropped into his stomach.

Blaise was gone.

23
TATEMAE

Tatemae (n.) *Japanese origin*
What a person pretends to believe; the behaviour and opinions one must display to satisfy society's demands

Two and a half hours until totality

'I am not a coward,' Blaise Ademola said to himself as he tore from Stonehenge, from his friends. Caeli's words rang through his head as he weaved through the ranks that were meant to be guarding him, his double-edged axe swinging by his side. He would show her he was fearless. He would prove to everyone and to himself.

He reached the battlefront in no time. It was nothing like how it had been at Stonehenge. There were pockets of fights everywhere, blades clashing and powers flying. Blaise needed in on the action while he had momentum.

Can't turn back, not now, he told himself.

'What a beautiful thing you are,' said a silky voice from beside him. Blaise turned to see a woman, or at least he thought it was a woman. There was something ethereal about her. The smoothness of her chalk-white skin or the intensity of her gaze made him unsure whether she was human or not, friend or foe. It wasn't until he noted the glossy, paper-thin wings that protruded from her back, their design and colour like that of a church's stained-glass window, that he recalled what Ziya had said earlier. Fae. Their team.

The faerie took a step closer and caressed the side of his cheek with the back of her hand. 'Too pretty to be out here,' she said, her voice dropping low, pulling Blaise in towards her. 'Why risk someone harming that face?'

Blaise shrugged her off. 'Looks aren't everything,' he said, staring at her through his eyebrows.

The faerie's expression turned cold. The sparkle of her eyes winked out and she stood to her full height. 'You dare insult me, Elemental? We offer you our support and this is how you repay the favour?'

Serena had said something about insulting the Fae. 'No,' said Blaise hastily, looking between her and the battles before him, unsure of which he would prefer to face. 'I'm just saying I can offer you more than my looks. I can help fight too.'

The faerie's ageless face softened and the mischievous glint in her eyes returned. 'Let us see what the best of the Elemental can do, then.'

Blaise rose to the challenge. His body ignited into a roaring flame, so bright and so hot that the faerie was forced to step back. He raised his arms outwards and found a parting between the row of centaurs before him. He hurled a fireball through it, which connected with a Nekro, exploding its body into charred chunks.

Blaise smiled to himself. He could do this. He threw another fireball skywards, casting a harpy out of the air where it fell like a blazing asteroid. His smile widened. He could feel his body growing more ardent as his confidence rose. He hoped the faerie was watching him, that she was impressed. She was shouting something, but Blaise couldn't hear or see her through the crackling of his flame and the mirage of heatwaves that rose from him.

The Woman of the Fire's counsel, spoken deep within the volcano cavern, returned to him as he burned.

'All it takes is a spark to start a fire . . . Without fear, without restraint, without concern for those in your path who cannot bear the heat.'

The two centaurs closest to him were making loud, disgruntled snorting noises. They reared back on their hind legs, shuffling forward eagerly. *I'm inspiring them*, Blaise thought, encouraged, gripping his burning pickaxe tighter. He advanced, making them surge again, deeper into the enemy lines.

'Wait!' Blaise called as a band of Nekro seized one of the silver-haired female centaurs in front of him. She had been too focused on Blaise to notice the Nekro that stabbed and sliced at her front legs. 'Wait!' Blaise shouted again, but the Nekro wouldn't listen. They crawled upon the fallen centaur like ants on a crumb, mauling her as she cried out in pain. The other centaur buckled too, collapsing to his knees even though no one had struck him down. Shock and grief played across his face in an awful dance.

As Blaise's fire faltered, he saw the billowing cloud of smoke that rose from their tails and hind legs. They had been burned, incinerated. He hadn't been inspiring them; he had forced them onwards, to their deaths, to avoid his heat.

'I didn't mean to . . .' Blaise started, but a Shadowless had already come to stand over the second centaur. The centaur did nothing as the Shadowless swung his blade and chopped down, severing his head from his shoulders.

Blaise's legs gave out. He turned back, hoping the faerie would come to his aid, but all he saw was a singed corpse where she had once stood, her pale face burned black in agony, her papery wings vaporised by Blaise's fire.

I can't do this. I can't do this. I need to get out of here. Get me out of here.

Blaise didn't realise his thoughts had translated into words, into shouts. 'Somebody get me out of here. I can't do this! Get me out of here!'

The Shadowless who had slain the centaur edged closer to him, eyes wide with glory and lips curved in excitement. 'That must be why they call it "friendly fire".' He raised his sword again. 'Sire ordered us to spare the other boy, but you . . . a Child of the Elements. He will immortalise me for this!'

A bellow escaped from Blaise. Blazing violent fire spat from his hands just as the Shadowless struck down. The fireball ripped through his centre, cremating him on the spot. He fell to the ground as nothing more than a bundle of smoking remains.

'*Get me out of here!*' Blaise screamed, squeezing his eyes closed as every cell of his body spasmed with the overwhelming sensation of fear. All-consuming, paralysing fear.

'Get me out of here! Get me out of here! Get me out—'

The noise shut off. The screams and cries and clashes of battle instantly vanished as though it had come from a speaker which had suddenly died. The overbearing glare of the sun was replaced by pale, white lights from all around, and cold, hard floor had traded the beaten soil beneath him.

'Blaise?'

He recognised the hesitant voice. Blaise cracked open his eyes to see that he was no longer on the battlefield, but instead hundreds of metres beneath it, in the impenetrable white walls of the Haven's laboratory. The glowing circle beneath him blinked out and just before him stood Ziya Parashakti.

'I brought you down,' she said, gesturing to the Haven's silver command disk in her hand. She kept her distance, her huge glossy eyes trained on the glowing red blade of his axe until its flames died out.

Blaise felt a wetness on his cheeks. He quickly wiped it away before Ziya noticed. Even though his legs felt like all the muscle and bone had been leached from them, he forced himself to his feet with the hilt of his axe. 'How did you hear me?' he asked, suddenly mortified.

Ziya's eyes flicked upwards. Blaise slowly approached her and followed her gaze. On the huge overhead display was the entire battlefield of Stonehenge, allowing Ziya to see all the chaos that unfolded on the land above the Haven. Its sound was muted, but Blaise could see it all, a live display of the whole area. He could see Althea Orenda casting spell after spell from her wand, deep in the thick of battle, calling out a name that Blaise assumed was Joe's, although he wasn't anywhere to be seen. He could see Serena Aevum on another smaller, separate screen, her body detonating with glorious, golden waves anytime anyone drew near. Then he saw in the very centre of Stonehenge his friends, running frantically across the circle of standing stones as they searched for him.

'Why did you leave them to go to the battlefront alone?'

Ziya asked, staring at the screen that now showed Caeli shooting into the sky to get a better view, like a falcon hunting for its prey.

'I wanted to help,' he said, trying to shake the ringing sound that lingered in his head.

'Then why did you beg to get out?'

Blaise bristled. 'I didn't . . .' He caught himself. He was tired of pretending like he wasn't scared. What did it matter if Ziya knew? He didn't care about her opinion, not really. Besides, she had already seen him screaming and crying. 'I feel powerless out there,' he finally admitted.

There was a beat before Ziya replied. 'I know how that feels,' she said softly. Blaise's eyes went to hers, but she didn't meet them.

Blaise had never really had much time for Ziya. He could hold his hands up and admit that. He didn't understand why Alexis and Demi always invited her to hang out with them. He found her amusing if not slightly irritating sometimes, in a way that was probably unintentional. She cared so little about the things Blaise did and so much about the things Blaise found totally dull. Until then, Blaise honestly thought he had nothing in common with her.

But Ziya had spent her whole life surrounded by people telling her she should be powerful, that she had been birthed into two of the most respected and formidable Elemental bloodlines their kind had ever seen, Aevum and Parashakti. She had been told that she was lesser because, despite that, she was alone in being powerless.

Blaise had been raised being told that he should and would be powerful, strong and important, mighty and feared and fearless. Yet he too, despite the powers that were at his very fingertips, felt just as Ziya did.

'I don't know if I can go back up there,' he whispered, holding his axe limply with one hand and stroking his amulet with the other.

'You must,' Ziya replied bluntly. She turned from him and began busying herself with the computers in front of her, tapping loudly as she muttered to herself. Blaise couldn't make out what she was saying, but her attention was locked on to the monitor, her eyes darting from side to side.

'What are you doing?' he asked, hoping to stall for time.

'Incantus called me earlier,' she said, not looking away. 'He asked me to contact the High Order Cabinet of High Councillors and find out what's going on by any means necessary. I told him I called twenty-seven times and they didn't pick up, so he told me to infiltrate their systems. I told him that was illegal, that I couldn't.'

Blaise found the way Ziya spoke mesmerising. It was so efficient, so straight to the point and focused. A bit hard to keep up with, even for him, but it was refreshing to hear only the concrete details and not all the emotional baggage that he so often preoccupied himself with.

'You must,' Blaise said back to her. 'Without their help, how the hell are we going to hold off Mortem? This need trumps any law.'

Ziya looked at Blaise, her head tilted at an angle. *She looks different with her hair down*, Blaise thought.

'*A duty to protect those who cannot protect themselves*,' Ziya recited. Blaise remembered Mortem saying that the first time they saw him. 'The High Order's first duty. By not breaking in to contact them, I'd be going against the most important law of an Elemental!'

Blaise didn't understand why she needed to justify it to him; it wasn't like he was going to snitch on her for it. 'Exactly,' he said, hoping to encourage her as he rounded the high tabletop to join her.

'Okay.' Ziya nodded to herself. 'I've got this. This I can do.' Her fingers typed away at the computer screens before her. Blaise thought she looked like she was enjoying herself, although he couldn't imagine what was fun about it. At least this would allow them to find out what was keeping the High Order and speed them along.

Ziya muttered to herself as she typed, narrating what she was doing. 'Tracing the network, locating the . . . Here! High Office of the Secretary-General of the High Order. Björn Kleine.'

Blaise vaguely recognised the name. The Secretary-General of the High Order had apparently requested multiple times to meet with the Children of the Elements during their training, but Incantus had declined. Blaise also knew the old man Teller Sagen had hated him – he said it on multiple occasions that the only reason Kleine had got the job was because of his powerful connections amongst the Elemental world, not based on his qualities or attributes. But it didn't matter what Teller thought. Kleine was the chief officer of the entire High Order. He would do his job and step in. He had to.

Blaise and Ziya saw him through the CCTV, a short, stern-looking elderly man with dark brown hair that crawled to the edges of his face, making him look a bit like a battered teddy bear. He was barking at a room filled with close to a dozen senior Elementals Blaise had never seen before. Ziya panned the camera to get a better look at them.

'Who are they?' Blaise asked, leaning closer.

'The High Order Cabinet, the heads of each of the main councils that make it up,' Ziya replied, having to raise her voice. The High Order were on their feet shouting at one another incoherently, gesturing and jabbing fingers as though they were weapons.

'So is this the High Order's headquarters?' Blaise asked. He slapped Ziya's back lightly. 'Good job, Zee.'

Ziya rubbed her back. 'Thanks.' She pointed to the screen. 'See the steel-grey walls behind them? I almost forgot that the institute had been rebuilt. Along with the destruction of the old High Order building, they tried to incinerate all evidence of what had once happened in the hopes that people forgot just how easily and how badly they had been hit. They all but erased people's memories.'

Blaise had no idea what she was talking about. 'How do you know all of this?' he asked, admiring for the first time her curiosity and knowledge of their world, for her passion that didn't begin and end with herself.

Ziya smiled slightly. 'People often underestimate me when they first meet me. They don't by our second meeting.'

She returned her attention to the monitor, as did Blaise.

Accusations and insults continued to be flung across the large circular office, which was mostly bare save for the huge round wooden table at its centre, and the dozens of framed certificates and qualifications splayed across the walls. Even with the volume turned down, the noise of their shouting was overwhelming. No one could hear each other. Blaise noticed

Ziya was scratching the edge of her thumbnail anxiously. He had to get them to stop.

'Can you teleport there?' Blaise offered, thinking it was a pretty good idea.

'No,' said Ziya. 'Even if I had taken an interest in the functioning of teleportation lines, which are utterly boring and confusing by all accounts, the secretary general's office is far too warded for me to break through anytime soon.' Ziya's attention snapped to Blaise. 'But I can *project* us there. That's how Incantus attends all of his meetings with the High Order: there but not. Present but absent.'

Blaise went to protest, to say that he didn't want to be involved at all, but it was too late. Ziya slammed her hand down on the keypad and stood back as the camera scanned their bodies. A few seconds later, and Blaise saw on the live video footage of Kleine's office that a virtual projection of themselves had appeared, standing on top of the large wooden table. The steel walls of the office replaced the Haven's lights around him, and the Cabinet of Elementals stood within reaching distance.

Blaise and Ziya were in the High Order headquarters without setting foot out of the Haven.

Gasps rang out as the High Order scrambled back to the edge of the office, knocking down many of the framed certificates and accreditations that had been hanging there. Their hands ignited with power as they took in the sight of them.

'Holy First Borns,' an elderly woman exclaimed, her fingers traded in for curved blades. 'What is this? Children?'

'I'm nineteen and three months, actually,' Ziya corrected matter-of-factly. 'And this is Blaise Ademola, Child of the Fire. He's almost eighteen, I believe.'

Everyone's eyes were on Blaise and on his bright red amulet. He wiped at the sweat on his brow and tucked his arms behind him, hiding his bloodied axe. Even though he knew he was still very much in the Haven, he felt a bit nauseous that the projection showed them standing on the table in the centre of the room. He was being gawked up at from every angle, and it was not with adoration like he was used to.

'Hello,' said Blaise, emulating Incantus as much as he could by making his voice sound deeper. He faltered, not knowing what to say next.

Ziya swept in. 'G-good afternoon, High Order High Councillors, and Mister Secretary-General.' She took an uneasy bow, clutching at Blaise's elbow to steady herself.

At least I don't look as nervous as her, Blaise thought.

Secretary-General Kleine barged past the others to stand before the virtual apparition of Blaise and Ziya. The fur that adorned the edges of his face was bristled; his dark eyes squinted. He opened his mouth, but Ziya spoke first.

'My name is Ziya Parashakti.' Whispers rang out amongst the councillors at her name, but she powered through. 'I am one of the Leaders of the Haven and we come on behalf of the heads of the Haven and the Sanctuario, Incantus Arcangelo and Serena Aevum. We are waiting for an update on your expected arrival at Stonehenge.' She swallowed hard and coughed again. She had got them to stop shouting, which counted for something.

Blaise sought to help out, not wanting to look awkward or unimportant beside her. 'Mortem's already arrived. The battle is in full swing and we expected your arrival hours ago. At this rate, we won't make it to the eclipse.'

A dark-skinned man with bright green eyes strode forward. He stood beside their projections to face Kleine. He reminded Blaise of Teller, somehow.

'This is a disgrace,' said the man to the secretary-general. 'How can we be still sat here hiding while Arcangelo and Aevum fight Mortem alone? It's an embarrassment that they have sent one of the Children of the Elements to retrieve us when he is desperately needed up there.'

Kleine, despite being a full foot shorter, didn't raise his head to look at the man's face and instead stared straight at his chest. 'We are not hiding, Wrought; we are strategising. This is a game of chess and we are in it for the long haul.'

'You heard the boy,' said Wrought, his voice edged with anger. 'He says they won't make it to the eclipse. They need our support, especially that of the Security Council's operatives. How can you justify anything otherwise? We cannot remain neutral at a time like this.'

'Remaining neutral is the only way I can ensure our safety,' Kleine barked. He prodded his fur-covered finger at Wrought's chest, and despite it looking like a light touch, Wrought went stumbling back into the Elementals behind him. Kleine advanced on Ziya next, slamming his hands against the table, making it shudder. 'How did you get in here? How much have you heard?' He couldn't actually touch her, but still she shuffled away to the edge of the table. 'When else have you and Arcangelo been listening in on my conversations? To spy on the Cabinet of the High Order is grievous crime.'

Blaise stood in Ziya's way.

'Don't threaten the girl,' Wrought growled, although he kept his distance. 'What do you fear she overheard?'

Kleine's head snapped to Wrought. 'Teller Sagen's no longer here to defend you, Wrought. You better watch yourself when speaking to me.'

Wrought paled and spoke no more.

'My grandson is fighting with the Haven,' said a tall, thin woman with a Californian accent and grey hair that had been clipped short. 'Meredith Coin, Deputy Secretary-General and High Councillor of the Security Council of International Elemental Operatives. It is a pleasure to meet you, Mr Ademola. I was so glad to hear that your quest was successful.'

Coin, as in Joe Coin. *They have the same eyes*, Blaise thought, *kind and sincere*. He wondered how Joe was doing on the battlefield. Joe wouldn't have left Caeli. He bet Joe wasn't shouting for someone to get him out. *No wonder Caeli chose him*.

'I know Joe,' said Blaise. 'He's a good guy. He and the rest of us could really do with your help.'

Meredith Coin turned to the secretary-general, her jaw clenched taut. 'There are hundreds if not thousands within the walls of the High Order at this time that can and want to help. This is the day that determines the fate of our people for ever.'

'This day is not determined by us!' Kleine roared.

The quieter comments and conversations from the other councillors were instantly silenced. Even Coin cowered back to stand beside Wrought.

Secretary-General Kleine moved to the centre of his office, his chest heaving. 'Sapientis Aevum and Incantus Arcangelo have hidden the truth of the Prophecy of Light and Darkness from us since its inception. Arcangelo refused to even let us *meet* the Children of the Elements. He told us to stay out of their quest – and now, all of a sudden, he wants *my* help?'

'Not *your* help,' snapped Wrought. 'The High Order's. And he doesn't want it; he needs it.'

'Our help won't make a difference,' Kleine retorted. 'Arcangelo said so himself. The fate of the Prophecy will unravel however it's supposed to. Our involvement won't tilt the scales either way except to aggravate Mortem and damage our community further. You may not want to believe it, but what I'm doing is for the longevity of the High Order and for all Elementals.'

No one was looking at Blaise now, so he felt no reason to stand with his back straight and his chin up. Who was he kidding? He wasn't Incantus. He wasn't strong here. He wasn't someone anyone ever listened to for ideas or inspiration.

He was only a pretty face, after all.

Caeli would have found a way to bully or berate them into submission. Alexis would've convinced them into helping with logic and careful tactics. Demi would inspire even the caretaker enough to join, but what could Blaise do?

The High Order council had fallen into a quiet acquiescence at Secretary-General Kleine's words. Some were even nodding. Coin and Wrought stood together, but Blaise couldn't tell if they were planning on speaking up again.

Blaise's lips felt like they were glued shut. He couldn't leave like this. They wouldn't survive without the High Order's aid. This was the only way he could actually help without being on the front lines, without being exposed to real danger that wouldn't wait until he was ready before it struck.

But before Blaise had the chance to speak, a strained cry slipped from Ziya's lips, something between a scream and a shout of frustration.

'None of this makes sense!' she shouted, her eyes darting about wildly. 'The High Order is supposed to help. You are supposed to help! What you say . . . it doesn't make sense. Of course you can help! You could deploy the Security Council operatives to keep the Shadowless and the Hybrids and the Nekro at bay. You could send the Health and Healing Council to recover the Elementals who have been injured. You could stand in the way of Mortem so that Incantus and Blaise and my friends can stay safely inside Stonehenge until the eclipse. There is so much you could do and you are doing nothing and it's so infuriating and irrational that I could burst!'

Ziya's outburst sparked the flame that Blaise kindled into an inferno. '*A duty to protect those who cannot protect themselves!*' he shouted. 'That is what you swear by!'

'Don't raise your voice at m—' Kleine began.

'You are cowards!' Blaise didn't know who he was shouting at. Perhaps it was them all.

He had been away from the battle for too long. What had he missed since he had been here listening to the High Order argue? Had any of his friends fallen? Were they all dead and he was wasting his breath? Where was Caeli? He needed to be with Caeli. Fire couldn't burn without air, and Blaise was done trying to pretend otherwise. 'We told you that Mortem will imprint all Elementals if he succeeds today, and still you do nothing!'

That got a few murmurs going. The High Councillors shifted on their feet, but still no one said anything.

Except for Kleine. 'You are just a child,' he said. He wasn't shouting, but somehow that made Blaise feel worse. 'There is much you don't understand about the decisions I have made to safeguard our community. I can understand your frustration, even if the way you have spoken to me is far from acceptable. But on this day, it is not our place to intervene and risk our own destruction just because you and your friends are not strong enough.'

Strong.

The word struck Blaise in the chest, forcing the air from his lungs. He had heard it so many times in his life. He had been haunted by it and fearful of it and raised to be it. He let himself be defined by it. He paled in the shadow of it.

No matter how big his muscles grew, he never thought he would ever truly become it.

And he was fucking tired of it.

If Blaise couldn't rely on the High Order to help Incantus and his friends, then *he* would have to come up with a way. He would have to return to the battle to save them himself.

I am strong enough. I am more than my fear. It's time I face it.

Ziya beat her fist down against the keyboard and together they watched as their projections vanished from the High Order's headquarters. They didn't stay to see their reactions. Ziya quickly exited the frame and their true surroundings of the Haven's laboratory returned. She then brought up the surveillance of the battle of Stonehenge.

Things had got worse. Much worse. Blaise gripped the tabletop as he accounted for all that he had missed. Caeli and the others were together now, weapons swinging and Gems glowing as they reached the battlefront without him. All around them, bodies littered the ground, Haven and Shadowless alike, making it impossible for them to move without tripping.

‘I am coming,’ Blaise whispered to himself, to *them*.

‘Are you going back up?’ Ziya asked him, no longer anxious to stand close to him.

‘Yes.’

‘I have to find a way to help you.’ Ziya shook her head furiously. ‘I have to find a way to replace the aid the High Order would have provided. I-I just don’t know how.’

‘Zee, you will be able to, I know you will.’ Blaise turned his full attention to her, seeing her for who she was for the first time. Not a character in his life, not someone unimportant or inconsequential, but a person, a complete, whole person who had their own weaknesses and strengths and ambitions and history. Blaise could see that now. He valued that now.

True strength wasn’t just physical, in the form of size and height and muscle. *This* was just as much a display of strength. ‘Zee, you are a mastermind. You know this. Everyone knows this. You’ll be able to think of something to help us.’

‘I can’t exactly put on a Haven suit and go out and fight myself,’ she said, her expression pulled together in tension, eyes squeezed shut in thought. ‘I’ll just be one more body to trip over.’

There was a pause. Then Ziya’s eyes shot open.

‘Zee?’ Blaise asked as her eyes found his. There was something in them, a sparkle of excitement, of hope. ‘Thought of something?’

Ziya smiled cautiously. ‘I think so . . . I know so. Maybe even two ways that I can help.’

When Blaise smiled, it was with his whole face, and what a beautiful smile he was sure it was.

‘I knew you could.’ He took a step back from her and flipped his axe in the air. When he caught it, his amulet sparked brightly and flames rippled down his arm, igniting the blade and incinerating the last of his fear. 'I'm ready, Zee. Send me back up there.'

24
YUÁNFÈN

Yuánfèn (n.) *Chinese origin*
A relationship made by fate or destiny;
the binding force linking two people

Two hours and fifteen minutes until totality

Alexis was at the battlefront of Demi's quarter with her and Caeli, their golden staffs alight with the radiance of the Elemental Gems, when Blaise appeared before them.

'Blaise!' Demi cried, rushing towards him. She enveloped him in a fierce embrace as Alexis inspected him over her shoulder, catching his eyes to see if they would reveal anything. Alexis had expected them to be filled with caution, with fear. What he found was the opposite.

'Where the hell did you go?' Caeli thundered, rearing up to stand before him.

'Doesn't matter,' Blaise replied, wringing his hands. 'I'm back now.'

Alexis didn't know what had gone on or where Blaise had been, but he could see that it wasn't something he wanted to discuss. 'All that matters is that you're here now.'

Blaise offered him a smile and nodded.

'Here,' said Caeli, thrusting the golden staff with the searing Gem of the Fire to Blaise's chest. 'Wherever you went, you left your staff lying around in Stonehenge for anyone to take.'

'Thanks for keeping it safe for me,' he said, taking it slowly. His fingers brushed hers and she recoiled. Alexis was convinced Blaise wanted to say something, but he appeared to decide against it. 'So what have I missed?'

'While you were gone, Incantus agreed to let us go to the battlefront to guard our army similar to how we guarded our quarter of Stonehenge,' said Alexis. 'That's easy enough – the tricky bit is ensuring we don't hurt our own with our defences or leave anyone outside. We'll mark the curved lines for our borders in front of Demi's and Caeli's quarters; Incantus and Serena are marking ours.'

Deep in the throes of battle, any semblance of order was all but gone in the fight for survival. Hundreds of pockets of smaller fights were taking place, dispersed across the field like grains of sand in the sea. The battlefield was covered with fallen Elementals and creatures alike.

'How are we going to get through all of this?' Demi asked, her cheeks washed of colour.

There was a flash of light. And another. Dotted before them, every time an Elemental from the Haven fell, their body flashed and they disappeared in the blink of an eye.

'Ziya,' said Blaise with a knowing grin.

From the laboratory of the Haven, she must be monitoring the entire battlefield, transporting any Elemental in a Haven or Sanctuario suit down to the Healing Sanctuary. Alexis had no idea how it was possible for one person to survey anything in this chaos, let alone from a distance – but if anyone could do it, it was Ziya.

'You ready?' Blaise asked, fidgeting on the spot beside Alexis. 'So we go, get our people out of the way, and then what?'

'Then I'll figure out a way to hold back the Shadowless,' Demi replied, sweeping her hair to the side to fan at the nape of her neck. 'Let's do this.'

Just before them, a member of the Sanctuario collapsed to her feet, buckling under the weight of the Hybrid that came at her. Demi pointed her staff at the half-horse, half-ram creature and the ground beneath its feet instantly turned to quicksand. It screeched, but it was unable to escape the sinking earth. By the time Demi solidified the ground, all that remained of the Hybrid was the curve of its bloodied horns.

'Cover me,' Demi ordered as she ran into the battle to help the Sanctuario woman to her feet.

Caeli chased after her, using her staff to conduct blades of wind that spun through the air like boomerangs, decapitating a Nekro that was clawing at the corpse of a centaur.

A Shadowless man suddenly appeared before Caeli, going from transparent to visible in an instant. He reached out and gripped a hold of her by the neck, strangling her so tightly that she let out a noise.

But that noise wasn't a gasp. It was a laugh.

'Trying to choke the Daughter of the Air?' Caeli's eyes darkened to a stormy grey. 'You fool.'

Before the Shadowless could realise his mistake, a roaring gale swept him up. A ragged sound escaped him as all the air was pulled from his lungs. He collapsed to the ground without even a scream. Caeli paid him no attention as she stepped over him to find her next target.

Blaise turned to Alexis, his mouth gaping open. 'I don't know whether to be turned on or scared . . .'

'How about you be helpful?' Alexis replied and kicked him forward, forcing him into action. Together, they advanced with their backs against each other and obliterated any Nekro or Shadowless that dared to draw close.

Blaise swept left as he headed towards the largest Shadowless in their path, an Elemental seemingly free from Mortem's imprinting. Webbing shot from the Shadowless's hand, pinning Blaise's staff and axe to the ground, but that didn't stop him. Blaise ran at him, fists roaring with flames. Alexis was forced to turn away just as they collided, for he had his own battles to focus on.

A mangled Hybrid with the body of a brown bear and pincers of a huge scorpion reared up on him. Its jagged claws sliced at Alexis, too fast for him to duck in time. The blades scraped his right temple, cutting through the skin just above his eyebrow. He gasped from the pain as tears sprang to his eyes, making it hard for him to see as he staggered backwards.

Incensed that he had let himself get hit, Alexis coated his head with ice and slammed it against the Hybrid with such a force that it dented the front of its skull. He sensed another attacker just behind him, this one with blood still pumping around its body. Without turning, he sent a high kick backwards and felt it strike true when it thudded into the throat of a Shadowless who slumped to the ground.

There was a squawk from above. A black-winged harpy

swooped towards Demi, its claws reaching out to slash at her face. Alexis wouldn't dare let anything touch her. He pointed his staff at it and rocketed an icy pike at its chest. Its lifeless body thudded to the ground at Demi's feet.

Demi shuddered from revulsion. She offered him a wave, but her face fell at the sight of him, dripping with blood where the Hybrid had scarred him.

'Cover us,' Demi ordered to Caeli and Blaise, who immediately swept ahead. She pointed a finger at Alexis as she strode towards him. 'You wait there.'

'Don't stand in this section!' Caeli shouted, projecting her voice so that anyone in their close vicinity could hear her. She gestured to the front line of the Haven's Elementals. 'You guys, come here! Demi's going to run her powers across your battlefront. Border it with your shields and don't let anyone go past this point.'

The Elementals rushed to obey, adorning the edges like stanchions cordoning a red carpet as Caeli and Blaise continued, following round the circumference of Demi's quarter, rescuing the Elementals of the Haven who fought beyond it.

Demi rested her hand against Alexis's forehead where it was bleeding more than he thought it would, making the right side of his face sticky with blood. Some had even seeped into his eye, forcing him to squeeze it shut.

'It's not as bad as it looks,' he grunted, wiping his eyebrow with the back of his hand. He made a move to rejoin the fight, but Demi clamped her hand around his jaw, forcing him still.

'How would you know? You can't even open your eye,' she countered, not loosening her grip. With her other hand, Demi withdrew a herbal-smelling bandage from her pocket.

'Eyes – *eye* on me,' she ordered as she applied a pale paste to his wound with her thumb.

They always are, Alexis thought as Demi began to wrap the bandage around his head, layer upon layer. Whether it was from her touch or from the balm, Alexis felt the pain from his forehead melt away.

And with the pain faded the battle around them. With Caeli and Blaise annihilating any Shadowless nearby, Alexis and Demi were given this moment uninterrupted. A moment of stillness in the anarchy where her hands were on his face and his eyes were locked on to hers.

'We're so nearly home, *agapi mou*,' she said to him, so softly that he was sure he had misheard her, that he'd dreamed it up entirely.

Agapi mou.

Did she think he didn't know what it meant? Didn't she know that he had spent countless days and nights over the years trying to learn Greek and Arabic so that one day he could speak to her in the languages she had been raised hearing? Didn't she know he had done that for her even before he realised he had loved her?

There's never been a time since knowing Demi Nikolas that I haven't loved her, Alexis admitted to himself, holding her hand against his cheek, even after she had finished bandaging him. He hadn't wanted to acknowledge the way his heart raced at the thought of her and eyes lit up when someone spoke her name. He hadn't wanted it to ruin their friendship and risk losing her. A tortured life adoring her from afar was better than a life without her, for that would be no life at all.

But she had called him *agapi mou*. My love. *Her* love.

'Demi . . .'

'Why did you leave me this morning?' The question came flying out of Demi's mouth, followed by another. She made no attempt to rescind them. 'Why didn't you do anything last night?'

A Nekro slipped through the ranks of Elementals, tearing towards them. Alexis didn't break eye contact with Demi as he swung his sword and severed it in half with almost no effort at all. She hadn't batted an eyelid either, her stare unbroken, unwavering.

'I was trying to respect you and your wishes,' said Alexis.

Demi's gaze dropped to his chest, his lips, and then back to his eyes. 'Respect was not what I wanted from you last night.'

A blush rushed to the surface of Alexis's cheeks, making Demi smile when she noticed it. That smile was all it took for Alexis to ignore everything going on around him. He would do whatever he had to in order to make her smile at him like that for ever.

He inched closer to her and said her name again, his voice lower this time, deeper, imbued with all the emotion he had been too afraid to reveal. He was just inches from her when she pressed her hand against his heaving chest.

In a small voice, Demi whispered, 'I think I die today.'

Alexis's heart stopped in his chest. He was sure that it had frozen, given up, no longer able to beat. His mouth opened and closed, but what combination of words was sufficient to reply to something like that?

Demi's eyes were locked on to Alexis's amulet as if she was seeing something behind it, recalling an old memory or a distant thought. He felt the warmth of her breath on his face when she spoke again. 'When I . . . *passed* at the waterfall, you all asked me if I'd seen something. I had. I didn't know if it was real or not and I didn't understand it at the time, but I knew it was important, whatever it was.'

Alexis's throat threatened to clamp shut. Of all the horrors he had witnessed, this was what made him most scared. He fought to find his voice. 'What did you see?'

Demi drew a ragged breath and pointed over his shoulder. 'I saw that.'

Alexis turned to follow her finger. She was pointing down the pathway they had created through the lines of Elementals, straight at Stonehenge, still adorned by the defences they had created with the power of the Gems.

'The last thing I saw before you brought me back was a single, great tree, and beside it a small pond,' said Demi, wringing her hands. She then continued cleaning the rest of his face, wiping the blood from around his eye with another damp cloth. 'It looks similar to how Stonehenge looks now, except it was an olive tree instead of an oak, and looking at it, I felt only peace, not fear as I do now. I know I'm already on borrowed time, but somehow, I thought I had more . . .'

'No.' The harshness of Alexis's voice caught Demi's attention. He shook his head, his jaw clamped shut. *No, I refuse to accept that*, he thought. He had lost her once already. He wouldn't let that happen again. He wouldn't let the Woman of the Earth's prophecy come true.

'*With water washing your roots, you will finally rest.*'

'No,' he said again, his voice light this time in outright denial as he stood straighter, lowering her hand from his face. 'We're not having this conversation now, because today is not the day you die. I won't allow it. If that means I have to starve this Earth of all its seas, I won't hesitate to do it.'

Demi must have seen the intensity in his blue-and-black-ringed eyes or felt the thundering beating of his heart beneath her palm. She dipped her head in a nod. 'Somehow, I don't doubt that you will,' she said.

She tiptoed and unwrapped the bandage from his head. It fell away, and she stood back impressed with what she saw. Alexis didn't need to touch his fingers to his head to know the bleeding had ceased and the wound was on its way to closing over.

'We will have our time, I promise you,' Alexis assured her. There weren't many things he was certain about, but he was certain about this. 'Because what I want to say to you and what I want to do with you is not anything I want to rush.'

Now it was Demi's turn to blush, and Alexis's turn to grin.

'Guys!' Blaise called from afar, tearing their attention from one another. He was rushing back to them from deep in the battle zone, Caeli at his side. Hordes of Nekro were ravaging the front of the Haven's Elementals, who desperately fought to keep them at bay.

'We've cleared all our people before this point of your section,' Caeli reported breathlessly. 'We have to create this divide now and move south-east to mine. Incantus and Serena have probably set the other two up for us.'

Alexis eyed the position of the moon. *How has time moved so quickly when I wasn't looking?* It was inching closer to the sun. The eclipse couldn't be more than a couple of hours away. Would they make it until then?

Demi clenched her jaw and gripped her golden staff with

both hands. Further up ahead, tides of Nekro were crushing each other to pile on to the Elementals of the Haven. Their shields buckled under the pressure, fighting to keep them contained, but with each second, they shuffled further back.

'Get behind me!' Demi ordered, darting to the centre of the battlefield where the Light and Dark Army met. She faced the surging passage of Nekro alone. With the Nekro almost on top of her, only a hand's reach away, Demi raised her staff into the air and drew a deep breath. The Earth Gem gleamed with power in her hold, supercharging her aura with a green light so bright that Alexis had to squint to see her.

Then, with an unrestrained cry, Demi struck her staff deep into the ground before her.

At its touch, a deafening boom exploded as the earth cracked apart at her feet. A fissure snaked out from either side of her, burrowing through the ground in a jagged, curved line across the battlefront. It swallowed any that stood in its path, taking them far beneath the surface of the earth. Another ripple followed and a series of stalagmites jutted out like serrated teeth, peaking over the trench like barbed wire and impaling any nearby Nekro.

Demi staggered, her shoulders sagging from exhaustion, knees going out from beneath her. She would have fallen into the crevice had her friends not been there to pull her back.

The Light Army cheered as their fighting paused for the first time in hours, allowing a brief moment of reprieve.

The Children of the Elements had created their first blockade against Mortem's army. The first step towards turning the tide and ensuring Stonehenge lay untouched until the eclipse began.

25
ICHARIBA CHODE

Ichariba chode (phr.) *Japanese origin*
'Though we meet but once, even by chance,
we are friends for life'

Two hours until totality

'I'm okay, just help me up,' Demi grunted.

Alexis took her into his arms, releasing her only when he was sure she could stand without her legs buckling. Even so, he kept his hand pressed against the small of her back, reminding her that he was there should she fall again.

Demi drew in a long breath through her nose. 'Incantus said they'll create makeshift barriers before our ranks on south- and north-west, ensuring our people don't venture beyond it. Boys, I think you should do your divisions quickly while Cae and I start on clearing people by her section.'

'Meet us as soon as you're finished,' said Caeli. She scraped her hair into a high ponytail, grimacing as she pulled on it with surgical precision. 'With any luck, we'll manage this whole thing before the eclipse.'

Alexis went to ask again how Demi was, but she ushered him off. 'Go.'

Alexis turned to Blaise and nodded. They darted through the hundreds of Elementals until they reached the oak tree that guarded Demi's quarter of Stonehenge. It was hurling thorns and whipping vines at the harpies flying overhead, slamming its great branches into any that dared to draw close. Alexis and Blaise rushed beneath its arms and passed through the centre of Stonehenge until they reached their sides, greeted by their defences still holding strong. Blaise easily strode through the blazing wall that curtained the monoliths, his staff pointed outwards like a rifle locked and loaded to fire.

'We good here?' Alexis asked, checking on the Elementals closest to his ice wall. Their numbers had grown sparse – only a dozen or so ringed lines of defence stood protecting Stonehenge from the Shadowless.

There was an explosion to Alexis's left, like that of a volcano erupting. Alexis felt the searing heat before he saw the glowing red-and-yellow flames pouring from Blaise's staff. It torrented across his battlefront in an arch, scorching any Shadowless, Nekro or Hybrid in its path. The wall of fire climbed high in the sky, too hot to cross but not so hot that it would burn the Haven Elementals stood behind it.

Only after he saw Blaise staggering back to Stonehenge with the assistance of a couple of Amazon warriors did Alexis finally take off. He slipped through the soldiers until he could get a closer look up ahead. He didn't want to chance making his division until he was confident there would be no collateral damage, and from what he could see, whatever walls or guards Incantus and Serena had made at the intersection between the warring armies had been quickly overrun.

Alexis swore under his breath. *God forbid it be easy*, he

thought, oddly calm despite the situation at hand. He caught the attention of a centaur who towered before him. Blood was splattered on his blond hair, which shimmered in the afternoon sun, but he looked free from injury.

'We are taking a beating up front, sir,' said the handsome centaur. 'It is impossible to maintain the barricade for any length of time.'

Alexis considered his options, none of which seemed great. 'You know what, could you give me a lift?'

Alexis grasped the centaur's fur-coated arm and hauled himself up until he was straddling his huge muscular hindquarters. Alexis unsheathed his sword so that he had a weapon in both arms. The centaur began galloping towards the front line, where the cries and clashes grew louder and louder. Alexis squeezed his legs as tightly as he could to keep himself from falling off.

'Are you sure this is safe for you, Lord Ocean?' the centaur asked, twisting his human torso to him.

'The name's Alexis Michaels,' he replied, preparing himself to jump. 'And it's not me you should be worried about.'

As the centaur skidded to a halt where the barriers fell to dissolution, Alexis dived into the midst of the warzone. He had no time to attend to the aching of his groin as an imprinted Shadowless came charging at him, jagged dagger raised in his hand.

Alexis beat the flat part of his bi-sword against his head, knocking him to the ground. The Elementals of the Haven spurred forward in a ring to guard him, relieving the pressure from the Nekro that surrounded them. Alexis sent a flurry of icicles from his staff at a harpy swooping his way, shooting it out of the sky. The centaur he had ridden on cantered over to cover his rear, standing at nearly double his height and protecting him with a beautifully intricate wooden bow and quiver of arrows.

'What's your name?' Alexis asked, slicing the head off a Nekro with his sword and kicking away its flailing body. He flipped the staff in his grip and a ring of water fountained from it. He manipulated its current to form a fishbowl over the head of a black-eyed Shadowless until she slumped unconscious. The young Sanctuario Elemental she had been brutalising offered Alexis a quick nod of thanks before he scrambled out of the pathway.

'Pamphilos, second child of Chief Sophos, truest descendants of the great Sagittarius,' the centaur said proudly, shooting down an eagle-panther Hybrid with astounding accuracy.

'Like the zodiac sign?' Alexis asked.

He could have sworn he heard Pamphilos sigh in exasperation.

'Stand clear!' Alexis swayed with the motion of the barrier. He looked from left to right to see that a haphazard barrier was somewhat standing. He had to do it here, now.

The powers of the Water Gem thrummed into him as he raised his staff into the air. He felt his lungs fill with liquid as he focused his Omni powers, making the Gem cast shards of blue light into the sky. Then, with both arms, Alexis lined up with the path and waited until the right moment.

He swung his staff in a perfect arc and a tidal wave of glistening water burst from the Water Gem. It tore away at the soil, digging up metres of earth as it burrowed deep into the ground. The flood consumed any in its path, swallowing Shadowless and Nekro in its insatiable appetite and drowning them in its unstoppable tide until it met with Blaise's wall of fire to the south and Demi's mighty trench to the north.

Alexis's knees went out from under him; then suddenly he felt weightless. Hairy arms swept him up before he could fall.

'Well done, sir,' said Pamphilos, holding him against his chest as he galloped back towards Stonehenge. As Alexis forced his stubborn lungs to breathe and tired eyes to open, he saw what all the splashing was coming from. The canal was acting with a mind of its own, whips of water lashing out as his subconscious fuelled it to harm any who was a threat to him.

With the soldiers of the Haven parting before the tall centaur, they reached Stonehenge in moments. The golden stallion gently placed Alexis on the ground.

'Thank you for carrying me,' said Alexis, pressing himself against the sturdy ice wall. The proximity of his element was already recharging his depleted energy levels. He extended his hand uncertainly. 'I don't know whether it's more appropriate to shake your hand or stroke your neck . . .'

Pamphilos chuckled. 'If you did either to some of the more secluded Centauroi Tribes, not even you would have a hand to keep.' He took a deep bow before him, so low that his mane fell free from his shoulders. 'I do hope we meet again, Sir Alexis, Son of the Seas.'

'Star sign, Pisces,' said Alexis, flashing him a smile. 'Keep safe, friend.'

Pamphilos returned the way they had come, back towards the enemy lines to guard it should any Shadowless slip past the stream. Alexis waited a moment longer before going to join his friends. He darted a look around before he bent down to feel at the base of his ice wall.

It was still there, what he and Ziya had hidden earlier that morning. It seemed intact, still functional should he need it later. He prayed he wouldn't.

'What are you doing, Al?' Blaise called from the centre of Stonehenge, his voice muffled through the frozen barrier that separated them.

Alexis shot to his feet and passed through it, joining him. 'Just catching my breath.'

'I saw what you did with your river, how you got it whipping out at the Shadowless like that.' Blaise fell in step with him as they crossed the stone ruins. 'How do you control it like that without concentrating on it?'

Alexis shrugged. He honestly didn't know. He assumed it was because he was in his Omni state with the Gem's full powers. Maybe it came from how deeply he understood his element, allowing him to exert his authority over it without explicit attention. The countless hours he had spent – after his nightmare awoke him – reading and revising and practising might have paid off in the end.

Alexis and Blaise started running when they saw that Caeli and Demi were in the midst of battle, barely ten metres from Stonehenge. The south-east section seemed to have taken the greatest hit of them all, with row after row of the Haven's Elementals succumbing to the ferocity of the Hybrids every couple of minutes.

Caeli and Demi were well past the Haven's front lines. They fought back to back, covering the other's rear, stabbing and slaying enemy after enemy. They were a stunning contrast, tall and short, blonde and brunette, offensive and defensive. Alexis and Blaise burrowed their way through to them, knocking Nekro aside as though they had never been there.

'Cae!' Blaise shouted as his entire body lit up with rolling crimson flames. She turned to him, her eyes wide in panic. Blaise threw his hands in her direction, and she spun out of the way just as the firebolt struck the place where she had just been standing. It incinerated the Hybrid that had been crawling towards her unnoticed.

Alexis leaped over the fallen carcass of a satyr and rolled to his feet beside the girls as Blaise crash-landed next to them.

'How the hell are we meant to create a barrier?' Caeli cried, her voice shrill. 'There is no battlefront. Our people are scattered everywhere! We'll be overrun in minutes.'

She clapped her hands together and a vicious gust of wind hurled into the Shadowless opposite her, throwing him away.

'We've still got to try,' replied Demi, sinking her dagger into the side of a Nekro. The remains of its entrails spilled out, but Demi had already moved on to her next target.

Caeli tutted patronisingly, but she was cut off before she could protest.

'Try or die,' Demi snapped. She stomped her foot and a well opened up beneath the Hybrid that Blaise had been trading blows with it, burying it six feet under.

Alexis recognised the look in Demi's eyes: the stubborn, unmoving, uncompromisable nature of her element. He knew that she wouldn't stop, not till the very end.

Caeli huffed, but soon complied. 'Fine, but we have to push back the Shadowless at least another twenty metres or so first.'

Just as the four friends went to embark on a rescue mission for whoever remained behind enemy lines, a loud, distant screeching stole their attention. Thousands of pounds of metal screamed as it scraped and crumpled together, forcing much of the battlefield to turn towards the west-facing sky to stare at the source of the noise.

A chain of transmission towers, at least a hundred feet tall, was floating across the fields, coated in a shimmering gleam of purple magic. They had been clearly ripped from the ground, half-shredded as dozens of high-voltage power lines dangled from the steel lattice towers. Blue-and-yellow electricity crackled violently around each body, striking at the battlefield beneath it erratically.

The enormous chain of pylons drew to a halt in the sky, just beyond the outskirts of the back of the Dark Army. Raeve's magic evaporated, and the towers toppled to the ground.

'What the hell is going on?' Blaise murmured, his bright aura withering as he crept closer to Alexis.

Alexis kept his sword poised, ready to strike at any Nekro that drew close while the others were distracted, but his eyes remained trained on the display, breath caught in his throat as the hairs of his body stood up.

The hanging steel power lines splayed outwards, flooding the atmosphere with the buzz of static electricity. They stretched out until they were pointed like great long arrows directly at the Children of the Elements.

Caeli grasped Blaise's arm as the electricity sparked, voltage climbing.

'What do we do?' Demi asked in a quiet voice, face aghast.

'I don't know,' Alexis answered. He watched as the electrical current raced up and down the wires, awaiting the order from Taranis to fire. Alexis gripped his staff and tried to collect the scattered parts of his mind to think of a way to defend themselves. Any water he poured would conduct it straight back to him. He could try to dismantle the pylons, but they were so far away, and by the time he tore them down, it would already be too late.

Think faster, think better. But nothing was coming to mind.

They were out of options.

And then it happened. In a flash of blue and yellow, the metal pylons exploded with an ear-splitting shriek. A mass of thick zigzagging bolts snaked across the battlefield impossibly fast. Alexis could only shield Demi from the blast, covering her body with his own, feeling the back of his neck prickle with the teeth of the sparks.

But then the heat, the current, the light disappeared.

Silenced. Swallowed.

A huge gaping hole opened up in the sky above the Elementals. Alexis cracked his eyes open to see what had spared them. He could only see a swirling flat red surface.

The partner of the portal popped open just beside the transmission towers, spewing the blue-and-yellow volts back at them. The ground trembled as the chain of pylons burst and collapsed into heaps, riddled with static energy that eventually sparked out.

The red portals disappeared, and the woman who stood before the Children of the Elements lowered her hands. She turned to them, ink-black hair pulling in the wind. A smile crept across her lips.

'Do you children always need saving?' said Valentina, brown eyes twinkling in the daylight, her shadow cast clearly behind her.

26
NEMESIS

Nemesis (n.) *Greek origin*
'To give what is due'; goddess of vengeance and retribution; the inescapable agent of someone's downfall

One hour and forty-five minutes until totality

'Valentina!' Demi cried. She grabbed her with both hands and pulled her into a bone-crunching embrace.

Valentina stiffened, looking more alarmed than she had moments before when devouring several thousand volts of electricity. She met Alexis's gaze over Demi's head and gave him the briefest of smiles, one that he returned in full.

As Demi drew back, Caeli cautiously approached Valentina.

Caeli then slapped Valentina hard across the face.

'Cae!' Demi gasped.

Valentina's head snapped back. Already, a red mark was blossoming on her pale face. She shoved Caeli back, but somehow, Caeli did not budge. 'What the hell? I just saved your pathetic life, *Doran*.'

Caeli shrugged and shot a look over her shoulder at the others. 'Just checking she wasn't imprinted again,' she said sweetly. 'She should be grateful I didn't break her nose like she did mine. You know, when she portalled Sinner to us. Remember him? Ugly bloke, almost killed Demi. Ring any bells?'

Alexis rushed to intervene when he noticed Valentina's jaw tick and her hands ball into fists at her sides. 'Val, what happened to you? Where did you go?'

Around them, the Elementals of the Haven surged back into action, engaging once again with the Shadowless to form a ring of protection around the quarrelling Elementals.

Valentina had found a change of clothes between leaving the Haven and returning for the battle. *Definitely an upgrade from the prison rags of Mortem's castle*, Alexis considered. A fitted black leather jacket wrapped around her thin frame, accented with intricate Chinese-style cloud patterns that were painted the same cherry red of her portals. It looked custom made and Alexis wondered if she had travelled back home to retrieve it especially for the battle – the commute wouldn't have taken long, after all.

She readjusted her sleeves. 'Would you like to have a nice little gossip or would you rather we win this battle?'

Alexis matched her cool glare. 'I was *this* close to saying it's nice to see you again.'

Valentina curtsied.

Blaise cleared his throat. 'Right, so we have a battle plan – create a barricade here to force back the Shadowless to safeguard Stonehenge.' He spoke matter-of-factly, his chin held high as though he was delivering orders. His previous interest in Valentina appeared utterly extinguished, much to Caeli's satisfaction, Alexis noted.

'That's brilliant; best of luck,' Valentina replied indifferently.

From the underside of her sleeves protruded two thin jian swords. The double-edged blades shimmered in the afternoon sunlight, their hilts buried somewhere in the design of her bespoke jacket. 'I'm off to kill Mortem.'

'Join the queue,' said Alexis, placing an arm on her shoulder as she went to turn. She froze at his touch and didn't move until he removed his hand from her. 'But the only one who can do that is Incantus. We need to stop Stonehenge from getting overrun by the time of the eclipse and we could really use your help.'

Valentina turned on him. Her voice held no malice, but Alexis could see the frustration behind her expression. 'Look, I don't expect any of you to understand this, with your perfect friendships and perfect homes and perfect guidance, but that man *abducted* me and then tortured me until he saw that the only way I would do as he asked was if I was imprinted.' Small cracks appeared in her rehearsed façade, revealing glimpses of the suffering beneath. She took a step towards them, the jian swords retracting beneath her jacket sleeves as she let out a long sigh. 'It's good to see you all again, it truly is. But altruism was not the reason I came back.'

Valentina spun on her heel, her long black hair swishing behind her. She held out her palm and a swirling red portal blinked into existence before her, a tunnel to somewhere beyond enemy lines.

'He's too dangerous to fight alone,' warned Demi.

Valentina didn't turn back, but Alexis heard her parting words before she vanished. 'So am I.'

*

Valentina knew better than to portal to any random point on the battlefield. Her teachers from the temple had repeatedly emphasised the importance of knowing where exactly she was portalling to, using horror stories of inexperienced portallers reappearing halfway through a wall as a means to get their point across.

But flair trumped safety in that moment, so Valentina opted for the dramatic exit.

She emerged from the red-glowing panel and found herself ensnared at the battlefront between the warring armies, staring down the barrel of the roaring tide of the Shadowless and Nekro.

She hadn't come alone.

'Do you have a death wish, blue-eyed boy?' she said, whipping round to face him, her jian sword jutting out of her sleeve as she did. She caught herself just as the blade kissed his neck beneath his jaw, deep enough to draw blood but not enough to cause any real damage. Not yet.

Alexis's eyes were trained on her. Despite a sword and staff in each hand, he made no move to defend himself. 'I'm not here to stand in your way. I didn't come to hurt you.'

He just doesn't get it.

Valentina's voice was clipped when she spoke, her patience wearing thin. 'I am neither a hero nor a villain. I'm just a woman seeking revenge. Don't be a fool and get in my way. You may not want to hit a girl, but I can easily kill a man.'

Valentina's sword didn't waver, not even as a line of blood welled around the silver blade and trickled down the front of Alexis's throat. She contemplated flicking her wrist and severing his pretty head from his shoulders. It didn't matter that he was one of the Children of the Elements, any move she made against him at this proximity would be fatal.

Alexis's eyes darkened, but not in anger – in question. As if he was reading her mind. It unnerved her, thinking that anyone had the ability to understand her thoughts. He had proven on more than one occasion that he had a way of understanding her where others couldn't.

She weighed up the benefits of killing him. Did she want to? Not really; she was actually quite fond of him. But would she? Absolutely, if necessary. He was a child of darkness.

No one had explicitly told her that, but having spent days silenced by the hand of cold shadow, she could recognise its presence. He was a child of Mortem Arcangelo and had inherited both of his powers. Alexis had the potential to imprint her just as Mortem had. She didn't think he would, but she had vowed to never again trust the word of a man.

'*Don't just prepare for the threat. Prepare for the potential of threat.*'

That was a lesson she could not forget from her callous training; one of the many she was grateful for in retrospect.

Finally, Alexis spoke, thick dark lashes closing over his eyes in a long blink. 'My friends have each other. You have no one. That is why I came.'

Although she knew it to be true, Valentina bristled. 'I don't need anyone.'

Alexis's eyes widened as he noticed something over her shoulder. Valentina sensed it a moment after. A huge, coiling Hybrid was slithering towards her, an unnatural combination of a serpent and a winged creature. It bared its venomous fangs as it tore through the air at them.

She flipped out of its way, as did Alexis. When it came at her again, she slashed through the scaled skin of its underbelly. It roared in anguish as blood spilled out, burning the spot where she had just been.

Valentina blinked a portal above herself and lunged through it, reappearing out of its partnered end just behind the flighted Hybrid. With both blades, she stabbed deep into its back, tearing a gaping line through its body as it collapsed to the ground.

She blew loose strands of hair from her face and wiped her blades against its carcass. Alexis stood seemingly unfazed by the commotion.

'I know you don't need anyone,' Alexis said, his eyebrow arched as though she had just validated his point. 'But you saved us. Twice. If there's anything I can offer you, whether that's my protection or my company, I'm here.'

Something inside of Valentina, something she had long turned her back on and abandoned, blossomed deep in the centre of her chest. It was a feeling she didn't realise how much she had missed until now.

The irreplaceable warmth that came from the realisation that she was *wanted*.

'Your honour might get you killed, Alexis Michaels,' she warned.

Alexis shrugged and came to stand beside her. He looked out on the battlefield, a vacant, unreadable look in his eyes. 'I'll add it to the list. I wasn't expecting to survive this day anyway,' he stated. 'Might as well die a hero.'

That was something Valentina vehemently disagreed with. If she had decided she wasn't going to kill Alexis, no one was allowed to. And if she was to be his friend, she would tell him what he needed to hear, regardless of whether he wanted to or not.

'This saviour complex you have isn't noble, not when you're so concerned with saving everyone else that you don't take the time and effort to save yourself.' Her words came out sharper than she'd expected. Alexis turned to her as if she had just struck him across the face, his dark eyebrows knitted together over light eyes. Valentina softened her voice, but still she went on. 'You would sooner make yourself a martyr than really try and heal because that way you won't be disappointed if you fail. Why do you constantly need to prove to yourself that you're not a bad person?'

Alexis's mouth opened and then closed again as he apparently ruminated on her words. Lucky for him, fate intervened and he was saved from answering.

A distant explosion shook the ground. Shimmering waves of golden energy billowed from an older, rounded woman with fair skin and greying red hair, who Valentina didn't recognise. Her purple robes were splattered with blood and dirt, but she looked far from tired, her skin radiant with energy and vitality.

Valentina hoped she would look like that in a hundred years.

Distracted by the woman, Valentina failed to notice the Shadowless that came charging towards her. He threw her to the ground, where her head smacked against the earth so hard that stars exploded across her vision. She felt his legs squeezing into her sides as he straddled her, too stunned to push him off.

'Not so self-righteous now, are you, princess?' said a voice she knew from Mortem's castle. One who had taken great pleasure in torturing her for hours into the night.

Then, the man's weight was gone in an instant.

Alexis's arm was wrapped tightly around his neck, hauling him away from behind. With his other hand, Alexis sent his sword stabbing into his side.

Only the blade didn't penetrate.

The man threw his head back, crunching into Alexis's nose. He barrelled out of his hold, just as Alexis swiped at his face. Again, the blade did not cut his skin, which gleamed with a metallic shine.

Valentina drew her dual blades and crouched like a wild cat ready to pounce. She shot forward, casting a portal and reappearing behind the man. Her blade barely made a dent in his shoulder.

The man sneered and unsheathed a bloodied machete. He beckoned her and Alexis towards him and they rushed to meet him. They parried blows, stabs for cuts, swings for punches.

Alexis was mesmerising to watch, Valentina found. He fought like a dancer – precise, agile, fluid. Yet nothing seemed to be slowing the Shadowless down and she could see Alexis growing increasingly infuriated beside her.

'We're going to take you captive again,' spat the man, laughing hauntingly. 'Where I get to play with you all night long.'

A fiery haze rippled across Valentina's mind. *I am going to claw his eyes out.*

The man's smile vanished when a stream of water surged into the back of him, sending him stumbling towards them. Valentina leaped to meet him, legs wrapping around his neck as Alexis disarmed him of his machete and swept him off his feet.

They crashed to the ground, Valentina still on top of him. 'I am no one's prisoner,' she said.

The Shadowless's eyes widened in fear, providing her

with the perfect targets. She plunged her dual blades into his unprotected eyes, feeling the tissue and muscles tear, taking pleasure when his whimpers of pain faded to nothing. Just like his name, his death would soon be forgotten, joining the ever-growing list of her fallen enemies.

Alexis stretched his arm out towards her and she took it before dusting herself off. He looked pale, but he didn't turn away from the sight of the mutilated Shadowless.

'Still want me to be your friend?' she asked him, expecting him to look at her differently now.

Alexis offered her a crooked smile. 'Seems safer than being your enemy.'

'Alexis! Valentina?'

Incantus Arcangelo stormed towards them, accompanied by the red-haired older woman. He looked angelic in his all-white Haven suit, a beacon of light and power. He opened his arms and Alexis ran into them, hugging his mentor fiercely. Alexis then allowed the woman to sweep him up and plant a kiss against his cheek.

'What the hell are you doing out here?' the woman asked in a thick Scottish accent, shaking him by the shoulders with so much vigour that his whole body jostled.

Alexis gestured to Valentina. 'Helping a friend,' he replied.

Incantus's eyes scanned over Valentina, taking in the sight of her custom outfit. 'You came back?'

She inclined her head to him. 'Duty told me to, sir, to repay my debt to you for taking me in and for leaving without a proper thank you.'

'You must be the friend my granddaughter mentioned,' said the gracefully dressed woman. 'Serena Aevum,' she added, introducing herself as she vaporised a Shadowless creeping towards them with a careless flick of her wrist.

Valentina bowed again; every Elemental knew of the famous Aevum bloodline of female-only spawn, powerful descendants from the last surviving grandson of the First Borns. 'An honour to meet you. Ziya showed me true kindness when I arrived at the Haven. Although it was only a brief encounter, I will remember her benevolence always.'

Serena's face split into a wide smile of pride.

'The portal you cast, saving them . . .' Incantus began. He paused to hurl a glowing beam of light at a harpy that was circling overhead, swiftly ending its alerting squawks. 'It was incredible. I offer my sincerest gratitude. Continue to do whatever you can to help out.'

He glanced at the moon, accounting for the little time that remained before the eclipse would begin. He turned to Alexis, opening his mouth to speak, but Alexis beat him to it.

'I know. I'll get back as soon as I can,' he said, his jaw taut in sullen concern for his friends.

Incantus nodded and cupped the nape of Alexis's neck in a warm, paternal embrace. The white-haired Elemental then took off in the direction of the collapsed transmission towers, thrashing through a group of Nekro as he likely searched for his former Leaders.

Serena lingered a moment longer, her eyes trained on Valentina as if she was seeing through the veneer. Did Serena see the hollowing envy that gripped Valentina when she watched Alexis and his mentor? Did she sense the violent energy that thrummed within her, waiting to be unleashed at the man she had returned to kill?

'I know who you are,' Serena stated. Valentina felt a lump form in her throat, one that was painful to swallow. She peered out of the corner of her eye to see Alexis preoccupied, defending them against a two-headed Hybrid, thankfully out of earshot. 'I know what it is like to try and escape a legacy, a name, that will always precede you. And I know why it is that you are here.'

Serena stepped closer towards her, taking Valentina's hands in her own and looking up into her eyes. 'We *will* take him down,' she promised. Her hands shook with conviction. It took a moment for Valentina to realise that Serena had turned her palm face up. Her sleeve fell away to reveal the symbol that branded her skin as if she were nothing more than a prized bull: the dragon curled into a circle, chasing the pearl of power and immortality. 'No one wants him dead more than I, but it is more important to save the lives of the innocent than to take the life of one guilty man. No matter how much we want to, only Incantus and the Children have the power to truly end him. But you can help me find my Akili, to see if he and the other two survived your attack.'

Tears of sorrow and tiredness stung Valentina's eyes as she pulled her hands away. She wished she could stay with Aevum and Arcangelo – to stay in their supportive presence and experience the alien feeling of what it was like to be respected and appreciated. Not because of the family she had been born into or the family she had married into, but by her own merits. The fact that both Incantus and Serena knew who she was, and maybe even what she had done, but still trusted her to stay to help them led Valentina to hold them in such high esteem that she had given no other.

And yet, it is not enough.

They wanted to save their friends. Valentina respected that, but she would not compromise her own mission for it. Killing Mortem was her priority, the only thing that kept her standing during her torture and after. She needed him to pay for what he did to her, and more importantly, who he took from her.

Serena slowly shook her head in dismay, knowing the decision was made. She didn't try to deter her any more. Instead, she merely darted a glance at Alexis and instructed, 'Return him to his friends before you go.'

Valentina nodded. With one hand, she cast a red portal in front of Alexis just as he started to say something to her. The threshold swept him up before she could hear it.

She then made another portal beside her.

'Your life is more important than his death, Nà Jìng,' said Serena Aevum.

A single tear fell at the name that had once been hers, belonging to a girl who had been hurt and defiled and abused. A naive, weak girl, who, for the longest time, thought she deserved her suffering, that it was a necessary punishment to make her strong.

Lì Nà Jìng was gone, dead, burned away with the ashes of her childhood.

Her name would no longer mean *beautiful*. No longer mean *elegant* or *quiet*. She had abandoned that girl along with the place she synonymised with oppression and sorrow. In time, she would learn to break those fallible associations, to rekindle her love for her culture – but, no matter how much time had passed, she would never again answer to that name.

Valentina.

That was her name now, one meaning strength, chosen to honour the only man who had ever truly cared for her, and who had paid the price of loyalty with his life.

27

BASOREXIA

Basorexia (n.) *Latin origin*
The sudden, overwhelming desire to kiss

One hour and twenty minutes until totality

Alexis saw red – literally.

He was swallowed up and thrown out of the portal before he could protest. He cursed as it blinked closed in front of him, snatching him away from Valentina. He wasn't granted the luxury to complain, however, not when Valentina had deposited him in the thick of the Shadowless army. She must have thought the Haven would be doing a better job of holding them than they currently were, or possibly she had decided that he was better off dead.

Does she know I heard Serena say her birth name?

He tucked that piece of information away. Right now, he needed to find Demi.

The moment the Nekro saw the glow of his amulet, they advanced on him. Alexis had neither the time nor will to make it a fair fight. In fact, it wouldn't be a fight at all.

It would be a *slaughter.*

He drew a deep inhale and leached the water from all

around him. The water that existed in every cell of the body, the water that lived in the brain. He stole it from the people and creatures around him like a petty thief, his for the taking and his for the discarding. His lungs ached from exertion, from the sheer gravitas and intricacy of the act he had never before performed, but he wouldn't allow himself to falter.

Between one beat and the next, Alexis found himself surrounded by a ring of dried-up corpses, devoid of water and life. Without a second glance at them, he took off.

He would not grieve these, nor any other who stood in the way of him and Demi. He had been foolish to leave her, thoughtless and reckless. Even if she did have Blaise and Caeli, they would not give their lives to protect her the way he would.

Alexis searched desperately, no opponent strong enough to keep him from her. Blood splashed against his face as he tore through enemy after enemy, matting his hair and painting his skin. Even connected to the Water Gem with his Omni powers, he could feel himself growing weaker. Every small and large manipulation of his powers was taking a toll, making him feel as though he was swimming against a tide and slowly sinking, slowly drowning from the inside.

Still, he could not stop.

Sink or swim. For now, he sought the latter.

It was as if she had been calling him, akin to how the roots of a tree would draw moisture from the soil. He located her aura, the brilliant green, the eternal, imposing strength of earth.

Demi was a small figure in the battle, but one that fought valiantly and viciously with the power of nature at her beck and call. The earth trembled beneath Alexis as he barrelled towards her.

'Lexi!' Demi exclaimed, snatching back her dagger from the shattered ribcage of a decomposing Nekro. 'Where have you been?'

Alexis instantly filled the space behind her, his broad back against hers. Each time they touched, a spark of vitality rippled through him and spurred him on, driven by the innate need to protect her. He wondered if she felt the same, if the ruthlessness of her fight was that much stronger now she had to guard him.

'Where are the others?' Alexis asked breathlessly, shouting over his shoulder. 'And what happened to the wind tunnel?'

They were surrounded by countless smaller battles. Whatever semblance of a pathway there had been from Stonehenge was lost. Haven Elementals had abandoned their posts to fend for themselves in the ravaged lands.

'Cae spotted a band of Sanctuario further along,' said Demi. She grunted as she stamped her boot against the ground. A huge stalagmite burst free from the earth before her, impaling a Hybrid several metres high. 'I said I'd cover it here while she goes ahead. Blaise went after her. Oh no . . .'

Alexis snuck a glance and caught what she had seen.

A group of Nekro had managed to break through the guarded battlefront south-east to where they stood. They burrowed into the free space, trampling over the Haven Elementals, whose cries were soon silenced by their animalistic growls. The Nekro then began to stampede towards Stonehenge. They flattened up against Caeli's force field, which lay just beyond the outermost stones, but Alexis wasn't sure how much pressure it would withstand before it shattered.

Alexis was torn between returning to Stonehenge to guard it before the Shadowless arrived with their powers, and rushing to Caeli and Blaise to ensure they were safe. The fiery detonations and thundering howls were growing increasingly frantic and desperate. In the sky above, the edges of the moon and the sun had snuck closer together and couldn't be further than a few minutes away from overlapping. How much longer would they last? How much longer would he last before his muscles gave out and heart seized up?

'*Lexi!*' Demi's voice was riddled with panic, soaked with fear. She pressed her back against his, her head resting between his shoulder blades. 'I know we said we would save this conversation for later . . . but I don't think we have a later.'

Alexis drew ragged breaths through lungs that felt as though they were coated in sawdust. He swung his staff in a wide arc. The Water Gem on its tip smacked into a Hybrid that was something between a wild cat and a bear, reducing it to a puddle of liquid.

'Don't give up on us now, Demi,' he begged, finding it ironic that as the Elemental with the power of water, he felt like he was going to pass out from dehydration. 'You promised me a lifetime of chasing sunsets, remember?'

Demi let out a choked sound behind him, somewhere between a laugh and a sob, and it took everything in him not to turn around and hold her in his arms. He heard her sniff, pulling herself together. 'I remember. We will. Tonight, once this is all over, you will hold me and I will kiss you as we watch the sun set on this horrid day, and neither of us will fear the darkness that follows. I have faith in us, in this world, in our fate.'

It was an image Alexis clung on to with everything he had.

He had always admired Demi's faith, more than anything, but he had never really shared it before.

Not until now.

What came next could only be described as divine intervention, or perhaps the most perfectly timed coincidence of all existence.

Hope came in the form of a short Indian woman.

Faith and power came in Ziya Parashakti.

Alexis saw her through Caeli's force field around Stonehenge, hunkered over one of the projectors that she must have taken from the Training Academy. For the first time ever, she was wearing the all-black Haven suit, silver command tablet in one hand and sword in the other, although she didn't appear to hold the latter with much confidence.

What the hell is she doing? Alexis thought, his grip on his sword and staff so tight that he felt the metal change shape.

The projector pulsed beneath her, shooting out rays of dark colour from its lenses; rays that soon formed figures – humanoid, faceless bodies. The holograms poured from it, one after the other, becoming solid, tangible. They strode from the centre of Stonehenge in the direction of Alexis and Demi.

Immediately, they were leaped upon by the Nekro, but the training bots, which had been clearly set to their highest difficulty level, dispatched them with ease. Whenever one fell, disintegrating to cubed pixels, another was there to take its place. Soon enough, the bots came to encompass the two fighting Elementals, forming a protective ring around them.

'Alexis! Demi!'

It was Ziya's high-pitched voice, spoken through a faceless training bot before them.

'Ziya?' Demi asked, utterly bewildered, looking between the training bot that had spoken and the real Ziya who stood in Stonehenge. 'Darling, it's not safe for you to be here!'

Alexis caught his breath beside Demi, wiping blood and sweat from his face.

'I had to help you!' Ziya replied, again through the bot. Around them, more and more deep grey figures had filed out in a curved line before the Elemental front line, burrowing across the battlefield. 'I thought there could be another way the projectors could help us, Alexis.'

Demi turned on him, eyeing his dark expression with a look of confused concern. 'What is she talking about?'

Alexis shook his head. 'Nothing.' He was too tired to put any authenticity in his lie, but he hoped the circumstances might spare him from having to explain himself. 'Ziya, you've been an incredible help, but you need to get back into the Haven.'

He looked through the rows of gunmetal bots back towards Stonehenge where he saw the real Ziya nod. The Haven disk in her hand flashed and she was gone, kilometres of earth separating her from harm's way.

'Was that Valentina who saved you?' came Ziya's voice from the bot.

'We haven't seen Caeli and Blaise in a long time,' said Alexis, cutting her off. Demi hadn't stopped staring at him, trying to pull out whatever it was he was keeping from her with a stubborn glare, but once they started jogging, she was forced to look away.

Panic built up in Alexis's chest as they passed countless fallen bodies of the Light Army, an array of dropped weapons and unmoving carcasses. Caeli and Blaise were nowhere to be seen. Five metres. Ten. Twenty.

He shared a solemn look with Demi. Neither of them dared speak it.

'They're up ahead!' came Ziya's voice from the bot they had just passed. Then the bot beside them added, 'They're with some of the Sanctuario, but they're surrounded on all sides!'

Alexis's and Demi's jog broke into a sprint.

'Show us!' Alexis bellowed, heart thundering in his chest, holding both weapons in one hand so he could grab Demi in the other and drag her along to keep up with him.

The faces of the bots bordering the walkway flashed in unison. Colour replaced the metallic grey to depict a live video of what must be happening further away. A video showing Caeli and Blaise, staffs in hand, glowing red and grey, projected for Alexis and Demi to watch as they ran.

28
CAFUNÉ

Cafuné (n.) *Portuguese origin*
The act of running your fingers through your lover's hair

One hour and ten minutes until totality

Blaise Ademola swore as the first of the Haven's training bots reached them. The corporeal projections hurled themselves at a Hybrid, which shattered into a hundred unmoving cubes, but not before they'd slashed the Hybrid's stomach open.

'What the hell . . . ?' Caeli murmured breathlessly, turning in a circle as the bots formed a protective guard around her and Blaise.

Her silver-blonde hair clung to her neck, dark and slick with sweat. Red blotches marked her angular face, burned from the unrelenting glare of the sun. Blaise staggered towards her, his lips cracked and bleeding, broad chest heaving.

'They are from the Haven,' Blaise gasped. His face lit up when he saw Alexis and Demi running towards them in the far distance through the cleared pathway. 'Cae! They've come!'

Blaise turned when he heard no response. 'Cae?'

Caeli was manipulating arrows with the wind, shooting them through the Nekro that were assaulting the training bots that guarded them. Her eyes were trained on something beyond, however. Blaise followed her gaze to the three Sanctuario members in their navy suits, still surrounded by Shadowless.

'I have to help them,' said Caeli, relinquishing hold of the whizzing arrows.

'I don't care about them; I care about us!' Blaise shouted, starting towards her. 'Don't you dare—'

'Already am.'

Caeli shot into the air before Blaise could stop her, soaring over the heads of the training bots, who could do nothing but watch her. Blaise saw her land beside the Sanctuario members, the Elementals furthest from Stonehenge. He didn't recognise any of them, but one had a deep gash that cut across her chest, and another was bleeding freely from one eye.

Caeli faced her palms outwards and erected a dome-shaped force field around them. Nekro collided against its hard surface, forcing it to shudder, but it held for now.

Blaise wouldn't wait to find out how long her shield lasted. He barged past the Haven's training bots that protected him, forcing his way towards her.

'You better not die before I get to you,' he muttered, unsure if he'd spoken the words out loud or not. He watched Caeli's arms tremble as she swept the air beneath the Sanctuario Elementals. She created an opening in her force field and sent them soaring towards the training bots where Blaise had just been. She nearly sagged to her knees once she dropped them off, but she clung to her staff to keep her upright.

Blaise knew a wind tunnel had to be created, but there were Nekro and harpies crawling over Caeli's force field like vicious vultures on a lone animal in the wild. There was no way she could hope to defend herself *and* finalise the defences before the Light Army *and* get back to safety.

Blaise thawed Caeli's fears with flame and fury.

'You are so damn reckless, Caeli Doran!' bellowed Blaise. His body was coated in rolling waves of red and purple as he incinerated the Nekro that beat down on Caeli's shield. 'Can't you ever do as you're told?'

Caeli found the strength to reply to that. 'Who are you to tell me what to do? I can handle myself. I am not yours to care for or look after; that's been made pretty damn clear.'

Blaise met her thunderous gaze through her bloodied force field. There was a tortured expression on her face, but Blaise couldn't decide if it was one of anger or fear. Potentially both. Whatever it was, she seemed to be done with waiting for Blaise to decipher it.

She shattered the remains of her shield and leaped into the air, staff in hand. With the training bots lining the pathway, it remained unobstructed, dividing the armies of Haven and Shadowless.

Caeli called on the power of the skies, on the emotions Blaise knew she stifled, and on her ambition so great, it must be suffocating. Blaise was certain he had been right earlier, that her fatal flaw was that she needed to feel important. He had never understood it before, had never tried to work out why she needed to constantly prove herself, to solicit admiration from others or seek academic validation to fill the hole in her chest. Maybe he never would.

Caeli seemed to take that pain and turn it into something wild. She took the carefully constructed order she had held on to in her life and let it unwind in chaos.

The Woman of the Air had told her to feel her emotions freely. Blaise watched as she did just that.

As she felt all of them. All at once.

Caeli screamed as she hurled her staff down. Hurricane winds burst from the Gem of the Air, blasting deep into the front of the Shadowless army, propelling away any in its path with a mighty gust and an even louder boom.

The air dispersed from beneath Caeli as she fell to the ground, breathless, energy spent. She made no attempt to catch herself, and fortunately for her, she didn't need to.

Blaise caught her. She tried to stand for herself, but he would not let her go, not even as the Shadowless began to recover and crawl towards them, only to be swept away by stray pelts from the rolling wind tunnel.

'You won't let me be yours!' The words tumbled out from Blaise like he couldn't hold them in any longer. His axe fell to the ground, clattering against her spear.

For the first time in a long time, Blaise let himself look into her stormy grey eyes. He averted them any chance he got, too afraid to catch her gaze, for he could deny many a thing, but he couldn't deny the ease with which it felt to get lost in her.

With her body so close to his, could she see the delicate fire within that braved the storm, fighting to stay alight no matter how harsh the winds worked to extinguish it?

'You won't let me see you, not really,' Blaise continued through shallow breaths, his hands splaying to cover her whole back. 'I don't blame you for that. I've been . . . I've been bad to you. I burn you to see if you care about me enough to stand the heat, and you push me away to see if I'll come back. I see that now. But I want you to know that I *do* want you to be mine.'

The air stilled around the Son of Flames and Daughter of Storm.

Caeli finally found her footing. Her face burned crimson and she tore her gaze away from him as if to gather the thoughts that seemed to scatter before her. 'I'm scared,' she whispered. 'I'm scared that it'll go wrong and ruin everything. I need you in my life, Blaise, no matter how crazy you drive me. But if you come close, you might not like everything you see.'

Blaise took her hand and placed it against his chest so that she could feel the racing beat of his heart. His bright eyes were locked on to hers. 'I'm scared too, but I'm done running from my fear. Stop thinking for once, Cae. Stop trying to control yourself and the people around you. I won't leave you. I *can't* leave you. Whether we work out or not, I promise to always stay. But Cae, today could be our last day. I don't want to spend another minute of it without you.'

Blaise felt the pressure in his chest ease with his declaration, as though he could breathe deeper, take in more air.

Maybe this was strength. Not in destruction, but in construction. In the building of something new. In the wild, bold, unabashed blazing of the fire. A fire that could be reignited by nothing more than a spark. In himself, in the knowledge that no matter if he was left alone, he would be strong enough to stand on his own.

Caeli's amulet seemed to know before she did what she really wanted, giving it away before the smile broke across her face. 'Oh for the First Borns' sake, just kiss me already.'

Blaise exhaled a laugh and pulled her to him. Their bodies slammed together and their lips finally met, crashing into one another with all the desperation and desire that had been building for far longer than either ever dared to admit.

Caeli pressed her hands either side of his face, holding him close to her as he wrapped his arms around her slender back. Without noticing, their amulets had found one another too, beating together once.

Upon their touch swept an explosion of wind and fire, rolling out from their bodies in a great ring that swept away anything and everything near.

When the fire finally died down, withering to wisps of burning red embers that were carried away by light gales, Caeli and Blaise parted.

'What took us so long?' Caeli breathed, pressing her forehead against his.

Blaise chuckled as he ran his fingers through her hair. 'You're a hard bird to catch,' he said. For that, he received another kiss.

'Well about damn time!' came Alexis's voice, riddled with equal parts relief and happiness. Demi stood beside him, smiling gleefully with tears in her eyes, bouncing on her feet in vicarious elation. Blaise wasn't sure how long they had been there, but it seemed only they were strong enough to withstand the power that had come from his and Caeli's union.

The two pairs rushed to meet one another, bodies slotting into each other, finding perfect harmony in the balance that could only be created when together. For the first time all day, the four friends found themselves laughing, hands reaching out to hold each other, check that each was safe and intact and *alive.*

The battlefield had been divided between light and dark. With the Shadowless army cut off from the Elementals by walls of fire, earth, water or wind, the Haven finally stood a chance of holding them back. They finally stood a chance of succeeding.

A screech tore across the entire battlefield. It was an awful sound. Tortured. Anguished. Panicked.

And it had come from Stonehenge, which meant only one thing.

The four friends looked to the sky. The moon had reached the edge of the sun, signalling the commencement of the eclipse, and of something else far more sinister.

Birthed from the darkness, the *Demons* came to life, and any hopes the Children of the Elements had of survival disappeared like shadows in the night.

PART III

29
LAKAS NG LOOB

Lakas ng loob (n.) *Filipino origin*
A person's inner strength; the quality of the mind or spirit that enables one to face struggle, pain, difficulty and uncertainty with courage and without fear

One hour until totality

Demi sucked in a haggard gasp and let out the faintest of whispers. '*Demons.*'

'*When you find that which you seek, the sky will grow dark, and your* Demons *will come to find you.*'

Alexis hadn't expected the meaning of Caeli's prophecy, spoken by the Woman of the Air, to be literal. It was a cruel joke, for the *Demons* were very much real, despite looking like something from a nightmare.

Or worse: from a hallucination.

Four colossal, obsidian creatures towered from the outskirts of the Dark Army, so great that the entire battlefield shuddered with each of their synchronised footsteps. They held a vaguely human shape, yet were christened by darkness. In the place where their face should have been was nothing but shadow, a vacuum, sucking in all light from around it like a black hole.

It was then, as Alexis stared at the *Demons*, that he realised how they had been made, or rather what they had been made from. The warriors of darkness had been constructed by all the shadows Mortem had stolen; they radiated with the very same aura Mortem did, the same aura Alexis had when he had used his powers of darkness to kill Sinner.

Perhaps Alexis's shadow, and the *Shadow Man* itself, was in there somewhere too. That was the cruellest joke of all.

In the gloom of the eclipse and at the sight of the *Demons*, the battlefield succumbed to an overbearing silence. For a moment, no one spoke, no one fought, no one moved – not even the Shadowless.

Then the footsteps of the *Demons* split the earth, crushing Shadowless and Haven Elementals beneath indiscriminately. And bedlam ensued.

Screams erupted as Elementals of the Haven fled their posts. A great deal of the Shadowless absconded too as the *Demons* took towards Stonehenge, leaving mostly the Nekro and Hybrids to decorate their feet like vermin following the tread of a giant.

All the breath that had escaped Alexis's lungs rushed back to him. Reality crashed down upon him, pulling him from his introspection to where he stood as a contender and not a spectator of the horror before him. He half-expected to be standing alone, but had he not learned already?

Demi was muttering a silent prayer at his side, her eyes squeezed shut and hand clinging to her crucifix as if she was sending a message. To her family or to her god, Alexis wasn't sure. Caeli and Blaise were to his right, no longer looking at the *Demons* but instead at each other. Tears brimmed their eyes, but nonetheless, they stayed. They always would.

The four goliath shadows split, altering their trajectory slightly. As three moved to encircle Stonehenge, it became painfully obvious that the Children of the Elements each had their own *Demon* to face. Alone.

As the realisation crept upon them that this could be the last time they were all together and that they were likely walking to their end, words once again failed them, for what was sufficient, what was *enough*, to say what they needed to say to one another? The nostalgic feeling of finality lay intermixed with the longing that they could have more time together. That they should have a lifetime together.

Alexis thought of all the things he wanted to tell the people before him.

I want to tell Caeli that she's always inspired me, that becoming her friend has been something I never knew I wanted or needed but now desperately can't go without. I want to tell Blaise that I have found a way to thaw the frozen part of myself that had believed the Shadow Man *when it said I would always be weak, and that has only been because of Blaise's company and his friendship and his strength.*

I want, I need, *to tell Demi that my past has been a noose around my neck. That most of my life I have waited for the hands of my shadow to shove me off the ledge. That on my very worst days, I wondered if I would take the leap myself.*

That those days are no more since she came into my life.

But to say those things was to say goodbye, and Alexis couldn't bring himself to do that. Not when there was still light in the sky and breath in his lungs.

Alexis swallowed the ball of barbed wire caught in his throat. 'It's not long until totality.' He glanced skywards to note the first contact – where a small bite had been taken out of the sun as the moon began to cover the edge of its disc. 'If we can somehow hold them off . . .'

The words died on his lips, for he was many things, but a believer was not one of them.

None of them were ready to leave, but he knew he had to be the first. He clenched his jaw and gripped his staff, forcing the Water Gem to glow valiantly. With nothing more than a nod and a small smile at Blaise and Caeli and Demi, he solidified the sight of them in his memory, and turned away.

It wasn't that he was the bravest of his friends or even that he thought they stood a chance at winning any more. But as he crossed through what remained of the battling armies on his journey to Stonehenge, Alexis understood that he had already defeated a great number of demons in his life. In a sense, he had spent his whole life fighting – perhaps it was poetic justice that this was how he was supposed to die too.

So be it.

Alexis didn't need to look to know that his friends had done the same, that they had moved to stand before their defences at Stonehenge alone and scared.

As the battlefield grew sparse and desolate, there was little that stood in the way of the *Demons*. Few remained, the training bots and gargoyles, the Elementals of the Haven and Sanctuario who didn't have much else to lose, battling against the hundreds of Nekro and Shadowless and Hybrids.

Alexis stumbled backwards as a *Demon* approached, edging closer to Stonehenge until eventually it stopped before him. It craned its empty face downwards, staring through Alexis, deep into his soul, dragging something from it, something he thought he had buried so deep that it would never again see the light of day.

It dragged forth the hallucinations.

It dragged forth the *darkness*.

Alexis felt it all simultaneously. He was unable to prevent the resurfacing of the shadows that had been concealed deep inside of him. The darkness that was inexplicably entwined with his psychosis in a way he couldn't understand and likely never would.

Was the *Shadow Man* a servant of the darkness sent to punish him, to *turn* him? Had Mortem been afflicted by the same torment, or was the *Shadow Man* his to command, the first of many things to be imprinted? Had that been why Mortem had turned to its power – to escape it? Had Alexis's psychosis, and all the pain and suffering that had resulted from it, been due to the dark power he had inherited?

Was it one and the same? Or perhaps its very existence had corrupted his mind past the point of sanity and reality?

The questions swirled around him, drowning him in the weight of their implications. In the very centre of the whirlpool of blackness was the *Demon*. At its command, Alexis was forced to experience the worst hallucinations that his fractured mind could torture him with.

His parents abandoning him, telling him that he wasn't their son. Telling him they had never loved him, that he was a charity case, that he was unlovable and unsavable. Jason proclaiming that he had no brother. Caeli, Blaise and Demi moving on without him with not so much as an afterthought. The sound of Demi's laugh as she ridiculed him. Her eyes no longer filled with affection when she looked at him. The disappointment in Incantus's voice as he blamed Alexis for their failure, for their deaths.

No more sunsets. No more light.

The last thing Alexis heard was the *Shadow Man*. It whispered into his ear, as real as it had been all those years ago. '*Let go.*'

Alexis squeezed his eyes shut. He tried to remember what was real. What wasn't just a projection of the darkness, of his fears.

Breaking though the black cloud like a star in the night came the memory of his friends' faces before him. The lightness that surrounded them. The love and hope and vitality. That was what was real. What was genuine. Not a hallucination or a delusion, but something tangible.

Alexis's love for them and their love for him thrummed through him, making the amulet on his chest and Water Gem on his staff burst with light like they never had before. Alexis pulled on the Gem's power and leaped up into the sky on a stream of water, rising to meet the vacant, hollow face of the *Demon*. With the staff shaking in his hands, barely able to withstand all its energy, he hurled everything that he could muster.

Alexis hadn't come all this way to fall victim to the enemy in his head once again. He simply wouldn't allow it.

A torrent of pure blue power shot from the Water Gem, exploding against the *Demon* and casting it off of its feet, taking with it the darkness of his hallucinations. The *Demon* crashed, causing a giant quake, crushing all that stood beneath.

Alexis was barely able to catch himself as he landed back on the ground. As he drew to his feet, booming flashes of red, grey and green quickly followed, lighting up the sky. The ground shook three more times as the *Demons* fell, skyscrapers blown down from the impact.

Alexis tore his gaze from his motionless *Demon* to survey the battlefield. *Where the hell are Incantus and Serena?* He could see no sign of them anywhere. Incantus would be losing his power now that the eclipse had begun and would be utterly powerless during the minutes of totality. He would have to remain close by Stonehenge for then. But why had he not come once the *Demons* appeared?

Unless he was unable to.

Maybe Incantus needed rescuing more than Alexis did.

The thought was snatched away the moment Alexis's *Demon* jerked up. Darkness gathered around it as it rose to its feet, revitalised with each passing minute as the sky grew darker.

Alexis cursed under his breath. Should Mortem come now, he could walk freely into Stonehenge with the Children of the Elements otherwise preoccupied and nothing would stand in his way. Alexis didn't know how Mortem had been powerful enough to construct such creatures of destruction, but he must be here somewhere, recovering his strength to charge Stonehenge when the time was right.

The *Demon* raised its hands and clouds of vicious shadow burst from it. It appeared that Mortem had bestowed his gift, or curse, of the power of darkness upon the *Demon*. *That's made this slightly more interesting*, Alexis considered.

He barely raised his staff in time to meet the onslaught. The two forces collided with an ear-splitting eruption that almost threw Alexis off his feet. He cried out as blades of shadow cut through his shield of ice and water, tearing through his Haven suit and slicing at his sides.

Alexis roared in pain as a dagger slipped through and sliced his forearm, almost forcing him to drop his staff. He gritted his teeth and splayed his other hand. His frozen dome-shield rocketed forward, striking the *Demon* in its mid-section and forcing it to double over.

Alexis wasted no time. He sprang into the sky, using the water vapour to support him as he grew great knives of ice from his clenched fist and swiped at the *Demon*'s neck. Instead of blood, wisps of darkness bled out, dispersing into the air like the fumes from a volcano.

The *Demon* thrust a mighty fist down upon Alexis just as he was about to stab his staff into the place where its heart would be if it were human. The blow was unlike anything that Alexis had ever felt before. Every muscle and bone throbbed with pain so intensely that he didn't even register his body slamming into the ground.

He couldn't remember how to breathe; he couldn't think straight. Had he not been in his Omni state or wearing the Haven suit, he would've died twice over already.

Alexis thought his battle against the Water Serpent had been deadly, but the Creature of his element was nothing more than a sea snake in comparison.

As the *Demon* stepped towards his battered body, Alexis used whatever strength he could muster to swing down the tip of his staff at its feet. Ragged stalagmites of ice burst from the Gem, burying deep into its ankle. A wave of darkness streamed from the wound as it stumbled back.

Spurred into action, Alexis manipulated a stream of water and whipped it around the *Demon*'s leg. With a cry, Alexis yanked it to the side, forcing the great shadow to be swept off its feet entirely. Pulling himself into a squat, Alexis sprang into the air. He raised his staff and brought it down in the centre of the *Demon*'s chest.

An omnidirectional wave of sapphire energy erupted from the Gem with a force so great that Alexis was hurled back from the blast.

Blackness consumed his vision, serrated with the futile splashes of the water's blue. It wasn't nearly as unpleasant as the sight that lay before his open eyes. Alexis considered keeping them shut. He would not see his worthless attempts at survival if he kept them closed. He would not see his death coming if he never looked.

There would be only the moments before, and the infinite moments after. To rest for ever seemed so much more forgiving.

Something cold and hard, something made of stone, would not let him fade away so easily. Oxygen was a distant memory at this point, but Alexis still fought for it to enter his lungs, even if his chest hadn't the strength to rise and fall. He cracked open his sore eyes and saw before him a small winged gargoyle. The stone creature was using its wings to shuffle Alexis's body awake and force him up. Alexis let it take his weight and push him into a seated position.

It peered at him knowingly. Alexis studied its face as though it would reveal who had conjured it, but nothing, not the spout of its nose that channelled rain away from buildings nor the vacancy of its eyes would help him know.

The gargoyle gave Alexis a parting huff from its wolfish mouth and took to the air towards the rousing *Demon*. With short stone daggers, the gargoyle stabbed repeatedly at its featureless face, but it served as no more of an annoyance or threat than a gnat, and was soon squatted as easily as one once the great *Demon* caught it in its fist, reducing its body to rubble and dust.

Out of luck, out of options, Alexis held his amulet in his bloodied, trembling hand, staring at the engraving of the water droplet within.

'Come on, help me out,' he pleaded, shaking the ancient stone, hoping that the Woman of the Water hadn't abandoned him. Not after visiting him in his dream, saving him from his nightmare. Not after helping spur the idea that he was yet to implement; the trap he had developed for Mortem upon his eventual attempt to enter Stonehenge. 'Please,' he said once more.

He let his amulet thud back against his chest as he gripped the staff with two hands. As the radiance of the Water Gem illuminated his face, he stared into the swirling coloured stone that he and his friends had so perilously ventured out to retrieve on a quest that now seemed so futile, so pointless.

What other secrets lay hidden beneath the surface of its powers? What else were they left to discover about the elements that had created this world and all else? Without realising, without even being consciously aware of what he was doing, Alexis reached forth and placed his hand atop the glowing stone.

Before he could stop himself, he tightened his grip around the Water Gem.

And crushed it in his palms.

As swiftly as he had succumbed to it, Alexis emerged from the trance. Sea-blue dust seeped through his fingers, the gleaming colour already diminishing.

A rageful scream escaped his lips as he condemned himself

for allowing Mortem or Akili Pierce or the *Shadow Man* to have entered his mind. Without his full powers, he had no hope. How could he have let someone drive him to an act of suicide without even realising? As he searched the scene around him, clinging on to his lifeless staff, he saw the *Demon* career towards him.

It had stopped in its tracks. Although it displayed no emotions and had no face, Alexis couldn't help but feel as though it was just as confused as he was.

He looked down and saw why.

The ashes of the Water Gem had begun to swirl around Alexis's body. They lapped around him like the current of a whirlpool, encasing him in a glowing blue vortex that accelerated with every circuit and slowly began to bleed into his body.

Alexis rose into the air, driven by the rivulets of energy. Painlessly, he felt his body transform into something . . . else.

The Gem's fragments seeped into his skin and ignited his amulet. His limbs grew longer, thicker, and his skin hardened to an ice that was hard as diamonds. In a final explosion of dazzling blue light, the *Demon* was sent hurtling away, and Alexis opened his eyes to see the extent of the Water Gem's hidden abilities.

Alexis thought he had been lifted hundreds of feet into the sky, but he hadn't – he had *grown*. Where the muscles and organs of his body should have been now coursed crystalline water; and instead of skin, his body was coated in a glimmering sheen of ice.

Now he was the ocean. He *was* the Water Gem.

Alexis stared in utter disbelief at his own transformation. He cradled his amulet, which had grown in size with him. The ancient stone moved like washing rivers, waves crashing over each other with every pulse. He was sure that somewhere deep within, looking back at him, was the Woman of the Water. And she was smiling.

Alexis wasn't the only one who had been turned from Elemental to some kind of majestic, cosmic angel. The Women of the Elements had answered all of their calls when they'd needed them most.

Blaise's body burned like a towering inferno, great flames of orange and red spitting from his arms, burning wisps of black ash billowing from the edges of his silhouette. The centre of his body burned the hottest violet, just like the Fire Phoenix had, coursing down his limbs in rolling waves that seared for ever.

To the south-east, Caeli's body had transformed into a ferocious tornado, gusts of winds wrapping around the space where her limbs had once been. She moved freely in the sky, her hair a mass of greyish torrents that flowed like smoke in the wind. The stormy currents that made up her body were spinning around with the density and wildness of a raging tempest, blowing away any and all that dared approach her.

And lastly, there was Demi. Tree roots and green vines twisted around her earth-darkened arms and legs like the tendons and sinew of muscle. A flurry of lush green leaves coated the skin of her face, the contours and curves of her bone structure displayed in the wildness of the nature that had grown. Lianas and woody vines draped over her head like hair, running down freely in loose curls.

This was the true extent of the Elemental Gems' power, Alexis realised. *This was what it was to be Omni: to be all present, all powerful. No longer will it be an onslaught. It will be a fight – a fair fight.*

Seventy per cent of the Earth's surface was water. Sixty per cent of the human body. Seventy five per cent of the brain. In this state, should Alexis desire, he could control the world and everyone in it.

But there was only one person Alexis wanted to control, and he was pulling the strings of the creature of darkness before him.

When the *Demons* took to their feet to face the Children of the Elements, Alexis could have sworn they looked scared.

'Come on then,' Alexis sneered, beckoning the *Demon* to him. 'Let's see if I can make a shadow bleed.'

30
TADHANA

Tadhana (n.) *Filipino origin*
An invisible force that makes things happen
beyond the control of mortals; destiny, fate

Forty-five minutes until totality

Threads of darkness burst from the *Demon* as it stormed at Alexis. He threw his arm to the side, and as he did, the swirling column of water hardened into a huge trident of jagged ice, inspired by the tail of the Creature of the Water. He slashed it down when the *Demon* was within range and marvelled when it sliced through its arm at the elbow seamlessly.

The *Demon* lurched back, cradling its severed limb as poisonous black mist bled from it, corroding the battlefield below. Alexis made haste and splayed his hands. A great beam of water flooded from him, but the *Demon* erected a wall of darkness just in time to shield itself.

Alexis threw himself into the *Demon* just as its barrier dissipated. The two giants grappled for dominance until they both fell to the ground with a resounding crash. The *Demon* was the first to get up. It slammed a fist into Alexis's back, jolting the breath from his lungs. As he tried to roll away, the *Demon*'s heel swung down, connecting with the side of his face. And then, with Alexis too disorientated to move or to raise a hand to defend himself, the *Demon*'s arm sharpened into a blade.

Alexis gasped, but that was all he could do before the blade buried itself deep into the space between his shoulder and his chest.

Alexis screamed, but the shadows stole his voice.

Swathes of pain exploded across his chest and rippled down his arm. Each came more violent than the last, more debilitating.

The *Demon* lowered his face close to Alexis's to watch his agony as it twisted the blade.

Instead of excruciating pain, Alexis felt only rage.

This prick.

His rage erupted from him in an almighty explosion of royal-blue power.

The *Demon* was catapulted hundreds of metres into the air, its body lacerated with a thousand stabs of ice. Alexis gritted his teeth and rose to his feet, blinking away tears that came as streams. The exhaustion from using so much power was taking its toll. He didn't know how this foreign magic operated, the rules and conditions of its use, but something deep within told him that his authority over it would not hold for ever. He felt his strength draining, mirrored by the faltering of the tide of water that made up his body, its colour fading and velocity slowing. His amulet pulsed, its power flickering in warning that it wouldn't last much longer.

He had to end this now.

The *Demon* was crashing back to the ground. Floods of shadow burst from its daggered arm and beat down towards

Alexis. He swung both arms up to meet it with a knee-shuddering stream of water. The two substances poured into each other, black and blue energy cascading from the sky where they met, but nothing could slow the *Demon*'s descent as it drew closer to Alexis by the second. Couldn't be more than five seconds left.

Alexis convulsed under the pressure, his entire body reverberating as he grasped on to his godlike, angelic form. Four.

He had to hold on. He had to keep to his feet. He had to keep his focus, even when his whole vision was filling with blackness. Three.

How could he redirect the *Demon*? How could he stop the unstoppable force with which it fell? Two.

Unless he didn't. Why wait for the darkness to come to him? He would meet it head on and face the shadows as he always had. One.

Alexis leaped into the air, cutting through the stream of blackness that bathed him. As he soared upwards, he fashioned an icy blade from his own arm, a vicious shard in place of his hand. His shoulder screamed in agony with every movement, but he would feel its pain later.

With everything he had, Alexis blindly swung his arm in a wide arc above his head. He didn't need to look up to know it had cut through the space that the *Demon*'s head now filled – straight through.

The stream of darkness abruptly ended. Gravity pulled them both to the ground, but once the dust had settled, only one of them was left standing – holding the head of the other in his hand.

Behind him, the *Demon* sank to its knees, blackness pouring from the place where its head should be like fumes from an extinguished fire. Almost in slow motion, the decapitated *Demon*'s body slumped to the side and stirred no longer.

Alexis took one last look at its featureless head still in his grasp. He raised it to eye level to inspect, but the dead shadow revealed nothing, not even in death.

'I guess shadows can bleed,' he said. He then spat at its face and tossed it away, hoping that all it represented would be discarded with it.

No longer able to ignore the unbearable exertion that had racked his body, Alexis collapsed to a heap. He felt as though he was drowning internally. The water that made up his angelic form was losing its current and its glow. The amulet hanging from his neck was gently calling the borrowed power home.

Muscle and bone replaced water and ice. Messy waves of dark hair threaded through his scalp, and even the cool feel of his Haven suit returned to dress his human frame. Despite having shrunk back to normal size, Alexis felt his chest expand as he drew a long, deep breath, the sensation familiar and human – but a stab of pain forbade him from fully filling his lungs.

Alexis peered down to see blood ebbing from the wound in his shoulder where the *Demon* had impaled him. Wisps of darkness corroded the flesh around it, but Alexis knew somehow that the infection would not spread the way it had with Demi when Sinner had shot her. He was already poisoned – there was nothing pure to taint.

A flash of aquamarine light stirred him as he was washing away the blood and darkness with a delicate shower. The essence of the water was reforming the ancient Gem's shape until it glinted atop the golden staff once again as though it had never been crushed.

The others, Alexis suddenly remembered, forcing himself to sit up even though his head was spinning dangerously. *How are the others?*

He needn't have worried.

Blaise was incinerating his *Demon*, hurling streams of scorching lava at it even as it lay motionless on the ground. It appeared as though Demi's *Demon* had long been dealt with, even before Alexis's. Bulging tree roots and vines had ripped free from the earth to claim their victim. Her *Demon* was ensnared within a thousand interlaced constraints, unable to move as Demi repeatedly clubbed its head. Finally, through the towering rocks of Stonehenge, Alexis was able to make out the violent torrents of wind that swirled around Caeli. Somewhere in the eye of the storm, brought to its knees by the sheer force of the gales, was her *Demon*.

The three of them looked exhausted and close to collapse, but Alexis was sure they would take their *Demons* down before long.

He gradually rose to his feet. *Where's Incantus? Why hasn't he come to us?* He gazed out across the fields of death and decay. The battleground had mostly been cleared due to the clash between the Children of the Elements and the *Demons*, either devastated by their powers or fleeing while there was still time, with Ziya bringing hundreds of Elementals down into the Haven within seconds for safe treatment.

The battlefield before Alexis's section lay quiet for the first time all day, cold and desolate, for the time being at least. While Nekro, Shadowless and Hybrids still battled those

Elementals that remained, there was something towards the back of the Dark Army that drew his attention.

Hundreds of metres over the landscape he saw flashes of light, white and golden light, and with each passing moment, the flashes grew fainter and more sparse.

The moon had crept over the sun slowly since the *Demons* had been conjured. It now obscured almost half of its light. How many minutes remained until totality began? What if Incantus wasn't back by then? Or worse, Mortem was.

As much as they had accomplished that day, feats beyond their wildest dreams and displays of power greater than anyone could have expected, Alexis was no fool. He knew they stood no chance against Mortem, even when combined. Not without Incantus.

Alexis had to do something to help him. His legs were moving before his mind had caught up. Already, he had bent down to retrieve his glowing staff and was staggering across the battlefield as quickly as he could. Some part of him was almost glad each time a Nekro or Hybrid or Shadowless braved him. It was something to distract him from the agonising pain of his shoulder. Even with the Water Gem in his grasp, the wound was taking far too long to heal.

Soon enough, he could make out Incantus's aura in the distance. He was bent over, but the sweat in Alexis's stinging eyes was making it hard to decipher any other detail.

Suddenly, the ground jolted beneath Alexis, almost forcing him off his unsteady feet. Great booming rumbles shook through the earth.

Alexis turned to see his *Demon*, the *Demon* he had slain and decapitated, now fully reformed. The eclipse was regenerating its body as it tore towards him. Alexis knew he couldn't withstand another assault, but nonetheless, he raised his staff before him as the giant shadow blocked out the remaining slivers of daylight.

But then it passed right by him.

The *Demon* bounded over him, paying him no more attention than it did any other soldier or creature on the battlefield. As Alexis stared after it, watching it flee from Stonehenge, he felt the ground tremor as the other three *Demons* hammered past him in quick succession.

For a painfully brief moment, Alexis wondered if his friends had chased them away, for it appeared as though they too had returned to their normal forms and were no longer visible in the sky. He almost felt a glimmer of hope in the pit of his empty stomach.

That sensation soon faded, as, Alexis realised with a jolt, had another. The far stronger sensation that had been coursing through his body, indiscriminate from the flow of his blood, ever since he had stepped into Stonehenge. His power. It had gone.

His power was gone.

Not gone. *Taken*.

Alexis was thrown to the ground. Something hard and sharp was digging into his back. His hands were wrenched behind him and a heavy set of shackles now chained his wrists together.

Alexis swore as he writhed on the ground. He tried to see the person who had attacked him.

'You should've killed me when you had the chance.'

Cold fury burned through Alexis's body at the recognition of who had spoken.

'There's still time,' Alexis seethed through gritted teeth.

Ezra Alastor sniggered humourlessly and took his knee off Alexis's back. 'Not without your powers, there isn't.'

Alexis didn't give Ezra the satisfaction of scrambling to his feet. He took his time turning over to inspect the tall, black-haired young man. Ezra's armour was free from any scratches or dents and not a speck of blood tainted his pale skin.

The cold metal of the shackles burned Alexis's wrists as they leached his powers. He had no idea how every morsel of his power could be nullified in an instant. To silence other Elementals' powers, yes, but *his*? A Child of the Elements? No matter how much he struggled against them, they would neither bend nor break.

Without access to his powers, he only felt the stabbing pain of his shoulder that much stronger. Stars danced tauntingly before his eyes, winking around the lean silhouette of Ezra as he grabbed Alexis by his hair and hauled him to his feet.

Alexis threw his head forward and crushed it against the bridge of Ezra's nose, hoping that if he hadn't broken it the night before, he certainly had this time. What was a little more discomfort when Alexis was already overcome with pain?

Ezra howled and with a whoosh and a glimmer of bronze, he teleported a safe distance away.

Alexis laughed almost deliriously. 'Take these manacles off me and let's have a real fight. You and me, Eczema. Without our powers, if you dare.'

There wasn't even a moment of consideration. Ezra vanished again, but this time, he reappeared right behind Alexis. His body pressed against Alexis's back, and his sword kissed Alexis's throat.

Alexis breathed deeply through his nose, fighting to keep still. He could see his golden staff lying just a few metres away, the Water Gem glowing expectantly at him, almost as though it was asking why he had abandoned its powers. If only he could get to it.

Alexis pressed faintly against Ezra's blade and Ezra practically moved it away from his neck. Had he intentionally done it so that Alexis wouldn't cut himself? Somehow, that infuriated him even more.

Alexis again leaned into the sword. This time, he felt the sharp sting as it sliced into the underside of his jawline. He could feel it wasn't a deep cut, but it was enough to draw blood.

Ezra's body stiffened behind him.

'Do it,' Alexis said, his jaw clenched tight. 'Or do you prefer to keep your sword clean like the coward you are?'

Ezra inhaled, but didn't reply. Then, as if he had suddenly become aware of his surroundings and of how close they were to the Water Gem, Ezra cracked the hilt of his sword against the side of Alexis's head, and everything went quiet.

Oceans of starlight. Fields of blackness.

A universe of nothingness and everything that seemed to last for ever, but also to have never existed at all. Not even for a moment of time.

Alexis wasn't sure how long he had been out, but when he stirred, a new scene lay before him. One so dire that Alexis wanted to close his eyes again and go back to the world between nowhere and somewhere else far away.

This whole time, Alexis had thought Mortem birthed the

Demons to destroy the Children of the Elements. But they were merely a distraction, a secondary objective of the *Demons*' mission.

Darkness was not the death of fire or water, earth or air. Darkness was the death of light. And the *Demons* had been created to destroy the Elemental that wielded it.

That was what Alexis had been brought here to watch. The dying of the light.

Before him, captured at the feet of Mortem, lay Incantus Arcangelo, and surrounding them in a ring stood the four *Demons*, poised to execute.

31
ANAGAPESIS

Anagapesis (n.) *Greek origin*
To no longer feel any affection for someone
you once loved

Fifteen minutes earlier; one hour until totality

Incantus Arcangelo ran his sword deep into the belly of the Shadowless before him, and with his other hand, a ray of bright light burst from his palm and hurled the wailing assailant away.

Piles of corpses surrounded him and Serena Aevum. Mangled, steaming, bleeding corpses.

'This has got to be our highest kill count in a battle so far!' Serena exclaimed between great gasps for air, wiping away the sweat that trickled down her flushed cheeks with the back of her hand. 'I've lost count of how many I've taken down, but I'm certain it's a greater number than yours.'

Of all his comrades over the years, Incantus had to admit, Serena was his favourite to fight beside. Only she could turn survival into a competition.

Incantus opened his mouth to retort, maybe even to boast, which was something he only ever did with her, but the air was punched from his chest by an invisible fist. A plunging coldness swept across his body, stealing not only his breath, but also his immortality and his powers. He didn't need to look to the sky to realise the eclipse had commenced.

'Ian?' Serena's cheerful tone was replaced with one of concern as she watched him stagger, the true number of years he had lived suddenly catching up with him. She placed a firm hand against his back.

A warm glow spread from it, infusing him with enough energy and strength to stand straight. He let it restore him momentarily before moving away, wanting Serena to conserve it for herself.

A haggard gasp then came from Serena's lips. 'Unholy First Borns!'

Incantus followed Serena's gaze to where four giant human shadows were slowly materialising in the distance. They towered over everything around them, leaving destruction in their wake as they encircled Stonehenge.

'The Children –' Incantus gulped – 'they need me.' He couldn't let them fight the *Demons* alone. They were some of the most powerful Elementals of all time, especially in their Omni states, but not even Incantus was confident they could battle the *Demons* and come away unscathed.

What if they think I've abandoned them? He took off, but didn't get far before Serena yanked him back.

Her tired face was one of painful confliction. Greying fiery hair curled at her temples. The deep wrinkles across her forehead and around her mouth were slick with sweat and blood. She looked . . . *scared.* Incantus didn't know if he had ever seen her scared before.

But it wasn't the *Demons* she was scared of. 'Akili . . .' she said faintly. Her eyes flickered towards the crumpled transmission towers barely a few hundred metres away.

It had been something Incantus had always known, how Serena had loved Akili in a different way to how she had loved him or even Teller, but it wasn't something he and Serena had ever really discussed.

'I've already lost Teller,' she said. She was far too stubborn to let her tears fall, but that didn't stop them from welling in her eyes. 'If totality comes and Akili is still imprinted, we may lose him for ever. I-I can't. He's the best person I've ever known.'

And the only person you have ever truly loved, Incantus thought to reply, but decided against.

Instead, he took her hands in his and said, 'In our youth, the five of us made a promise to each other.' Serena tore her eyes from him to blink away tears at the mention of the Quinate. 'We promised that if any one of us was to be imprinted and it came down to ending our life to save another, we should not hesitate to act. Akili has lived a long and full life. The Children . . . they are only children. Akili would want us to save them. Without them, today is lost.'

There was a thunderous noise. Incantus heard it somewhere behind him, and before he spun to see it, he couldn't imagine what the source could be. A dam bursting beneath the weight of a flood or a volcano erupting? A hurricane rolling across the skies or the very earth cracking underfoot?

In a way, it was all of them.

He blinked in disbelief as the Children of the Elements transformed. Power coursed in waves in and around them, morphing them into divine, eternal Elemental beings. They rose as tall as the *Demons*, their bodies made up of fire or water, wind or earth. Like nothing Incantus had ever seen or could have ever anticipated. With abilities he never knew they had.

With a resounding explosion, Incantus and Serena saw the bluish creature that had once been Alexis blast back the *Demon* that stood opposing him, throwing it away from Stonehenge.

'Where the hell did they learn that one?' Serena demanded, slapping Incantus's arm in what looked like equal parts awe and envy.

'Not from me,' Incantus admitted, a flutter of hope rising in this chest, thawing the icy drain on his powers. 'They are so much more than we imagined the Children of the Elements to be. And they are far from needing saving from a couple of old-age pensioners like us.'

Serena grinned. 'Call me old again and I'll be the one that takes you out, Wonder Boy.'

Together, Incantus and Serena turned from Stonehenge and took off back in the direction of the crashed transmission towers. Serena dragged him onwards, supporting him as he felt his powers and energy trickling away, but their pace didn't slow for a single moment.

Eventually, after what felt like hours later, they reached the cusp of the battlefield and found it littered with the bodies of both the dead and dying. At the very edge, just beyond the shattered static pylons, lay the fallen Leaders of the Haven.

'Help me,' Akili Pierce whispered in a ragged exhale. His eyes flickered between the blackness that infected them and the true brown underneath. Wisps of smoke drifted from his charred body, but he was alive, fighting strong against the darkness that desperately attempted to shatter his resistance.

On either side of him, writhing on the ground, were Taranis

and Raeve. Incantus could sense the mental paralysis Akili cast over them to keep them unconscious, but he didn't know how much longer they would stay that way.

These were his Leaders. Leaders who had created the Haven with him and who had provided him with a family again. Incantus's heart ached to see them like this. Serena had already rushed to Akili's side. Incantus dropped to his knees beside them and tentatively searched their faces.

'I'm holding on,' Akili said through gritted teeth, wincing as though daggers were slicing his insides. 'Get one of the kids first.'

'Just stay with us, love,' Serena uttered, cradling his face.

Akili struggled to meet her eyes. 'I'm trying, Sere. Please forgive me for hurting you.'

Serena held him that much tighter. 'You could never hurt me.'

Incantus fought to call his powers back to him, seeking all that hadn't yet been snatched away by the eclipse. His palms lit up with a flickering white glow that illuminated the Leaders' faces and displayed the blackened veins that ran beneath the surface of their skin.

'Will it work, Ian?' Serena asked, studying him anxiously.

Incantus shut his eyes to hold his focus. 'The darkness is so strongly woven into their minds. I can't risk causing what happened to *her* to happen to them.'

Even now, a lifetime later, Incantus could not bring himself to speak her name when talking of her end. An end he had caused.

Nevertheless, Incantus knew better now than he did then. This time, he pulled on the threads of darkness that had been infused into Raeve with surgical delicacy, careful to not sever the cords that were tethered to her mind and her soul. It was like clipping an aneurysm, only there were hundreds of them scattered all across her aura and they shifted with each heartbeat. If he worked too quickly, then the thread would snap and cause even greater damage; but too slowly, and it would give the darkness time to work its way deeper into her mind.

The darkness sought to destroy its host one way or another. Incantus couldn't, *wouldn't*, let it.

But just as he began to feel his cleansing take effect, that the darkness within her was withering away, a wave of shadow roared into the side of him and Serena. They flew through the air and crashed heavily onto the ground in a tangled heap.

Incantus's eyes adjusted to see Mortem standing over the fallen Leaders, robes of darkness sweeping from him. Akili's resistance grew futile until his eyes once again were coated in an opaque black. Alongside Raeve and Taranis, Akili rose to stand guard before Mortem, whose eyes twinkled in the half-light.

Serena got to her feet quicker than Incantus. Her hands ignited with a golden burst of energy, but before she could throw her powers, streaks of electricity, purple magic and telepathic pain beat into her chest.

She let out a guttural scream, but somehow managed to stay standing. Even as they intensified their attack, three of the strongest Elementals of their age, Serena Aevum did not fall. It was only when Mortem sent a great surge of shadow that she finally succumbed and fell to the ground in silent anguish.

Incantus crawled towards Serena's smouldering, broken body. He placed his hands on her and pulled on his own fading life force to restore her. A dagger of darkness came flying at him, forcing him to rear back and defend himself before he could finish reviving her.

Mortem was taunting him, waiting to engage him in battle. He smiled handsomely, but Incantus no longer felt any love or affection for him. He felt only anger and a sad sense of injustice. He dragged himself to his feet, letting Serena's shivering hand fall from his own.

The two Arcangelo brothers eyed one another as they circled each other like wolves, with nothing but their powers at their disposal.

'Mother always said that birth and death are the gates that border all life,' Mortem recalled. He gestured for the Leaders to give them space. 'Today will no longer mark only the day of your birth, but the day of your death too.'

'You had to wait until I was almost powerless to take me on,' Incantus sneered, his hands slowly flickering alight. 'You were always living in my shadow and now you seek to steal that too. I loathe you no more than I pity you.'

Mortem's smiled twisted into something much darker. 'I do not want your shadow.' Long tendrils of darkness seeped out from beneath his plated armour. 'I want your corpse at my feet. I have taken everything from you,' he jeered. 'Your love. Your friends. Your family. Just as I promised.'

'There is still one thing you are yet to take,' Incantus replied, narrowing his eyes in challenge. 'Me.'

Mortem twisted his hand sharply, sending a stream of darkness snaking towards Incantus. It blew up in size and reared up in front of him, viper-like. It bared venomous fangs and spat black acid, which Incantus narrowly dodged.

Incantus brought his hands together to form a sharpened white blade. He tore through the middle of the apparition, reducing it to wisps that dissipated in the air like ash. Incantus flung himself at Mortem, throwing him to the ground. As Incantus rose up to stab him with his blade, Mortem unleashed a powerful silhouette of shadow from his body that hauled Incantus off his feet.

Again, the two brothers got up, wiping away the blood that smeared their faces. Mortem shed the black cloak from his shoulders. The robes fell off him, revealing his true muscular frame. He was getting stronger with each passing minute, his eyes gazing hungrily, waiting for the moment he could put an end to it all.

'They all look up to you like you are some sort of angel,' Mortem seethed, bitterness besieging his voice as he licked blood from his lips. 'They don't know you like I do. The things you've done. You are just as dark as me, brother. I wonder what your friends and students would think if they knew the truth of your secrets. What would *Alexis* think?'

The name was poison in his mouth.

Incantus roared in anger, streams of light bursting from his hands and tearing into Mortem.

'How dare you liken me to you?' Incantus bellowed, hauling blasts of starlight at Mortem, forcing him to retreat. 'How dare you speak of what you made me do? How dare you speak of the son you abandoned?'

A tidal wave of darkness spewed from Mortem in retaliation, overpowering Incantus's assault. The waves encircled him like a whirlpool. Even as Incantus shot desperate rays of light against the swirling blackness, it would not break.

And then the tide turned and the spinning shadows came crashing down. They broke against Incantus's body and spat him out until he crumpled on the ground. He tried to get up, but a boot whirred across his vision before it connected with the side of his face.

Incantus sprawled on his back, feeling nothing but a numb pain and an annoying loud ringing in his ear. He could only watch as Mortem raised a sword of darkness over him and plunged it down.

There was a flurry of white. It lunged against Mortem's hand, sinking in sharp teeth. Mortem came unbalanced, pulled by the creature as his sword disintegrated mere inches from impaling Incantus.

There was only one creature that would stand between Incantus and a blade.

Mortem roared in pain, but Gibbous did not let go, growling fiercely as he yanked Mortem further from Incantus. The dire wolf trembled with fear, but he held his ground and gnashed relentlessly at Mortem. Gibbous sank low, steadying himself for barely a moment before he pounced again.

But that moment was all Mortem needed.

A long blade of darkness blinked into Mortem's uninjured hand. As Gibbous dived through the air, Mortem snuck the blade under and slashed it in a great arc.

The knife cut deep across Gibbous's belly.

A whimpering howl escaped from the dire wolf's lips as he landed, staggering for a moment before collapsing in anguish, blood gushing freely from the wound, splashing his coat red. He tried to back away as Mortem advanced, wincing with every movement, but his body was too weak. He was left helpless on the ground, waiting until Mortem finally landed the finishing blow.

A thousand lifetimes of pain coursed through Incantus, but that could not compare to the ache in his chest as he crawled towards Gibbous, his most loyal companion. Mortem glanced over his shoulder and threw back a dozen chains of darkness to ensnare him. Even in this state, Incantus ripped through each restraint with his bare hands, but they both knew he would not reach Gibbous in time.

Mortem turned back, his sword glinting in the fading sunlight as he raised it over Gibbous, ready to swing down for the execution.

Until another animal came to stand in his way.

His own. Crescent.

The black wolf trembled as it stood over his injured brother, his body a barrier between them. Gibbous was nudging the black wolf away with his nose, but Crescent didn't move an inch, his eyes trained on Mortem's, lips pulling back to utter a low, warning growl.

'You stupid dog.' Mortem tutted as he shook his head. He had not lowered his sword. 'Remember which hand feeds you.'

Crescent howled, and the sound was as if he was shredding the muzzle of fear that had kept him enslaved for a lifetime of servitude. He leaped into the air in an ultimate act of disobedience, the claws of his front paws rushing to tear at the face of the person that had showed him less compassion in decades than Incantus had in the last few hours.

But not even the black dire wolf was quick enough, not with the eclipse in Mortem's favour.

Mortem sank his blade deep into Crescent's chest without hesitation, without remorse.

Crescent slumped over Mortem's shoulder, and Incantus watched helplessly as the life left his eyes. Mortem threw his body aside and he rolled to a stop inches before Gibbous, his eyes open but unseeing, his lips parted but chest unmoving. Gibbous nuzzled his brother's face and pressed the side of his head against his for warmth as they would when they were pups: a time before Ian had become Incantus and Nero had become Mortem.

With the partially eclipsed sun now just a crescent in the sky, the black wolf released his last breath, and Gibbous let out a single, weak howl to signal the end of the battle before totality had even begun.

A series of great tremors shook the earth, but Incantus barely felt them as he tore through the last of the shadow chains. Mortem hadn't delivered a killing blow to Gibbous, but if Incantus didn't heal him soon, he may very well die of blood loss or perhaps heartache. Incantus was forced to stop beside Serena, however, when the sky drew darker still. Something other than the moon was obscuring the last of the sunlight.

The tremors had come from the *Demons*. Now, all four of them stood in a circle surrounding him, mammoths to a man.

Mortem sneered as he approached them, evaporating the sword of darkness he had formed to kill Crescent, no longer concerned that Gibbous would pose any threat. The Leaders stood motionless beside him, but with a gesture of his hand, they began to advance towards Stonehenge.

Incantus tried to stop them from leaving, but a translucent

dome of darkness fell over him and Serena, sealing them within. It burned his hands as he tried to break through. He had little more strength than an old man now, and every small move caused his tired body to ache.

'Your benevolence really is boring, Ian,' Mortem said, finally addressing them as he walked around the dome. 'It makes you predictable. You had to protect your precious Children by keeping them in Stonehenge, so I sent the *Demons* after them. You had to save the Leaders, so I make them the perfect bait to trap you.' He paused as something caught his attention.

Incantus followed Mortem's gaze to the faint flash of bronze light. Ezra Alastor stepped out from the portal, but he was not alone.

Mortem grinned. 'Speak of the devil.'

Alexis Michaels slumped to the ground before Ezra. He was bruised and battered, groaning slightly in pain. A fresh wound bled freely from his jaw, but what concerned Incantus more than anything was that his entire torso was soaked red from a much deeper injury to his right shoulder.

Ezra failed to look at his old mentor, not even as he threw down the golden staff that housed the Water Gem and took a cautious step back.

Incantus could barely tell if Alexis was conscious, for his amulet hung dull from his neck. But then Alexis stirred and struggled to his knees with his hands tied behind him. Incantus could see the change in his expression as he processed all that he saw.

Two wolves that lay silent, Gibbous's white coat splashed crimson, his head lowered over the unmoving body of his brother, whimpering quietly. Incantus and Serena trapped within a dome of darkness, the *Demons* standing like mountains around them, ready to obliterate.

Incantus's gaze met his nephew's. There was too much to say, and not nearly enough time to say it.

'You had your time in the light,' said Mortem, addressing his brother and his son. 'Now it is time for the Dark Age.'

32

SIB NCAIM

Sib ncaim (v.) *Hmong origin*

To part ways and never meet again; a separation of two persons or things after a brief encounter

Twenty minutes until totality

Alexis grunted insolently as Ezra retightened the shackles that bound his wrists. 'You traitorous prick.'

He stared at Incantus and Serena captured before him, equally as helpless. Mortem was circling the dome that entrapped them, admiring his *Demons* of shadows while he taunted Incantus.

'Look what you've done,' Alexis muttered through gritted teeth, his eyes prickling at the sound of Gibbous's whimpering, almost bringing him to tears. 'Was it all worth it?'

'Shut your mouth, Alexis,' Ezra hissed.

'Make me, Eczema.'

Ezra cracked an elbow to Alexis's jaw, rocking his head to the side. Alexis spat blood, and maybe a tooth. A wiser man might've conserved his energy and remained silent to avoid further conflict, but Alexis was unable to bite his tongue. He didn't think it worthwhile to spend his last few moments pleading. He would rather spend it fighting in whatever way he could.

'What did he promise you? What was enough to condemn us all? To betray the Leaders who taught you and turn in the man who gave you a home? Was it respect? Or power?' Alexis tried to crane his head to look back at Ezra, who had fallen silent, keeping close to Alexis's back. 'How can you look at yourself in the mirror and see that you're as responsible for our deaths as he is?'

Ezra yanked Alexis by the shackles and jostled him, almost making him fall over. He leaned in, his breath hot by Alexis's ear, making him flinch. 'How did you expect to ever survive against him? Even if I'd wanted to come back, I couldn't have. He would never let me leave, and Incantus wouldn't take me back after what happened to Sagen.'

'Then why did you come to the Haven and warn me not to trust the High Order?'

Ezra's eyes grew wide as he glanced at Mortem. He was still speaking to Incantus and Serena, but the fear that struck Ezra at the prospect of Mortem overhearing what Alexis had said couldn't be masked.

Ezra's response was barely a whisper. 'It was side with the champion or die with the victims.'

Alexis was close now. He could see Ezra teetering on the brink of action. Of redemption. What else could Alexis say to encourage him, to free him so that he could grab his staff and save Incantus and Serena?

Alexis recalled what Ziya had told him about Ezra after they first met.

'Then you are no different to the mindless Nekro that killed your parents.'

Ezra drew a sharp breath as if he had been hit by a physical blow. He looked at Alexis incredulously. It was bold, and perhaps foolish for Alexis to have said such a thing, but Alexis held his stare, refusing to take it back.

Have I ruined my chance of escape? Has my audacity cost us all our lives?

'Silence the prisoner,' came a bark from Mortem. He glared at them from a distance, eyes squinted in mild irritation.

Ezra slammed the hilt of his blade against Alexis's burned shoulder. Alexis would have screamed from the pain, but he didn't want to give either Mortem or Ezra the satisfaction.

'Do you recognise the power of the shackles?' Mortem asked loudly, directing his question to Serena Aevum. 'They've inhibited the powers of one of the *Children of the Elements*. How astonishing. And what about my *Demons*? She spent *years* working on these, while stripping my prisoners' powers from them and amplifying mine – not that she had much of a choice.'

There was only one person Mortem could be talking about. Serena's daughter – Aadya Parashakti. *Ziya's mother.* She was still alive? All this time.

Does Ziya know? Alexis wondered when Serena had learned of this. He recalled how he had seen Serena become enraged at Mortem at the start of the battle after she had tended to Akili – so much so that she had forced Mortem to retreat. Death trembled in the face of a mother's rage, it appeared. Although now that rage seemed to have crumpled into despair.

Serena slumped against Incantus's heaving shoulder and did not reply. Alexis observed Incantus console her as he regarded the eclipse. Shadow bands began to undulate across the darkened battlefield in the final few minutes of daylight, the sun now almost completely obscured.

As they all looked to the sky, Alexis felt the touch of a cold, slick hand against his own. It was followed by a faint clicking noise that came from his shackles. He tried not to draw attention to himself as he wriggled his fingers behind his back to feel that the bindings had been loosened somewhat.

Ezra? Did he just . . . ?

Alexis strained to peer back at him, but the black-haired Elemental didn't catch his eye. He was looking intently at Mortem, beads of sweat running from his temples and dripping from his jawline.

'Ezra,' called Mortem. Alexis felt him jolt behind him. 'Portal us all closer to Stonehenge. I want them to see us walking towards it in their final moments, knowing that they have failed.'

A huge bronze portal split the sky above them. The flat circular panel stretched wide to encompass them all, including the four *Demons*. The portal aperture flew down to swallow them and it spat them out in the exact same arrangement much closer to the ancient ringed stone structure.

Nekro, Hybrids and the remainder of the Shadowless were charging all around them towards Stonehenge. From where they were, Alexis could see his friends desperately fighting to protect the perimeter against the imprinted Leaders, their defensive structures just about withstanding.

Demi against Akili; Blaise against Raeve; Caeli against Taranis.

Alexis's heart yearned for them. He wished he had told them that he had left, seeing how they now had to work overtime to cover his section too. They were holding their own against the Leaders with their full powers at their disposal, but he feared they wouldn't last much longer.

Demi and the others noticed the sudden reappearance of the *Demons* much closer, of a captured Alexis and Incantus and Serena, but Stonehenge was too swarmed by enemies for them to leave their posts to come to their aid.

Ezra stumbled from Alexis's side, looking expectantly at Mortem for praise for his actions. But Mortem didn't move so much as an inch in his direction, paying him no more consideration than he would any other member of his army.

Ezra turned to retreat, his head lowered in defeat.

Until a portal appeared.

It bloomed into existence at Ezra's feet, engulfing his left leg up to his knee. Had it been bronze, Alexis would've paid it no attention, for it was far more convenient to portal than to walk. But it wasn't bronze.

The portal was blood-red.

Ezra noticed a moment later that his leg had passed the threshold of the portal, but he wasn't fast enough to pull it out. His eyebrows shot up, his mouth opening to shout. And then the portal abruptly winked closed, and as it did, Ezra's leg was severed with it.

His scream finally came as he collapsed into a puddle of his own gushing blood. Despite the gruesomeness of it all, Alexis smiled to himself.

She definitely knows how to make an entrance.

A tall red portal manifested in the middle of them all and out from it stepped Valentina, her jian swords drawn from the underside of her sleeves, both pointed at Mortem.

'You,' Mortem seethed at her.

Daggers of shadow grew from his body and he thrust them at her in the blink of an eye. A portal opened before Valentina, which swallowed the daggers and spat them straight back out at him. While he was distracted defending himself from his own assault, Valentina took off in a sprint towards him, her blades ready to slash at his body. Mortem dived under them, only marginally quicker than her.

Mortem wielded his scythe of shadow. Tendrils of darkness simultaneously trailed out from behind him as he and Valentina duelled, moving to strike her down. She just about sliced through them in time.

As Valentina took a moment to catch her breath, Mortem reinforced the dome of shadows that encased Incantus and Serena with a discarded wave of his hand. Alexis watched as the four towering *Demons* loomed over the dome, pressing against its surface with their giant hands, crushing it to the ground.

Incantus and Serena instantly shot to their feet to meet the surface, their hands illuminated white and gold to hold it at bay. All the while, Alexis struggled to free himself from the shackles, but they were still too tight and his powers were still out of reach. As was his staff carrying the Water Gem – although not by much. It lay only a few feet away. He fell to his front and crawled to it as fast as he could.

Valentina again lurched into battle. Mortem was far more experienced, but her powers went a long way to providing her with the element of unpredictability. She created a small red portal in front of her blades, and when she stabbed into it, they sliced through Mortem's back from the partnered portal behind him.

'Say his name,' she seethed, disappearing seconds before

Mortem's curved blade would've carved her in half. 'He was a good man. Innocent. Say. His. Name!'

'I don't bother to learn the names of all the people I slay,' Mortem retorted, advancing on her. 'Least of all a pathetic old mortal, whom history will discard as easily as I did.'

Valentina flung herself at Mortem, diving beneath his scythe. With one sword, she sliced at his chest, and with the other, she stabbed at his side, burying its blade several inches deep.

'His name was *Valentino*,' she spat, her free sword now swinging towards his head.

'Enough!' Mortem screamed.

An omnidirectional wave of black erupted from him. It collided against Valentina's thin frame and sent her somersaulting through the air, pulling her blades from Mortem's flank, until she struck the ground hard. When Mortem reached her, he snapped the blades of her jian swords at her wrists and dragged her to her feet by the throat.

Valentina frantically tried to writhe free, but Alexis saw the muscles of Mortem's forearms flex as he tightened his chokehold. Already, the stab wound in Mortem's side and his various other injuries had started to close over, the skin stitching together with threads of shadow, his healing accelerated by the eclipse.

'Alexis . . .' a breathless voice gasped, wrenching Alexis's gaze from the unfolding scene. 'Help me.'

Ezra lay in a pool of blood, his armour now far from pristine.

With the amount of blood he had lost, his face was paler than ever. He wouldn't last for much longer.

Alexis heard Valentina's desperate gasps for air somewhere behind him.

He made up his mind on which portaller he would try to save. He ignored Ezra's cries and continued crawling towards his staff to help Valentina.

A series of roars exploded, so great, so primal that Alexis cowered on the ground as it shook him to his core. It had come from the *Demons*. They were still slamming down against the dome that trapped Incantus and Serena.

The two elder Elementals were on their knees, their faces scrunched in exhaustion. Serena's energy and what remained of Incantus's powers were barely shielding them, but they couldn't hold out for ever. The total eclipse was almost upon them. Incantus was close to collapse, and Serena didn't seem far behind him.

The *Demons* were beating them. Alexis would lose them too. Then all would be lost.

'Come on, Lexi,' Alexis muttered, ignoring the stabbing in his shoulder each time he dragged himself a foot further. 'Come on. You can do this. You have to do this.'

Valentina's gasps were growing fainter. Sparks of red flickered around her fingertips as she clawed at Mortem's face, but it wasn't enough to conjure a portal. Alexis's eyes were trained on her, but she was looking at someone else.

She was looking at Serena Aevum, and the old woman was staring straight back at her, as if they were the only two people there.

And then between one moment and the next, one woman was gone, and what followed could only be described as a supernova: the explosion of a star that would never again shine.

*

I see her. I recognise her. I was *her.*

She reminds me so much of myself. Raised in a world where people knew me by my surname better than my first. Always Aevum, never Serena. A world who only cared about the legacy I came from and the powers I had.

I knew the girl all too well and the reasons why she acted as she did. Why she was so desperate to succeed, to prove herself, to finally become her own person.

That was why I had to save her. No one had invested in her future, not in the way she really needed.

I would, because I wish someone had for me.

I glanced at the man beside me, a person who I cared for just as much as any person could care for another. Even as his power dampened, totality almost upon us, Ian still didn't give up. He still kept fighting, as I would have.

The Demons *that bore down on us were not just creatures of shadow. They were born from Mortem, yes, but sustained and supported by something else. I knew that, because I had given birth to the power that now amplified theirs. Aadya's powers.*

Only I was able to destroy them. And I was willing to die to kill Mortem's children so that I could finally avenge my own.

I let my body glow with the energy that fuelled it. A gold that shone brighter and brighter, limitless, unbound. Free, just like me.

They say a star shines strongest in its final moments, that light is brightest when surrounded by darkness. I always planned on going out with a bang.

The prophecy my father had told me as a young woman had, of course, come true, as did they all, no matter how hard we tried to escape them. The prophecy that I would meet my end on my own terms – not by old age or by a sword, but at my own hands, when I was ready, to spare a girl who hoped to escape what I couldn't – I thought it had been about my Aadya. But if I couldn't save her, at least I could save this girl.

'Serena! No!' Incantus cried, but I couldn't see him over the glow of my body. He knew what I was doing. He knew what it would cost.

But, I had to do it. For the eclipse. For the Quinate. For this girl and every other who grew too tall to let a man talk down to her, too proud to permit them to strike her down. This was for us all, to show them that we will always be more than the demon that tries us.

'It is my time,' I said, closing my eyes, knowing that when I reopened them, Teller and Darcy and my sister would be there waiting to greet me wherever our souls ended up.

And so I let go.

I let go of my memories and my aspirations. I let go of my hopes and fears. All that I'd ever been and all that I could be. I let it all go . . . and oh how liberating it was.

From my body came an explosion of pure energy. It burst into the sky and disintegrated the Demons *where they stood, reducing them to nothingness, clouds of fragmented darkness.*

And I went with them.

I died the way that I lived.

Brightly. Limitless. Unbound.

And free.

33
ESHAJŌRI

Eshajōri (phr.) *Japanese origin*
'People who meet always part'; the concept that expresses the idea about the impermanence of all things, that every human relationship will end someday due to the transient nature of life

Five minutes until totality

Serena's self-sacrifice lit up the sky like nothing the world had ever seen before.

The explosion of energy was more powerful than any nuclear bomb. It vaporised the *Demons* and eradicated them in an instant, gone for ever without a trace.

Alexis felt his body jolt with a sudden influx of energy as if Serena had channelled some of herself directly into him. The whole scene was flooded with streaks of golden light, too bright for Alexis to see through. Even so, he crawled the last few feet to where he knew the Water Gem was and he beat his amulet against it.

Alexis's entire body pulsed with enough power to shatter the shackles that bound his wrists and inhibited his powers. He could finally breathe again.

There was a groan. A figure rose to their feet, a man, tall and broad. Frantic, furious. Fearful.

Alexis swung his staff with everything he had. A riptide of water burst from the Gem and beat into Mortem just as he came into view, launching him far away before he could even throw up a shield.

'Incantus?' Alexis called out blindly, fumbling around until the smoke and gold dust finally cleared.

Incantus was on his knees, his palms to the ground where Serena had just been, seeking the last of her body's warmth. The only thing that remained of her was the golden Aevum brooch. It lay singed on the earth, the intricate 'A' surrounded by two angel wings in the shape of a clock.

Incantus's eyes were glowing behind closed eyelids, flickering back and forth. It was just as they had been when Teller passed. He was watching Serena's entire life play out in front of him in seconds, processing the light of her life force now that it was no longer contained in her physical body.

Ragged gasps were all that could be heard until the distant clashing of battle resumed. Alexis briefly checked on Valentina before going to Incantus's side. She was choking, quivering hands clutching her bruised throat. She watched him approach through teary eyes.

Without a word, he knelt and cupped his hands and poured a stream of clear water into them. Valentina took a long sip while she stared at Incantus.

'Why?' she asked Alexis. Her voice was barely a whisper, one that sent her into another choking fit as she rolled onto her back.

Alexis didn't know, and so he said nothing. He left Valentina reluctantly once she nodded to let him know she would be okay, and drew closer to his mentor. Incantus looked wearier and older than ever. The most human Alexis had ever seen him. As the sky fell darker still, Incantus didn't raise his head. He was in some sort of daze, his eyes unseeing, his expression vacant. He didn't even register Alexis's approach.

Alexis placed his hand on his mentor's slumped shoulder and squeezed it gently. 'Don't let it be in vain,' was all he could bring himself to say.

Incantus's pale blue eyes found his. His voice sounded empty when he uttered, 'I am so tired, Alexis.'

Alexis nodded. *So am I*, he wanted to admit. He wanted to stay there with his mentor, his uncle, until eternal sleep found him too.

'We didn't come this far just to come this far,' he replied instead. He didn't know where he found the strength – perhaps it was a gift from Serena. It was one he wouldn't dare waste.

Incantus's mouth pressed into a line of conviction and the light returned to his eyes in a blaze. 'No, we didn't.' They grabbed hold of one another and drew to their feet, each supporting the other, determined that this day was not yet lost.

Until Alexis heard a scream. A blood-curdling, ear-splitting scream that cut across the entire battlefield in waves. He recognised the voice and turned to find the source of the cry that had originated from the very centre of Stonehenge, a place that, despite Serena's self-sacrifice and the eradication of the *Demons*, was so overrun with the Dark Army that he almost couldn't see what had happened. Almost.

Caeli Doran stood with her arm extended in front of her, staring in horror at the place where her hand should have been.

But no longer was.

She screamed over and over again, the sound rising higher and higher, unable to tear her eyes away. Before her stood a Shadowless man, his sword soaked with her blood, a self-satisfied grin plastered across his face from having hurt one of the Children of the Elements.

His smile vanished the moment Demi stepped between them.

Demi didn't raise her hands. She didn't shout. She didn't say anything. Instead, she gazed at the man with the incalescent fury of the hearth, with the thunderous power of the tide, and the raging chaos of the tempest.

With her dark hair coiling behind her in the wind like snakes, Demi pulled not on the power of the earth, but on its corresponding state of matter. On solid. To go beyond her element to also wield the state of matter it represented was a feat that so far only Alexis had managed with the manipulation of blood.

Alexis stared as the Shadowless's body solidified into stone, his dying expression of panic freezing upon his face.

Demi's love for her best friend had turned the man into a statue, and her anger had caused her to strike him down with the sweep of her hand, crumbling his body to rubble at her feet.

A quote Alexis had once read from the psychologist, Carl Jung, rose to the forefront of his mind then. '*No tree, it is said, can grow to heaven unless its roots reach down to hell.*'

It seemed Demi Nikolas's roots reached much further down than he had ever thought.

All those hours of defensive fighting, of differentiating between human and other, living and dead. All to spare her soul from further ruin, to distance herself from and redeem herself for the single act of murder she thought she was guilty of, but never truly was.

It had all been for nothing.

No, not nothing. It had all been for Caeli. The guilt Alexis knew Demi would feel would have to wait, for the moon did not stop to grace them with the time to process any of what had just happened.

Blaise was holding Caeli in his arms, incinerating any Nekro that dared to draw near, his eyes not leaving hers. Alexis saw Caeli then grab him by the collar and hold out her stump to him, but Blaise shook his head and shouted something in refusal.

Caeli moved before Blaise could, for she had always been quicker than he. She snatched his burning hand and forced it against her severed arm. A sonic explosion erupted from her in a sweeping gale as the fire cauterised her wound.

Caeli was screaming, Blaise was sobbing, and Demi was fighting to defend them both. Alexis had to join them; he had to save his friends. They wouldn't last much longer against the incessant tide of enemies. Even as Caeli drew to unsteady feet and started fighting back one-handed, how could they hope to survive until the eclipse?

Three figures came to stand in Alexis's way, blocking him from his friends.

The Leaders of the Haven.

'Go!' Incantus shouted, pushing Alexis from his side. 'Help them!'

'But . . .'

'Your friends need you!'

Alexis's feet would not permit him to move. To help them

was to doom Incantus. How could Incantus face off against all three Leaders? And yet Caeli's howls of anguish rang out over and over again. The total eclipse would start any second and he had to be waiting inside Stonehenge for Incantus.

Alexis tore from Incantus's side, narrowly missing a hex Raeve hurled his way. As he rounded clear of the battle, he glanced back to see Incantus single-handedly taking on all three Leaders, his dying powers somehow still holding up.

Beams of light surged from Incantus in all directions. He dived out of the way of a searing streak of lightning that cracked towards him and flung a ray of light into Taranis's face.

The youngest Leader fell. A line of light snaked from Incantus towards him. It illuminated his face, seeping through his skin as it searched for the darkness inside to destroy. Akili came charging at Incantus, but Incantus sent a shockwave at him, throwing him into Raeve as they both toppled over.

Alexis finally reached the ice wall at Stonehenge, tearing through the Nekro and Shadowless that were breaking through what remained of his frozen barrier.

'Lexi!' Demi cried, catching sight of him over her shoulder.

He wanted to go to her more than anything, but she was conducting her oak tree to thrash at the Nekro and he had his own quarter to protect now that he was back.

'Cae?' he called, unable to turn around to check on her properly.

'Don't!' he heard her sob over the howling winds. She likely knew the three worded question he wanted to ask, and how far from okay she was. She wouldn't let him ask her again and he knew better than to.

'Serena?' Blaise shouted in question.

Alexis's silence was his answer. Although he couldn't see Blaise, he could feel the heat of his fire burn more ardently in response.

Beaded blobs of sunlight were all that remained around the tiny sliver of the sun that was left exposed. They flickered out and disappeared by the second.

Through the waves of Shadowless and Nekro, Alexis fought to see how Incantus was faring. Taranis lay unconscious on the ground and the tendrils of white light Incantus had encased him with were slowly retracting. Incantus was just about to conjure another rivulet of light to throw at Akili when a cloud of blackness rolled towards him.

'Look out!' Alexis bellowed, allowing Incantus to turn and duck under the shadow blade just in time. Emerging from the greater cloud came Mortem, darkness pouring from every inch of his body.

When the two Arcangelo brothers faced each other once more, neither of them spoke a word as waves of light and darkness erupted from their palms. It crashed in the space between them soundlessly, exploding into the sky, causing the entire battlefield to flicker between light and dark.

Alexis heard Incantus roar, and somehow that supercharged his own assault too. Alexis fought indiscriminately with whoever stood before him, imprinted or otherwise. Bones cracked and flesh tore to ribbons at his hands, splattering his face with blood, but he couldn't take his eyes off the eclipse or Incantus.

Only a single bead of light was visible now, glinting behind the blackness of the moon like a diamond ring, the last glimpse of stunning, bursting light.

Despite everything, Incantus seemed to be withstanding. His stream of power was prevailing, forcing Mortem's shadows back towards him. Mortem had his back to Stonehenge, far too preoccupied to make any attempt to flee.

'Alexis!' sobbed a robotic voice. Something ploughed through a Shadowless that had snuck through a crack in his ice wall. It was one of the training bots from the Haven, its voice belonging to Ziya.

'There's no time!' Alexis shouted. *It has to be now.* He had to leave his friends; it was the only way to save them. He swept away the sheet of snow that covered what he and Ziya had planted that morning. He then tore from Stonehenge, burrowing through Shadowless to join Incantus. 'Turn on the projector now!'

Alexis didn't need to check to see that the bot Ziya controlled had finally set the plan into action. He heard the whirring of the Haven projector start up behind him.

Alexis spared one last glance over his shoulder at Stonehenge. As always, he searched for Demi. Perhaps that would be how he spent his last moments of daylight.

Over the swarm of black, he couldn't see her. She and Caeli and Blaise must have already regrouped to cover the space he had just defended.

Please know I haven't abandoned you. Please know that what I'm about to do is for you. Everything I do is for you.

It was Demi who Alexis was thinking of when the sky finally went dark.

The temperature plummeted. The sound of the animals and Hybrids on the battlefield fell silent in an instant. Even the bloodstained grass and what remained of the flowers shrivelled up. The moon had completely engulfed the sun and only its glimmering corona provided the slightest illumination on the land.

It was enough for Alexis to see the horror that unfolded before him as he ran as fast as he could from Stonehenge.

The light that once shone so boldly and brightly from Incantus's body diminished until it vanished entirely. Not a glimmer or a spark remained. Nothing. His hands fell to his sides. He was mortal now, powerless. And he was at the mercy of Mortem.

Mortem terminated his stream of darkness. Wisps withered away around him like smoke in the wind. Alexis could see it now, the unabashed, unquestionable sense of victory that emanated from him as he strode towards Incantus.

Incantus did not move to defend himself. It seemed as though he knew that he too was out of time.

Incantus looked past Mortem. His eyes fell upon Alexis, who was racing across the battlefield towards him, screaming '*No!*' over and over again as if that would stop the inevitable. They both knew he wouldn't reach them in time, but still Alexis ran, his heart hammering in his chest, his breath caught in his lungs, unable to look away.

Alexis never thought he would beg Mortem for anything, but he found himself pleading now. 'Please, no! *Please* don't!'

But it was of no use.

Mortem Arcangelo drew from his hands a dagger of darkness.

And my brother plunged the blade into my chest.

The blow struck me harder than I had thought it would.

Incantus Arcangelo. Angel of Day. Bringer of Light. It made poetic sense that I fell by darkness.

Mortem glowered as I sank to my knees. The dagger dissipated, but still I felt the hole it had made in my chest. He stood perfectly still before me, a shadow frozen in time, patiently waiting until I found his eyes to prove to him that after all of these years, he had finally won.

I raised my head. For one last time, I looked at him, hoping to recognise something of the person I had once loved more than anyone in the world.

I saw only shadows.

And then . . .

I saw light.

The light of life. Of my life. And what a life it had been.

I saw the people I had loved. The people I had lost. I saw her.

All I saw was her. My Midnight.

I fell to the ground without a word, my body cold, beaten and tired, and utterly vacant of light.

In the end, the darkness had got me too.

34
HELIOPHILIA

Heliophilia (n.) *Greek origin*
The desire to stay in the sun; the love of sunlight

Seven minutes left of totality

Dead. Incantus Arcangelo was dead. And Alexis wanted to be too.

Alexis's legs swept from beneath him. The breath deserted his chest. The world didn't grant him the privilege of slowing down, but he no longer wished to keep up with it.

The scene replayed itself over and over in his mind. The force of Mortem's stab; the crumpling of Incantus's body; the expression on his face when he closed his eyes, somewhere between disappointment and acceptance.

'*Dad!*' came a heart-wrenching cry, shattering the stillness that had befallen the battlefield.

A figure raced past Alexis. Ziya. Actually her in the flesh. She had no holographic bots to protect her and no sword to defend herself with, but she didn't seem to care. She tore across the fields until she reached Incantus's body, where she collapsed in a heap and wept, the noise of devastation unlike anything Alexis had ever heard before.

Alexis watched hopelessly as she positioned herself so that she was covering Incantus from Mortem, from the man who had taken away every single adult she had ever loved. Her mother. Her grandmother. And now Incantus too: the man who treated her as his daughter, the man she regarded as her father.

'*Rakshasa!*' Ziya spat at Mortem, cradling Incantus's head in her lap. '*Demon.*'

Mortem peered down at her, his head tilted in mild interest. 'Angel or demon, good or bad – what does that matter when you are dead on the ground?'

Ziya didn't answer him. She had gone utterly still, holding Incantus's face to her as though Mortem didn't deserve to look upon him, her shoulders suddenly no longer shaking from the sobs that had ripped through her.

Mortem took a moment to observe the destruction he and his army had caused. Stonehenge stood behind him, just metres away, closer than he likely would have thought. The Children of the Elements were nowhere to be seen, nor were any of his Shadowless. The battlefields surrounding Stonehenge had been utterly deserted.

Only Alexis remained, on his knees, staring at the ground before him. He lay just outside the outermost monoliths of Stonehenge, utterly disinterested in it, unconcerned by the absence of his friends, who appeared to have abandoned him when totality struck and Incantus fell.

Alexis didn't raise his head to look at Mortem, but he felt him turn his attention back to Ziya.

'Parashakti and Aevum blood runs through you, girl. You know what your ancestors were capable of and yet you settle for *this*. A life stolen away from what was rightfully yours. If you join me, you could be so powerful. As powerful as your mother and grandmother, perhaps more so.'

Alexis raised his head slightly to see Mortem stretch his hand towards Ziya in offering. He watched from a distance as she hesitated, and that was enough to reawaken him from his stupor. He would not let her fall the way everyone else around them had.

His brain reignited, cogs clicking into action and beginning to turn. His body was crippled by ice, but he fought to thaw it, bit by bit. All the while, he watched and prayed for Ziya to resist Mortem's invitation to embrace the thing she'd never had but had always desired.

Please don't leave me too, Ziya.

Something glinted on the ground beside Ziya. The Aevum brooch, now hers. It glowed a faint gold with the remnants of her grandmother's energy. She had died trying to stop Mortem. As had her mother.

And Alexis feared so would she.

Mortem shook his head in apparent disappointment once he realised Ziya had made her decision. 'Pity,' he said, looking away. 'I no longer need you now anyway.'

With that, he turned and walked through the pristine wall of ice into a vacant Stonehenge.

Alexis staggered to his feet. Blood pumped through him in hot bursts. Adrenaline. Fury. Power. Purpose. He rushed to Ziya, coming to a halt just beside her.

'*Hurry!*' she ordered Alexis, her eyes still on Incantus, rocking him back and forth. Alexis peered over to see that she clung to a handful of small, pale yellow healing crystals and was holding them fiercely against Incantus's chest. Alexis wanted to tell her that it was useless, that the crystals' power only went so far, but the words never found a voice. He wouldn't be the one to steal Ziya's hope from her, even if it was wasted. Let her think Incantus was merely sleeping. Let her believe they still had a chance, if only for a few more minutes.

With her spare hand, Ziya fervently beckoned Valentina to her, who was rousing not a few feet away. She would likely ask her to portal her back into the Haven where she could spend her last few minutes with her sister, or to shelter in the White Room that had housed the Gems to be spared from Mortem's imprinting powers. Alexis didn't blame her.

Alexis couldn't bring himself to look upon Incantus's face now. At the man who had cared for him as if he was his own, from the very first day they had met. Who had taught Alexis everything he knew about a world too magical to be conjured by the darkness of his mind. A man who he'd confided in and found comfort with and trusted above anyone else.

Alexis gritted his teeth and brushed his sweat-soaked hair from his eyes.

He would stand where Incantus had fallen. Even if he was undeserving of it, he would try to keep alight the torch of hope Incantus had irrevocably ignited in his heart and mind.

'Light will always find a way through the darkness, and if you can't find it, become it.'

With his staff in his hand – the Water Gem at its tip, gleaming under only his touch – Alexis followed Mortem into Stonehenge.

35

APHOTIC

Aphotic (adj.) *Greek origin*
Lacking light; that not reached by sunlight

Five minutes left of totality

Mortem stood in the very centre of the ring of ruins. Blood and dirt darkened his face, accentuating the blueness of the inner part of his eyes. His armour was battered and his curling hair was matted. But, supported by the shadow of the eclipse that plunged the world into a temporary darkness, he had never looked more powerful.

He smiled when Alexis entered the arena. The thin scar down his neck gleamed in the dim light. Alexis wondered how many more scars he had and where he had got them from. He wondered who had managed to inflict a wound upon one of the most powerful Elementals in the world, running so deep that it was still prominent after all these years.

I'd like to shake their hand, he thought.

When Mortem noticed Alexis staring, he turned his head to obscure his scar, almost as though he was ashamed. Alexis planned on inflicting a matching one on the other side, only he intended for his cut to run much deeper, and prove far more fatal.

With the silence drumming in his ears louder with every step he took, Alexis waited until Mortem finally spoke, somewhat grateful that there was an end to the suffocating intensity of their wordless reunion.

Mortem tutted. The sound echoed within the vacant structure. He shook his head, looking at Alexis like he was a poor, misunderstood and misled child.

'This world has descended into chaos,' he said thoughtfully, staring at the eclipse. 'Our predators? Ourselves. Mortals treat this world as if its resources are inexhaustible. Elementals are starting to do the same. I am here to bring order to the chaos.' He stretched his arms wide. 'As long as people are free to make the wrong decision, they will continue to do so. It is for that reason that I am removing their free will.'

Alexis gripped his staff that much tighter when Mortem began walking around the inner ring of rocks. Mortem was enjoying himself now, clearly thinking the day had already been won. For that reason, despite the fear that was mounting within him, Alexis forced himself to stay rooted still and allow Mortem to come to him.

'I will imprint every person on Earth who has so much as a drop of Elemental blood so that I can lead our people into a new age – an age where darkness shall be worshipped – and in doing so, shall save this world from itself.'

Mortem drew to a stop just a metre away from Alexis. This was the closest Alexis had ever been to him. He'd never realised just how tall Mortem was; how similar he looked to Incantus; how similar he looked to *him*. Mortem's eyes bored into the younger Elemental's, apparently expecting him to submit as every other person did.

But Alexis had back pain, and he had no intention of bowing.

'Listening to you speak is more painful than being stabbed,' Alexis exhaled disinterestedly, rolling his injured shoulder. Mortem's expression turned hard. 'You can't lie to me, *Nero*. I know the type of person you are. You don't care about the world or the people in it; you only care about control. About making sure there is no one who has the potential to challenge your powers or question your authority.'

Despite how casual he tried to sound, Alexis's heart beat faster than ever. Waves of nerves crashed through him. He tapped the fingers of his spare hand to his thumb, but still the panic grew. There was so much he wanted to ask him, a lifetime's worth of questions.

Why are you the way you are? How did I manage to escape you? Who was my mother and what happened to her?

Alexis had had enough of being in the dark. He wanted to know everything, even that which would hurt him the most.

Besides, it was working. He was stalling him.

Of all the responses Mortem could have given, Alexis hadn't expected him to laugh. 'You think you are so different from me, blinded by the arrogance of the light in which you think you bathe.' His chuckle subsided and the humour faded as swiftly as it had come. 'How long do you intend to keep up this charade? It is futile and utterly pathetic. I can see how death and darkness clings to you, child. Admit it to me now, for we are the only two people here – didn't you enjoy killing Sinner and the others? Didn't you savour the taste of the shadows? Have you not been craving it since?'

Mortem's eyes were bright with delight, so much so that Alexis couldn't meet them. He didn't trust himself to answer.

Mortem leaned even closer. 'The sins of the shadow hide from the light. So I ask again, are you going to die lying to yourself? Ashamed of who and what you truly are. You are no good, Alexis – have you not realised this already? You are no *hero*.'

And that was it. As simple as that: Alexis had been unmasked easily by the man who didn't know him at all and yet knew him better than anyone else ever could.

Alexis wanted to be a hero.

He wanted nothing more. That was why he ventured out on the quest for the Elemental Gems in the first place, and one of the reasons he said he would fight today. He desperately wanted to atone for his misdeeds, for the pain he had inflicted upon his family due to his illness, by doing something heroic and *good*. By doing something that would justify all the suffering. For a while, he thought he had.

But somewhere along the way, Alexis had stumbled and then altogether fallen into the darkness that so readily welcomed him.

Maybe his father was right. Maybe he was no hero.

But that didn't mean he was a villain.

'I have been haunted by your shadow for as long as I can remember,' Alexis said, mustering strength he didn't know he had from a place he hadn't known existed. Was it coming from the Water Gem? His parents? His friends? Only the tapping of his fingers to his thumb was getting him through this. 'Your memories haunted my nightmares. Your shadow haunted me in the daylight. For my entire life, you have been trying to turn me, to make me like you, and although I might have lost my way at times, I know exactly who I am.'

There was a look on Mortem's face. It had slipped through to the surface at the mention of the memories that had plagued Alexis. It looked like . . . *fear.*

Mortem lashed out, his hand finding Alexis's neck. Alexis felt the wind escape him as his throat was crushed and he was lifted into the air.

'You will die alone, with none of your little friends to save you. Abandoned once again.'

Mortem was right about many things, but he wasn't right about this.

I don't need anyone to save me, Alexis decided.

Alexis cracked his staff against the side of Mortem's face. It wasn't hard enough to force Mortem to drop him, but it gave Alexis a moment to take a desperate breath. He remembered the first thing Akili had taught him in training: the importance of breathing, it being the first and last thing someone did in their life. He also taught him how it was tethered to not only their state of mind but also to their innate abilities. How it channelled their powers. With a short inhale, Alexis launched a stream of ice-cold water into Mortem, forcing him to crash backwards.

Each gasp ached as though he were swallowing razors, but Alexis forced himself to breathe as Mortem scrambled to his feet. Mortem looked at him with pure, unquestionable hatred, his loathing more evident than it had been even when he faced Incantus.

What have I done to you to make you despise me so much?

But he had no time to ask. Great curved blades of darkness ripped towards him, so powerful that they tore through his constructed ice shield as if it were made of tissue. One grazed his arm while another tore through his hip, the pain searing and forcing him back.

Mortem drew his wicked scythe of shadow, its curved tip pointed directly at Alexis. Alexis did the same with his staff and pointed it at his father. The two met in the middle of Stonehenge.

Alexis parried a blow, then drew a sharp icicle from his hand and dug it into Mortem's shoulder. First blood.

Mortem grunted in pain and sent Alexis flying into one of the monoliths with a roundhouse kick to the side of the face.

There was a loud popping sound in Alexis's ear . . . and then *nothing.* Nothing but excruciating, nauseating pain that tipped him over at every futile attempt to get back up. He was vaguely aware of the warm sensation of blood trickling down his neck. He had burst his eardrum and the lack of noise from one side was throwing him off balance as he staggered to his feet.

'I have waited a century for this moment!' Mortem bellowed, flipping his sword in his grip.

Mortem charged and his sword dug into the rock where Alexis's head had been just moments before. Alexis swept his staff in an arc, catching Mortem behind the knees and forcing him down. Raeve had drilled into them during their training that while a weapon was useful, its greatest utility was to channel their powers. With that in mind, Alexis called on the power of the Gem to rain down a small flood onto Mortem's head.

Mortem thrashed in the waterfall, his movements erratic and unpredictable. A wild tendril of darkness snaked from his sleeve and flew at Alexis. It coiled around his staff and snatched it from his hand, sending it clattering to the ground.

Weaponless, Alexis stumbled backwards as Mortem parted the waterfall with a cutting sweep of darkness. '*Survey your surroundings*,' Alexis heard, almost as if Incantus was still there to remind him.

Alexis ran and leaped from one of the fallen monoliths in the centre of Stonehenge to propel him into the sky. He reared his arm back ready to blow, shards of ice protruding from his knuckles, but just before he landed, Mortem dived out of the way.

Fatigue was crippling his body and sparks were starting to dot his vision, but Taranis's intensive conditioning at the end of every day enabled Alexis to stay on his feet. The lessons from the Leaders of the Haven were the only thing keeping him alive. They had to be enough.

'You never deserved your life,' Mortem spat as he lashed a whip of shadow at Alexis. Alexis shuddered under the strike, barely shielding himself from it with a weak tide of water. 'You did this to yourself!' Another whip. 'You asked for this!' Another. 'You should have been the one to suffer!'

The last lash ripped through Alexis's defence. It lacerated the side of his face, just at the edge of his jaw and down his neck. A cut to match Mortem's.

'Then why did you have me?' Alexis cried. He knew he was losing, that he had to get away. He had to do something. But even in the face of death, he had to know why he wasn't good enough. Why the person who had given him life so desperately wished he hadn't. What had he done to deserve it? Was that how his mother felt too?

'What did you do to my mother?'

Mortem shook his head, halting for just a moment. His eyes bore deep into Alexis's before he delivered the final blow, one that cut deeper than any blade ever could.

'*You* killed your mother.'

36

ILMESTYS

Ilmestys (n.) *Finnish origin*
Vision, apparition, manifestation; phenomenon, spectacle, sight; revelation

Three minutes left of totality

A pressure had been building within Alexis. Anger, fury and hatred had been bubbling inside of him as he battled Mortem, fuelling his body and slowly taking control of his mind without him realising. It clawed at his insides. It *shouted* at him. He heard great crashes in his head like the breaking of tides against the cliffside.

But now those crashes became clearer; they became synchronised. Alexis realised all at once that the sound wasn't the pumping of blood at all. *Words.* The crashes of the tide were words. And they said the same two words over and over again.

'*Let go.*'

This time, Alexis listened.

This time, Alexis submitted to the darkness.

He reached into the darkest depths of his abilities. Past the water that swirled inside of him, well beyond where the light could reach. Lying there, just as they had been the last time he had used them to slay Sinner, were the shadows.

I killed my mother.

It couldn't be true. Alexis couldn't have. He couldn't believe that he had.

Was that why Mortem despised him so much? Why Alexis, for as long as he could remember, knew deep down at his core that no matter how much he tried to be good, it would never be enough?

Alexis couldn't face the reality of it and so he dived underwater to escape. He extended his arm towards the shadows and the cold ripple of their power shuddered into him, all too eager to see the light.

A tendril of darkness poured from Alexis's hand. He commanded it to form a dagger, and then he hurled it straight at his father.

The blade sank deep into Mortem's torso and he pitched backwards. He let out a gasp and stared incredulously from the blade to Alexis. A roar of fury escaped him as he yanked the dagger out and flung it away.

Just like that, reality was no longer something Alexis could evade.

Mortem swept towards him in the blink of an eye, far faster than Alexis could react. He delivered an uppercut deep into Alexis's stomach, so hard that Alexis heard the snapping of a bone, which silenced the scream in his throat. Grabbing him by his hair, Mortem slammed his knee into Alexis's face once, twice, three times, before pushing him away.

Alexis stumbled backwards, blindly searching for his staff as blood and sweat obscured his vision. But Mortem was once again in his way. His hand reached out and his blackened fingers dug straight into the stab wound the *Demon* had made in his shoulder.

Alexis let out a scream like never before. His body shuddered beyond his control as if he was being electrocuted, every nerve cell firing in pain in unison. And then, probably to silence him more than anything, Mortem picked Alexis up and flung him across the circular arena.

Alexis crashed into one of the fallen rocks, smearing blood all across it.

'You chose your path,' Mortem heaved as Alexis dragged himself out of sight, cowering behind the large monolith. 'Don't you dare try and use *my* powers against me.'

Alexis clung on to consciousness with everything he had left. He was experiencing more pain than he thought the human body could bear. He fought to stay focused through it. He couldn't think about how his shoulder was in agony or how his staff was way out of his reach or how Mortem was waiting for him to come back out so he could finish him once and for all.

What Alexis had to concentrate on was his proxy.

Alexis pressed his trembling, bleeding hands together, wincing with every move. He held his breath in anticipation as he summoned his proxy.

His mirror image appeared before him, and Alexis had to reach out with a bloodied hand to silence its gasp. Its eyes were huge as they searched his body, its hands immediately going towards the streams of blood that dyed Alexis's torso crimson.

'You know I'm f-fine,' Alexis stuttered, every whisper

hurting as his cracked rib scraped against his lung. 'Otherwise you'd be d-dead.'

His proxy placed its hands either side of his face. Although the proxy's touch was cold, Alexis felt relief at its contact and almost slumped into its hands.

'Hiding?' Mortem taunted from afar, sending shivers down Alexis's spine. 'Is this the training you have received? It is no use. You'll be dead before the eclipse is over, long before I imprint your friends – if they survive. I think I'll make them fight each other to the death, starting with your little green-eyed girl first.'

'Lexi, stay awake,' the proxy whispered to him, wiping the tears that escaped his half-closed eyes. 'Hurry, do it now.'

Alexis choked back a sob and nodded. His proxy presented both its palms to him.

'This is going to hurt,' Alexis warned, pressing his hands against the proxy's.

Upon their touch, the proxy was absorbed back into Alexis for less than a second before he put his hands together to release it again. He didn't have time to process the proxy's memories and he ignored the incoming stream of information from its experiences.

When he reopened his eyes, his reflection reappeared. Now that they had synchronised, when the proxy crouched before him, its appearance was identical, down to the smears of blood and the tears in its Haven suit. As always, the only thing that could never be replicated was his amulet, which remained solely against Alexis's chest.

'You've got less than a minute,' the proxy said uncomfortably, although it didn't quite experience the pain to the extent Alexis did. 'Good luck.'

‘And to you,’ said Alexis.

With that, Alexis dragged himself away from Mortem and out of Stonehenge.

Alexis’s proxy limped to its feet, raising its blood-soaked face to look at Mortem, who stood in the very centre of Stonehenge, his hands to the sky.

‘All those years of experience and you still can’t finish me off?’ the proxy jibed, pouring as much emotion into its voice as possible to mimic the real Alexis. If Mortem realised it was a proxy, it would all be for nothing. It had to make it convincing and hold his attention for a few more moments to give Alexis time to escape unnoticed. The proxy pointed a quivering finger at the scar on the side of Mortem’s face. ‘Don’t make me give you another one.’

Mortem growled and charged at Alexis’s proxy.

Step one, to distract Mortem, was a success. It hadn’t prepared for step two: survive more than five seconds.

The proxy darted across Stonehenge towards Alexis’s fallen staff, but it had only run a few metres before Mortem was upon it. Huge talons of shadow burst from his fingers as he swiped across the proxy’s face, cutting through skin and bone.

The proxy screamed as it fell to the ground, lashing out wildly with its legs. One kick connected with Mortem’s knee, forcing it to bend at an awkward angle. As Mortem buckled, the proxy scrambled towards the staff. It grabbed it with both hands and swung it into the side of Mortem’s face, where the Water Gem cracked against his cheekbone.

Mortem bellowed, and bursting from his back came great

wings of shadow. Tendrils and snakes of darkness coiled around the proxy's limbs, splaying it in the air.

No matter how much it shook the staff, the Water Gem would not glow in its hand.

Mortem reared up before the proxy. 'Your time is over,' he seethed. 'I can now finally be free of you.'

And then, Mortem's eyes flickered towards the proxy's chest. To what should have been there. Then to the Water Gem, where it remained dull and powerless in its possession.

Fearful realisation flooded Mortem's eyes.

Alexis's proxy smiled weakly and spat blood at his face.

Mortem hurled its body into the wall of ice Alexis had constructed at his quarter of Stonehenge. The proxy crashed into the barrier, sending cracks splintering across its length. The fractured wall shattered with an ear-splitting sound, raining down great slabs into a jagged heap on the ground.

Stonehenge *flickered.* The entire stone structure jittered between being there one moment and vanishing in the next.

Mortem spun around as swathes of darkness seeped from him, pouring from every orifice. He tore to the central altar stone of Stonehenge and unleashed his powers up to the sky in the last few seconds of the eclipse.

And

nothing

happened.

There was a dying whirring sound and a small trail of smoke, which came from the collapsed ice wall where the proxy lay. Beside its crumpled form was one of the Haven's projectors. The light from its camera lens finally faded, and with it, the entire projection of Stonehenge where Mortem was currently standing disappeared too – as though it had been nothing more than a hallucination all along.

With the projection gone, Mortem turned to see where he really stood: several metres away from the real Stonehenge, where its stones glowed white and hung in the air as the eclipse sat directly above it. Through Alexis's shattered ice wall, Mortem saw that in its centre were the four Children of the Elements.

And standing between them, held by them, was Incantus Arcangelo.

The elements of water and earth, fire and air were drawn into his broken body, combining to form a light so bright that no shadows could evade it.

Mortem screamed as Incantus unleashed the power of light from Stonehenge and everything flashed white.

PART IV

37
EPOCHAL

Epochal (adj.) *Greek origin*
Highly significant or important, especially in bringing about or marking the beginning of a new era; monumental

Blaise didn't know how they did it. How they'd won the Battle of Stonehenge. It had all happened so fast.

He lay there on a bed in the Healing Sanctuary as the healers fussed over him. They asked him questions he didn't hear and shone lights in his eyes that he didn't register. All Blaise could do was replay the final minutes of the battle over and over in his head, trapped in those awful moments when the world had succumbed to the shadow of the eclipse: the lull in the chaos once the last of the Shadowless had been struck down; Valentina and Ziya stepping through a portal carrying a motionless Incantus between them; Alexis emerging from what appeared to be a replica of Stonehenge.

Caeli had been wailing, and Demi . . . Demi had had a look in her eyes that Blaise hadn't ever seen before. He was convinced that had Alexis not shown up at that exact moment, stumbling towards them, beaten and bloody almost beyond recognition, Demi would have left Stonehenge and sacrificed all of Elemental-kind to go after him.

The last thing Blaise saw before his vision was blinded was a cloud of blackness pouring from Mortem's mouth. And then he was in the Haven . . . and there was just as much chaos there.

Incantus and the Children of the Elements had been sent to separate rooms within the Healing Sanctuary, which seemed so odd to Blaise after the ordeal they had suffered together. He flexed his fingers. He felt relatively unscathed, save for a few superficial cuts and bruises, and a strange, unshakeable cold pang deep in his chest that hadn't been there moments ago. Shock, perhaps.

He wasn't able to rest in bed as the healers lathered him up with balms and placed pale yellow crystals around him. He felt his hearing return with a pop and his eyes snap back into focus. He felt their hands all over his body, jostling his limbs as they accounted for every wound. Blaise *felt*, which meant he was still alive.

Some part of him knew that it was over, but he couldn't slow the momentum that carried his mind and his body at lightning speed. He had to do something. If he stayed still like the healers were ordering, he feared he would explode. Even though he couldn't do anything to help the hundreds of injured Elementals that now swarmed the Sanctuary, he had to make sure to check on his friends.

Blaise went to Caeli first. He soon wished he hadn't.

'Get back!' a healer warned, ushering Blaise away from the roaring, thundering sound behind the door to Caeli's room.

'What are you doing to her?' Blaise demanded, not budging.

All he could hear over the howling winds was Caeli's panicked shrieking. 'Let me through!'

'She's not letting us get near to her,' the healer said. She, like all other healers, was dressed in plain beige scrubs that reminded Blaise of Akili Pierce's robes. Her dark hair was cut short and she clutched a large bag at her side. 'If we don't sedate her, she'll destroy half the Sanctuary!'

Caeli Doran had saved Blaise's life. Moments before that man had carved her hand off, she had pointed to Blaise. He had been battling Raeve, desperately keeping her at bay by blindly hurling fireball after fireball at her. Raeve had been so wickedly quick, dodging each one, flinging targeted hexes his way that he barely incinerated in time. With both his and Alexis's sections to defend, he could barely keep up with her. He had to watch her every move.

That was why it had been so easy to fall under her immobilising spell – her Concilium charm. All it took was for Raeve to suddenly go still and look into Blaise's eyes. That was it. He was immobilised, his mind and body no longer wanting to move. Even as she approached him, swords at her sides, he made no attempt to stop her. She was going to kill him and he would do nothing about it.

And then a gust of wind had rolled across Stonehenge and torrented into Raeve. She was thrown back, her eye contact severed. Blaise had turned to Caeli. Her arms were still outstretched in his direction, and Taranis, who she had been battling, was nowhere to be seen.

'Thank you . . .' he'd started, before he noticed something. Her arms were just beyond the force field that guarded her section. He opened his mouth to shout, but already it was too late.

A burly man stomped up to Caeli, raised his blade high, and swung it down. Between one second and the next, Caeli's hand dropped away as easily as if she had been holding an apple and had decided to let go.

Blaise would never be able to forget the sound that escaped from Caeli. The pure, unrestrained scream that had somehow settled itself in Blaise's mind. Even now, as Blaise stood with the healer on the other side of Caeli's private room, his ears still rang with the noise.

'I'll go in,' he said to the healer. 'Give me as many sedatives as she needs and I'll get through to her.' He noted the healer's apprehension. 'She won't let anyone else near her, and in this state, I don't know what she'll do. Give it to me! Only I'm strong enough. I can help her. I need to help her.'

The door to Caeli's room was shuddering violently as Blaise reached out for it, barely held by its hinges. The healer tucked three amber-coloured pebbles into Blaise's pocket. 'Knock them lightly against her cerebellum, just above the top of her spine.' Blaise looked at her with confusion until she lightly demonstrated by tapping the lower back of his head. 'Here. One should do it, but I've never tried to sedate a Child of the Elements before. Be quick and call us in as soon as she's out.'

'Her hand! Do you have it?' Blaise asked. He had to shout now as the thundering only increased, making the walls and ceiling shake around them. 'Can you get it back on somehow?'

The healer's eyes fell to the ground and she shook her head. 'If it had been a clean cut, then maybe. But where it's been burned so badly . . .'

Blaise's breath hitched in his throat. What would he say to

her? What *could* he say? How would Caeli, who spent her entire life practising to be perfect, be able to deal with this?

How would she be able to forgive me for being the reason for it?

Blaise threw the door open before he could turn back. He was violently swept inside, pulled by a force he couldn't resist. He collided with the back wall and clung to a groove there as his eyes adjusted to the whirlwind that was roaring around Caeli.

In its eye, she sat crouched on her knees, screaming into the winds over and over as her intact left hand repeatedly dug into her scalp and came away with clumps of long, silvery hair.

'Cae!' Blaise bellowed. He forced himself away from the wall, shielding his face from the torrential gusts that beat against him.

'I can't live like this,' Caeli screeched to no one, to everyone. She was staring at her severed arm, transfixed on where the flesh had been cauterised by Blaise's flame to stop its bleeding. 'I can't do this!'

Blaise fought his way towards her. He struggled to keep his footing, taking small steps so that he wasn't hurled away. 'Cae, you're going to destroy the Healing Sanctuary if you don't stop this! Please stop – everything is going to be okay!'

Caeli shot to her feet then. Her eyes flashed a dark, stormy grey and a rush of wind threw him into the far wall again. 'How is everything going to be okay? Look at me! Look at what I lost for you!'

Blaise couldn't. He just couldn't.

Then there was a flash of bright red at Caeli's side. Caeli noticed it a second too late. Valentina stepped out from the portal and knocked her closed fist into the back of Caeli's head.

Instantly, the rolling winds around the room ceased and fell apart. Blaise slumped to the floor as he watched Caeli's tear-filled eyes roll to the back of her head, all anger fading from them.

Valentina caught Caeli as her knees buckled and she went to the ground with her, the amber stones clattering from her hand. She cradled Caeli's head, the action delicate, intimate almost, not at all what Blaise would have expected from a stranger who so clearly appeared to despise her.

'I'm sorry, Doran,' Valentina whispered, stroking a flyaway strand of hair from Caeli's face. She tentatively placed Caeli's injured arm across her body before she caught Blaise's eye.

Blaise wasn't Alexis; he knew he wouldn't be able to read the emotion of her face, so he didn't bother trying. Instead, he crawled towards them and took Caeli's weight from Valentina, shifting it so that she was lying across them both, her legs atop Valentina's, her head in Blaise's lap.

Even as the healers rushed in, neither Blaise nor Valentina moved, remaining shoulder to shoulder, silenced and struck still by all the unanswered questions that encircled the three of them. Questions of *What if?* and *What now?* Questions Blaise couldn't bring himself to ask. Questions that changed everything between himself and Caeli.

It was a long time later that Blaise finally left Caeli's room, realising that his presence was only making it harder for the healers to do their jobs. Valentina left at the same time, although she went another way and without a word, vanishing as if she had never been there at all. Blaise wasn't one to keep secrets, he could admit this, however he found himself oddly protective of that moment they had shared and he knew he wouldn't tell it to anyone, not even Alexis.

Alexis.

Blaise started running before he knew it. He had to find him. Blaise had to make sure he was all right. That he was alive.

He didn't know where he was going. He hadn't spent too much time in the Healing Sanctuary aside from now and again during his training, but it had never been for long. He knew it wrapped around the entire circumference of the Haven's core, as did all the other sanctuaries, but he honed in on the power of his amulet to lead him to his friend.

Every hall and corridor was packed with people in various states of recovery: some slumped against the sides of the walls; others running up and down corridors. It was a maze, and Blaise was only grateful to be tall enough to see over most of the crowds as he waded through the chaos. He rounded a corner and almost knocked over a muscular black girl with dreadlocks, who stood hunched over someone in a hospital bed.

'Althea?'

Althea Orenda's face and arms were lacerated, but that wasn't what most startled Blaise. It was the tears that were streaming down her cheeks as she turned to him, and the sight of the person who lay unmoving in the bed behind her.

Blaise's heart thundered in his chest as he took two cautious steps towards her to better see who was half-concealed by a bed sheet dyed red with blood.

'Althea?' he asked again, this time with a different question in his voice.

Althea closed her eyes, her long eyelashes glistening with tears. She finally stepped aside to allow Blaise to see who it was, but some part of him already knew that only one loss could bring her such pain. The loss of her best friend.

Joe Coin's arms were crossed over his chest, his eyes closed, his fluffy golden hair splayed out like a halo above his head. He could be sleeping, if not for the blood that spilled from the stab wound through his heart.

'I lost him,' Althea muttered, her Southern accent heavy with heartbreak. She was usually so mischievous, so brazen. It was one of the things Blaise had found most attractive about her over the summer. Now, that glimmer, that unshakeable confidence and spark, had been stripped away, dying with Joe. 'I thought he might've gone to check on Caeli, but I knew he would never leave without telling me. It wasn't until those *things* came and everyone fled that I finally found him, buried beneath the corpses.'

She stroked her bloodied hand against the side of Joe's face. Even though Blaise had been jealous of Joe, he had never resented him. He had tried, but he couldn't. Blaise's heart was laden with sadness as he mourned the loss of a person whom, had circumstances been different, he could have been friends with.

Blaise wanted to ask how he had died, especially with powers like his, but he knew he shouldn't. There was much he wanted to know. How Caeli would take it, and would it change anything between them? Would she grieve him? He pushed the thoughts from his mind.

Blaise placed his hand on Althea's shoulder. 'Joe was a great guy,' he said. There was more to say, but Blaise didn't know how.

Althea leaned her head against Blaise's hand. 'He really was.'

Blaise stayed with Althea until a healer arrived to see her for her injuries while another took Joe away.

It took Blaise a further half an hour of searching to finally find Alexis's room. The only reason he had was because of Demi.

'Let me see him!' she howled at the three healers who stood before her. Blaise wasn't sure if they were meant to be guarding Alexis's room or pacifying Demi, but all three healers appeared to quiver before her. 'I need to be with him! He needs me!'

'Ms Nikolas, you have suffered many great wounds,' said a thin elderly lady with kind eyes. 'We need to make sure you are not suffering from any major injuries, internal or external, that you might not be feeling at this moment. Adrenaline is a powerful thing.'

Demi splayed her arms wide. Blaise wondered if she meant to prove that she was fine, still standing, but all it did was confirm what the healer had said.

Demi was hurt far worse than Blaise had realised. He didn't know if it had been during her fight with Akili Pierce or sometime before, but her Haven suit had been torn to shreds, barely clinging to her. She was standing at an awkward angle, all her weight on one leg. Cuts and scratches and bruises were scattered all over her body, up to her face and neck.

'Please let me see him,' Demi pleaded. 'Please. I don't want him to be alone. Just tell me he is okay.'

The two healers either side of the elderly lady exchanged a look with one another. Blaise rushed in before Demi caught it.

'Dee.'

'Oh, Blaise.' Demi reached out for him and wrapped her

arms around his mid-section, squeezing him so tightly that the air was forced from him. 'Lexi –' She started, her voice cracking and eyes filling. 'They won't let me see him. They won't tell me if he's still alive, but he must be. I would feel it if he wasn't. I would know it here.'

She placed her hand over her heart. Her knuckles were split and dark purple, and at least one finger was bent at a crooked angle, yet all of Demi's injuries seemed secondary to the pain she was feeling within.

'You would,' Blaise assured her, although he wasn't sure if he was telling the truth. 'It's Al. Nothing can stop him.' He hated to admit this next part, but he knew Demi wouldn't tell anyone. 'He's the strongest one of us. If anyone can make it, he can.'

Demi nodded adamantly. Even with a split lip, she smiled. 'Of course. He's going to be fine.'

The door to Alexis's room burst open as a healer rushed out, her face buried in her hands as she tore down the corridor. What Blaise and Demi saw within stripped away the hope that had so briefly provided them with comfort – the hope that Alexis would indeed be all right.

Half a dozen healers surrounded him, their hands hovering over his body, shouting warnings and calling out injuries. Blaise caught only glimpses of him, but for the most part, he was glad. More wires and tubes than he could count were stabbed into Alexis at his arms and legs. The room glowed with yellow lights, but the panic of the healers dulled them so much that Blaise feared the healing crystals had already been used up before they had managed to take any effect. Even as the healers jostled Alexis's body, shoving a wide breathing tube down his throat and wrapping soaked bandages around his limbs with brutal urgency, Alexis's eyes remained closed, the amulet on his chest barely alight.

'It's not enough!' one of the healers shouted, throwing something over his shoulder. The blackened gauze squelched as it hit the far wall. He packed more and more clean ones to a mangled, weeping hole at the top of Alexis's chest. 'I don't know what we can do! We're losing him.'

A noise escaped Demi. It was the slightest of sounds that came from somewhere deep within, a single syllable. '*Oh.*'

That was it, the last of her resistance, the end of her fight. She stood impossibly still, frozen in shock, her green eyes wide and unmoving and haunted.

'Get out of my way!'

Blaise recognised the voice behind him. A voice that commanded power; one that he thought he'd never again hear.

'Incantus?'

Incantus Arcangelo staggered past them, shoving away the hands of the healers that gently tried to redirect him, guided by the weeping healer who had fled Alexis's room moments before. His chest had been haphazardly bandaged, as though someone had started to work on him but had been interrupted. Beneath the bandages, Blaise could see that his skin was faintly glowing, healing itself now that his powers were returning as the eclipse faded.

Incantus glanced once at Demi and Blaise in the doorway.

'Please leave,' he said.

It was an order as much as it was a plea. He didn't wait to see if they had obeyed him. He limped past the healers, his hands already glinting with a white glow that outshone the yellow crystals. The healers made space for him as he stood at the foot of Alexis's bed.

Blaise and Demi remained loitering just beyond the doorway to Alexis's room, so he couldn't see Incantus's expression, but he could see the way his shoulders rose and fell just once as though he had taken a deep breath and had decided something.

Incantus rounded the bed and muttered something to the healers around him. Just as Incantus leaned over Alexis's body, his glowing hands lowering to his chest, someone closed the door to the room and sealed Blaise and Demi from seeing anything further.

Demi collapsed to the ground. Whatever had been keeping her standing had emptied out the moment Alexis was shut off from her. She went out cold, fainting from shock or pain or some twisted amalgamation of them both. Blaise didn't have the strength to carry her.

He let a pair of healers rush forth and scoop her up and carry her away. He allowed himself to be led away, away from his best friend who was dying – or maybe had already died – away from the flashes of light that escaped through the cracks of the closed door that separated them.

Blaise let himself be taken away.

In the week that followed, Blaise spent as much time as he could with Caeli and Demi. Even though Demi still wasn't speaking to anyone, not even to her parents or sister, who were staying in the Haven with her now, Blaise would rather sit and talk at her than be by himself.

It had been a surprise for Blaise to see Demi's parents and

younger sister the morning after she passed out, and an even greater surprise for Demi, even though she was the one who had asked Ziya to bring them there. Blaise had knocked on the door to Demi's room in the Healing Sanctuary, and a short, stocky Egyptian man had opened it. At Demi's bedside was her mother, who rushed over with the biggest smile on her face to wrap Blaise in a bear-tight embrace and kissed both his cheeks. Tucked into Demi's bed, curled up next to her, was a young girl Blaise assumed to be Kallisto, Demi's younger sister, who waved at him excitedly.

Demi was still speaking then, but she only allowed her family, Caeli and Blaise to see her outside of the healers. Mr and Mrs Nikolas had sat at Demi's bedside and told her everything, answering every question she and Caeli and Blaise had asked, showering them all with praise and admiration for all that they had achieved.

Blaise hadn't expected it to hurt so much, to hear them explain that they had departed from the Earth Tribe once they had been informed they were pregnant with one of the Children of the Elements. It was harder still to sit there and watch them apologise to their daughter for keeping the truth from her and to see her forgive them immediately for acting in accordance with the Prophecy. But the greatest sting came when they assured her that, no, they wouldn't dare leave without her, that they had made a new home together in Protegere and had no intention of returning to the Earth Tribe where they had been raised.

Blaise didn't tell anyone, but that night, he had cried for hours alone in his room until he finally fell asleep.

In the days that followed, the Healing Sanctuary had fallen

into a routine, and a calmness and order settled in. Blaise's physical wounds had been seen to and he was allowed to move freely around the Haven before the others. With Demi spending so much time catching up with her family, and Caeli refusing to go out in public, Blaise spent a lot of time alone, wandering throughout the many levels of the Haven, unable to sit and do nothing.

Now, he was on his way back from one of the Training Academy rooms when he bumped into Ziya. After the battle, no one really set foot onto this level of the Haven. They had seen enough fighting to last a lifetime, but for Blaise, it was a great way to spend his time and keep himself occupied. Even though all of his wounds had been healed, something inside of him still wasn't right. He couldn't put a finger on what it was, but he put it down to trauma, which he was working through with one of his healers. Talking, though, was not one of his strengths. Strength was his strength.

After at least a couple of hours of weightlifting, Blaise left the Academy and was halfway across one of the bridges of the hive when Ziya raced past him.

'Zee! Nearly knocked me over the bloody side.' He threw his arms up and gestured to the ground floor of the Haven far below. 'Surviving the battle only to fall to my death would be insanely embarrassing.'

Ziya waved dismissively at him. 'It's enchanted so that you can't actually fall,' she reminded him, and Blaise did recall her telling him that at least once or twice before.

'Oh yeah, my bad. How are you?'

Ziya held up the Haven command disk, which Blaise was convinced was glued to her hand at this point. He guessed that was the price of being the only Leader of the Haven, tasked almost single-handedly with its daily functioning. No wonder she went everywhere with a run.

Ziya took a deep breath, and Blaise thought to himself, *Here we go.*

'Busy,' she said. 'Still co-ordinating with healers from across the globe to come here to help, including the witches and sorcerers from the Coven Academies – those that Raeve trusted, at least. Obviously, the High Order have been refused access to the Haven. They said that staying impartial with regards to Mortem was to ensure the survival of our government, as he'd promised he would spare them from being imprinted. Secretary-General Kleine said it was part of their bigger plan to betray him, but we're still not letting them in. The High Order have enough to deal with anyway, with the Security Council operatives tracking down any Shadowless who may have escaped, and the Erasers working overtime on any mortal who might have seen the light from Stonehenge – if it wasn't disguised by the Maya force that prevents mortals from accurately perceiving our world, of course. And then there's the issue of the natural disasters that . . . you know . . .'

Ziya didn't continue. Blaise nodded, knowing what she meant but glad she didn't say it. He changed the subject. 'Any updates on Al?'

Ziya's expression softened. 'Yes. I just spoke with the healers, who told me that Alexis should awaken from the coma any day now.'

A tension in Blaise's chest that had settled there a week ago finally unwound and lifted. 'That's amazing! I'll tell the girls. Dee will be so happy.'

Ziya beamed. 'Good. Okay then, I'll see you around.'

'In a bit, Zee.'

Blaise reached the level of the Healing Sanctuary and immediately made his way to Alexis's room. As of two days ago, he had been allowed to set foot inside it, but that came with strict instructions that he touch nothing. He gently creaked the door open and nodded to the healer inside.

'Looking good?' he asked.

'Looking better,' the healer replied. He gave Blaise a slight smile and added, 'I'll be back in half an hour. Call us immediately if there are any changes.'

'Will do.'

Once the healer had left, Blaise pulled up a chair and plonked it at Alexis's bedside. He did indeed look better. His skin looked less papery and pale, and most of the cuts along his face and arms had closed over and healed without a trace. He was still surrounded by healing crystals and coated in masks and bandages, but his breathing was much stronger and more stable.

'Hello, handsome. I heard you'll be waking up soon.'

Silence. Well, not silence, but just the steady bleep of the heart monitor.

'Saw Incantus the other day,' Blaise went on, fiddling with one of the many IV tubes that ran off Alexis. 'Looks . . . well, he still looks rough, like he's aged ten years in a day, but at least he's still alive, which is a feat, considering what he did for you. How he survived, nobody knows, not even himself. Oh, guess what? You'll never believe this.'

Blaise sat back and put his feet up on Alexis's bed, accidentally knocking over one of the pulsing yellow crystals.

He wasn't sure if Alexis could hear him somehow, but he spoke loudly just in case he could.

'Taranis woke up earlier and it was *not* good. Incantus must have told him that they never recovered Akili's and Raeve's bodies. He thinks they were destroyed alongside Mortem because of how close they were to Stonehenge and how much darkness he had imprinted in them. Either way, I think Taranis had a bit of a breakdown.'

Blaise couldn't sit still, so he got up and started pacing around Alexis's bed. He hoped that if he knocked the bedframe slightly, Alexis might wake up. He leaned in close and blew a puff of air at Alexis's face, but got no reaction. 'Basically, Taranis went from bed to bed apologising to anyone he might have hurt. He full on sobbed when he saw me and Caeli. It was really sad, actually.'

Blaise brushed Alexis's dark hair away from his eyes so that when he did wake up, he could see straight away. Blaise had hoped that by some miracle, when he arrived, Alexis would be sat up and talking, ready to take the mick out of him or say something sarcastic. He tried not to be too crestfallen. Alexis needed to be surrounded by positivity, and Blaise wouldn't let himself get angry or upset nearby. Instead, he would just keep him in the loop with everything that had happened to save himself from the epic run-down Alexis would otherwise be sure to demand when he awoke.

If he finally bloody wakes up. Lazy bastard.

'Anyway,' Blaise continued, perching at the foot of his bed now. 'Incantus asked Taranis if he wanted the Erasers to remove his memories of the time he'd spent imprinted, but he said no. I would've said yes, personally. Why would you want to remember that? Either way, that's all I've got for you. Caeli's the same. And Demi . . .'

Blaise stared at the ceiling. He cleared his throat to remove the lump that had snuck up on him, lodging itself there. 'Demi could really do with seeing you. So could I.' Tears formed before he could suppress them. 'So now would be a really great time to wake up. Come on, show me those beautiful blue eyes.'

Nothing. Not a flicker of his eyelashes or a twitch of his face.

Blaise let out a long breath. 'Okay. I'm . . . I'll be back again tonight. Be good until then. I miss you, Al. So much.'

Blaise lingered for a moment more and then got up. He returned the healing crystal to its previous position on the bed. He turned to leave, wondering what he was going to do with the rest of his day. Spend some time with Caeli, if she would let him. Put the TV on for Demi; something funny to make her smile. Probably go back to the Training Academy to work out some more.

As Blaise made it to the doorway, something small and hard smacked into the back of his head.

'What the f—?'

It clattered to the ground, a small healing crystal. He turned back.

Alexis waved casually, the faintest of smiles playing on his lips.

'What was that about my *beautiful blue eyes*?'

38
VEMOD

Vemod (n.) *Norwegian origin*
A tender sadness or passive melancholy;
the calm feeling that something emotionally
significant is over and will never return

Alexis Michaels had been balancing on the fine line between life and death, waiting for a strong tide to knock him aside. In truth, some part of him did not mind which way he fell.

When he finally stirred awake to the sight of tubes and healing crystals all around him, he could not deny the regret that nestled in his chest, making him feel as though he had made the wrong decision in returning.

That feeling abated, however, when he saw Blaise standing before him, and it vanished altogether when the Boy of Flames called him a '*cocky prick*' before breaking down in an overwhelming flood of tears.

They didn't speak much for a while. Nevertheless, Alexis let Blaise cling on to him for the longest time, not wanting to tell him that the force with which he held him made him wince.

'So, what have I missed?' Alexis asked, his voice raw.

'I bet Caeli twenty pounds that that would be the first

question you asked,' Blaise said with a laugh, wiping the tears from his eyes aggressively. 'You've been out for a week now, so I'll see what I can remember. As soon as the eclipse was over and Mortem had been destroyed, Incantus's powers and strength started to come back—'

'Incantus is still alive?' Alexis interrupted, attempting to sit upright. He grimaced, rising no more than a couple of inches before a stabbing pain forced him back down. Stars decorated the periphery of his vision as he slumped back against his pillows. No pain was enough to wipe the smile from his face, however.

'Yeah, I don't know how, but that guy is indestructible,' Blaise marvelled. 'Ziya got the healing crystals to him just in time, I guess. She's really something, you know? So much more than meets the eye.' Blaise folded his muscular arms across his chest and his gaze flickered to Alexis's bandaged shoulder. 'What proved a bigger challenge was saving you. No healer's hand or crystal had any effect on that stab from your *Demon*. Your blood was black and it smelt like . . . it smelt like death.'

Alexis shifted in his bed and peered beneath the layers of interlapping dressings laden with syrups and small yellow stones. He was shirtless, but most of his upper torso was encased in tight, moist bandages that smelt herbal, medicinal.

'Do you have a mirror?' he asked.

Alexis had never been overly precious about his looks, but he was glad when Blaise brought a small hand-held mirror and he saw that most of his injuries had healed and faded altogether. His broken nose and cracked ribcage, even the scar from his jaw that matched Mortem's. The only thing that remained was the jagged black mark at the intersection of his shoulder and breastplate.

Alexis could still feel the sharp pain if he concentrated on it, and it set his teeth on edge. It was sharp, spiteful, existing deep beneath layers of muscle as if Mortem's fingers were still dug inside, ripping him further apart. Somehow, Alexis knew it wouldn't ever fade. A scar to represent all that he had endured, to symbolise the pain inside that wasn't as visible.

'How did they save me?' Alexis asked, although deep down, before Blaise reluctantly told him, he already knew that only one person was powerful enough to have done so.

Blaise drummed his fingers anxiously against Alexis's mattress. He glanced at him only fleetingly as he told him. 'Incantus used his own life force to save you. He . . . he sacrificed his immortality to do so.'

Alexis looked away, staring at a distant point on the sandy-beige walls. His father had almost murdered him, and his uncle had given up his immortal life to save him. He didn't know what to say to Blaise, let alone what he would say to Incantus when he saw him. What combination of words could express his gratitude and his guilt and his adoration for an act Incantus truly didn't have to do, not now that the Prophecy had been settled and he was free to live a life away from service?

'And he's . . . ?'

'He's okay,' Blaise reassured him, nodding as he did so. 'Looks a bit weary, a bit older and not as godly, but still him. Still got that twinkle in his eye and that smile that makes the girls blush.'

The girls.

‘Demi? Caeli? Where are they? How are they?’ Alexis brushed the healing crystals off him and reached for the catheters and IV drips that stabbed into him. Blaise caught his hand just before he ripped them away.

‘Don’t be an idiot,’ he said, not unkindly. ‘I’ll get them.’

Blaise left and didn’t come back for what felt like an eternity, even though the clock on the wall read only nineteen minutes. When he returned, he was with a girl Alexis knew to be Caeli Doran, and yet, somehow, she was someone else entirely.

‘Cae,’ said Alexis, extending his hand to her.

Almost as if she had forgotten, she extended her arm for him to take. The crushing realisation struck her then. Together, they stared at where her right arm ended just above her wrist. She swiftly tucked it behind her back.

‘Did you . . . want to talk about—?’ Alexis began.

‘No,’ she interrupted. Her eyes dared him to ask again, but Alexis knew better than that.

‘Okay,’ he said. He patted the side of his bed and shuffled across to make space for her.

‘I’m really glad you’re okay,’ she said, taking a seat. She leaned towards him, and Alexis thought she was going in for a hug until he heard a rattle just above his head. He watched as she unhooked one of his IV tubes and dragged the drip towards herself. She fiddled with the box until she found a new needle to replace the one that had gone into Alexis.

Alexis didn’t know Caeli to do anything without overthinking it a hundred times, but that had been *before*. He couldn’t assume anything was the same as it had once been. He offered to help her with whatever she was doing, but she turned away from him, clearly not wanting his help.

After a couple of painful minutes struggling by herself, Caeli managed to fix the needle to the drip and injected it straight into a vein in her arm.

'Cae,' said Blaise, grimacing in discomfort. 'I don't think you should be doing that.'

Alexis saw the anger flash in Caeli's bloodshot eyes. 'For the rest of my life, I am going to be walking around like this!' she screamed, suddenly furious, waving her bandaged arm in the air like it was a weapon. 'I'll have to relearn how to do everything with just my left hand: how to eat and write and use my powers and wipe my arse. And it was done to me by a man whose name I don't even know! So don't even think about telling me how you think, in your perfectly abled body, *I* should be dealing with this.'

'I'm just trying to help,' Blaise said softly, and it was the softness of his voice that allowed Caeli's anger to diffuse into sadness. He pulled her close and stroked through her long, silvery hair as she wept until she eventually drifted to sleep from the morphine on Alexis's bed.

'How are you, Blaise?' Alexis whispered, not wanting to disturb her.

Blaise shrugged. 'Holding down the fort,' he said, and he didn't elaborate further.

There was only one person Alexis was yet to ask about – the person whom he cared most for.

'Demi?'

Blaise wrung his hands together and cringed. 'Not great, Al. Not great. You genuinely looked like you were dead, or at least headed that way. When we heard that you probably wouldn't make it, she went into shock. She's confined herself to a private room where she is healing from her injuries, only letting me and Cae and her family come to see her.'

'Her family have been here?' Alexis forgot to keep his voice low and Caeli stirred on the edge of his bed, frowning in her sleep. They waited a beat until she relaxed before they risked speaking again.

They were more than just neighbours – the Michaels and the Nikolas families were as close as could be, and had been so ever since they had moved onto Valerian Lane almost a decade ago. Alexis knew that Demi's parents must've known about the Elemental world, that they were probably a part of it, but to know that they had been here in the Haven made it feel like his two lives had collided.

Had they known who Alexis was the first time they'd seen him, wearing an amulet that so closely resembled their daughter's? Was that why they had moved onto the same street in the first place? Had Geb and Petra ever disclosed anything to Alexis's parents about it? Did Kallisto have powers too?

'They've been around all week,' Blaise replied, making extra effort to whisper. 'They are, like, the nicest people ever. You can see where Dee gets it from. You know what I mean.'

That brought a faint smile to Alexis's face and a warmth to his heart. He could see them now in his mind's eye, the Nikolas family together, standing outside their home, which Stephanie Michaels had always admired, for its exterior was decorated with dozens of winding vines and bright cherry blossoms and hanging wisteria. Alexis longed to see them too, for they were as close to a second family as he could ask for. He knew with certainty that with them here, after weeks of Demi missing them, she was in the best position possible to recover.

Blaise, however, did not seem to share in Alexis's joy.

'What?' Alexis asked hesitantly. 'Is she not okay?'

Blaise winced. 'During the battle, when we synchronised with the full powers of the Gems and went Omni, our elements had . . . I don't know how to put it lightly. I'm not good with words like you are, so I'm just going to say it. A few days ago, we found out that we had caused disturbances with our elements across the world. Big ones.'

'Disturbances?' Alexis dared to ask.

Blaise nodded solemnly. 'Wildfires, tsunamis, hurricanes, earthquakes,' he said.

Alexis sucked in a breath. *How could I have done this without realising?* He glanced at his amulet, which lay untucked above the layers of bandages, sitting at the centre of his chest. While he'd conjured his powers at his every convenience, how many people had he unwittingly hurt?

His throat had closed up, but he forced himself to speak. 'Was it bad?'

'Yeah,' groaned Caeli. She sat up groggily, forfeiting any futile attempt at sleep. 'Incantus hadn't told us, but when he realised we found out, he assured us that he had already put preventative measures in place within both Elemental and mortal communities. Either way, Dem didn't take it well. Since then, she hasn't spoken a word. Not to us or her parents or Kallisto, not even to ask to eat. I don't think she's used her powers since either.'

Caeli and Blaise stayed with Alexis for a few hours longer, updating him on anything else he had missed, but Alexis couldn't process much of it. His mind wouldn't allow him to think of anything other than Demi. The thought of her suffering brought him a pain deep in his soul, one that far surpassed any broken bone or torn muscle. One that couldn't be masked with morphine or healing crystals.

He had to see her, Alexis decided, no matter the cost, no matter the risk to his recovery. He wouldn't rest that night until he did. When the healers arrived later and started fussing over him, Alexis would go along with their tests and answer their questions, waiting for a chance to be left alone. Then he would go to Demi, once everyone was fast asleep, when no one could stop him.

Caeli and Blaise refused to leave until Alexis explained how he had done it. How he had managed to trick the most powerful dark Elemental in the world. For Caeli's benefit, Alexis went into detail about how he thought of the trap to use a projector from the Training Academy to create the scene of Stonehenge, inspired by what the Woman of the Water had said to him.

Just as he had expected, Mortem had fallen for the illusion, believing himself to be in the true centre of the ancient ruins when he attempted to unleash his powers. With the aid of his proxy, Alexis had managed to sneak out of the projection to join the Children of the Elements in the true Stonehenge on the other side of his wall of ice. He admitted that he hadn't expected to see Incantus there with them.

After Blaise delivered a scolding lecture to Alexis for not being let in on the plan, Caeli finally suggested they all get some rest, for which Alexis was grateful. He wished Caeli and Blaise goodnight and watched as the couple walked away, their arms intertwined, heads rested together, sleepily falling into step with one another.

Half an hour later, when the healers next checked on him, Alexis had feigned sleep as planned in the hope that they would leave him at peace for the rest of the night.

That might have worked had it actually been a healer that had come to see him.

'You might be able to fool my brother, but you'll have a harder time fooling me, Alexis Michaels.'

Alexis opened his eyes. In the dim light, Incantus looked the same as ever. Just as tall and just as broad. It wasn't until Alexis's eyes adjusted to the darkness that he saw the lines that now creased his mentor's face and noted the grey that had replaced his white hair and dark stubble.

Incantus looked ... mortal. Still beautiful, still handsome, but human. While he didn't reflect his true age – over one hundred – Incantus now looked somewhere in his fifties.

Incantus reached out and pressed his palm against the side of Alexis's face. Alexis leaned into the touch with his eyes squeezed shut, stifling the surge of emotions it evoked.

'I'll take you to her,' Incantus said softly.

Incantus helped Alexis into a wheelchair and covered him up with the tatty, brown blanket that he rarely parted from. Without a word, he slowly wheeled Alexis through the corridors of the sleeping Healing Sanctuary until they eventually reached a closed door to another large room that must be Demi's.

'Incantus,' Alexis began, feeling Incantus step away from

behind him, the warmth of his body and glow of his light retracting as he parted.

Incantus placed his hand against Alexis's good shoulder and squeezed it slightly. 'Not tonight,' he said. 'Neither you nor I are strong enough to have this conversation now. This night is reserved for you and for her.'

With that, Incantus left, and Alexis slipped into Demi's room. She was alone, curled into a ball in a bed that seemed far too large for her, illuminated only by a faint night light in the corner of the room. Dozens of vases of flowers adorned the sides of her room and Alexis could see the framed photos that had come straight from the walls of the Nikolases' home on Valerian Lane.

Demi in her father's lap as a baby with bright green eyes to match the amulet that was far too large for her then. Demi swinging between her parents' arms. Demi and Kallisto gardening with their mother in their new home in Protegere. Demi's first day of secondary school. Demi doing Kallisto's hair for a concert. Demi on the beach somewhere with sand all over her thighs, her skin tanned, hair sun-dyed with ribbons of blonde, smiling so widely that her eyes crinkled. In all of these photos, these snapshots across the years of her life, she was smiling.

Will she ever smile like that again? Alexis thought. It was swiftly followed by another thought. A promise to himself and to her that he would do everything in his power to make sure she did.

He wheeled himself over to her, and with everything he had, tearing stitches and straining taut muscles, Alexis slipped into the bed next to her. He was careful not to wake her as he draped his arm over her and pulled her in close, desperate for the heat of her body. Desperate to hold her in his embrace, so much so that it brought tears to his eyes.

When Demi woke many hours later and turned over to see Alexis praying beside her, she uttered her first words in days.

'Don't ever leave me like that again, Lexi.'

From that point on, somehow, Alexis knew that everything would start to get better.

39
HÜZÜN

Hüzün (n.) *Turkish origin*
A feeling of deep spiritual loss but also a hopeful way of looking at life; a shared feeling of melancholy – a poetic suffering, a permission to feel deeper, to ache

'Welcome, Mr Michaels. My name is Olivia Kefi. Thank you for coming to see me. Please come in.'

Alexis's new psychological healer was a high-spirited, pretty young woman with blonde hair and honey-brown eyes. 'Thank you,' he replied. His right arm had been put in a cast and sling a couple days after he had awoken from his coma, so he shook her outstretched hand with his left and smiled back at her before following her into the cosy, well-lit, plain-walled room. Inside, there was only a chair, which Kefi took, a small sofa opposite, and a glass table separating them.

Alexis was grateful for the arm sling hanging across his chest. In a way, he thought his injured wound served as a barrier between himself and the healer, who to him, was a therapist no different to those he had encountered in his childhood. Back when his parents had still been desperately searching for a solution to his problems.

Over a decade later, and here he was again, meeting

another who had been assigned to help him, and likely couldn't.

Where to sit? Alexis thought, eyeing up the sofa, wondering if his choice would indicate something about his personality. To choose to sit at the far end of the sofa might suggest he was avoidant; too close to Kefi, and it could look like he was overcompensating. He sat in the middle. There was a pillow at one end that he wanted to pick up and hug in front of him, but he knew that might make him look like he had something to hide. He very much did, but that was not the image he was trying to project.

'Can I just say,' began Kefi, adjusting her loose beige top, 'I'm such a huge fan of yours! I, like everyone else, am extremely grateful for everything you have done for our people. I hope that in these sessions, I can repay all that you have given us, and support you on this journey of recovery.'

Kefi's infectious smile and comforting presence helped go some way in thawing Alexis's anxieties. He hadn't chosen to come to see her voluntarily – Incantus had made it mandatory that all who'd fought in the battle had to receive support from the psychological healers too. When Alexis had protested, he'd assumed that Incantus thought that it was because he had never had therapy before and had his concerns or his doubts, rather than it being quite the opposite. Regardless, now he sat in a room in the west wing of the Healing Sanctuary for his first session of many, and the only way he could fast-track a way out of this was to utter lies through his smiling lips and gritted teeth.

'Thank you so much,' Alexis replied, nodding as he did. 'I'm looking forward to mending this –' he gestured to his temple – 'just as much as mending this –' he lifted his bandaged arm. He didn't have to feign a wince from the action.

Kefi sat back in her chair and Alexis mirrored her. 'So, this is the first of our individual sessions together. I want to reassure you that there is no set timeline for grief. It doesn't have to be public, and you don't have to prove it to anyone, not even me. We all take different lengths of time to recover from pain or trauma, and so we'll work at whatever pace suits you best. I heard that your group sessions weren't as productive as Mr Arcangelo was hoping for.'

Alexis stifled a smile at the memory of the initial session he had shared with Blaise, Caeli and Demi with another, more senior healer. It seemed that, in the presence of one another, they had spent more time making inappropriate, dark jokes to entertain themselves than anything else, and so group therapy had been swiftly put to a stop for now.

'Everyone has their own way of healing,' Alexis said lightly.

'True, so let's discover yours,' Kefi answered, her eyes meeting his with an intensity that made his coy smile falter. Despite her youth and her unabashed positivity, there was something about her that Alexis knew better than to underestimate – a wisdom. He didn't know if she had any powers – to specialise as a healer, it was not a necessity – but Alexis found himself sitting up slightly as she went on. 'Before we get started, can you please share with me if you have any current or pre-existing conditions that would be worthwhile me knowing?'

Alexis smiled innocently. 'No.'

His first lie. It wasn't that Alexis didn't value or respect Kefi or what she was doing; quite the opposite, actually. But somehow, miraculously, he had managed to get through this entire ordeal without anybody learning of his past, of the hallucinations and the *Shadow Man*. Nor did anyone know that he had used his powers of darkness twice: the first time to kill Sinner, and the second against Mortem. Alexis wished to keep it that way.

'Okay,' Kefi replied, giving nothing away as to whether or not she believed him.

Alexis noticed that she had nothing to write or take notes with. He had had enough assessments in his youth and seen plenty of shows and films that displayed what a typical therapist's office should look like: wooden bookshelves filled with textbooks for psychology and psychiatry, for diagnoses and treatment plans. Worksheets of Rorschach inkblots or handouts for homework diary entries to record the patient's thoughts. A well-placed tissue box. Perhaps a pendulum or a metronome, if they were old-school.

Sheltered by his sling, Alexis tapped his fingers to his thumb as he wondered what style of therapist Kefi was. Maybe there was a healing crystal she could beat against his head to pacify his panicked thoughts as easily as it mended broken bones or cut skin.

Kefi seemed to hear Alexis's questions even if he hadn't spoken them aloud. 'So I tend to take a holistic approach to recovery by incorporating techniques from a range of therapies that you may have heard of in your world, while also employing a specialised branch of Elemental healing – one that focuses on reading the aura map of your body and of where you may be harbouring your pain.' Alexis couldn't mask his interest, and nodded as Kefi spoke. 'I studied closely under the late Mr Pierce, and he trained me to use my powers to learn and manipulate the energy patterns that we emit and absorb. Different emotions and sensations resonate at different frequencies, and with that, at different temperatures. While we explore your thoughts and feelings, following all that you've endured, that you've *survived*, I'll work on re-channelling these lower energies into more positive ones. Sound okay?'

Alexis made a humming noise at the back of his throat. Had circumstances been different, he might have been excited to begin this. But all he felt in that moment was fear, and he did his very best to disguise it the only way he knew how. With a smile.

'Sounds great!'

Kefi tilted her head slightly and took the smallest of inhales. Was she reading him now? Could she feel somehow that what he said and what he felt did not align?

'So, to start off, please tell me a little bit about you?'

The question was an anchor, one that wrapped a chain around Alexis's ankle and pulled him down, down, down beneath the surface of consciousness. He faded from the room, from Kefi and from the Healing Sanctuary and from his body. He sank deep into the depths of his mind as he thought of all the ways that he could answer her question.

I am Alexis.

I am a murderer, a liar, a fraud, a person with an illness, but not an ill person. I am a son, a brother, a friend, a fighter. I am a villain masquerading as a hero, or perhaps a hero who can't seem to shed his villainy. I have urges to be violent, to hurt and be dark, and desires to be kind and gentle and loving.

I am Alexis, and I don't know who I am.

Please tell me this: how much pain is needed to fill this hole in my heart because I fear I have overpaid my debt?

It was the only truth he had admitted thus far, and none of it made it past his lips. He knew that to be discharged, he had to play the game.

'I'm Alexis, and I'm getting better.'

And so he went on lying, to Kefi, to everyone. When he spoke of the quest and the battle, he cried at the moments he thought Kefi expected him to. He identified his goals and formulated an action plan to achieve them, and, somehow, he managed to hold fast through every session they shared over the following days and weeks.

Besides, Alexis hadn't attempted to drown Kefi like he had his last therapist, so by all accounts, he considered this a success.

When it was reported that he had made an incredible journey to recovery, Alexis had again lied by agreeing with the statement – only this time, the person he had lied to was himself.

Oh well, he thought. *We all lie to ourselves from time to time.*

If he wasn't mistaken, he heard another voice in his head, one that did not belong to him, also agree.

40
HEIMWEH

Heimweh (n.) *German origin*
Homesickness; nostalgia; a longing for home

It was close to a month after the summer solstice and Alexis missed his family desperately.

He longed for the tight squeeze of his mother's embrace and for the warmth of his father's presence. He even missed Jason, which he never thought he would. It was the subtleties of their relationship that Alexis was eager to return to, the humour one moment and the bickering the next. He knew with utmost certainty just how much Jason would love everything about the Elemental world, but he had to remind himself that he would never be able to tell him. That was yet another thing Alexis would have to keep from them when he returned home.

Alexis ascended the grand marble spiral staircase that wrapped around the hive of the Haven. He was still wearing his black suit from the funeral earlier that day, unsure as to what the respectable length of time was before he could change out of it.

He didn't mind though. Black was his colour.

Incantus had directed the funeral for all those who had fallen in battle or succumbed to their injuries. While the magical creatures asked to dispose of their deceased in accordance with their own traditions, it was customary for Elementals to cremate the dead when the last of those who'd fought in a battle succumbed to any related injuries from it, allowing the soul to be freed from the physical body to permeate the natural world around them.

It was swelteringly hot in the enchanted Garden in mid-July, but not a single person in attendance complained. The Elementals of the Sanctuario had returned from their home beneath the moai on Rapa Nui, the giant monolithic figures of Easter Island. Together, they stood alongside the Haven in the glade, surrounded by the magical forest, and watched as Blaise ignited the multi-tiered pyres until it became a towering inferno.

Alexis didn't know if it was from the smoke that billowed or the weight of his grief, but he couldn't bring himself to join in on the celebrations that followed. Serena Aevum had apparently ordered the Sanctuario to sing and dance on the day they buried the fallen. She had told them that if she died, she would come back to haunt whoever failed to rejoice.

Yet even as the Haven and Alexis's friends conformed to the celebrations as the pyres blazed on, joining in with hymns they didn't understand and swaying to the rhythm of the drums they didn't recognise, Alexis could only stand and watch as Serena Aevum's chamber went up in flames.

There had been nothing of her body that remained, so in its place, Ziya burned her most treasured items, all except the Aevum brooch, which Incantus said now belonged to her. Ziya held Parvati by her side, and together they sobbed for their grandmother. Valentina was there too. She had stayed in the Haven after the battle and had formed a particularly close friendship with Ziya that Alexis found equally as endearing as it was unexpected.

During the funeral, it was the only time in the last month that Alexis had seen Valentina shed a tear as she placed a beautiful meihua flower on Serena's belongings. Alexis had researched the symbolism of the Chinese plum blossom afterwards and learned that it represented hope, beauty, resilience in the face of adversity and the transitoriness of life. He couldn't think of a better way to encapsulate Serena.

Alexis sniffed at the collar of his shirt, and even though the funeral had been hours earlier, it still smelt of smoke. He hoped Incantus wouldn't mind. His mentor had called him to his office that afternoon. Alexis prayed that it was to tell him that he was finally discharged from the Healing Sanctuary and was signed off by all of his healers – physical and psychological.

Just as he was about to knock on the tall, white-glowing door, Alexis heard a shout from someone inside. It was too erratic and panicked to be Incantus. It took Alexis a moment to realise who it was.

'But why me?' Taranis pleaded. He sounded drunk, each word slurring into the next. 'Raeve was bringing a Coven Academy to the Haven. Akili could have helped so many people with their trauma. He could have helped you! They were both stronger than me, more useful and more resistant to him!'

Alexis heard Taranis weep again. Incantus hadn't yet said anything.

'I didn't deserve to be saved, sir! I remember everything I did, the people I killed – even Sophos, my own great uncle. If the Centauroi discover this, our alliance will be destroyed and they could declare war. I attacked the Elementals I swore to train and protect! I was stuck inside my own body, watching helplessly but unable to stop. Even now, some of them still look at me with fear.' There was a slamming sound, like the slap of a hand against something solid, possibly Incantus's table. Gibbous barked, making Alexis jump even though he was on the other side of the door. 'I should have been destroyed with the rest of them,' Taranis muttered. 'With Raeve.'

Chair legs scraped against the floorboards. There was a shuffle of footsteps; then came a muffled sigh as Taranis cried into what Alexis assumed was Incantus's shoulder.

Alexis's heart lurched for his former Leader. He couldn't imagine how he would be able to cope if only he had survived out of his friends – or even if he would want to. It must be infinitely harder for Taranis to go on without Raeve and Akili after decades living and working together. Despite how drastically different they were, as teachers and as people, Alexis had always admired the rare, faultless quality of their camaraderie, the way one might find beauty in the mismatch of colours in a mosaic.

'Take as much time as you need, Taranis,' said Incantus, speaking for the first time since Alexis had begun eavesdropping. 'Travel, see your family, focus on your research into dimensional teleportation. And then, if and when you are ready, we will be here waiting for you.'

Taranis sniffed loudly. 'Don't you need me?'

'We'll always need you, but not more than you need to heal,' Incantus replied. 'Ziya and I will manage the Haven and

Sanctuario in the meantime. You go and remember what it feels like to bask in the glow of sunlight.'

There were faint footsteps towards the door. Alexis rushed back as far as he could until he heard the door folding away, and then he spun on his heel and casually looked up as if he had only just arrived.

Taranis stood before him, cloaked in layers of clothing that hung from his lean frame. His hair was unwashed, face unshaven. He had always been known in the Haven as one of the most striking Elementals, but Alexis almost couldn't recognise that person now.

'Alexis!' Taranis stumbled over and embraced him tightly, forcing Alexis to hold his breath so that he wouldn't go light-headed from the smell: a deadly combination of alcohol and days of not showering. 'I must apologise for not seeing more of you and the others. I've been struggling, if I'm being honest.' He frowned, clearly trying not to cry. 'I didn't know if you wanted to ever see me again after what I did. I am terribly sorry.'

Alexis gave up on trying to hold his breath. He placed his hands on his Leader's shoulders. 'It is not your fault, what happened to you. We don't blame you. You were forced to do something. We know you didn't choose to do any of it. We don't need to forgive you, but you need to forgive yourself.'

Alexis peered at Incantus over Taranis's shoulder and saw his mentor smiling to himself as he brushed the fur between Gibbous's eyebrows. Taranis extended his arm for Alexis to shake, and when he did, a slight burst of electricity zapped him. Alexis grinned, glad to see a glimmer of Taranis's spark back.

The door to Incantus's library-esque office swung shut

behind Taranis as he exited, leaving Incantus and Alexis alone together. 'Like I have told you many times before,' Incantus said admiringly, doing his best to conceal his walking stick behind his desk. He too was still wearing his clothes from earlier, a black shirt that looked slightly loose around his torso and arms but had probably been snug prior to the eclipse. 'You have a beautiful and rare ability to make others feel better about themselves. You would make a fine healer should you wish to specialise in the field.'

Gibbous slowly drew to his feet and padded over to Alexis. He nuzzled into Alexis's hand until the Elemental took a seat on the cracked coffee-coloured leather sofa beside the fire, where he then propped Gibbous's head on top of his lap and stroked him diligently. Gibbous had healed well, considering his wounds, but he too was more frail than he had been before and spent even more time sleeping.

Perhaps he is also in grief, Alexis wondered. *Perhaps we all are.*

'My mother the surgeon would love that,' Alexis said with a chuckle, tickling Gibbous's ear and making him whine contentedly. 'Although I wouldn't exactly say I'm best placed to give advice on how to be happy and heal.'

'I would say that surviving what you have and still having it in your heart to help others is exactly what makes you perfect for it,' said Incantus with a lift of his chin. 'Hurt people heal people, or at least they try their very best to, for only they have a true knowledge of how to cope with a pain others blissfully believe cannot be felt so deeply.'

Alexis ruminated on Incantus's words, hoping to find the truth in them. Incantus slowly lowered himself into his seat behind his desk, his sharp inhale from the strain barely audible over the crackling of the fire. 'How did you find the service?' he asked.

'Beautiful,' Alexis replied. 'The Aevum women though ... They were –' he thought of a polite way to put it – '*unique*.'

Incantus chuckled. 'How diplomatic a descriptor. Far kinder than how Serena would describe her own sisters.'

Before the funeral had officially begun, the Children of the Elements had met at least a dozen women who'd introduced themselves as Serena's half-sisters. When Blaise had asked where they had been during the battle, they explained that Stonehenge was not the only site where the Shadowless had been sent.

Apparently, Mortem had deployed his loyal followers to execute those Elementals he feared had the potential to repel his imprinting powers. The all-female children of Sapientis Aevum were encompassed within that group.

The sisters hadn't stayed for long. In Alexis's opinion, they showed little to no love or affection for each other, for Serena, or for Ziya and her sister. They mostly spent their time looking supercilious in their elaborate gowns decorated with an excessive number of jewels, keeping together but exchanging few words.

'Serena never had much love for them,' Incantus disclosed. 'They took everything she offered without a second thought and always resented how she was her father's favourite.'

'He wasn't there though, was he?'

Sapientis Aevum. He hadn't even bothered to attend his eldest daughter's funeral. Incantus shook his head. He didn't look surprised. 'I asked, of course, but he said he was preoccupied with more important deeds to make an appearance. Please don't tell Ziya of this.'

'I won't,' Alexis promised. Alexis's thoughts went to Ziya, then to Valentina, and finally to the fellow portaller she had grievously maimed and he had left for dead. 'Still no sight of Ezra?'

'Gone,' said Incantus with a raise of his eyebrows. 'If he was imprinted with darkness in as high a concentration as Akili and Raeve, his body might have been destroyed. If he wasn't, then he must have teleported away before risking arrest, although I don't know how far he would have made it with the amount of blood he lost.' Incantus studied Alexis then. 'Are you pleased about this?'

Alexis had told Incantus and his friends about what Ezra had done, how he had loosened his shackles to enable him to escape. His friends had said it wasn't enough to redeem him for his betrayal, although Alexis had a harder time thinking of it in such black-and-white terms. Therefore, all Alexis gave in response both then and now was shrug.

Incantus changed topic and gestured to him with an upturned hand. 'How is your shoulder? Is it still causing you pain?'

Alexis could lie to Blaise and Demi when they asked, and especially to Caeli after what she had gone through, but he didn't want to lie to Incantus, not when they shared the same wound, the same pain.

The blade of darkness had torn muscles and severed nerves. It twinged Alexis whenever he over-extended his arm or carried a heavy load, serving as a constant reminder of how close he had come to death at the hands of the man that had given him life. It would heal with time, as long as he kept doing the physiotherapy exercises and applying the healing creams. In the meantime, however, for the next few months, it would have to be something he learned to deal with, alongside all the scars the eye couldn't see.

'I'm learning to live with the pain,' he said.

'I wish you didn't have to,' Incantus replied with a deep exhale, his head tilted as he watched Alexis stroke Gibbous's sleeping face.

Me too, Alexis thought.

'Olivia Kefi has told me about your remarkable recovery,' Incantus said encouragingly. 'She is one of our finest healers, and Akili's unspoken favourite student, so I trust her word. Therefore, you have earned the right to enter and leave the Haven as you wish. So long as you remember that you are always wanted and welcome to come back.'

Alexis's beaming smile was a genuine one that he made no attempt to mask. He knew he wasn't leaving the Haven or the Elemental world for good, but he still felt as though this moment was the end of something significant, probably the most significant chapter of his entire life. And he had no idea what the next would bring.

'I also wanted to say thank you again.' Incantus rose to his feet and walked around his desk until he was standing opposite Alexis. While Incantus's glow had dimmed and his body had grown tired, he was still as angelic as ever, or at least he was to Alexis. Alexis just hoped that he knew that too. 'What you did saved us all from Mortem. You were the beacon of light in a sea of darkness. I am so very proud of you. In the future, however, you have to promise me that you won't ever put your life at risk like that again. I know why you did. I know it was to keep us safe – it's something I've done numerous times myself. But you should always tell someone of your plans, just in case they go wrong. I trust that you can understand that, especially seeing that you *always* demand to know everything.'

Alexis clenched his jaw to steel himself, hoping that Incantus's words and the emotion they carried would pass over him. 'You gave up your own immortality to save me, Incantus. You didn't need to – Mortem was gone and the Prophecy was settled, and yet you did it anyway . . .' Alexis's throat tightened. 'I don't know how I can ever repay you.'

Incantus clasped his hands behind his back and stared into the white fire. 'Not even our kind are meant to live for ever. As much as death takes from us, it also grants us something more important than anything else – *meaning.* It gives us a purpose, a reason to live our lives to the fullest, knowing that they are finite, knowing that they will expire. All things must come to an end, even the most wondrous of things, yet it is that very impermanence that gives all things, all lives, their beauty.'

He turned his head so that he was looking at Alexis again. 'I have lived a meaningful life of love and beauty and light, so when my time comes, I will be ready. But until then, I still have a lot of light yet to bring and I don't plan on going anywhere anytime soon.'

'I still can't believe you survived,' Alexis admitted with a deep exhale. 'I really thought we had lost you.'

'Me too.' Incantus's hand went to his chest where Mortem's blade had penetrated him. His eyebrows furrowed slightly. 'I truly don't know how I survived. My soul should have left my body, but something wouldn't let it. Whoever or whatever is responsible for granting me this, I must have faith that it is for a reason.' Incantus took hold of Alexis's hands and infused them with an evanescent glow. 'Anyway, go and tell your friends the good news,' he said, waving a grinning Alexis away.

Alexis shot to his feet, disturbing Gibbous, who huffed before slumping to his usual resting spot in front of the hearth. Just before he went, Alexis caught sight of Incantus's knitted brown blanket that had been slung over Gibbous's huge bed.

Alexis was sure it had once belonged to Darcy Raphe, and that that was the reason Incantus couldn't bear to be separated from it, why he always had it close by. He recalled the night after he had awoken from his coma, how Incantus had draped it over him, letting it provide him warmth.

Widow was the name given to a person who had lost a spouse, and *orphan* was for a child whose parents had died, but there was no such title for those who had lost everything.

'What did you do with the ashes?' Alexis asked delicately, recalling the stone urns that had sat directly beneath the hundreds of individual pyres.

Incantus didn't move for a while, as if contemplating whether or not to tell Alexis. Eventually, he said, 'I took them away, one by one, to give them the respect they deserved. There is a place here in the Haven where they are kept together, a place I call the Shrine of Fallen Heroes. If you like, one day I can take you there.'

Alexis could see it now, a vague conceptualisation of such a place. An endless crypt decorated with lanterns and candles that never went out, with more urns than he could count. He could see Incantus too, carrying empty urns for Serena Aevum and Akili Pierce to place beside Teller Sagen and Darcy Raphe. Four-fifths of the Quinate, reunited in eternity. With only Incantus left to go on in their stead.

‘I would like that very much,’ said Alexis.

As soon as Alexis had parted from Incantus, he felt the creeping return of the cold pressure in his chest. It was an unsettling sensation that he hadn’t been able to shake since awakening. He’d felt it even as he lay unconscious for days on end.

There was one thing that his mentor had said that stuck in his head more than anything.

‘*You were the beacon of light in a sea of darkness.*’

The fake Stonehenge. The power of the shadows at his hands, conjuring a blade of hatred and fury and spite.

The door was opening again, but it wasn’t memories that seeped out.

It was a voice.

It was *the* voice. The *Shadow Man*’s.

Alexis clamped his hands over his ears, but it was not enough to silence it.

‘*You cannot confine me to the dark for ever.*’

And it wasn’t the first time it had spoken. It had returned the day Alexis had awoken from his coma, clinging to his aura, breathing against the back of his neck like a cold whisper. It had lingered throughout the entire night as he’d tried to sleep with Demi in his arms, keeping him awake no matter how many hours he spent praying for it to go away.

It hadn’t. Some part of him had known it wouldn’t. For a while he’d thought it belonged to Mortem, to the darkness, but with them now both gone and the *Shadow Man* back, Alexis was left utterly uncertain.

Somehow, that was worse. His only hope was that the hallucinations remained just auditory and wouldn’t spread to plague his other senses as his psychosis once had. He couldn't picture himself ever being truly happy again if they did.

'*You were the beacon of light in a sea of darkness.*'

Incantus's words couldn't have been further from the truth.

41

ZEMBLANITY

Zemblanity (n.) *Nova Zembla origin*
The inevitable discovery of what we would rather
not know; the opposite of serendipity

'Let's go away!' Blaise suggested, jumping to his feet and shaking Demi's and Caeli's shoulders in excitement.

'Where?' Demi asked, a smile creeping across her face.

'Anywhere!'

Caeli stared at Blaise through her eyelashes. 'We've literally travelled to the four corners of the world and you want to go away again?'

Alexis didn't know whether Blaise was resistant to Caeli's sarcasm or maybe he just didn't notice it. Blaise circled the huddled group of friends and leaned in again as if telling them a secret. 'We've been stuck healing in this place for weeks, and now that we're allowed to leave, you're telling me you don't want to get out of here? What's the point in saving the world if we can't go out and see it?'

Alexis tilted his head at him. 'That was quite poetic from you.'

'Thanks … I think,' Blaise replied. 'It's also my birthday soon. The big one-eight.'

Caeli was unable to stop herself from correcting him. 'You're a mid-August Leo – your birthday is still over a month away.' She pulled a face at Blaise, but for the first time in a long time, the glint in her eyes had returned, sparked by his enthusiasm. 'Any thought as to where?'

'Somewhere hot,' Blaise decided.

'With no people,' Alexis added.

'And with a cute little old town to wander through,' Demi chimed in, finger pointed in the air as if that was non-negotiable.

Caeli acquiesced as though she were a parent who'd reluctantly agreed to order a takeaway despite there being food in the fridge. 'Fine. But I'm not walking through any forests or climbing any mountains or going into any volcanoes. I am sitting on the beach with a drink in one hand and a book in the other.'

Alexis's heart did a little flutter at the prospect. 'That sounds like heaven'

Blaise nudged Demi. 'Sounds boring. Who goes on holiday to read?' he asked, a genuine quizzical look on his face.

'It's fine – we'll build sandcastles or something,' Demi offered and patted his arm. 'Let's meet in the laboratory in thirty minutes. I want to see Incantus before we go. I'm not sure when I'll next be in the Haven once we come back from our holiday.'

'Half an hour,' Alexis agreed.

They all drew to their feet, causing the others in the coffee shop in the Haven's plaza to stir. As they began to make their way out, Alexis caught sight of a figure hidden in shadow, tucked into the far corner of the room, their long legs stretched out along the wooden bench.

'Hey, Val.'

Valentina leaned forward, emerging from her cover.

'Spying on us?' Alexis asked lightly as he approached her.

'Observing you,' Valentina answered, her eyes softening the way they usually did with him. She gestured a lazy hand after the others, who had gone on ahead without him. 'Off on another world-saving quest already?'

'Hero complex – can't help it,' Alexis said with a shrug.

Valentina smirked. 'I can't relate.'

'I think you can,' Alexis replied. He tucked his hands into his pockets. 'I'm sorry that I've not checked in much. Demi keeps saying that the six of us should have dinner sometime. I'd really like that.'

Valentina inclined her head. 'That's very kind of you both. I shall consider it, if only for an excuse to irritate *Doran* for a few hours. Ziya was looking for you by the way. You'll likely find her hanging around your room.'

'Oh, thanks.' Alexis turned to go, knowing Valentina wasn't one for sentimental goodbyes.

Valentina caught his arm, then quickly retracted her hand. 'I wanted to ask you something before you left,' she said, her voice lilting with intrigue. She made no attempt to fold her legs to let him to sit on the bench, so he was forced to stand awkwardly before her. 'How did you know that Mortem would fall for the projection you cast? It was a risky trap, considering you had only met him once. How did you know he would believe what he saw?'

The question was a key – one that unlocked the door to all the memories Alexis had suppressed from that horrid, horrid day, if only for a moment.

The sight of Mortem and the Shadowless appearing. Joe Coin dying in front of him and the look on the imprinted man's face as he took his last breath. Blood. Pain. Exhaustion. Crying on the ground as he begged for it all to stop, and then the realisation that it wouldn't. The Leaders, their faces twisted in torture. The *Demons.* Gibbous whimpering for his fallen brother. Serena's sacrifice. Seeing Incantus die, or nearly die. Caeli's screams and Blaise's tears and Demi's revenge.

And finally, the memory that had haunted Alexis most of all. His confrontation with Mortem. It didn't matter how many weeks had passed, the memories still served to make him feel cold all over, flaring the pain that continued to haunt his body.

Valentina was looking at him with her head tilted. Alexis cleared his throat, slamming the door closed to that part of his mind. 'I just know him. I mean, I don't . . . but I guess I know what he's like. The type of person he is. He saw what he wanted to see and was so carried away with it that he didn't stop to question it. I thought he would fall for it because, if I hadn't had come up with it myself, I would have too. Sometimes it's hard to differentiate between reality and what is just in your head.'

Alexis forced himself to stop. Valentina's silence had a way of making him say more than he intended to in order to fill the empty space. He offered her a smile, trying to make it look as natural as possible. He patted the pockets of his shorts and said, 'Anyway, I've got to go and get packed.'

'Yes, of course,' Valentina said, thoughtful behind her pristine expression. 'Enjoy your trip, and hopefully I'll see you again soon, blue-eyed boy.'

With a circular motion of her index finger, Valentina

manifested a deep-red portal into the space beside him. Trusting that it would take him to his room, Alexis stepped over the red threshold and reappeared instantly in the corridor of the Children of the Elements' dormitories.

Alexis had been packing for less than ten minutes before there was a knock at the door.

When Ziya entered his room, he was sitting beside the narrow pool that arced across his room, his feet submerged beneath the cool liquid.

'Hey, you caught me with my clothes on!' he said, making Ziya blush. She walked over and took a crossed-legged seat by the poolside, unusually quiet as she shuffled a few inches away to ensure there was enough distance between them.

'How are you?' she asked. The question seemed perfunctory, rather than because she was particularly interested to know.

Alexis tried to catch her eyes, but they were fixed on the slight swimming pool beside them. 'I'm doing okay,' he said slowly. *Did she hear about the holiday? Is she upset she hasn't been invited?* 'How are you? Every time I've seen you recently, you've looked distant.'

'It's been hard,' she admitted. She let her hand fall beneath the pool's surface, wetting the hem of her sleeve before she pulled it away. 'Especially after Incantus told me that Mortem had been keeping my mother alive all these years as a prisoner. He said he and the High Order will continue to search for Mortem's castle, but the chances of tracking it down are slim. If my mother wasn't dead before, then she almost certainly is now. I haven't told Parvati that though. With Incantus and

I taking on the responsibility for both the Havens, without letting the High Order help out, I've been busy though. It's been stressful, but good.'

'Silver lining, I guess,' Alexis replied, trying his best to fill his voice with enthusiasm. He took her hand in offer of condolence, his eyebrows frowning in confusion as she withdrew from his touch. 'I'm so sorry for what happened to your mother and grandmother.'

Ziya nodded. She brushed her long dark hair with her fingers, clearly unsure of what to do with it being down from the bun where it was usually tightly kept. 'I guess I won't be seeing much of you any more,' she said quietly.

'Why not?'

'The Prophecy is done; your role as the Children of the Elements is over.' Ziya picked at her fingernails. 'You don't need me – us – any more.'

'Ziya, we've never hung around with you just because we needed to. We spent all of our time with you because we wanted to.' He smiled at her, even if she couldn't see it. 'You are our friend. You always have been. So I hope you don't mind, but you won't be getting rid of us that easily.'

Alexis saw her visibly relax, as though the weight of servitude had been lifted from her shoulders, a weight that Alexis long ago should have relieved her of, whether it was self-imposed or otherwise.

Alexis's phone buzzed in his pocket. 'Sorry, I've actually got to go.'

Ziya grabbed his arm just as he went to stand, pulling him back down.

'What is it, Ziya?' he asked as softly as he could.

Ziya wiped her palms down her jeans. 'You asked Incantus to look into your parents – your birth parents.'

It wasn't a question, but Alexis felt the need to clarify. 'Yeah . . . months ago,' he answered, unsure of where she was going. Had she found something about his birth mother? The person Mortem said Alexis had murdered? Alexis wasn't sure if he wanted to know anything about her, for that would make her a person, it would make her real, and that seemed so much harder to accept somehow.

Ziya shuffled closer to him. 'Incantus passed the task on to me. Well, like he already told you, we found nothing about who your mother could be, but I did manage to find out some stuff on your adoptive parents. Stephanie and Jackson Michaels.'

She paused as she waited for his response. He leaned back slightly, caught off guard by the mention of them, addressed in full name. 'Yeah,' he said, pressing her to go on, observing her through squinted eyes. 'Just tell me.'

'Well . . .' she began, unfolding her legs and bringing her knees to her chest. 'I could be wrong, but I triple checked and I'm never usually wrong. Alexis, I'm sorry to inform you that there aren't any legal documents to prove that they adopted you.'

Alexis lightly blew air from his nose. *Is this a joke?*

No, Ziya didn't make jokes.

'What?'

'You have an adoption certificate . . . but I think it was forged – really well,' she continued, picking at her lips. 'That's not the weirdest thing. After you were adopted . . . you all disappeared. And I mean completely disappeared. No card payments, no sightings. Nothing. It wasn't until your brother Jason was born nearly a year later that you suddenly reappeared again.'

Alexis's frown hadn't left his face, and holding the expression was beginning to brew a headache that he knew he wouldn't be able to shake for hours. 'Maybe they had to disappear. For my dad's job, if he went undercover or something. He's quite a high-profile detective and criminal profiler.'

It dawned on him how he sounded, like he was trying to explain away something he knew absolutely nothing about. He couldn't quite get his head around what she was saying. That his parents may not have legally adopted him. That they'd vanished from their lives straight after. Surely there had to be a logical explanation that didn't conclude they had kidnapped him.

'Maybe it was a different system abroad,' he suggested. 'They said it was after that huge tsunami in Australia that they adopted me. If I was born in South America, in the Water Tribe that likely exists close by to where the Water Gem was kept, perhaps that could explain the papers getting lost somehow across three continents.'

Ziya shrugged, as if it was indeed a possibility. She had never been good at lying, however. It was clear that she didn't seem to think that was the case.

'There's something else, isn't there?' he asked, his gaze steady, unbreaking. Part of him felt bad for putting her under pressure, but the rest of him was desperate to find out everything she had learned. He could feel his body growing more tense, more agitated, his headache worsening, pounding now.

'During the battle, I was surveying and recording

everything – including what was happening inside the projection of Stonehenge . . .' Ziya's voice grew quieter as she trailed off. 'I saw everything.' Her eyes finally met Alexis's. 'Everything.'

And there it was. The secret he had so cautiously concealed from everyone, the detail he had omitted in every retelling of his fight against Mortem.

'So you saw me use it then?' he asked, his voice carefully controlled. While she may not have done it consciously, Ziya leaned away from him slightly. As if he was someone to be feared.

'But it's gone now, isn't it?' she said, not really a question but more of a statement to be confirmed. She looked unsettled by his stillness. She was likely used to him smiling or laughing and making others feel happy. She didn't seem to recognise this side of him. The darker side. The side he had buried so well and so convincingly. 'All traces of darkness were destroyed with Mortem, right?'

'All except the shadow that hides within us,' whispered the *Shadow Man.*

Alexis couldn't see it, but even its voice was chilling enough to send shivers down his spine.

Alexis smiled, a perfectly practised, rehearsed, convincing enough smile. 'Of course they were,' he said. He got to his feet, moving so quickly, it made Ziya startle. He couldn't sit around and continue the conversation any longer. He couldn't talk about it to death like he knew she wanted to. Not when his friends were waiting for him. It wasn't something he wanted her to know in the first place.

'Thank you for coming to see me,' Alexis said as he helped

Ziya to her feet. 'But I'm really running late, and Cae's going to berate me if I hold them up – not that we need to go through customs or airport security!' He laughed.

Ziya didn't laugh with him. She hesitated for a moment before turning and starting towards the door, Alexis just behind her, his bag slung over his shoulder. 'If you want to talk about anything, Alexis—'

'I appreciate your concern, but everything's okay now,' he assured her easily, hoping that she couldn't hear the thrumming of his heartbeat somehow. 'I can trust you to keep these pieces of information secret, can't I? I'm sure the right to privacy and confidentiality isn't something that can be broken by a Leader of the Haven.'

Ziya nodded. 'Of course.'

He'd have to take her word for it for now. 'Perfect. Thank you, Ziya. For this and for everything. You're a good friend.' Alexis gave her a fleeting hug and parted. 'See you soon,' he called over his shoulder.

'Bye,' Ziya called back, standing alone in the corridor.

Alexis turned the corner. It was only after ensuring that he was out of sight from any prying eyes that he threw himself against the hard wall, and slammed the side of his head against it.

Pain exploded across his head, blurring his vision, but it was far more welcome than the *Shadow Man*'s voice that it chased away. Alexis could hear it retreat, silenced for now by the all-consuming agony. He touched his head and his fingers came away smudged with blood, but thankfully it was just behind the hairline of his right temple, easily concealed for now, so long as it didn't get worse.

He tapped his fingers to his thumbs as he tried to tidy away his thoughts, as he grappled at the secrets and revelations and realisations that were unravelling. They scattered before him, slithering away from his grasp. Why couldn't he get to them? Why couldn't he rein them in like he usually could?

One thought taunted Alexis more than any other, even more than the return of the *Shadow Man* and of what that meant regarding the aetiology of his psychosis. It was what Ziya had said about his parents. That they had forged his adoption certificate. That they hadn't legally adopted him and had disappeared for nearly a year after.

A final question crossed his mind. It was spoken by his own consciousness and by the *Shadow Man* in perfect synchrony, invading every cell in his body and replacing his previous obsession of finding out who his birth parents were.

Now, his newest obsession was, *Did my parents abduct me?*

42

DÈS VU

Dès vu (n.) *French origin*

The awareness that this moment will become a memory

Caeli threw her hands up as soon as Alexis entered the top-floor laboratory. 'Alexis! You're late!' she scolded.

Alexis jogged over, his bag swinging in his hand. He settled beside Demi. 'I know, I know. Sorry, lost track of time.'

Demi's hand brushed his knuckles. 'Always waiting for you, we are,' she said, a smile in her eyes.

'And I always come for you, in the end,' he replied, a smile of his own blossoming, eclipsing the fears and insecurities that had settled minutes before.

Demi's eyes fell to their hands, hanging barely a few centimetres apart, close enough to feel the warmth from one another. Her mouth went to open in reply, but then something seemed to catch her attention. Her eyes narrowed, and it took Alexis a moment too long to realise that she must've seen the dried blood that painted his fingertips. He shoved his hands into his pockets, and thankfully any question Demi might've had was interrupted by the opening of the doors to the laboratory.

In walked Incantus. His gait was still slightly unbalanced,

but if he was in any pain, he didn't show it. He had changed into a loose white shirt and an old pair of blue jeans, and he radiated a brightness stronger than that of the white walls of the laboratory as he drew closer to them. 'Brilliant, you're all here. Are you packed and ready to go?'

'We are,' Blaise announced, jiggling his suitcase in one hand and taking Caeli's hand in the other. 'Where are we off to?'

'I know a place in Italy,' Incantus said, clasping his hands and tucking them beneath his chin. He looked as though he was reminiscing, the ghost of a grin on his face. 'Where the forest meets the water, and the air is so fresh, it feels like it's never been breathed before. I can give you the name of the little lodge I once stayed in, if you like?'

'That would be wonderful,' Demi said, beaming. She took a final sweep of the laboratory. 'I'm going to miss this place.' She turned to Incantus. 'I'm going to miss you.'

Incantus placed his hand on her shoulder. 'The Haven will always be here, as will I. My greatest dream and deepest desire is for you to live your lives however you wish, just so long as you know your way back to us.'

Demi nodded. Alexis could see that her eyes were glistening. *This trip will be good for her*, he thought. It would be good for them all. A chance to truly recover and to realise that all they had sacrificed had been worth it.

They were no longer children – they had traded in their childhood for survival. But that didn't mean that they had learned everything about themselves, or about each other, for that matter.

Thankfully, they had a lifetime for that.

'Before you go,' Incantus began. He pulled out a camera

from his pocket and smiled shyly. 'I was hoping that we could get a photograph together. Something for us to hold on to; something that will last long after we are gone. Perhaps my mortality is making me a little sentimental, but I wish there had been more photos of the Quinate, for only Teller was blessed with the ability to remember us in perfect detail in those moments that ever so quickly became memories.'

'Of course we can,' said Demi, taking his hand and pulling him into the middle of the four friends. Caeli levitated the camera into the air, floating it further back so that it would capture them all.

'Did you make sure the flash is on?' Caeli asked, fixating over her curtain fringe while she tucked her amputated hand behind Blaise's back.

Blaise gently put his hand on top of her arm and brought her close to him until Caeli was grinning unabashedly. The pair stood within one of Incantus's open arms. Demi wrapped her arms around Alexis's waist as they shuffled close to Incantus's other side. The top of her curly hair tickled Alexis's chin as he drew in the smell of her, praying that this would be the first of many times that he would be held by her. That she would care enough to notice even the smallest things about him, and that he would care enough to hide even the biggest things from her.

He had saved her a dozen times, catching her when she fell, bringing her back when she was almost gone.

But she had saved him a thousand more times. Every day, in fact, from the moment he had first met her. That was something not even the *Shadow Man* could take from him.

As Incantus and the Children of the Elementals huddled together, Alexis felt his heart catch in his throat as he realised how lucky he was for the life he had. Like Incantus said, this moment would one day become a memory. He prayed it would be one he never forgot. One that was filled with happiness and affection. With love and friendship.

And above all, with light.

And yet, as Alexis smiled at the camera, there was one thing that he had not yet come to realise. It was something that was lying dormant beneath the surface of his consciousness, buried deep not just within him, but within all four of the Children of the Elements.

A power they thought they had destroyed, and yet it would soon begin to tear them apart from each other, corrupting their friendship and poisoning their minds without them even realising.

Alexis was right to appreciate the moment while it lasted. For when Incantus clicked his fingers and the camera flashed a white light, the darkness trapped inside Alexis, Demi, Caeli and Blaise rose to the surface, and for a single, fleeting moment, their eyes and amulets shone black, and their shadows blinked away.

EPILOGUE

Stephanie and Jackson Michaels were speaking in hushed tones in the kitchen of their home, a single light illuminating the room so as to not stir their children. With the severity of what they were discussing, they did their best to stay discreet. They didn't want to risk being overheard. Not by their children; not by anyone who could be listening in.

Alexis lay awake in his bed upstairs. He had been back home for a couple of days following his trip with his friends, but no matter how much his body needed to rest, his mind would not. He didn't want to sleep, even if he could. He didn't want to dream. He didn't want to remember. For it was at night, when the world was cast into darkness, that the *Shadow Man* spoke the loudest and the memories of what he had seen and done came back to haunt him.

Even though his parents were whispering downstairs, Alexis could hear them. His senses had been made acute ever since tapping into his Elemental abilities. He could barely make out what they were saying, yet he could hear the fear that made their voices shake.

It was gone two in the morning. *What are they discussing so late? And why are their hearts beating so quickly?*

Alexis slipped out of bed and silently descended the stairs.

He would say he was thirsty and needed a glass of water if they caught him. Masked by the shadows, Alexis relied on his spatial memory to take him safely down, his eyes adjusting to the darkness by the time he reached the bottom step.

He pressed himself up against the cool wall of the living room, careful that his parents couldn't see him in the reflection of the conservatory windows. His father paced around the kitchen, looking out beyond the tall glass panels at the garden, while Stephanie sat on one of the bar stools, her leg bouncing restlessly.

'Love, are you sure?' Jackson asked, desperation creeping into his voice. His body moved past the closed glass door that divided the kitchen and the living room, forcing Alexis to shuffle back so he wasn't seen.

'Jackson!' Stephanie hissed, before instantly lowering her voice. 'I know what I saw. It's not just once or twice; it's been a few times now. Wherever I go. Even Jason has noticed them. They just stand there, watching me from a distance for hours into the night, even after I come back from a late shift.' Her breath shook as she exhaled. Alexis could make out that her hands were trembling, the cup of tea between them failing to provide her with any warmth.

Who the hell are 'they' and what do they want with my mother? Alexis thought, protective fury igniting his senses instantly.

Stephanie Michaels was not a woman who scared easily. It made watching her now all the more worrisome. 'I wouldn't have noticed them if you hadn't taught me these things to look out for the last time we ran.'

'Have any of them approached you or the boys?' Jackson asked. He gestured for her to have a sip of her tea. She obliged, pausing for a brief moment to collect herself.

'No. But last night, when you were still at work, they were outside the house again. So I went out with one of your horrible guns . . .'

'*Stephanie.*'

'But they disappeared!' She swivelled on her bar stool so that she was facing him. 'It's like they're just observing us for now, figuring out whether we're a threat or waiting for a signal or something.' Her breath caught in her throat. 'Babe . . . I'm scared.'

Jackson walked over and dropped to his knees before her. He placed his large hands over hers, rubbing them as though to warm them. With a gentle kiss to her fingertips, he looked up at his wife. 'I thought we had put an end to this. Are you one hundred per cent sure it's them again?'

Alexis pressed his ear closer to the doorframe, blocking out the sound of his drumming heartbeat, listening intently for the words that escaped his mother's mouth.

After hearing what she said, he darted from the wall, racing silently up the staircase. He burst into his parents' bedroom and rushed over to their front window to stare out onto the lane. He looked past their long drive over towards the trees of Protegere Forest that stood opposite their cul-de-sac.

He stood there for a moment, panting against the glass. And then something caught his attention, a disturbance in the bushes. He wiped away the condensation from his breath, squinting into the darkness. For the first time ever, he hoped that he was just hallucinating. That his mind was playing tricks on him. But deep down, he knew that what he was seeing now was real.

A tall, pale-faced man was staring straight at him, his face barely illuminated by the streetlight above.

A gasp tore from Alexis's chest. The strength of his legs betrayed him and his knees almost buckled. He managed to stay standing, barely, but his body was turning cold all over as goosebumps rolled over the surface of his skin.

After a couple of seconds, the man retreated behind the treeline, disappearing from sight, obscured by the shadows as if he had never been there at all. But Alexis knew, and the man knew that Alexis knew.

A silent acknowledgement that something new, something dark, had just begun.

An icy shiver slipped down Alexis's back. He couldn't stand there any longer. He sprinted back to his room, climbing under the covers as he tried to block it out. Now he wanted to sleep. Nightmares were better than reality.

The words that his mother had uttered to his father just before replayed in his head, echoing against the walls of his mind, bringing forth a fear so great that it took his breath away. No matter how hard he tried, Alexis couldn't forget what she had said.

'They know who we are. They know what we've done. Alexis can never find out.'

ACKNOWLEDGEMENTS

Who else to start with but Olivia? Words can't express just how grateful I am that you came into my life on that random trip in India (can you believe we met in India?!). This book would not be a thing and my dreams would not have been realised if I hadn't met you. You were the one who told me to revisit that book I was so passionate about. You were the one who listened to me rambling about potential plots and storylines for hours on end. You are the one who reassures me, motivates me and defends me, and who makes sure that I stand up for what I believe in. Thank you for being my muse, my love, my friend, my travel partner and my unofficial personal assistant.

I want to thank my family. Thank you to my dad (he wants everyone to know his name is Theo) for always encouraging me to stop working and rest, even if I ignore you, and for selling copies of my book to anyone who comes to our restaurant for a nice quiet meal. Thank you to my mum, Stella, for shouting about my achievements and providing me with support and comfort whenever I need it (and for reluctantly participating in my TikToks). I'm honoured to say that I have the best guides and role models in both of you. Thank you to my brothers and their wonderful partners for celebrating every win, and for keeping me grounded and grateful. To my cousins, uncles and aunties (Greek and Cornish and American!) and to my northern family for every hug, message and shameless brag. The love and support you have shown me is so pure and bright. I consider myself lucky to call you family.

Thank you to my four-legged siblings: Monty, my angel in heaven and inspiration for Gibbous; Coco, my own personal cuddly bear; Rocky, my chaotic new armrest.

Thank you to my publisher, Simon & Schuster, who made my dreams come true. The hugest thank you to the superstar editor that is Tierney Holm. I have adored every minute of our work together as we have transformed this story into the book is today. Thank you to Yas Morrissey, my fairy godmother, with whom it all began! A huge thank you to the boss-lady MD, Rachel Denwood; powerhouse Publishing Director, Ali Dougal; Laura Hough, Dani Wilson, Hannah Taylor, Leanne Nulty, and Kate Dewey in sales; Sean Williams in design; Nicholas Haynes in export; Maud Sepult and Emma Martinez in rights; Daniel Fricker and Miya Elkerton in marketing; Lizzie Irwin and Jess Dean in publicity; and Sophie Storr and Bassia Ossowka in production. A big thank you to my copyeditor, Veronica Lyons, and proofreader, Sally Critchlow, for the polishing. So much gratitude also goes to my foreign publishers for publishing this series in different languages around the world, especially to De Saxus for organising my unforgettable first international trip to France.

I am so incredibly grateful to my friends. Your company gets me through the bad days and helps me treasure the good. I hope to make a lifetime of memories with you all. To all of my friends and followers from social media. I've gone from posting videos in which I yap about books to seeing people yap about my book! Thank you for screaming about every snippet I post and thank you to my awesome subscribers for making me feel so cherished and loved. The publishing world was a scary, intimidating place when I first stepped into it. I knew very few people, but what I soon learned about this community was just how supportive everyone is. To my author friends, thank you for sharing your company and wisdom with me.

Thank you to Dr Korallo for introducing me to the world of clinical psychology and teaching me about therapy! Thank you to my friends at work who put up with my (part-time) shenanigans and are always proud to see me succeed. Thank you to my students for making my days enjoyable. I am so proud of you all and so grateful for your support! P.S. thank you also for asking me to sign your copies of the book; a much healthier gift than wine and chocolate.

Thank you to my agent, Safae El-Ouahabi at RCW. I treasure our long conversations and feel so at ease speaking with you about anything on this wild ride that is publishing. I hope to make magic together going forwards.

A special thank you to Alex Forrest for another stunning set of internal illustrations, and to Katt Phatt for creating the most eye-catching FIRE cover!

Thank you to the composers who got me through writing this outrageously epic fantasy battle: Harry Gregson-Williams (for the entire Narnia soundtrack), Hanz Zimmer, Ludovico Einaudi and John Williams.

To the booksellers far and wide: thank you for making space for my fantasy series. From independent bookstores to high-street chains, thank you for putting me on your shelves and tables and for recommending me. I wouldn't have reached so many readers without you.

With love and light always,

Andy

PRAISE FOR THE SERIES

'Explosive, action packed and full of twists I didn't see coming, all while bringing together my favourite found family and sweeping romance – truly everything I love all in one book.'
Bea Fitzgerald, author of *Girl, Goddess, Queen*

'Absolutely enchanting and nothing short of epic. Andy effortlessly transports you back to the golden age of YA fantasy.'
Bill Wood, author of *Let's Split Up*

'Andy Darcy Theo is such an exciting new voice in YA. This series is truly thrilling.'
Juno Dawson, author of *Her Majesty's Royal Coven*

'Breathtaking and exhilarating.'
Rosie Talbot, author of *Sixteen Souls*

'This series establishes Andy Darcy Theo, not only as one of the freshest voices in YA literature, but one of the most vital. I couldn't put these books down!'
Sasha Peyton Smith, author of *The Rose Bargain*

'With prose that is lyrical yet accessible, Theo evokes a sense of nostalgia which reminds you of your love for classics in the fantasy genre, whilst still feeling fresh and modern.'
Busayo Matuluko, author of *'Til Death*

'A full-throttle roller-coaster ride complete with swoon-worthy romance, vibrant magic and sharp insights into mental health. Above all, this book understands what it is to face your fears and come of age – my teenage self would have gone absolutely feral for it.'
Ella McLeod, author of *Rapunzella, Or, Don't Touch My Hair*

'Exhilarating, electrifying and unputdownable. I devoured it in one sitting. A breathtaking debut from one of the most exciting voices in YA!'
Danielle Jawando, author of *And the Stars Were Burning Brightly*

ABOUT THE AUTHOR

Andy Darcy Theo is the bestselling author of the Descent Into Darkness series. The first book in the series, *The Light That Blinds Us*, was an instant TikTok sensation. He is a British-Greek Cypriot with an educational and occupational background in clinical psychology and teaching. When he is not teaching, learning or reading, he is developing this compulsive, character-driven fantasy series, which he first started writing at age thirteen.

Andy can be found on TikTok, Instagram and Twitter:
@andydarcytheo and be contacted via his website
andydarcytheo.com